Florida Stories

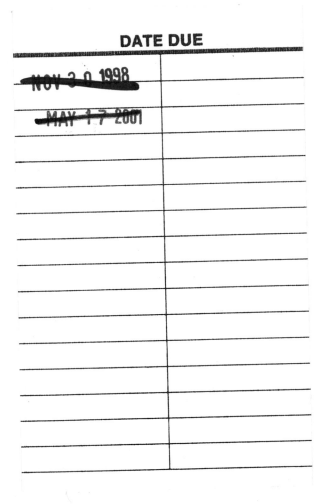

Florida Stories

edited by
Kevin McCarthy

University of Florida Press
Gainesville

Illustrations by Jeanne Van Riper

The stories included in this volume are reprinted with permission as indicated below:

Harry Crews, chapter 1 of *Karate Is a Thing of the Spirit*. Copyright 1971 by Harry Crews. Reprinted by permission of William Morrow & Co.

Edwin Granberry, "A Trip to Czardis," *The Forum* 87 (April, 1932): 248–51. Reprinted by permission of Current History, Inc.

Ernest Hemingway, "After the Storm" from *Winner Take Nothing*. Copyright 1933 Charles Scribner's Sons; copyright renewed © 1961 Mary Hemingway. Reprinted with the permission of Charles Scribner's Sons, an imprint of Macmillan Publishing Company.

James Leo Herlihy, "The Day of the Seventh Fire," as found in *A Story That Ends with a Scream and Eight Others* (Simon and Schuster, 1967). Reprinted by permission of the author.

Zora Neale Hurston, "The Conscience of the Court." Reprinted from *The Saturday Evening Post* © 1950 by permission of the Curtis Publishing Co.

Donald Justice, "The Artificial Moonlight." From *The Sunset Maker*. Copyright © 1987 by Donald Justice. Reprinted with the permission of Atheneum Publishers, an imprint of Macmillan Publishing Co.

MacKinlay Kantor, "No Storm on Galilee." Reprinted from *The Saturday Evening Post* © 1941 by permission of the Curtis Publishing Co.

Ring Lardner, "The Golden Honeymoon" (Copyright 1922 Ellis A. Lardner; copright renewed 1950) from *How to Write Short Stories*. Copyright 1924 Charles Scribner's Sons; copyright renewed 1952 Ellis A. Lardner. Reprinted with the permission of Charles Scribner's Sons, an imprint of Macmillan Publishing Co.

John D. MacDonald, "Kitten on a Trampoline." Reprinted from *The Saturday Evening Post* © 1961 by permission of the Curtis Publishing Co.

Theodore Pratt, "Five to Seven, Palm Beach." From *Florida Roundabout*, 1959. Reprinted by permission of Mrs. Belle J. Pratt.

Marjorie Kinnan Rawlings, "A Plumb Clare Conscience" from *When the Whippoorwill*. Copyright 1940 Marjorie Kinnan Rawlings; copyright renewed © 1968 Norton Baskin. Reprinted with the permission of Charles Scribner's Sons, an imprint of Macmillan Publishing Company.

Isaac Bashevis Singer, "Alone." From *The Collected Stories of Isaac Bashevis Singer* by Isaac Bashevis Singer. Copyright © 1964 by Isaac Bashevis Singer; renewal copyright © 1981, 1982 by Isaac Bashevis Singer. Reprinted by permission of Farrar, Straus and Giroux, Inc.

Gore Vidal, "Erlinda and Mr. Coffin," first published in *New World Writing* by New American Library. Reprinted by permission of William Morris Agency, Inc. on behalf of the author. Copyright © 1952 by Gore Vidal.

Philip Wylie, "Widow Voyage." From *The Big Ones Get Away*, 1939, published by Farrar & Rinehart, Inc. Reprinted by permission of Harold Ober Associates. Copyright © 1939 by the Curtis Publishing Company. Copyright renewed 1967 by Philip Wylie.

Contents

Introduction

OST PEOPLE, if they think of Florida, think of Disney World or Cape Kennedy or college students on the beach at Fort Lauderdale. They don't usually think of literature, but there is a body of literature set in Florida by distinguished authors that deserves to be better known. The purpose of this collection of Florida short stories is to make the public aware of well-written, entertaining literature set in Florida.

Short stories by and about Floridians have delighted readers of all ages from the sixteenth century, when returning Spanish seamen told of a legendary Fountain of Youth, to the present day's science fiction tales of moon shots from Cape Kennedy.

From its beginnings as an outpost of the Spanish Empire, Florida has provided fiction writers with an abundance of legends and myths and tragic histories to draw on. Tales revolved around Spanish conquistadors, English pirates, and Seminole Indians (the last of whom played an especially important role in many stories about Florida); around the natural disasters that have struck (the hurricanes, yellow fever epidemics, and fires that have wiped out towns and forests); and around the animals—alligators, wild bears, panthers, dolphins, deer, and manatees—that have enhanced the state's exotic reputation.

Florida evolved in a manner different from that of other states on the eastern coast, primarily because its geography oriented it to the Caribbean and Latin America. And while France to a small extent and England to a greater extent played roles in its settlement, Spain shaped its history for two hundred years and made it a colony often at odds with those to the north.

Instead of trying to define what length of residence makes someone a "Florida author," we have chosen stories that are set in Florida or off its coast and that present some important aspect of its history or inhabitants. They are by writers who have lived in Florida for some or all of their careers; a few visited for a short time or knew the state from their reading. Each has taken a particular place and built a story on it. The stories present a rich variety of people: condemned prisoner, shipwreck scavenger, karate devotee, moonshiner, devoted servant, eccentric. The diversity of Florida is represented— beach and ghetto, farm and ocean—and the span of time extends from the sixteenth century to the present. Collectively the stories allow Florida to be seen in all its variety and richness.

Listed in order of their approximate dates of action, the authors, stories, and settings included in this volume are as follows:

Andrew Lytle, "Ortiz's Mass," sixteenth-century, Tampa

Sarah Orne Jewett, "Jim's Little Woman," 1800s, St. Augustine

Stephen Crane, "The Open Boat," 1897, off Daytona Beach

Ring Lardner, "The Golden Honeymoon," 1920, St. Petersburg

Ernest Hemingway, "After the Storm," 1925, off Key West

Edwin Granberry, "A Trip to Czardis," 1930, southwest Florida

Marjorie Kinnan Rawlings, "A Plumb Clare
    Conscience," 1930, Ocala
Philip Wylie, "Widow Voyage," 1935, Miami
James Leo Herlihy, "The Day of the Seventh Fire," 1936,
    Key West
MacKinlay Kantor, "No Storm on Galilee," 1940, Lake
    Okeechobee
Gore Vidal, "Erlinda and Mr. Coffin," 1950, Key West
Zora Neale Hurston, "The Conscience of the Court,"
    1950, Jacksonville
Theodore Pratt, "Five to Seven, Palm Beach," 1955, Palm
    Beach
Donald Justice, "The Artificial Moonlight," 1958, Miami
John D. MacDonald, "Kitten on a Trampoline," 1960,
    Sarasota
Isaac Bashevis Singer, "Alone," 1960, Miami Beach
Harry Crews, first chapter of *Karate Is a Thing of the
    Spirit*, 1970, Fort Lauderdale

Stephen Crane

(1871–1900) was a writer and reporter when he was sent in 1896 via Jacksonville, Florida, to cover a military operation in Cuba. En route he almost lost his life in a shipwreck off Daytona Civil War novel, *The Red Badge of Courage* (1895). After his harrowing experience off Florida, he went on to cover the Greco-Turkish War (1897) and the Spanish-American War

Beach. That experience formed the basis of one of the most frequently anthologized stories in American literature, "The Open Boat." Crane had already published his novel about life in New York's Bowery, *Maggie: A Girl of the Streets* (1893), and his

(1898).

Crane waited in Jacksonville for over six weeks for a ship. He left on the steamer *Commodore*, which struck a sandbar on the St. Johns River and developed a leak in the engine room. Water flooded part of the ship and overwhelmed the pumps. Crane and three others boarded a dinghy shortly before the steamer sank and tried to make their way to shore; three men reached safety, but one drowned. Local newspapers at first wrote that Crane had drowned in the shipwreck, but later headlines claimed "Stephen Crane Safe." The exposure he suffered during several long nights in the dinghy contributed to the tuberculosis that killed him three years later.

Crane wrote "The Open Boat" soon after his experience, using many of the details he witnessed and imbuing the narrative with the helplessness, despair, hope, and exhaustion that he and the others felt so deeply. More than a straightforward narrative of the shipwreck, the story deals with the thoughts and daydreams of the correspondent (Crane) as he wavers between hope and despair. It deals with the struggle of several men for survival and how, even in the midst of mortal terror, some men are capable of heroic, unselfish acts. Crane used the fact that the best swimmer among the four drowns, while the one who cannot swim survives, to emphasize the theme of the interdependence of mankind and of nature's

indifference to their abilities.

The shipwreck took place on a part of the Florida coast long known for shipwrecks. The Mosquito Inlet Lighthouse, which the men in the story see and discuss several times, could not help sailors in a ship hit by huge waves or buffeted by a hurricane. Early in the story, the cook and the correspondent argue about the difference between a life-saving station and a house of refuge, an important distinction.

The correspondent was right when he explained that houses of refuge don't have crews to rescue shipwrecked victims. Houses of refuge were wooden-frame houses built along Florida's east coast. Unlike a lighthouse, which often had several keepers working different shifts, a house of refuge had at most one keeper, perhaps with his family. Houses of refuge were designed to feed and shelter around twenty persons for ten days and were used in place of life-saving stations in Florida because there weren't enough people along the coast in the nineteenth century to staff volunteer crews to operate lifeboat stations. One nineteenth-century house of refuge survives today at Gilbert's Bar near Stuart, Florida.

Stephen Crane

The Open Boat

A TALE INTENDED to be after the Fact. Being the Experience of Four Men from the Sunk Steamer *Commodore*

I

NONE OF THEM knew the color of the sky. Their eyes glanced level, and were fastened upon the waves that swept toward them. These waves were of the hue of slate, save for the tops, which were of foaming white, and all of the men knew the colors of the sea. The horizon narrowed and widened, and dipped and rose, and at all times its edge was jagged with waves that seemed thrust up in points like rocks.

Many a man ought to have a bath-tub larger than the boat which here rode upon the sea. These waves were most wrongfully and barbarously abrupt and tall, and each froth-top was a problem in small boat navigation.

The cook squatted in the bottom and looked with both eyes at the six inches of gunwale which separated him from the ocean. His sleeves were rolled over his fat forearms, and the two flaps of his unbuttoned vest dangled as he bent to bail out the boat. Often he said: "Gawd! That was a narrow clip." As he remarked it he invariably gazed eastward over the broken sea.

The oiler, steering with one of the two oars in the boat, sometimes raised himself suddenly to keep clear of water that swirled in over the stern. It was a thin little oar and it seemed often ready to snap.

The correspondent, pulling at the other oar, watched the waves and wondered why he was there.

The injured captain, lying in the bow, was at this time buried in that profound dejection and indifference which comes, temporarily at least, to even the bravest and most enduring when, willy nilly, the firm fails, the army loses, the ship goes down. The mind of the master of a vessel is rooted deep in the timbers of her, though he command for a day or a decade, and this captain had on him the stern impression of a scene in the grays of dawn of seven turned faces, and later a stump of a top-mast with a white ball on it that slashed to and fro at the waves, went low and lower, and down. Thereafter there was something strange in his voice. Although steady, it was deep with mourning, and of a quality beyond oration or tears.

"Keep 'er a little more south, Billie," said he.

"'A little more south,' sir," said the oiler in the stern.

A seat in this boat was not unlike a seat upon a bucking broncho, and, by the same token, a broncho is not much smaller. The craft pranced and reared, and plunged like an animal. As each wave came, and she rose for it, she seemed like a horse making at a fence outrageously high. The manner of her scramble over these walls of water is a mystic thing, and, moreover, at the top of them were ordinarily these problems in white water, the foam racing down from the summit of each wave, requiring a new leap, and a leap from the air. Then, after scornfully bumping a crest, she would slide, and race, and splash down a long incline and arrive bobbing and nodding in front of the next menace.

A singular disadvantage of the sea lies in the fact that after successfully surmounting one wave you discover that there is another behind it just as important and just as nervously anxious to do something effective in the way of swamping boats. In a ten-foot dingey one can get an idea of the resources of the sea in the line of waves that is not probable to the average experience, which is never at sea in a dingey. As each slaty wall of water approached, it shut all else from the view of the men in the boat, and it was not difficult to imagine that this particular wave was the final outburst of the ocean, the last effort of the grim water. There was a terrible grace in the move of the waves, and they came in silence, save for the snarling of the crests.

In the wan light, the faces of the men must have been gray. Their eyes must have glinted in strange ways as they gazed steadily astern. Viewed from a balcony, the whole thing would doubtlessly have been weirdly picturesque. But the men in the boat had no time to see it, and if they had had leisure there were other things to occupy their minds. The sun swung steadily up the sky, and they knew it was broad day because the color of the sea changed from slate to emerald-green, streaked with amber lights, and the foam was like tumbling snow. The process of the breaking day was unknown to them. They were aware only of this effect upon the color of the waves that rolled toward them.

In disjointed sentences the cook and the correspondent argued as to the difference between a life-saving station and a house of refuge. The cook had said: "There's a house of refuge just north of the Mosquito Inlet Light, and as soon as they see us, they'll come off in their boat and pick us up."

"As soon as who see us?" said the correspondent.

"The crew," said the cook.

"Houses of refuge don't have crews," said the correspondent. "As I understand them, they are only places where clothes and grub are stored for the benefit of shipwrecked people. They don't carry crews."

"Oh, yes, they do," said the cook.

"No, they don't," said the correspondent.

"Well, we're not there yet, anyhow," said the oiler, in the stern.

"Well," said the cook, "perhaps it's not a house of refuge that I'm thinking of as being near Mosquito Inlet Light. Perhaps it's a life-saving station."

"We're not there yet," said the oiler, in the stern.

II

As the boat bounced from the top of each wave, the wind tore through the hair of the hatless men, and as the craft plopped her stern down again the spray slashed past them. The crest of each of these waves was a hill, from the top of which the men surveyed, for a moment, a broad tumultuous expanse, shining and wind-riven. It was probably splendid. It was probably glorious, this play of the free sea, wild with lights of emerald and white and amber.

"Bully good thing it's an on-shore wind," said the cook. "If not, where would we be? Wouldn't have a show."

"That's right," said the correspondent.

The busy oiler nodded his assent.

Then the captain, in the bow, chuckled in a way that expressed humor, contempt, tragedy, all in one. "Do you think we've got much of a show, now, boys?" said he.

Whereupon the three were silent, save for a trifle of hemming and hawing. To express any particular optimism at this time they felt to be childish and stupid, but they all doubtless possessed this sense of the situation in their mind. A young man thinks doggedly at such times. On the other hand, the ethics of their condition was decidedly against any open suggestion of hopelessness. So they were silent.

"Oh, well," said the captain, soothing his children, "we'll get ashore all right."

But there was that in his tone which made them think, so the oiler quoth: "Yes! If this wind holds!"

The cook was bailing: "Yes! If we don't catch hell in the surf."

Canton flannel gulls flew near and far. Sometimes they sat down on the sea, near patches of brown sea-weed that rolled over the waves with a movement like carpets on a line in a gale. The birds sat comfortably in groups, and they were envied by some in the dingey, for the wrath of the sea was no more to them than it was to a covey of prairie chickens a thousand miles inland. Often they came very close and stared at the men with black bead-like eyes. At these times they were uncanny and sinister in their unblinking scrutiny, and the men hooted angrily at them, telling them to be gone. One came, and evidently decided to alight on the top of the captain's head. The bird flew parallel to the boat and did not circle, but made short sidelong jumps in the air in chicken-fashion. His black eyes were wistfully fixed upon the captain's head. "Ugly brute," said the oiler to the bird. "You look as if you were made with a jack-knife." The cook and the correspondent swore darkly at the creature. The captain naturally wished to knock it away with the end of the heavy painter, but he did not dare do it, because anything resembling an emphatic gesture would have capsized this freighted boat, and so with his open hand, the captain gently and carefully waved the gull away. After it had been discouraged from the pursuit the captain breathed easier on account of his hair, and others breathed easier because the bird struck their minds at this time as being somehow grewsome and ominous.

In the meantime the oiler and the correspondent rowed. And also they rowed.

They sat together in the same seat, and each rowed an oar. Then the oiler took both oars; then the correspondent took both oars; then the oiler; then the correspondent. They rowed and they rowed. The very ticklish part of the business was when the time came for the reclining one in the stern to take his turn at the oars. By the very last star of truth, it is easier to steal eggs from under a hen than it was to change seats in the dingey. First the man in the stern slid his hand along the thwart and moved with care, as if he were of Sèvres. Then the man in the rowing seat slid his hand along the other thwart. It was all done with the most extraordinary care. As the two sidled past each other, the whole party kept watchful eyes on the coming wave, and the captain cried: "Look out now! Steady there!"

The brown mats of sea-weed that appeared from time to time were like islands, bits of earth. They were travelling, apparently, neither one way nor the other. They were, to all intents, stationary. They informed the men in the boat that it was making progress slowly toward the land.

The captain, rearing cautiously in the bow, after the dingey soared on a great swell, said that he had seen the lighthouse at Mosquito Inlet. Presently the cook remarked that he had seen it. The correspondent was at the oars, then, and for some reason he too wished to look at the lighthouse, but his back was toward the far shore and the waves were important, and for some time he could not seize an opportunity to turn his head. But at last there came a wave more gentle than the others, and when at the crest of it he swiftly scoured the western horizon.

"See it?" said the captain.

"No," said the correspondent, slowly, "I didn't see anything."

"Look again," said the captain. He pointed. "It's exactly in that direction."

At the top of another wave, the correspondent did as he was bid, and this time his eyes chanced on a small still thing on the edge of the swaying horizon. It was precisely like the point of a pin. It took an anxious eye to find a lighthouse so tiny.

"Think we'll make it, captain?"

"If this wind holds and the boat don't swamp, we can't do much else," said the captain.

The little boat, lifted by each towering sea, and splashed viciously by the crests, made progress that in the absence of sea-weed was not apparent to those in her. She seemed just a wee thing wallowing, miraculously, top-up, at the mercy of five oceans. Occasionally, a great spread of water, like white flames, swarmed into her.

"Bail her, cook," said the captain, serenely.

"All right, captain," said the cheerful cook.

III

It would be difficult to describe the subtle brotherhood of men that was here established on the seas. No one said that it was so. No one mentioned it. But it dwelt in the boat, and each man felt it warm him. They were a captain, an oiler, a cook, and a correspondent, and they were friends, friends in a more curiously iron-bound degree than may be common. The hurt captain, lying against the water-jar in the bow, spoke always in a low voice and calmly, but he could never command a more ready and swiftly obedient crew than the motley three of the dingey. It was more than a mere recognition of what was best for the common safety. There was surely in it a quality that was personal and heartfelt. And after this devotion to the commander of the boat there was this comradeship that the correspondent, for instance, who had been taught to be cynical of men, knew even at the time was the best experience of his life. But no one said that it was so. No one mentioned it.

"I wish we had a sail," remarked the captain. "We might try my overcoat on the end of an oar and give you two boys a chance to rest." So the cook and the correspondent held the mast and spread wide the overcoat. The oiler steered, and the little boat made good way with her new rig. Sometimes the oiler had to scull sharply to keep a sea from breaking into the boat, but otherwise sailing was a success.

Meanwhile the lighthouse had been growing slowly larger. It had now almost assumed color, and appeared like a little gray shadow on the sky. The man at the oars could not be prevented from turning his head rather often to try for a glimpse of this little gray shadow.

At last, from the top of each wave the men in the tossing boat could see land. Even as the lighthouse was an upright shadow on the sky, this land seemed but a long black shadow on the sea. It certainly was thinner than paper. "We must be about opposite New Smyrna," said the cook, who had coasted this shore often in schooners. "Captain, by the way, I believe they abandoned that life-saving station there about a year ago."

"Did they?" said the captain.

The wind slowly died away. The cook and the correspondent were not now obliged to slave in order to hold high the oar. But the waves continued their old impetuous swooping at the dingey, and the little craft, no longer under way, struggled woundily over them. The oiler or the correspondent took the oars again.

Shipwrecks are *apropos* of nothing. If men could only train for them and have them occur when the men had reached pink condition, there would be less drowning at sea. Of the four in the dingey none had slept any time worth mentioning for two days and two nights previous to embarking in the dingey, and in the excitement of clambering about the deck of a foundering ship they had also forgotten to eat heartily.

For these reasons, and for others, neither the oiler nor the correspondent was fond of rowing at this time. The correspondent wondered ingenuously how in the name of all that was sane could there be people who thought it amusing to row a boat. It was not an amusement; it was a diabolical punishment, and even a genius of mental aberrations could never conclude that it was anything but a horror to the muscles and a crime against the back. He mentioned to the boat in general how the amusement of rowing struck him, and the weary-faced oiler smiled in full sympathy. Previously to the foundering, by the way, the oiler had worked double-watch in the engine-room of the ship.

"Take her easy, now, boys," said the captain. "Don't spend yourselves. If we have to run a surf you'll need all your strength, because we'll sure have to swim for it. Take your time."

Slowly the land arose from the sea. From a black line it became a line of black and a line of white, trees and sand. Finally, the captain said that he could make out a house on the shore. "That's the house of refuge, sure," said the cook. "They'll see us before long, and come out after us."

The distant lighthouse reared high. "The keeper ought to be able to make us out now, if he's looking through a glass," said the captain. "He'll notify the life-saving people."

"None of those other boats could have got ashore to give word of the wreck," said the oiler, in a low voice. "Else the life-boat would be out hunting us."

Slowly and beautifully the land loomed out of the sea. The wind came again. It had veered from the northeast to the southeast. Finally, a new sound struck the ears of the men in the boat. It was the low thunder of the surf on the shore. "We'll never be able to make the lighthouse now," said the captain. "Swing her head a little more north, Billie," said the captain.

"'A little more north,' sir," said the oiler.

Whereupon the little boat turned her nose once more down the wind, and all but the oarsman watched the shore grow. Under the influence of this expansion doubt and direful apprehension was leaving the minds of the men. The management of the boat was still most absorbing, but it could not prevent a quiet cheerfulness. In an hour, perhaps, they would be ashore.

Their back-bones had become thoroughly used to balancing in the boat and they now rode this wild colt of a dingey like circus men. The correspondent thought that he had been drenched to the skin, but happening to feel in the top pocket of his coat, he found therein eight cigars. Four of them were soaked with sea-water; four were perfectly scatheless. After a search, somebody produced three dry matches, and thereupon the four waifs rode in their little boat, and with an assurance of an impending rescue shining in their eyes, puffed at the big cigars and judged well and ill of all men. Everybody took a drink of water.

IV

"Cook," remarked the captain, "there don't seem to be any signs of life about your house of refuge."

"No," replied the cook. "Funny they don't see us!"

A broad stretch of lowly coast lay before the eyes of the men. It was of low dunes topped with dark vegetation. The roar of the surf was plain, and sometimes they could see the white lip of a wave as it spun up the beach. A tiny house was blocked out black upon the sky. Southward, the slim light-house lifted its little gray length.

Tide, wind, and waves were swinging the dingey northward. "Funny they don't see us," said the men.

The surf's roar was here dulled, but its tone was, nevertheless, thunderous and mighty. As the boat swam over the great rollers, the men sat listening to this roar. "We'll swamp sure," said everybody.

It is fair to say here that there was not a life-saving station within twenty miles in either direction, but the men did not know this fact and in consequence they made dark and opprobrious remarks concerning the eyesight of the nation's life-savers. Four scowling men sat in the dingey and surpassed records in the invention of epithets.

"Funny they don't see us."

The light-heartedness of a former time had completely faded. To their sharpened minds it was easy to conjure pictures of all kinds of incompetency and blindness and, indeed, cowardice. There was the shore of the populous land, and it was bitter and bitter to them that from it came no sign.

"Well," said the captain, ultimately, "I suppose we'll have to make a try for ourselves. If we stay out here too long, we'll none of us have strength left to swim after the boat swamps."

And so the oiler, who was at the oars, turned the boat straight for the shore. There was a sudden tightening of muscles. There was some thinking.

"If we don't all get ashore—" said the captain. "If we don't all get ashore, I suppose you fellows know where to send news of my finish?"

They then briefly exchanged some addresses and admonitions. As for the reflections of the men, there was a great deal of rage in them. Perchance they might be formulated thus: "If I am going to be drowned—if I am going to be drowned—if I am going to be drowned, why, in the name of the seven mad gods who rule the sea, was I allowed to come thus far and contemplate sand and trees? Was I brought here merely to have my nose dragged away as I was about to nibble the sacred cheese of life? It is preposterous. If this old ninny-woman, Fate, cannot do better than this, she should be deprived of the management of men's fortunes. She is an old hen who knows not her intention. If she has decided to drown me, why did she not do it in the beginning and save me all this trouble. The whole affair is absurd. . . . But, no, she cannot mean to drown me. She dare not drown me. She cannot drown me. Not after all this work." Afterward the man might have had an impulse to shake his fist at the clouds: "Just you drown me, now, and then hear what I call you!"

The billows that came at this time were more formidable. They seemed always just about to break and roll over the little boat in a turmoil of foam. There was a preparatory and long growl in the speech of them. No mind unused to the sea would have concluded that the dingey could ascend these sheer heights in time. The shore was still afar. The oiler was a wily surfman. "Boys," he said, swiftly, "she won't live three minutes more and we're too far out to swim. Shall I take her to sea again, captain?"

"Yes! Go ahead!" said the captain.

This oiler, by a series of quick miracles, and fast and steady oarsmanship, turned the boat in the middle of the surf and took her safely to sea again.

There was a considerable silence as the boat bumped over the furrowed sea to deeper water. Then somebody in gloom spoke. "Well, anyhow, they must have seen us from the shore by now."

The gulls went in slanting flight up the wind toward the gray desolate east. A squall, marked by dingy clouds, and clouds brick-red, like smoke from a burning building, appeared from the southeast.

"What do you think of those life-saving people? Ain't they peaches?"

"Funny they haven't seen us."

"Maybe they think we're out here for sport! Maybe they think we're fishin'. Maybe they think we're damned fools."

It was a long afternoon. A changed tide tried to force them southward, but wind and wave said northward. Far ahead, where coast-line, sea, and sky formed their mighty angle, there were little dots which seemed to indicate a city on the shore.

"St. Augustine?"

The captain shook his head. "Too near Mosquito Inlet."

And the oiler rowed, and then the correspondent rowed. Then the oiler rowed. It was a weary business. The human back can become the seat of more aches and pains than are registered in books for the composite anatomy of a regiment. It is a limited area, but it can become the theatre of innumerable muscular conflicts, tangles, wrenches, knots, and other comforts.

"Did you ever like to row, Billie?" asked the correspondent.

"No," said the oiler. "Hang it."

When one exchanged the rowing-seat for a place in the bottom of the boat, he suffered a bodily depression that caused him to be careless of everything save an obligation to wiggle one finger. There was cold sea-water swashing to and fro in the boat, and he lay in it. His head, pillowed on a thwart, was within an inch of the swirl of a wave crest, and sometimes a particularly obstreperous sea came in-board and drenched him once more. But these matters did not annoy him. It is almost certain that if the boat had capsized he would have tumbled comfortably out upon the ocean as if he felt sure that it was a great soft mattress.

"Look! There's a man on the shore!"

"Where?"

"There! See 'im? See 'im?"

"Yes, sure! He's walking along."

"Now he's stopped. Look! He's facing us!"

"He's waving at us!"

"So he is! By thunder!"

"Ah, now, we're all right! Now we're all right! There'll be a boat out here for us in half an hour."

"He's going on. He's running. He's going up to that house there."

The remote beach seemed lower than the sea, and it required a searching glance to discern the little black figure. The captain saw a floating stick and they rowed to it. A bath-towel was by some weird chance in the boat, and, tying this on the stick, the captain waved it. The oarsman did not dare turn his head, so he was obliged to ask questions.

"What's he doing now?"

"He's standing still again. He's looking, I think. . . . There he goes again. Toward the house. . . . Now he's stopped again."

"Is he waving at us?"

"No, not now! he was, though."

"Look! There comes another man!"

"He's running."

"Look at him go, would you."

"Why, he's on a bicycle. Now he's met the other man. They're both waving at us. Look!"

"There comes something up the beach."

"What the devil is that thing?"

"Why, it looks like a boat."

"Why, certainly it's a boat."

"No, it's on wheels."

"Yes, so it is. Well, that must be the life-boat. They drag them along shore on a wagon."

"That's the life-boat, sure."

"No, by ——, it's — it's an omnibus."

"I tell you it's a life-boat."

"It is not! It's an omnibus. I can see it plain. See? One of these big hotel omnibuses."

"By thunder, you're right. It's an omnibus, sure as fate. What do you suppose they are doing with an omnibus? Maybe they are going around collecting the life-crew, hey?"

"That's it, likely. Look! There's a fellow waving a little black flag. He's standing on the steps of the omnibus. There come those other two fellows. Now they're all talking together. Look at the fellow with the flag. Maybe he ain't waving it."

"That ain't a flag, is it? That's his coat. Why, certainly, that's his coat."

"So it is. It's his coat. He's taken it off and is waving it around his head. But would you look at him swing it."

"Oh, say, there isn't any life-saving station there. That's

just a winter resort hotel omnibus that has brought over some of the boarders to see us drown."

"What's that idiot with the coat mean?   What's he signaling, anyhow?"

"It looks as if he were trying to tell us to go north. There must be a life-saving station up there."

"No! He thinks we're fishing. Just giving us a merry hand. See? Ah, there, Willie."

"Well, I wish I could make something out of those signals. What do you suppose he means?"

"He don't mean anything. He's just playing."

"Well, if he'd just signal us to try the surf again, or to go to sea and wait, or go north, or go south, or go to hell—there would be some reason in it. But look at him. He just stands there and keeps his coat revolving like a wheel. The ass!"

"There come more people."

"Now there's quite a mob. Look! Isn't that a boat?"

"Where? Oh, I see where you mean. No, that's no boat."

"That fellow is still waving his coat."

"He must think we like to see him do that. Why don't he quit it. It don't mean anything."

"I don't know. I think he is trying to make us go north. It must be that there's a life-saving station there somewhere."

"Say, he ain't tired yet. Look at 'im wave."

"Wonder how long he can keep that up. He's been revolving his coat ever since he caught sight of us. He's an idiot. Why aren't they getting men to bring a boat out. A fishing boat—one of those big yawls—could come out here all right. Why don't he do something?"

"Oh, it's all right, now."

"They'll have a boat out here for us in less than no time, now that they've seen us."

A faint yellow tone came into the sky over the low land. The shadows on the sea slowly deepened. The wind bore coldness with it, and the men began to shiver.

"Holy smoke!" said one, allowing his voice to express his impious mood, "if we keep on monkeying out here! If we've got to flounder out here all night!"

"Oh, we'll never have to stay here all night! Don't you worry. They've seen us now, and it won't be long before they'll come chasing out after us."

The shore grew dusky. The man waving a coat blended gradually into this gloom, and it swallowed in the same manner the omnibus and the group of people. The spray, when it dashed uproariously over the side, made the voyagers shrink and swear like men who were being branded.

"I'd like to catch the chump who waved the coat. I feel like soaking him one, just for luck."

"Why? What did he do?"

"Oh, nothing, but then he seemed so damned cheerful."

In the meantime the oiler rowed, and then the correspondent rowed, and then the oiler rowed. Gray-faced and bowed forward, they mechanically, turn by turn, plied the leaden oars. The form of the lighthouse had vanished from the southern horizon, but finally a pale star appeared, just lifting from the sea. The streaked saffron in the west passed before the all-merging darkness, and the sea to the east was black. The land had vanished, and was expressed only by the low and drear thunder of the surf.

"If I am going to be drowned—if I am going to be drowned—if I am going to be drowned, why, in the name of the seven mad gods who rule the sea, was I allowed to come thus far and contemplate sand and trees? Was I brought here merely to have my nose dragged away as I was about to nibble the sacred cheese of life?"

The patient captain, drooped over the water-jar, was sometimes obliged to speak to the oarsman.

"Keep her head up! Keep her head up!"

"'Keep her head up,' sir." The voices were weary and low.

This was surely a quiet evening. All save the oarsman lay heavily and listlessly in the boat's bottom. As for him, his eyes were just capable of noting the tall black waves that swept forward in a most sinister silence, save for an occasional subdued growl of a crest.

The cook's head was on a thwart, and he looked without interest at the water under his nose. He was deep in other scenes. Finally he spoke. "Billie," he murmured, dreamfully, "what kind of pie do you like best?"

V

"Pie!" said the oiler and the correspondent, agitatedly. "Don't talk about those things, blast you!"

"Well," said the cook, "I was just thinking about ham sandwiches, and—"

A night on the sea in an open boat is a long night. As darkness settled finally, the shine of the light, lifting from the sea in the south, changed to full gold. On the northern horizon a new light appeared, a small bluish gleam on the edge of the waters. These two lights were the furniture of the world. Otherwise there was nothing but waves.

Two men huddled in the stern, and distances were so magnificent in the dingey that the rower was enabled to keep his feet partly warm by thrusting them under his companions. Their legs indeed extended far under the rowing-seat until they touched the feet of the captain forward. Sometimes, despite the efforts of the tired oarsman, a wave came piling into the boat, an icy wave of the night, and the chilling water soaked them anew. They would twist their bodies for a moment and groan, and sleep the dead sleep once more, while the water in the boat gurgled about them as the craft rocked.

The plan of the oiler and the correspondent was for one to row until he lost the ability, and then arouse the other from his sea-water couch in the bottom of the boat.

The oiler plied the oars until his head drooped forward, and the overpowering sleep blinded him. And he rowed yet afterward. Then he touched a man in the bottom of the boat, and called his name. "Will you spell me for a little while?" he said, meekly.

"Sure, Billie," said the correspondent, awakening and dragging himself to a sitting position. They exchanged places carefully, and the oiler, cuddling down in the sea-water at the cook's side, seemed to go to sleep instantly.

The particular violence of the sea had ceased. The waves

came without snarling. The obligation of the man at the oars was to keep the boat headed so that the tilt of the rollers would not capsize her, and to preserve her from filling when the crests rushed past. The black waves were silent and hard to be seen in the darkness. Often one was almost upon the boat before the oarsman was aware.

In a low voice the correspondent addressed the captain. He was not sure that the captain was awake, although this iron man seemed to be always awake. "Captain, shall I keep her making for that light north, sir?"

The same steady voice answered him. "Yes. Keep it about two points off the port bow."

The cook had tied a life-belt around himself in order to get even the warmth which this clumsy cork contrivance could donate, and he seemed almost stove-like when a rower, whose teeth invariably chattered wildly as soon as he ceased his labor, dropped down to sleep.

The correspondent, as he rowed, looked down at the two men sleeping under foot. The cook's arm was around the oiler's shoulders, and, with their fragmentary clothing and haggard faces, they were the babes of the sea, a grotesque rendering of the old babes in the wood.

Later he must have grown stupid at his work, for suddenly there was a growling of water, and a crest came with a roar and a swash into the boat, and it was a wonder that it did not set the cook afloat in his life-belt. The cook continued to sleep, but the oiler sat up, blinking his eyes and shaking with the new cold.

"Oh, I'm awfully sorry, Billie," said the correspondent, contritely.

"That's all right, old boy," said the oiler, and lay down again and was asleep.

Presently it seemed that even the captain dozed, and the correspondent thought that he was the one man afloat on all the oceans. The wind had a voice as it came over the waves, and it was sadder than the end.

There was a long, loud swishing astern of the boat, and a gleaming trail of phosphorescence, like blue flame, was furrowed on the black waters. It might have been made by a monstrous knife.

Then there came a stillness, while the correspondent breathed with the open mouth and looked at the sea.

Suddenly there was another swish and another long flash of bluish light, and this time it was alongside the boat, and might almost have been reached with an oar. The correspondent saw an enormous fin speed like a shadow through the water, hurling the crystalline spray and leaving the long glowing trail.

The correspondent looked over his shoulder at the captain. His face was hidden, and he seemed to be asleep. He looked at the babes of the sea. They certainly were asleep. So, being bereft of sympathy, he leaned a little way to one side and swore softly into the sea.

But the thing did not then leave the vicinity of the boat. Ahead or astern, on one side or the other, at intervals long or short, fled the long sparkling streak, and there was to be heard the whiroo of the dark fin. The speed and power of the thing was greatly to be admired. It cut the water like a gigantic and keen projectile.

The presence of this biding thing did not affect the man with the same horror that it would if he had been a picnicker. He simply looked at the sea dully and swore in an undertone.

Nevertheless, it is true that he did not wish to be alone with the thing. He wished one of his companions to awaken by chance and keep him company with it. But the captain hung motionless over the water-jar and the oiler and the cook in the bottom of the boat were plunged in slumber.

VI

"If I am going to be drowned—if I am going to be drowned—if I am going to be drowned, why, in the name of the seven mad gods who rule the sea, was I allowed to come thus far and contemplate sand and trees?"

During this dismal night, it may be remarked that a man would conclude that it was really the intention of the seven mad gods to drown him, despite the abominable injustice of it. For it was certainly an abominable injustice to drown a man who had worked so hard, so hard. The man felt it would be a crime most unnatural. Other people had drowned at sea since galleys swarmed with painted sails, but still——

When it occurs to a man that nature does not regard him as important, and that she feels she would not maim the universe by disposing of him, he at first wishes to throw bricks at the temple, and he hates deeply the fact that there are no bricks and no temples. Any visible expression of nature would surely be pelleted with his jeers.

Then, if there be no tangible thing to hoot he feels, perhaps, the desire to confront a personification and indulge in pleas, bowed to one knee, and with hands supplicant, saying: "Yes, but I love myself."

A high cold star on a winter's night is the word he feels that she says to him. Thereafter he knows the pathos of his situation.

The men in the dingey had not discussed these matters, but each had, no doubt, reflected upon them in silence and according to his mind. There was seldom any expression upon their faces save the general one of complete weariness. Speech was devoted to the business of the boat.

To chime the notes of his emotion, a verse mysteriously entered the correspondent's head. He had even forgotten that he had forgotten this verse, but it suddenly was in his mind.

> A soldier of the Legion lay dying in Algiers,
> There was lack of woman's nursing, there was
> dearth of woman's tears;
> But a comrade stood beside him, and he took   that
> comrade's hand
> And he said: "I shall never see my own, my native
> land."

In his childhood, the correspondent had been made acquainted with the fact that a soldier of the Legion lay dying in Algiers, but he had never regarded the fact as important.

Myriads of his school-fellows had informed him of the soldier's plight, but the dinning had naturally ended by making him perfectly indifferent. He had never considered it his affair that a soldier of the Legion lay dying in Algiers, nor had it appeared to him as a matter for sorrow. It was less to him than breaking of a pencil's point.

Now, however, it quaintly came to him as a human, living thing. It was no longer merely a picture of a few throes in the breast of a poet, meanwhile drinking tea and warming his feet at the grate; it was an actuality—stern, mournful, and fine.

The correspondent plainly saw the soldier. He lay on the sand with his feet out straight and still. While his pale left hand was upon his chest in an attempt to thwart the going of his life, the blood came between his fingers. In the far Algerian distance, a city of low square forms was set against a sky that was faint with the last sunset hues. The correspondent, plying the oars and dreaming of the slow and slower movements of the lips of the soldier, was moved by a profound and perfectly impersonal comprehension. He was sorry for the soldier of the Legion who lay dying in Algiers.

The thing which had followed the boat and waited had evidently grown bored at the delay. There was no longer to be heard the slash of the cut-water, and there was no longer the flame of the long trail. The light in the north still glimmered, but it was apparently no nearer to the boat. Sometimes the boom of the surf rang in the correspondent's ears, and he turned the craft seaward then and rowed harder. Southward, someone had evidently built a watch-fire on the beach. It was too low and too far to be seen, but it made a shimmering, roseate reflection upon the bluff back of it, and this could be discerned from the boat. The wind came stronger, and sometimes a wave suddenly raged out like a mountain-cat and there was to be seen the sheen and sparkle of a broken crest.

The captain, in the bow, moved on his water-jar and sat erect. "Pretty long night," he observed to the correspondent. He looked at the shore. "Those life-saving people take their time."

"Did you see that shark playing around?"

"Yes, I saw him. He was a big fellow, all right."

"Wish I had known you were awake."

Later the correspondent spoke into the bottom of the boat.

"Billie!" There was a slow and gradual disentanglement. "Billie, will you spell me?"

"Sure," said the oiler.

As soon as the correspondent touched the cold comfortable sea-water in the bottom of the boat, and had huddled close to the cook's life-belt he was deep in sleep, despite the fact that his teeth played all the popular airs. This sleep was so good to him that it was but a moment before he heard a voice call his name in a tone that demonstrated the last stages of exhaustion. "Will you spell me?"

"Sure, Billie."

The light in the north had mysteriously vanished, but the correspondent took his course from the wide-awake captain.

Later in the night they took the boat farther out to sea, and the captain directed the cook to take one oar at the stern and keep the boat facing the seas. He was to call out if he should hear the thunder of the surf. This plan enabled the oiler and the correspondent to get respite together. "We'll give those boys a chance to get into shape again," said the captain. They curled down and, after a few preliminary chatterings and trembles, slept once more the dead sleep. Neither knew they had bequeathed to the cook the company of another shark, or perhaps the same shark.

As the boat caroused on the waves, spray occasionally bumped over the side and gave them a fresh soaking, but this had no power to break their repose. The ominous slash of the wind and the water affected them as it would have affected mummies.

"Boys," said the cook, with the notes of every reluctance in his voice, "she's drifted in pretty close. I guess one of you had better take her to sea again." The correspondent, aroused, heard the crash of the toppled crests.

As he was rowing, the captain gave him some whiskey and water, and this steadied the chills out of him. "If I ever get

ashore and anybody shows me even a photograph of an
oar—"

At last there was a short conversation.

"Billie . . . . Billie, will you spell me?"

"Sure," said the oiler.

VII

When the correspondent again opened his eyes, the
sea and the sky were each of the gray hue of the dawning.
Later, carmine and gold was painted upon the waters. The
morning appeared finally, in its splendor, with a sky of pure
blue, and the sunlight flamed on the tips of the waves.

On the distant dunes were set many little black cottages,
and a tall white wind-mill reared above them. No man, nor
dog, nor bicycle appeared on the beach. The cottages might
have formed a deserted village.

The voyagers scanned the shore. A conference was held in
the boat. "Well," said the captain, "if no help is coming, we
might better try a run through the surf right away. If we stay
out here much longer we will be too weak to do anything for
overselves at all." The others silently acquiesced in this
reasoning. The boat was headed for the beach. The correspondent wondered if none ever ascended the tall wind-tower, and
if then they never looked seaward. This tower was a giant,
standing with its back to the plight of the ants. It represented
in a degree, to the correspondent, the serenity of nature amid
the struggles of the individual—nature in the wind, and
nature in the vision of men. She did not seem cruel to him
then, nor beneficent, nor treacherous, nor wise. But she was
indifferent, flatly indifferent. It is, perhaps, plausible that a
man in this situation, impressed with the unconcern of the
universe, should see the innumerable flaws of his life and
have them taste wickedly in his mind and wish for another
chance. A distinction between right and wrong seems
absurdly clear to him, then, in this new ignorance of the
grave-edge, and he understands that if he were given another
opportunity he would mend his conduct and his words, and

be better and brighter during an introduction, or at a tea.

"Now, boys," said the captain, "she is going to swamp sure. All we can do is to work her in as far as possible, and then when she swamps, pile out and scramble for the beach. Keep cool now and don't jump until she swamps sure."

The oiler took the oars. Over his shoulders he scanned the surf. "Captain," he said, "I think I'd better bring her about, and keep her head-on to the seas and back her in."

"All right, Billie," said the captain. "Back her in." The oiler swung the boat then and, seated in the stern, the cook and the correspondent were obliged to look over their shoulders to contemplate the lonely and indifferent shore.

The monstrous inshore rollers heaved the boat high until the men were again enabled to see the white sheets of water scudding up the slanted beach. "We won't get in very close," said the captain. Each time a man could wrest his attention from the rollers, he turned his glance toward the shore, and in the expression of the eyes during this contemplation there was a singular quality. The correspondent, observing the others, knew that they were not afraid, but the full meaning of their glances was shrouded.

As for himself, he was too tired to grapple fundamentally with the fact. He tried to coerce his mind into thinking of it, but the mind was dominated at this time by the muscles, and the muscles said they did not care. It merely occurred to him that if he should drown it would be a shame.

There were no hurried words, no pallor, no plain agitation. The men simply looked at the shore. "Now, remember to get well clear of the boat when you jump," said the captain.

Seaward the crest of a roller suddenly fell with a thunderous crash, and the long white comber came roaring down upon the boat.

"Steady now," said the captain. The men were silent. They turned their eyes from the shore to the comber and waited. The boat slid up the incline, leaped at the furious top, bounced over it, and swung down the long back of the waves. Some water had been shipped and the cook bailed it out.

But the next crest crashed also. The tumbling boiling flood

of white water caught the boat and whirled it almost perpendicular. Water swarmed in from all sides. The correspondent had his hands on the gunwale at this time, and when the water entered at that place he swiftly withdrew his fingers, as if he objected to wetting them.

The little boat, drunken with this weight of water, reeled and snuggled deeper into the sea.

"Bail her out, cook! Bail her out," said the captain.

"All right, captain," said the cook.

"Now, boys, the next one will do for us, sure," said the oiler. "Mind to jump clear of the boat."

The third wave moved forward, huge, furious, implacable. It fairly swallowed the dingey, and almost simultaneously the men tumbled into the sea. A piece of life-belt had lain in the bottom of the boat, and as the correspondent went overboard he held this to his chest with his left hand.

The January water was icy, and he reflected immediately that it was colder than he had expected to find it off the coast of Florida. This appeared to his dazed mind as a fact important enough to be noted at the time. The coldness of the water was sad; it was tragic. This fact was somehow mixed and confused with his opinion of his own situation that it seemed almost a proper reason for tears. The water was cold.

When he came to the surface he was conscious of little but the noisy water. Afterward he saw his companions in the sea. The oiler was ahead in the race. He was swimming strongly and rapidly. Off to the correspondent's left, the cook's great white and corked back bulged out of the water, and in the rear the captain was hanging with his one good hand to the keel of the overturned dingey.

There is a certain immovable quality to a shore, and the correspondent wondered at it amid the confusion of the sea.

It seemed also very attractive, but the correspondent knew that it was a long journey, and he paddled leisurely. The piece of life-preserver lay under him, and sometimes he whirled down the incline of a wave as if he were on a hand-sled.

But finally he arrived at a place in the sea where travel was beset with difficulty. He did not pause swimming to inquire what manner of current had caught him, but there his progress ceased. The shore was set before him like a bit of scenery on a stage, and he looked at it and understood with his eyes each detail of it.

As the cook passed, much farther to the left, the captain was calling to him. "Turn over on your back, cook! Turn over on your back and use the oar."

"All right, sir." The cook turned on his back, and, paddling with an oar, went ahead as if he were a canoe.

Presently the boat also passed to the left of the correspondent with the captain clinging with one hand to the keel. He would have appeared like a man raising himself to look over a board fence, if it were not for the extraordinary gymnastics of the boat. The correspondent marvelled that the captain could still hold to it.

They passed on, nearer to shore—the oiler, the cook, the captain—and following them went the water-jar, bouncing gayly over the seas.

The correspondent remained in the grip of this strange new enemy—a current. The shore, with its white slope of sand and its green bluff, topped with little silent cottages, was spread like a picture before him. It was very near to him then, but he was impressed as one who in a gallery looks at a scene from Brittany or Algiers.

He thought: "I am going to drown? Can it be possible? Can it be possible? Can it be possible? Perhaps an individual must consider his own death to be the final phenomenon of nature.

But later a wave perhaps whirled him out of this small deadly current, for he found suddenly that he could again make progress toward the shore. Later still, he was aware that the captain, clinging with one hand to the keel of the dingey, had his face turned away from the shore and toward him, and was calling his name. "Come to the boat! Come to the boat!"

In his struggle to reach the captain and the boat, he reflected that when one gets properly wearied, drowning must really be a comfortable arrangement, a cessation of hostilities accompanied by a large degree of relief, and he was glad of it,

for the main thing in his mind for some moments had been
horror of the temporary agony. He did not wish to be hurt.

Presently he saw a man running along the shore. He was
undressing with most remarkable speed. Coat, trousers, shirt,
everything flew magically off him.

"Come to the boat," called the captain.

"All right, captain." As the correspondent paddled, he saw
the captain let himself down to bottom and leave the boat.
Then the correspondent performed his one little marvel of the
voyage. A large wave caught him and flung him with ease
and supreme speed completely over the boat and far beyond
it. It struck him even then as an event in gymnastics, and a
true miracle of the sea. An overturned boat in the surf is not a
plaything to a swimming man.

The correspondent arrived in water that reached only to
his waist, but his condition did not enable him to stand for
more than a moment. Each wave knocked him into a heap,
and the under-tow pulled at him.

Then he saw the man who had been running and undressing, and undressing and running, come bounding into the
water. He dragged ashore the cook, and then waded toward
the captain, but the captain waved him away, and sent him to
the correspondent. He was naked, naked as a tree in winter,
but a halo was about his head, and he shone like a saint. He
gave a strong pull, and a long drag, and a bully heave at the
correspondent's hand. The correspondent, schooled in the
minor formulae, said: "Thanks, old man." But suddenly the
man cried: "What's that?" He pointed a swift finger. The correspondent said: "Go."

In the shallows, face downward, lay the oiler. His forehead
touched sand that was periodically, between each wave, clear
of the sea.

The correspondent did not know all that transpired afterward. When he achieved safe ground he fell, striking the sand
with each particular part of his body. It was as if he had
dropped from a roof, but the thud was grateful to him.

It seems that instantly the beach was populated with men
with blankets, clothes, and flasks, and women with coffee-

pots and all the remedies sacred to their minds. The welcome of the land to the men from the sea was warm and generous, but a still and dripping shape was carried slowly up the beach, and the land's welcome for it could only be the different and sinister hospitality of the grave.

When it came night, the white waves paced to and fro in the moonlight, and the wind brought the sound of the great sea's voice to the men on shore, and they felt that they could then be interpreters.

Harry Crews

(1935–) has spent most of his life in the South, first in southern Georgia, growing up among tenant farmers, and later in Florida as a student, teacher, and writer. After serving in the productive writing career. He has written thirteen books and numerous essays, most of which take place in the South he knows so well.

The selection from Crews is

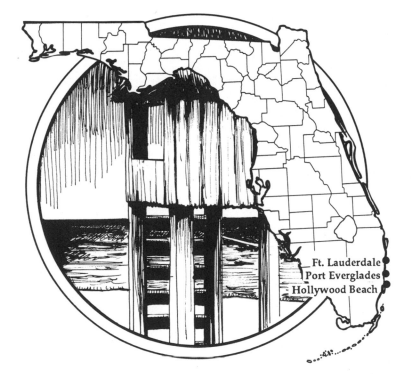

Ft. Lauderdale
Port Everglades
Hollywood Beach

Marine Corps, he earned his master's degree from the University of Florida, taught at Broward Community College in Fort Lauderdale, and returned to the University of Florida in Gainesville to teach creative writing and to continue a very the first chapter of *Karate Is a Thing of the Spirit* (1971), the only excerpt from a longer work in this collection, but Crews considers it complete in itself. The novel is the story of a young drifter who wanders into a commune of karate devotees in

Fort Lauderdale. This chapter shows a former beauty queen demonstrating the power of a karate kick on a young man who had the gall to stare at her naked body. Like much of Crews's fiction, the story emphasizes the value of self-discipline and skill in a flawed world and shows the motives that might lie behind the avid pursuit of such discipline. Crews's prose captures the dedicated rituals of the group of karateka as well as the struggle of a young man to find his place in their harsh world.

Among the writers in this collection, Crews would rank second only to Marjorie Kinnan Rawlings in the significance he gives to place in his writings. He noted in *The Writer* (June 1971, p. 9) that "a sense of place had made a piece of writing come together, jell for me. Place, for me, has always been that important. Until I have *place* firmly in my head, until I begin to smell it and taste it, until it lives in the ends of my fingers, a story simply will not come alive for me." He used his actual home address and phone number in a novel, *The Hawk Is Dying*, because that made the story more authentic for him. He set the story printed here in Fort Lauderdale because he knew the area well and because it represents the contrasts he needed for the story. In a part of southern Florida known for free-spirited students' spring break and lavish high-rise condominiums, the karate devotees practice their deadly skills, oblivious to the luxury steamers nearby and contemptuous of a world that has no need for their skills.

In the novel from which this chapter is taken, John Kaimon spends much of his time trying to find a place where he belongs, just as Crews spent a year and a half motorcycling around the country trying to find the same thing. At the end of the novel, Kaimon decides to leave the karate group and join the beautiful young woman pregnant with his child in seeking a better life. He has come to understand himself better, has decided that he does not fit in with the karateka, and is ready to move on.

Harry Crews

Karate Is a Thing of the Spirit,
Chapter 1

ROM THIS distance it sounded like the barking of a dog. At regular intervals the sound —hoarse, abrupt—came to her over the sand dunes. It was the only sound anywhere. She had been walking for almost an hour: north on U.S. 1, then east on Andrew Johnson to Hollywood Beach and through the retirees and their wives burnt to the color of cork, paunched, sunvisored, greased with Coppertone and Johnson's Baby Oil, through their beach chairs and umbrellas and blankets and wailing transistors, their pinched leathery faces squinting in her direction, their eyes rolling to follow her, not believing her even though they saw her nearly every morning and knew who she was, knew that she was lethal, knew that she taught killing techniques gently.

Then after she had left old men and women—stretched, desiccated and dying, on their individual beach towels—she followed the beach north past Dania, past the Municipal fishing pier and finally onto the deserted, wooded area just south of Fort Lauderdale that had once been the Niggerbeach before the federal courts enlightened the city. Now it was just a stretch of nothing. Rolling sand dunes, brightly decorated with Budweiser cans and Schlitz cans and glinting Sprite bottles, a place where high-school boys came now and again to race their cutdown beach buggies and grope their adolescent squealing sweethearts among the stunted windbent Australian pines.

And pockmarking the beach like abandoned bunkers on a battlefield were homosexual meatracks. The meatracks were little nests made by dragging dead limbs and driftwood and wrecked pieces of cars (the beach buggies often exploded in mid-flight or rammed a tree). On any given day one was apt to discover a lean golden homosexual in the bottom of a nest naked and lonely, dreaming of love.

This place—this beach—was everybody's place because it was nobody's place. Someday a great South Florida Hotel with a lobby like the harem of an Eastern Prince would rise on this stretch of sand. But for the moment, it lay abandoned and forgotten.

With the same measured stride she walked on, a slender blond girl, well-made, with long legs and sharply defined, athletic calves. She walked with her head just turned from the sea, putting her right ear toward the regular, barking sound, which was louder now. She always walked with her face slightly turned to the left because she was totally deaf in her left ear, the eardrum having been blown out by a well-executed roundhouse kick to the head during the first few seconds of a fight at a karate tournament in Atlanta, Georgia.

The whole inside of her head had rung like a bell tower, but she had fought on to win, managing in the process to smash her opponent's instep into a bloody pulp. Her performance had earned her the right to private lessons in the master's room in the dojo.

There, not fifty yards away beside a sea-stripped Australian pine, turned the color of salt by the sun and wind, she saw a man standing on the lip of a meatrack. His back was to her. He was thin, deeply tanned, and wearing a black abbreviated pair of nylon swim trunks.

He looked like an animated anatomy chart. His greased, rippling body was a shimmering of the sun. He shifted and she saw his face. His gaze down into the nest was deeply fond. His eyebrows were golden. He hooked his thumbs on each side of the swimsuit and as he slowly pushed them down his shining hips, he descended into the nest and out of her vision behind the candy-striped door of an abandoned beach buggy.

But she hardly noticed the man go over the lip of the nest. She could see the master now and his coarse explosive bark had already struck the responsive chord in her that obliterated the world. He was her heart's focus now. She had no peripheral vision, no peripheral feeling. She felt her body ache for contact. She watched with a love that was beyond pride, beyond all that her mother (who was determined that someday she would walk down that long runway at Miami Beach with Bert Parks singing "There she comes, Miss America") beyond all that her mother had said her fantastic body could accomplish.

She could see them all now. They were lined up on the beach, nine students in a single row in front of the master. He was on his knees in front of them. Between his knees was a pile of stones. It was morning, the sun no more than three hours high, but the air was already alive with the summer heat.

All of them, including the master, had removed the top part of the gi, and they were dressed now only in the flowing white trousers, cinched and double-knotted at the waist with the karate belt. Lined up in descending order of rank, there was a purple belt, two blue belts, two green belts and four yellow belts. The kneeling master's belt was black.

The students were going through the formal, ritualized movements of the Heavenly Kata of Japan. The master was breaking stones. Every time the master struck a stone, he kyaied. And every time the sound of the kyai—the fierce, abrupt roar of the karateka—tore from the master's throat, his students, locked and synchronized like a machine, made one of the hundred blocks and punches of the Heavenly Kata of Japan. And the stones, without exception, as they were struck, parted cleanly.

She walked straight to them and stood behind the master. He did not address her, nor did any of the students' eyes follow her movements. None of them blinked. They were taught that when two karateka of equal ability meet in a fight to the death the first one who blinks dies. Consequently, during kumite and kata, they tried not to blink.

Their eyes were glazed and they appeared as blind men. Their faces were leached of color. Their mouths were slack. Strings of ropy spit hung from the chin of the purple belt. Still the hoarse bark of the master never hesitated. And the nine students, as though their bodies were somehow operated by the master's kyai bouncing back out of the scorched wall of Australian pine, never missed a move either.

Then the kata was finished, the last block made, the last punch thrown. They all stood frozen in the sun. The master sat easy on his heels with his legs doubled under him. His swollen hands were open on his knees. His face was tranquil. He seemed about to smile.

"Rai!" cried the master.

The students bowed stiffly from the hips, but then resumed their unmoving stance, their fists clenched in front of them. They did not appear to be breathing. She knew that some of them could no longer think, no longer knew where they were. Or even who they were.

They had been here since just before daylight staring into the sun rising over the glittering ocean. Their eyes blinked rapidly now that they were out of kata. But it was all reflex. They were not aware of their stinging gritty eyes, nor were they aware of their numb muscles or bleeding feet.

Karate filled them full. There was room for nothing else. Their hearts pumped small images of Dhourma, the legendary monk who brought karate from India through the Himalayas to China.

But like all good monks everywhere, she thought, the toughest test yet remained. It was time.

She took one step forward and removed the yellow top of her bikini. Her breasts burst free in the sun. The nipples—the color of brown sugar —trembled. They stood at right angles to her rippling rib cage. Not an eye moved. She turned and went knee-deep into the waveless ocean, bent and dipped salt water high over her shoulders. The water converged between her high easy breasts and ran down the indentation of her muscled belly and finally into the yellow triangular bikini bottom. In a single slipping graceful movement she got out of the bikini pants and was naked. The hair at the base of her belly was high and curling and blond.

She walked up on the sand and dropped the bikini pants with the top just behind the master. He sat as before, his hands thicker, more swollen now. She did not look at him. She moved slowly before the students. The drops of salt water caught and held the sun where they hung on her skin.

She was just turning at the end of the line when she saw the movement. It was hardly movement at all: the quickest flutter of an eyelid, the marginal sliding of a blue eye in her direction, the blue desperate focus on her swelling nipples.

But it was enough. She saw. And the student, one of the yellow belts, saw she saw. And then his humiliation was complete: his gaze, open and with infinite sadness, fell full upon her triangular puff of golden hair.

She kicked him in the sternum. She screamed — kyaied — and from where she stood, in a single sweeping movement she caught him in the middle of the chest with the steel-hard point of her heel. He buckled. Went to one knee, but rose again. His right eye was suddenly shot with blood. He bowed to her.

The master did not watch. His gaze was lost somewhere in the middle distance, his hands limp but swelling on his knees. She smiled. The student rapidly closed and opened his blood-red eye. The eye was watering badly. She waited until the eye closed again—until she knew the boy had no depth perception—and then she threw the same roundhouse kick she had hit him with before, an Okinawan reverse roundhouse that led with the point of the heel. But as soon as the kick started, the bloody eye snapped open; the boy dropped into a nekoashi dachi—a fighting cat stance—and was waiting, poised, when her back was exposed to him at the crucial moment of the kick.

He worked to her short ribs with a flying front snap kick.

When he fell back into the cat stance, he left the print of his five toes in her side. A half-moon of blood appeared where the nail of his big toe had driven against a rib. He smiled. Tears ran down his cheek from the bloody eye. She bowed to him. But her smile was gone. Her lips were thin and blue as ice.

"Rai!" cried the master.

She and the boy bowed to each other. She picked up the triangular pants and stepped into them. No one breathed while she pushed her trembling breasts into the yellow top and fastened it behind her.

The master stretched his neck and cried: "Prepare for kumite!"

Four students stepped forward, turned, and faced four students. The girl still stood in front of the yellow belt whose eye had moved to follow her and whom she had kicked.

"To the stones!"

They turned and, paired together, trotted off down the sand. The master did not go with them. He rose—not stiffly, but like a spring uncoiling—and shook his legs, swung his arms, rolled his head. Twenty yards away was a high tower made of plywood and metal pipes. It was painted red. He went to the tower, climbed to the top, and sat down. At one time the tower had belonged to a black lifeguard who tended a flock of black sunbathers lying about over the glittering beach or surfacing like seals in the blue water. But they were gone now. And they would not return.

The lifeguard stand was a sturdy thing (it had survived several direct hits by wildly careening beach buggies in the middle of the night). From the top of it he could see his students now spread out over the long line of enormous granite boulders, some of them weighing as much as fifty tons, that formed the south jetty of Port Everglades, the deepest port in Florida.

A huge white luxury ship of the Cunard Line was just leaving Fort Lauderdale, steaming out of Port Everglades under its own power but followed by tugboats and fireboats. The sound of tug whistles shook the air and great streams of water from the fireboats waved like lengths of ribbon against the sky.

With a sudden effort of will, the master gave himself tunnel vision, blocking out the white liner and the boats following it, so that all he saw was his students shining under the sun where they had taken fighting stances facing each other on the uppermost levels of the granite boulders.

The master took a deep breath. "Adshumi!" His diaphragm slammed upwards and the word—the signal to begin fighting—burst from his throat and out over the rocks like the report of a gun.

The girl, who stood farthest from the master, was the first to react. Out of pride—which she recognized as pride and immediately hated herself for—out of pride, because she had missed with it earlier, she again threw the Okinawan reverse roundhouse. This time the boy made himself take the blow without blocking or flinching. He had no chance against her anyway. The brown belt that was not hanging about her smooth bare hips, but hanging back in her room at the dojo, had him intimidated. But that was not what kept him from trying to at least partially block the kick. He had to be kicked—*he ought to be kicked*—because he could not forget her trembling brownsugar nipples and gleaming loins.

For the first time the Cunard Line steamer answered the screaming tugs and spraying fireboats. A valve opened on top of the liner's center red and black smokestack and her whistle—low as a groan—shook the air.

Edwin Granberry

(1897–), a Mississippi-born writer, spent much of his life in Florida, attending the University of Florida and teaching literature and writing at Rollins College in Winter Park. Over a long

Trip to Czardis" has given him the most acclaim.

Originally printed in *Forum* magazine in 1932, the story won the O. Henry Memorial Prize and has been reprinted many

writing career he published four novels, two plays, many articles and short stories, and translations from French; he even coauthored the "Buz Sawyer" comic strip for thirty years. However, his story "A

times in anthologies. It is a moving story, full of restraint and drama, about a young mother and her sons saying goodby to their husband and father, who is to be executed for a murder of which he has been convicted. The prison is located in the town of Czardis, whose name sounds Greek or Russian, and it is indeed an alien place to a rural family; the town will always seem so to the boys who will remember it as the place where their father died. At the end of the story, the older boy realizes that he must take over his father's role as head of the family; the family must pull together and stand firm against the stares and remarks of their neighbors.

Thirty-four years after the appearance of this story, Granberry used it as an epilogue in a novel of the same name that answered the questions of many readers about what had happened before the story begins. A rich landowner, Ponce Logan lived on a ranch with his childless wife, Lenora, his foreman, Jim Cameron, and Jim's wife and two sons. In a moment of weakness, Ponce told Jim of his sterility and asked Jim to father a child with Lenora. Jim refused, but later, when Ponce was away, Lenora seduced Jim and became pregnant. When Ponce returned and learned about the pregnancy, he threatened to kill Jim. Still later, when Jim and Ponce were alone in a boat on the Gulf of Mexico, Ponce killed himself in a moment of despair. Jim refused to tarnish Ponce's reputation by revealing that Ponce had committed suicide, and he was condemned to death for Ponce's murder.

While one does not have to know the plot of the novel that Granberry wrote around this story, knowing it helps to keep the reader from being distracted by questions regarding Jim's conviction and possible innocence. "A Trip to Czardis" is probably the most moving story in this collection, not only because it is a story of a young boy having maturity thrust upon him (as are the stories by Crews, Justice, and Kantor) but also because it is set in a state that today has one of the largest number of condemned criminals on death row.

Edwin Granberry

A Trip to Czardis

I T WAS STILL dark in the pine woods when the two brothers awoke. But it was plain that day had come, and in a little while there would be no more stars. Day itself would be in the sky and they would be going along the road. Jim waked first, coming quickly out of sleep and sitting up in the bed to take fresh hold of the things in his head, starting them up again out of the corners of his mind where sleep had tucked them. Then he waked Daniel and they sat up together in the bed. Jim put his arm around his young brother, for the night had been dewy and cool with the swamp wind. Daniel shivered a little and whimpered, it being dark in the room and his baby concerns still on him somewhat, making sleep heavy on his mind and slow to give understanding its way.

"Hit's the day, Dan'l. This day that's right here now, we are goen. You'll recollect it all in a minute."

"I recollect. We are goen in the wagon to see Papa—"

"Then hush and don't whine."

"I were dreamen, Jim."

"What dreamen did you have?"

"I can't tell. But it were fearful what I dreamt."

"All the way we are goen this time. We won't stop at any places, but we will go all the way to Czardis to see Papa. I never see such a place as Czardis."

"I recollect the water tower—"

"Not in your own right, Dan'l. Hit's by my tellen it you see it in your mind."

"And lemonade with ice in it I saw—"

"That too I seen and told to you."

"Then I never seen it at all?"

"Hit's me were there, Dan'l. I let you play like, but hit's me who went to Czardis. Yet I never till this day told half how much I see. There's sights I never told."

They stopped talking, listening for their mother's stir in the kitchen. But the night stillness was unlifted. Daniel began to shiver again.

"Hit's dark," he said.

"Hit's your eyes stuck," Jim said. "Would you want me to drip a little water on your eyes?"

"Oh!" cried the young one, pressing his face into his brother's side, "don't douse me, Jim, no more. The cold aches me."

The other soothed him, holding him around the body.

"You won't have e're chill or malarie ache to-day, Dan'l. Hit's a fair day—"

"I won't be cold?"

"Hit's a bright day. I hear mournen doves starten a'ready. The sun will bake you warm. . . . Uncle Holly might buy us somethen new to eat in Czardis."

"What would it be?"

"Hit ain't decided yet. . . . He hasn't spoke. Hit might be somethen sweet. Maybe a candy ball fixed onto a rubber string."

"A candy ball!" Daniel showed a stir of happiness. "Oh, Jim!" But it was a deceit of the imagination, making his eyes shine wistfully; the grain of his flesh was against it. He settled into a stillness by himself.

"My stomach would retch it up, Jim. . . . I guess I couldn't eat it."

"You might could keep a little down."

"No . . . I would bring it home and keep it. . . . "

Their mother when they went to bed had laid a clean pair of pants and a waist for each on the chair. Jim crept out of bed and put on his clothes, then aided his brother on with his. They could not hear any noise in the kitchen, but hickory firewood burning in the kitchen stove worked a smell through the house, and in the forest guinea fowls were sailing down from the trees and poking their way along the half-dark ground toward the kitchen steps, making it known the door was open and that within someone was stirring about at the getting of food.

Jim led his brother by the hand down the dark way of yellow-pine stairs that went narrowly and without banisters to the rooms below. The young brother went huddling in his clothes, aguelike, knowing warmth was near, hungering for his place by the stove, to sit in peace on the bricks in the floor by the stove's side and watch the eating, it being his nature to have a sickness against food.

They came in silence to the kitchen, Jim leading and holding his brother by the hand. The floor was lately strewn with fresh bright sand, and that would sparkle when the daybreak got above the forest, though now it lay dull as hoarfrost and cold to the unshod feet of the brothers. The door to the firebox of the stove was open, and in front of it their mother sat in a chair, speaking low as they entered, muttering under her breath. The two boys went near and stood still, thinking she was blessing the food, there being mush dipped up and steaming in two bowls. And they stood cast down until she lifted her eyes to them and spoke.

"Your clothes on already," she said. "You look right neat." She did not rise, but kept her chair, looking cold and stiff, with the cloth of her black dress sagging between her knees. The sons stood in front of her, and she laid her hand on first one head and then the other and spoke a little about the day, charging them to be sober and of few words, as she had raised them.

Jim sat on the bench by the table and began to eat, mixing dark molasses sugar through his bowl of mush. But a nausea began in Daniel's stomach at sight of the sweet, and he lagged by the stove, gazing at the food as it passed into his brother's mouth.

Suddenly a shadow filled the back doorway and Holly, their uncle, stood there looking in. He was lean and big and dark from wind and weather, working in the timber as their father had done. He had no wife and children and would roam far off with the timber gangs in the Everglades. This latter year he did not go far, but stayed near them. Their mother stopped and looked at the man, and he looked at her in silence. Then he looked at Jim and Daniel.

"You're goen to take them after all?"

She waited a minute, seeming to get the words straight in her mind before bringing them out, making them say what was set there.

"He asked to see them. Nobody but God Almighty ought to tell a soul hit can or can't have."

Having delivered her mind, she went out into the yard with the man, and they spoke more words in an undertone, pausing in their speech.

In the silence of the kitchen Daniel began to speak out and name what thing among his possessions he would take to Czardis to give his father. But the older boy belittled this and that and everything that was called up, saying one thing was of too little consequence for a man, and that another was of no account because it was food. But when the older boy had abolished the idea and silence had regained, he worked back to the thought, coming to it roundabout and making it new and as his own, letting it be decided that each of them would take their father a pomegranate from the tree in the yard.

They went to the kitchen door. The swamp fog had risen suddenly. They saw their mother standing in the lot while their uncle hitched the horse to the wagon. Leaving the steps, Jim climbed to the first crotch of the pomegranate tree. The reddest fruits were on the top branches. He worked his way up higher. The fog was now curling up out of the swamp, making gray mountains and rivers in the air and strange ghost shapes. Landmarks disappeared in the billows, or half seen, they bewildered the sight and an eye could so little mark the known or strange that a befuddlement took hold of the mind, like the visitations sailors beheld in the fogs of

Okeechobee. Jim could not find the ground. He seemed to have climbed into the mountains. The light was unnatural and dark, and the pines were blue and dark over the mountains.

A voice cried out of the fog:

"Are worms gnawen you that you skin up a pomegranate tree at this hour? Don't I feed you enough?"

The boy worked his way down. At the foot of the tree he met his mother. She squatted and put her arm around him, her voice tight and quivering, and he felt tears on her face.

"We ain't come to the shame yet of you and Dan'l hunten your food off trees and grass. People seein' you gnawen on the road will say Jim Cameron's sons are starved, foragen like cattle of the field."

"I were getten the pomegranates for Papa," said the boy, resigned to his mother's concern. She stood up when he said this, holding him in front of her skirts. In a while she said:

"I guess we won't take any, Jim. . . . But I'm proud it come to you to take your papa somethen."

And after a silence, the boy said:

"Hit were Dan'l it come to, Mamma."

Then she took his hand, not looking down, and in her throat, as if in her bosom, she repeated:

"Hit were a fine thought and I'm right proud . . . though today we won't take anything. . . . "

"I guess there's better pomegranates in Czardis where we are goen—"

"There's no better pomegranates in Czardis than right here over your head," she said grimly. "If pomegranates were needed, we would take him his own. . . . You are older'n Dan'l, Jim. When we get to the place we are goen, you won't know your papa after so long. He will be pale and he won't be as bright as you recollect. So don't labor him with questions . . . but speak when it behooves you and let him see you are upright."

When the horse was harnessed and all was ready for the departure, the sons were seated on a shallow bed of hay in the back of the wagon and the mother took the driver's seat alone. The uncle had argued for having the top up over the seat, but she refused the shelter, remarking that she had always driven under the sky and would do it still today. He gave in silently and got upon the seat of his own wagon, which took the road first, their wagon following. This was strange, and the sons asked:

"Why don't we all ride in Uncle Holly's wagon?"

But their mother made no reply.

For several miles they traveled in silence through their own part of the woods, meeting no one. The boys whispered a little to themselves, but their mother and their uncle sat without speaking, nor did they turn their heads to look back. At last the narrow road they were following left the woods and came out to the highway, and it was seen that other wagons besides their own were going to Czardis. And as they got farther along, they began to meet many other people going to the town, and the boys asked their mother what day it was. It was Wednesday. And then they asked her why so many wagons were going along the road if it wasn't Saturday and a market day. When she told them to be quiet, they settled down to watching the people go by. Some of them were faces that were strange, and some were neighbors who lived in other parts of the woods. Some who passed them stared in silence, and some went by looking straight to the front. But there were none of them who spoke, for their mother turned her eyes neither right nor left, but drove the horse on like a woman in her sleep. All was silent as the wagons passed, except the squeaking of the wheels and the thud of the horses' hoofs on the dry, packed sand.

At the edge of the town the crowds increased, and their wagon got lost in the press of people. All were moving in one direction.

Finally they were going along by a high brick wall on top of which ran a barbed-wire fence. Farther along the way in the middle of the wall was a tall, stone building with many people in front. There were trees along the outside of the wall, and in the branches of one of the trees Daniel saw a man. He was looking over the brick wall down into the courtyard. All the wagons were stopping here and hitching through the grove in front of the building. But their Uncle Holly's wagon and their own drove on, making way slowly as through a crowd at a fair, for under the trees knots of men were gathered, talking in undertone. Daniel pulled at his mother's skirts and whispered:

"What made that man climb up that tree?"

Again she told him to be quiet.

"We're not to talk today," said Jim. "Papa is sick and we're not to make him worse." But his high, thin voice made his mother turn cold. She looked back and saw he had grown pale and still, staring at the iron-barred windows of the building. When he caught her gaze, his chin began to quiver, and she turned back front to dodge the knowledge of his eyes.

For the two wagons had stopped now and the uncle gotten down and left them sitting alone while he went to the door of the building and talked with a man standing there. The crowd fell silent, staring at their mother.

"See, Jim, all the men up the trees!" Daniel whispered once more, leaning close in to his brother's side.

"Hush, Dan'l. Be still."

The young boy obeyed this time, falling into a bewildered stare at all the things about him he did not understand, for in all the trees along the brick wall men began to appear perched high in the branches, and on the roof of a building across the way stood other men, all gaping at something in the yard back of the wall.

Their uncle returned and hitched his horse to a ring in one of the trees. Then he hitched their mother's horse, and all of them got out and stood on the ground in a huddle. The walls of the building rose before them. Strange faces at the barred windows laughed aloud and called down curses at the men below.

Now they were moving, with a wall of faces on either side of them, their uncle going first, followed by their mother who held to each of them by a hand. They went up the steps of the building. The door opened, and their uncle stepped inside. He came back in a moment, and all of them went in and followed a man down a corridor and into a bare room with two chairs and a wooden bench. A man in a black robe sat on one of the chairs, and in front of him on the bench, leaning forward, looking down between his arms, sat their father. His face was lean and gray, which made him look very tall. But his hair was black, and his eyes were blue and mild and strange as he stood up and held the two sons against his body while he stooped his head to kiss their mother. The man in black left the room and walked up and down outside in the corridor. A second stranger stood in the doorway with his back to the room. The father picked up one of the sons and then the other in his arms and looked at them and leaned their faces on his own. Then he sat down on the bench and held them against him. Their mother sat down by them and they were all together.

A few low words were spoken, and then a silence fell over them all. And in a while the parents spoke a little more and touched one another. But the bare stone floor and the stone walls and the unaccustomed arms of their father hushed the sons with the new and strange. And when the time had passed, the father took his watch from his pocket:

"I'm goen to give you my watch, Jim. You are the oldest. I want you to keep it till you are a grown man. . . . And I want you to always do what Mamma tells you. . . . I'm goen to give you the chain, Dan'l. . . . "

The young brother took the chain, slipped out of his father's arms, and went to his mother with it. He spread it out on her knee and began to talk to her in a whisper. She bent over him, and again all of them in the room grew silent.

A sudden sound of marching was heard in the corridor. The man rose up and took his sons in his arms, holding them abruptly. But their uncle, who had been standing with the man in the doorway, came suddenly and took them and went out and down through the big doorway by which they had entered the building. As the doors opened to let them pass, the crowd gathered around the steps pressed forward to look inside. The older boy cringed in his uncle's arms. His uncle turned and stood with his back to the crowd. Their mother came through the doors. The crowd fell back. Again through a passageway of gazing eyes, they reached the wagons. This time they sat on the seat beside their mother. Leaving their uncle and his wagon behind, they started off on the road that led out of town.

"Is Papa coming home with Uncle Holly?" Jim asked in a still voice.

His mother nodded her head.

Reaching the woods once more and the silence he knew, Daniel whispered to his brother:

"We got a watch and chain instead, Jim."

But Jim neither answered nor turned his eyes.

Ernest Hemingway

(1899–1961) is the writer most often associated with Key West, partly because of his well-preserved house there, now a museum, and partly because of the town's annual Hemingway Key West from 1928 to 1940, producing some of his most important work and doing much to foster the Hemingway mystique of safari hunter and deep-sea fisherman. Among his

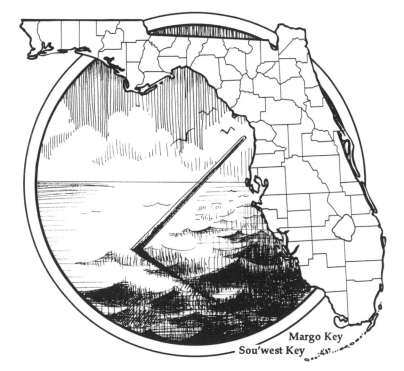

Margo Key
Sou'west Key

Days Festival. In his full life, he worked as a reporter in Kansas City, served with an ambulance crew in Italy during World War I, and worked as a writer and reporter in various European cities after the war. He lived in many awards were the Pulitzer Prize for Literature in 1953 and the Nobel Prize for Literature in 1954.

"After the Storm" (1932), one of his few stories set in Florida, is based on a true story

Hemingway heard from a ship's captain about the sinking of a Spanish liner. A sponge-fisherman, after he flees a barroom fight, discovers a boat sunk in a fierce storm off the Florida Keys. Like other Hemingway heroes, he uses brute force to try to solve his problems, whether man-vs.-man conflicts on land or man-vs.-sea conflicts offshore. He realizes in the end that he will not recover any of the cargo from the ship, partly because he was unprepared to enter the ship and partly because others, like the Greeks in the story, were quicker to reap the rewards of people's misfortunes. In any case, the fisherman stoically accepts his fate and holds no grudges.

The story recalls an important but disparaged episode in the state's history—wrecking. During the nineteenth century, when a ship ran aground or became disabled on the reef along the Florida Keys, wreckers sped out to the site to see what they could salvage. They usually had a license that allowed them to work on the wrecks, where they were expected first to rescue the crew and only then the cargo, which they would take ashore to auctions in Key West. There the wreckers would claim a high fee for the salvage operations, from which they became wealthy and the town prosperous. Some unscrupulous wreckers would set up false lights on the beach to lure unsuspecting ships onto the deadly reefs. Indeed, the salvagers in Hemingway's story might not have bothered informing the authorities of their work on the sunken boat; instead, they simply stripped her of her valuables before the narrator was able to return to the boat with the proper equipment and do the looting himself.

Ernest Hemingway

After the Storm

I T WASN'T about anything, something about making punch, and then we started fighting and I slipped and he had me down kneeling on my chest and choking me with both hands like he was trying to kill me and all the time I was trying to get the knife out of my pocket to cut him loose. Everybody was too drunk to pull him off me. He was choking me and hammering my head on the floor and I got the knife out and opened it up; and I cut the muscle right across his arm and he let go of me. He couldn't have held on if he wanted to. Then he rolled and hung onto that arm and started to cry and I said:

"What the hell you want to choke me for?"

I'd have killed him. I couldn't swallow for a week. He hurt my throat bad.

Well, I went out of there and there were plenty of them with him and some came out after me and I made a turn and was down by the docks and I met a fellow and he said somebody killed a man up the street. I said "Who killed him?" and he said "I don't know who killed him but he's dead all right," and it was dark and there was water standing in the street and no lights and windows broke and boats all up in the town and trees blown down and everything all blown and I got a skiff and went out and found my boat where I had her inside of Mango Key and she was all right only she was full of water. So I bailed her out and pumped her out and there was a moon but plenty of clouds and still plenty rough and I took it down along; and when it was daylight I was off Eastern Harbor.

Brother, that was some storm. I was the first boat out and you never saw water like that was. It was just as white as a lye barrel and coming from Eastern Harbor to Sou'west Key you couldn't recognize the shore. There was a big channel blown right out through the middle of the beach. Trees and all blown out and a channel cut through and all the water white as chalk and everything on it; branches and whole trees and dead birds, and all floating. Inside the keys were all the pelicans in the world and all kinds of birds flying. They must have gone inside there when they knew it was coming.

I lay at Sou'west Key a day and nobody came after me. I was the first boat out and I seen a spar floating and I knew there must be a wreck and I started out to look for her. I found her. She was a three-masted schooner and I could just see the stumps of her spars out of water. She was in too deep water and I didn't get anything off of her. So I went on looking for something else. I had the start on all of them and I knew I ought to get whatever there was. I went on down over the sand-bars from where I left that three-masted schooner and I didn't find anything and I went on a long way. I was way out toward the quicksands and I didn't find anything so I went on. Then when I was in sight of the Rebecca Light I saw all kinds of birds making over something and I headed over for them to see what it was and there was a cloud of birds all right.

I could see something looked like a spar up out of the water and when I got over close the birds all went up in the air and stayed all around me. The water was clear out there and there was a spar of some kind sticking out just above the water and when I come up close to it I saw it was all dark under water like a long shadow and I came right over it and there under water was a liner; just lying there all under water as big as the whole world. I drifted over her in the boat. She lay on her side and the stern was deep down. The port holes were all shut tight and I could see the glass shine in the water and the whole of her; the biggest boat I ever saw in my life

laying there and I went along the whole length of her and
then I went over and anchored and I had the skiff on the deck
forward and I shoved it down into the water and sculled over
with the birds all around me.

I had a water glass like we use sponging and my hand
shook so I could hardly hold it. All the port holes were shut
that you could see going along over her but way down below
near the bottom something must have been open because
there were pieces of things floating out all the time. You
couldn't tell what they were. Just pieces. That's what the birds
were after. You never saw so many birds. They were all
around me; crazy yelling.

I could see everything sharp and clear. I could see her
rounded over and she looked a mile long under the water. She
was lying on a clear white bank of sand and the spar was a
sort of foremast or some sort of tackle that slanted out of water
the way she was laying on her side. Her bow wasn't very far
under. I could stand on the letters of her name on her bow and
my head was just out of water. But the nearest port hole was
twelve feet down. I could just reach it with the grains pole and
I tried to break it with that but I couldn't. The glass was too
stout. So I sculled back to the boat and got a wrench and
lashed it to the end of the grains pole and I couldn't break it.
There I was looking down through the glass at that liner with
everything in her and I was the first one to her and I couldn't
get into her. She must have had five million dollars worth in
her.

It made me shaky to think how much she must have in
her. Inside the port hole that was closest I could see something but I couldn't make it out through the water glass. I
couldn't do any good with the grains pole and I took off my
clothes and stood and took a couple of deep breaths and dove
over off the stern with the wrench in my hand and swam
down. I could hold on for a second to the edge of the port hole
and I could see in and there was a woman inside with her hair
floating all out. I could see her floating plain and I hit the
glass twice with the wrench hard and I heard the noise clink
in my ears but it wouldn't break and I had to come up.

I hung onto the dinghy and got my breath and then I climbed in and took a couple of breaths and dove again. I swam down and took hold of the edge of the port hole with my fingers and held it and hit the glass as hard as I could with the wrench. I could see the woman floated in the water through the glass. Her hair was tied once close to her head and it floated all out in the water. I could see the rings on one of her hands. She was right up close to the port hole and I hit the glass twice and I didn't even crack it. When I came up I thought I wouldn't make it to the top before I'd have to breathe.

I went down once more and I cracked the glass, only cracked it, and when I came up my nose was bleeding and I stood on the bow of the liner with my bare feet on the letters of her name and my head just out and rested there and then I swam over to the skiff and pulled up into it and sat there waiting for my head to stop aching and looking down into the water glass, but I bled so I had to wash out the water glass. Then I lay back in the skiff and held my hand under my nose to stop it and I lay there with my head back looking up and there was a million birds above and all around.

When I quit bleeding I took another look through the glass and then I sculled over to the boat to try and find something heavier than the wrench but I couldn't find a thing; not even a sponge hook. I went back and the water was clearer all the time and you could see everything that floated out over that white bank of sand. I looked for sharks but there weren't any. You could have seen a shark a long way away. The water was so clear and the sand white. There was a grapple for an anchor on the skiff and I cut it off and went overboard and down with it. It carried me right down and past the port hole and I grabbed and couldn't hold anything and went on down and down, sliding along the curved side of her. I had to let go of the grapple. I heard it bump once and it seemed like a year before I came up through to the top of the water. The skiff was floated away with the tide and I swam over to her with my nose bleeding in the water while I swam and I was plenty glad there weren't sharks; but I was tired.

My head felt cracked open and I lay in the skiff and rested and then I sculled back. It was getting along in the afternoon. I went down once more with the wrench and it didn't do any good. That wrench was too light. It wasn't any good diving unless you had a big hammer or something heavy enough to do good. Then I lashed the wrench to the grains pole again and I watched through the water glass and pounded on the glass and hammered until the wrench came off and I saw it in the glass, clear and sharp, go sliding down along her and then off and down to the quicksand and go in. Then I couldn't do a thing. The wrench was gone and I'd lost the grapple so I sculled back to the boat. I was too tired to get the skiff aboard and the sun was pretty low. The birds were all pulling out and leaving her and I headed for Sou'west Key towing the skiff and the birds going on ahead of me and behind me. I was plenty tired.

That night it came on to blow and it blew for a week. You couldn't get out to her. They come out from town and told me the fellow I'd had to cut was all right except for his arm and I went back to town and they put me under five hundred dollar bond. It came out all right because some of them, friends of mine, swore he was after me with an ax, but by the time we got back out to her the Greeks had blown her open and cleaned her out. They got the safe out with dynamite. Nobody ever knows how much they got. She carried gold and they got it all. They stripped her clean. I found her and I never got a nickel out of her.

It was a hell of a thing all right. They say she was just outside of Havana harbor when the hurricane hit and she couldn't get in or the owners wouldn't let the captain chance coming in; they say he wanted to try; so she had to go with it and in the dark they were running with it trying to go through the gulf between Rebecca and Tortugas when she struck on the quicksands. Maybe her rudder was carried away. Maybe they weren't even steering. But anyway they couldn't have known they were quicksands and when she struck the captain must have ordered them to open up the ballast tanks so she'd lay solid. But it was quicksand she'd hit

and when they opened the tank she went in stern first and
then over on her beam ends. There were four hundred and
fifty passengers and the crew on board of her and they must
all have been aboard of her when I found her. They must have
opened the tanks as soon as she struck and the minute she
settled on it the quicksands took her down. Then her boilers
must have burst and that must have been what made those
pieces that came out. It was funny there weren't any sharks
though. There wasn't a fish. I could have seen them on that
clear white sand.

Plenty of fish now though; jewfish, the biggest kind. The
biggest part of her's under the sand now but they live inside
of her; the biggest kind of jewfish. Some weigh three to four
hundred pounds. Sometime we'll go out and get some. You
can see the Rebecca light from where she is. They've got a
buoy on her now. She's right at the end of the quicksand right
at the edge of the gulf. She only missed going through by
about a hundred yards. In the dark in the storm they just
missed it; raining the way it was they couldn't have seen the
Rebecca. Then they're not used to that sort of thing. The captain of a liner isn't used to scudding that way. They have a
course and they tell me they set some sort of a compass and it
steers itself. They probably didn't know where they were
when they ran with that blow but they come close to making
it. Maybe they'd lost the rudder though. Anyway there wasn't
another thing for them to hit till they'd get to Mexico once
they were in that gulf. Must have been something though
when they struck in that rain and wind and he told them to
open her tanks. Nobody could have been on deck in that blow
and rain. Everybody must have been below. They couldn't
have lived on deck. There must have been some scenes inside
all right because you know she settled fast. I saw that wrench
go into the sand. The captain couldn't have known it was
quicksand when she struck unless he knew these waters. He
just knew it wasn't rock. He must have seen it all up in the
bridge. He must have known what it was about when she
settled. I wonder how fast she made it. I wonder if the mate
was there with him. Do you think they stayed inside the

bridge or do you think they took it outside? They never found any bodies. Not a one. Nobody floating. They float a long way with life belts too. They must have took it inside. Well, the Greeks got it all. Everything. They must have come fast all right. They picked her clean. First there was the birds, then me, then the Greeks, and even the birds got more out of her than I did.

James Leo Herlihy

(1927–   ) is one of a group of writers who settled in Key West to write, as did Hemingway, Robert Frost, Elizabeth Bishop, and Tennessee Williams. Unlike the writers who used Key West as both a playwright and an actor. Among his novels are *All Fall Down* (1960) and *Midnight Cowboy* (1965); among the plays he wrote or coauthored are *Moon in Capricorn* (1953) and

Key West

as a haven from distractions but wrote about other places, Herlihy set some of his best work there. Born in Michigan and educated in North Carolina, he used his talents to write fiction and work in the theater *Blue Denim* (1958).

For "The Day of the Seventh Fire," published in the first issue of *Florida Quarterly* (1967), Herlihy used the setting of his adopted Florida home. Like much of his work, the story deals with people isolated from the mainstream of life but quite content to live solitary lives dignified by self-respect and order. The first paragraph of the story alludes to one of the worst hurricanes to hit the Florida Keys, the Labor Day hurricane of 1935, which destroyed the railroad that Henry Flagler had built to Key West in 1912. The so-called Overseas Railroad was expected to open up the Keys to development and commerce, but after the hurricane the train company gave up and abandoned the line. The town of Key West, which had had such high hopes of being connected by rail to the mainland, settled in for a long bout of hopelessness compounded by the economic depression that gripped the rest of the nation.

Some of the residents of Key West, described in the second paragraph of the story, went "stir crazy" in the isolation and insularity of the island. Writers like Thomas McGuane in his novel *Ninety-two in the Shade* have dealt with this phenomenon and with what happens to even ordinary people over long periods of solitude, and the two spinsters in Herlihy's story might have been so affected. Bizarre as their attempts to shoot a suspected prowler may seem, the sisters are endearing in their affection for and loyalty to each other and in their equanimity in the face of misfortune. When an arsonist burns their house, they are much less distraught than one might expect, partly because the house had become a bone of contention between them anyway and partly because they are able to put a proper value on material goods.

James Leo Herlihy

The Day of the Seventh Fire

EY WEST in 1936 was a dismal place. A bad hurricane had blown away the railroad, cutting off the island's one connection with the mainland. There were no jobs to speak of in that Depression year. Not much food either. A good fisherman always had something to set on his table, and you could get in line for sugar and grits and certain staples the Government was handing out; but many people had taken to eating grass and weeds, boiling the stuff with nothing to flavor it but a bird shot out of a tree with a BB gun. Some looked to Roosevelt for help and others said there'd be no letup at all: they blamed the bad times on a grand conjunction of certain heavenly bodies, claimed there was nothing to do but sit tight and wait for that movement of the stars.

There were those who believed in neither God nor Jupiter nor Roosevelt Himself and among this faction were a number who went berserk altogether: one old man took off all his clothes, ran into the swamps and died there a week later, stark-naked and alone; a middle-aged teacher surprised her students and colleagues one Monday morning by walking into the grade school dead-drunk, her hair freshly dyed the color of ripe tomatoes and twirling a loaded pistol round her forefinger; and so on. Nothing made sense any more.

Summer came and hot weather made things worse. There were reports of Peeping Toms and even rapes, countless minor burglaries and, by the end of September, seven cases of arson. A church, a hotel, and five residences had burned, most of them right to the ground. A firebug on the loose, along with all the other summer miseries, caused people to squint through suspicious eyes at old friends and neighbors and even at close relatives until, at the scene of the sixth fire, the maniac was apprehended.

Now, after a quarter of a century, the first six burnings of that evil summer have been pretty much forgotten on the island. But the seventh has not.

Even nowadays, on certain breezeless summer nights of talk and recollection, people huddled together on moonlit front porches of rickety old Bahama shacks will tell about that seventh fire and the events leading up to it. Many of the details seem petty or peculiar or a little absurd. But even the poorest listener of the bunch will not allow one word to go past his ear; for if there is one thing that can gladden the heart even more than a tale of love, it is one of revenge.

IN THOSE DAYS there lived on the island, in a fine old house at the end of Cocoa Lane, a pair of old-maid sisters known as the Wiltons, Miss Erna and Miss Dolores, daughters of brave Captain Willy Wilton who was killed in the Spanish-American War.

Captain Willy left these ladies rich, just as rich as could be. Their lives were therefore a subject of more than routine interest in the town, and a body of common knowledge had grown up about them. The one tough and central fact, like the heartbeat of all else known about the Wiltons, was this: they were devoted to one another. They got along like sweet teeth and taffy and that was all there was to it.

Miss Erna, the taller, the elder, the stronger, was raw-boned and had a long face; at seventy-six, she was agile as an eagle scout.

It might be said of Miss Erna that she was beloved on the Keys but not well-liked: people in general do not cotton to stinginess, and stinginess was Miss Erna's main flaw. Another factor sometimes operating in her disfavor has to be touched upon briefly: a fondness for scatological words. She often wrecked an entire conversation by maneuvering to create a context in which to wedge one of them in (her favorites were pee and poop) and a listener often found himself so embarrassed he could only stand there wondering what to do with his face.

But in spite of all, her loyal devotion to Miss Dolores commanded the island's respect. For Miss Dolores was the favorite of everyone, especially of children. She was kind-hearted, plump and pretty, an excellent smiler. At seventy-one she had eaten herself into the shape of a dumpling, but still she was a dashing thing to look at: painted her face, put bluing in her hair, and wore a black patch over her left eye. (No outsider knew for certain, but the patch was said to hide an enormous brown wart.)

All this charm, quite sufficient in itself, was further enriched by a smooth tongue and a keen and original sense of justice. These gifts sustained her in a brief political career: in 1924, ran for mayor on her own ticket, Children's Suffrage, won seventeen votes on a platform that called for a lowering of the voting age to seven; in 1926, decrying the Movie Matinee Situation—slogan: *Saturdays Are Too Far Apart!* —proposed all Wednesdays be declared legal holidays, claimed to have in her possession letters of support from Mary Pickford and the Pope, was defeated again; in 1928, after a brief flurry in the primaries, was dissuaded from running again by certain constituents who had since graduated from grammar school; finally, declaring that children as a pressure group cannot properly support a politician—"You grow too fast and before my very eyes become the opposition!"—retired from the political arena.

Some believed Miss Dolores's wart had been the sole reason for which so splendid a creature had never married. Others claimed she had chosen to remain a spinster because no man alive would wait on her hand and foot as Miss Erna did.

The elder of the Wiltons was always seen offering her arm to Miss Dolores at street corners. She was the carrier of parcels, the keeper of books, the lighter of lamps, the leader of the way. And it was her hand, the big, red-knuckled hand of Miss Erna, that carried Miss Dolores's hot-water bottles, emptied the slop jars, massaged away her headaches, and fanned the air for her at all hot-weather funerals.

Miss Dolores loved food; therefore the sisters ate good. Their tastes ran to poultry and fish, goat cheese and chocolate candy. They used cigarettes (Miss Erna blew perfect smoke rings) and rum in moderate quantities (a gallon of good Cuban stuff would last them six months). And Miss Dolores even managed to get hold of enough mad money so that she always had a twenty-five-cent piece to slip into the hand of a child or a poor person.

But still it was true, as any shopkeeper or tradesman would tell you, that in spite of these indulgences, her sister Erna was far from being a spendthrift. No house painter now living on the island could remember earning so much as a dollar on her property. If the house itself had not been sturdy, made of ironwood and teak, it surely would have gone to ruin along with the iron gates out front, which were rusty and had for years hung useless in a half-open position. The sisters kept no servants at all, not even a yard-man. The Captain's beautiful garden had long since gone to jungle and become a mating place for spiders and mosquitoes and snakes. Certainly such a state of affairs can be attributed only to a terrible kind of parsimony in a rich old woman.

But since this defect, critical as it was, never seemed to show itself in Miss Erna's behavior toward her beloved Dolores, anyone would have sworn that all the demons of hell might break loose in Key West without marring even the surface of their profound compatability.

Until 1936 came along.

And then, perhaps inevitably, Miss Erna's selfish streak and the scandalous decline of that house on Cocoa Lane did at last set Miss Dolores's teeth on edge.

Earliest evidence of the rupture was gathered by Mrs. Emory P. Badin, the sisters' closest neighbor on the Lane. One morning in June, standing against a high board fence near the

Wilton outhouse, she overheard a certain private conversation:

Miss Dolores wanted to move. Wanted to move into one of the little cottages the Captain had left them, one that had always been her special favorite, a bright, airy place with a tiny garden facing the water on Garrison Bight. The issue itself was innocent enough, but the tone of the quarrel aroused considerable alarm.

"I'm warning you, sister," Miss Dolores had said, "last night I had an insight sharp as an ax, so take your choice: either we move out of this house, or something dreadful befalls us!"

"Something dreadful?" croaked Miss Erna.

"Oh, Lord knows what! The place'll burn up, or we'll be eaten alive by rats. Or murdered in our sleep. How would I know? The point is, we've got to move into that cottage on the Bight. I want to start in raising parakeets and flowers, and hang yellow curtains at the windows, and . . ."

"Yellow curtains, parakeets? Dear girl," said the older woman, "make sense!"

"I am fed up with broken shutters and hideous, scampering little feet in the night. I say we move, move this summer, or die some horrible death. Now that's straight from m'guardian angel, and you can take it or leave it."

(Miss Dolores did have a reputation for prognostication: if ever she stopped you on the street and said *Something fascinating is in store for you,* sure as shooting you would break an arm or win money on the Cuban lottery.)

But Miss Erna was unimpressed. "I never heard such fooltalk," she declared. "Move out of Papa's house? Why, Dolores Wilton, I'd as soon run naked down Duval Street and . . . "

(Oh yes, can just *hear* it, the neighbors said: that foul tongue on her!)

"I don't wish to hurt your feelings, Sister, but I can only assume you begrudge me the money it would cost to make the move."

Miss Erna clapped one hand over her own mouth, as if to hold back a hemorrhage; for this thrust, like truth, went straight to the heart of the old woman. Mrs. Emory P. Badin claimed she heard a high, sad, moaning sound from the elder of the Wiltons, and then: *"Et tu, Brute?"*

KEY WESTERS, sensitive to omens that summer, shook their heads. "Tch-tch, even the Wiltons have taken to scrapping —and that's *bad* news!"

On still another June morning, the younger of the ladies was seen running down Caroline Street, long blue hair undone, wind billowing her gone-with-the-wind skirt, and crying to beat the band. She had even forgotten her eye patch.

A moment later, long-legged Miss Erna in hot pursuit emerged from Cocoa Lane, easily overtook her sister and led her back home. But not before several neighbors had caught the gist of the quarrel. Mrs. Emory P. Badin heard Miss Dolores call her sister a miser. This brought gasps of disbelief, but the truth of it seemed to be shored up by Mrs. Jesús Ramirez, who quoted something even worse from Miss Dolores: "I just pray that firebug burns *our* place down before they catch him!"

For two weeks the sisters were not seen in the streets at all. This aroused much speculation. Some guesses were mild: "Oh, Miss Erna'll step out for them rents come first of the month, you'll see." On the other end of the spectrum was the theory that they'd murdered one another. But only certain girl children, who love nothing so much as the thought of bloodshed, had any real faith in the notion.

One Saturday morning two such creatures, little flowers of the fifth grade, stopped out front of the place, and one of them said, "I always sniff when I come by here lately." Her friend asked what for and she said, "Oh, to see if the Wiltons are dead yet, that's all."

At that moment, a light, fairy-queen voice from behind the aralia hedge said, "No, they're not, dear." And Miss Dolores appeared before them.

The girls froze in their tracks.

Miss Dolores said, "Now can't you understand that just that kind of behavior gives a bad reputation to *all* children?

Where do you think prejudice *starts?*" She smiled benignly, gave them each a quarter, and dismissed them. "Jane Withers is at the Palace; go there at *once* and learn sweetness!"

THAT AFTERNOON the Wiltons were seen together rent-collecting and dime-store shopping as usual. (It turned out that Miss Erna'd had a touch of the flu.) People said the old woman appeared skinny with worry that day; and she was especially solicitous of her baby sister's comfort—even ordered the floorwalker at Woolworth's to bring out a stool for her to rest on.

Miss Dolores accepted the stool with grace, but the salesgirls, gathering round for their usual chat, thought she seemed unhappy, preoccupied; even her famous smile was lackluster.

She said, "Now, girls,"—many of them had been her followers in the old Children's Suffrage movement—"how many of you would have guessed that your leader would one day become a peculiar old woman living in a dilapidated house where children pass by each morning—and sniff to see if she's dead yet? Just raise your hands!"

Silence fell.

Miss Erna, pretending to be busy at the hardware counter, looked as guilty as a caught thief.

A CERTAIN EVENT took place the following evening that put the fear of God into Miss Erna Wilton. The next morning she took Miss Dolores by the hand and together they marched into the sheriff's office where the entire story was repeated in detail:

Miss Erna had been clearing the supper dishes that night when a piercing scream issued from Miss Dolores's bedroom. She grabbed a frying pan in one hand, a bread knife in the other, and thus armed, flew to her sister's side.

She found Miss Dolores seated on her bed in an attitude of horror, hands crossed over her bosom, eyes closed, her breath coming in short gasps. Miss Erna questioned her, but she seemed unable to answer or even to hear. At length, she pointed toward the open window. Miss Erna, swallowing her own fear, went to the window and shouted in her most intimidating voice, *"Who is it? Who's out there?"*

She stood there for a long moment, studying the darkness. "I see you, Mr. Evil," she bluffed; and then, with candy-coated malevolence, "Please don't go 'way. I got a big jagged bread knife here, and I'm just dyin' for a chance to stick it in your gizzard. You hear me out there?"

After a moment in which there was no sound at all from the garden, Miss Erna moved to her sister's side and placed her arm about her shoulder. "What was it, little baby? Tell Erna what you saw at the window."

Miss Dolores made much of her inability to speak; and then she whispered, "It was the same one, been here a time or two before. I just didn't want to frighten you is all."

"Who?" said Miss Erna. "What're you saying, girl?"

Miss Dolores fanned out her fingers, and her right eye opened wide. "A man!" she said. "It seems like every time I go to close the shutters, he's waiting there for me with some ghastly fever in his eyes."

The sheriff promised to keep a sharp eye on Cocoa Lane, but Miss Erna wanted every assurance she could get. Key West that summer had already seen a number of unsavory goings-on, and she was determined her pretty sister would not be among the victims.

That afternoon the Wiltons were seen in Thompson's Hardware on Caroline Street making a purchase of two large cowbells. On the way home, they stopped at each house on Cocoa Lane and told their story.

"If you'll excuse me for stating my honest opinion," said Miss Dolores in several of her neighbors' parlors, "I think it's just some poor lonesome wretch that likes to watch ladies take their clothes off. A peeper? Isn't that what they call such persons? And of course that old house is *perfect* for them, set off all alone with a big yard around it and plenty of bushes to hide in. The shutters are all nicely broken up, too, so they can get a real good eyeful, but I doubt they's any real *danger*."

All the women protested that there was very grave danger

indeed! Miss Dolores rather enjoyed the proceedings. At each house her story changed slightly. She seemed to have learned that the less she made of the whole thing, the more terrifying its effect upon her listeners. By the time the Wiltons arrived at the home of Mr. and Mrs. Emory P. Badin, Miss Dolores was in high spirits, chattering away gaily about how trivial the whole thing seemed to *her*.

Poor Miss Erna was more alarmed than ever.

By the end of the afternoon she had exacted promises from every man on the lane: when they heard the bells clanging (and she took the bells out of her bag at each house and gave a few sample clangs) they were to come a-running with shotguns and knives and big sticks, whatever weapons they could find.

ON THAT very night, at a few minutes after ten, the first alarm was sounded; the Wiltons were calling for help.

Men came running down the lane in all states of disarray: clothed, semiclothed, some in pajamas, others in robes. Miss Erna gave orders from the kitchen porch: "Emory P. Badin, you search the stable. No, wait; I'd better send somebody with you. Juan, you go with Emory. Mr. Fisher and Nat Spatafora, the outhouse. I'd come with you, men, but I got to stay with sister. . . . Jesús Ramirez, you take that stick and poke around behind my pandanus bushes."

In a few minutes the search was over.

No peeper, no prowler of any kind, was apprehended.

One by one and in twos, the men—nine of them all together—filed in through the kitchen porch to discuss the event with Miss Erna. Various views were exchanged and strategies proposed against future emergencies; and then talk got around to other summer happenings. One man told a rape story and Miss Erna was fit to be tied. She paced and swore and went to the window shouting threats and imprecations into the dark. The men found her anger awesome; and while they were enjoying the spectacle of it, another figure appeared in the door of the back hall and gradually drew all of their attention.

Miss Dolores stood there, smiling and calm— and wearing a new, emerald-green patch over her left eye. She was in full makeup, her blue hair carefully arranged in big, loose, upswept curls, and dressed in her best satin robe, a lovely dark blue thing that clung to her plump body like light and shadow on a nude. The men stared as she greeted them one by one, like a grand hostess at an impromptu party. And then she suggested that her sister might choose to reward their bravery with a thimbleful of rum.

Miss Erna brought out the jug and liberal quantities of the stuff were poured into glasses. Some of the men laid their weapons on the floor, and soon they were all sitting about in the great old kitchen, drinking and talking. This went on until long past midnight. Tales were told of the old days on the island, tales of wreckers and pirates, of ghosts and Chinese slaves; and some of the new legends of this very summer were reviewed and enlarged upon. The truth was told and lies were told; and each man contributed and each man believed, or seemed to. It was better than any party, Miss Dolores declared: more urgent, more exciting. Each man was at his best; for having responded to the ladies' bell of alarm he felt himself brave. And Miss Dolores, surrounded by a posse so fine and gallant, felt stirrings within herself that had been unfelt (but not forgotten) for a long, long time.

Miss Erna next morning at breakfast let it be known that she herself had not enjoyed the proceedings one iota, said the men had left a "certain odor" in the kitchen that would take days to get rid of. Miss Dolores laughed at this in a way that made the old woman fierce with anger. She rebuked Miss Dolores for appearing in such a "preposterous getup" the night before, and made a number of sharp comments on her behavior in general. But Miss Dolores, for some dark and worrisome reason, was imperturbable. She spent the day happily making new eye patches in a whole rainbow variety of colors.

And that night at about nine-thirty, the urgent *clang-clang-clang* of cowbells was heard once again through the neighborhood of Cocoa Lane.

As THE SUMMER wore on, there were more and more of these unfruitful searches through the acre of jungle that surrounded the Wilton house. But the procedure became less and less partylike until at last it had achieved a kind of ceremonial dullness; fewer and fewer of the men responded to the clanging of the bells. Finally, on one sad Tuesday night toward the end of July, only one man roused himself; a Cuban gentleman named Juan who was so decrepit with age that any prowler worth his salt could have made mincemeat of him with just one arm and no weapon at all.

Nor had the atmosphere inside the Wilton house undergone any improvement; Miss Erna had begun to suspect that the peeper had been invented by Miss Dolores for the sole purpose of deviling her. One morning she even hinted aloud at this possibility.

"Damn funny, isn't it," she said, "how this bozo never shows his face to *me?*"

Miss Dolores considered this with a judicial frown; and then she said, "I can think of *one* explanation. Maybe he's not there at all. Perhaps I've lost m'mind and gone *se*-nile."

ONE EVENING early in August, the island's sixth great fire of the summer took place: the splendid old Cunningham home on Eaton Street. This event drew a large crowd. Even the Wiltons, who rarely set foot outside after dark, managed to get there while the blaze was still high, accompanied by several of their Cocoa Lane neighbors. Later they would be able to claim they'd actually seen the roof of the place cave in. It was a magnificent and terrible sight. Women wept and trembled and their men stood by sober and silent while firemen poked at the catastrophe with tiny, ineffectual streams of water; the best they could hope for was to keep the thing from spreading through the neighborhood.

The most sensational feature of the spectacle on Eaton Street was the apprehension of the firebug.

This was a tall and spindly, curiously sweet-faced boy of twenty who had been seen watching several of the earlier burnings that summer. Word got around that he was vagrant in the town, had wandered in some months earlier from the Carolinas. On this night, under questioning by the sheriff, he admitted setting all six fires. As the young criminal was being handcuffed, a confused smile played on his mouth: it was as if some colossal joke had gone seriously awry and he was trying to remember what had happened to spoil it.

Miss Dolores, who had maneuvered her way into listening range, came forward as the boy was being carted off. She laid a firm forefinger on the sheriff's heart. "Be gentle with him," she said, "and you may learn something about purity." The sheriff said, "Oh sure, Miss Dolores, we'll just coddle him to death." Miss Dolores seemed pleased with this answer. "It's all right," she told her neighbors, "I've interceded."

A little later, she collared one of the Cunninghams, a fat and weeping girl of fourteen. "Now, Sadie, listen to Miss Dolores," she said. "Tell your grandmother this: when the new house is ready, I'm presenting her with yellow curtains throughout—just the kind I'm going to have." The little girl stopped crying. She looked at the old woman and said, "What?" Miss Dolores cupped a gentle hand over the girl's mouth. "No, no!" she said. "I insist! It's the least I can do; yellow is the color of sunshine."

Then she continued moving about in the crowd gathering and disseminating bits of information: the Cunninghams had got out of the place in time and no one was harmed; a servant had risked his life to save an armful of Kewpie dolls and souvenir ashtrays while forty thousand in cash had gone up in smoke; a cat was thought to be trapped in the attic; later, the cat was reported safe and sound in the arms of an Episcopalian altar boy; and there developed a controversy over whether or not it was the same animal at all, and whether or not the altar boy was Episcopalian; and so forth. These items she collected and reported faithfully to her sister.

Miss Erna was less impressed with these details than with the blaze itself. She frowned and stared and murmured about "judgments" and the "anger of God." And then, just when the worst of it seemed to be over, something took place that struck Miss Erna far more profoundly even than the fire itself.

She saw, standing some five yards from herself and her sister, a peculiar-looking little man of some forty-odd years, staring at Miss Dolores—staring with the wide-eyed audacity of a child, but with none of a child's innocence. And then the man caught Miss Dolores's eye; caught it, yes; and what was more appalling, he held it, held it for a long nightmare moment in which that lady lifted the rose-colored patch over her left eye and returned the stare with such intense concentration that a kind of spell seemed to have been placed upon her mind.

Perhaps this bewitchment even extended itself to Miss Erna, for the older woman was so immobilized by her own fascination with these locked eyes that she was unable to speak until the moment had ended. The man disappeared into the crowd before Miss Erna could manage to begin her questioning.

"What was that? Who was that man?"

She squeezed Miss Dolores's arm, and would have repeated the question; but suddenly the reason for her own terror had arranged itself in words, and she was able instead to supply an answer. "It was him," she declared in a furious whisper. "It was him at your window!"

Miss Dolores was scared stiff. "Oh sister, oh sister!" She murmured these words over and over again like an incantation against the spell of her own fear. And she pressed herself close to Erna Wilton, hiding herself in the old woman's anger and indignation.

LATER THAT NIGHT, Miss Erna, carrying a kerosene lamp, a shotgun and an old porcelain slop jar, led the way upstairs to the room above Miss Dolores's. This had been their father's bedroom, and for many decades no one had slept in it.

The old lady, exhilarated by danger, was more agile than ever: moved like a young man, carried her shotgun like one, and her voice had deepened half an octave. "Might as well throw out them cowbells altogether. No man alive any more is got guts enough to do his duty. But here's an old maid that has, by God! Oh, I'm dyin' to get a potshot at that son-of-aseacook."

Her plan was this: Miss Dolores would sleep safely in Captain Willy's old bed, while she herself stood watch at the darkened window, directly above her sister's first-floor bedroom. A lamp left burning down there would lure the wicked prowler into target range, and then, *"Pow"*—she'd "pin his guts to the mahogany tree!"

"Oh, isn't it a pity?" Miss Dolores whimpered as her sister spread fresh linen on the bed. "Isn't it a pity we don't just check into the La Concha Hotel for a few days until we could get the little cottage ready? Isn't it a pity we're so cussedly stubborn we have to stay on in this old death-trap till we're carried out by the undertaker?"

Miss Erna gave no sign of having heard this talk at all. "Quit chattering, babylove, and hop in."

Miss Dolores lay flat on her back and pulled the covers up to her chin. "Poor old God," she said, "tries so hard to warn us; sends His angels to whisper in our ears. And we just never ever listen till finally He has to scream His lungs out and *hit us on the head!"*

Miss Erna took her place on a straight-backed chair next to the window. "I'm not sure whether to capture him and take him in—or just kill him outright!"

"Sister," said Miss Dolores, "may I ask when you plan to sleep, or have you given that up altogether?"

"Oh, in daylight's plenty of time for sleep. A little catnap now and then, just enough to keep m'eyes sharp."

"Well, I'd like to ask a favor. Tonight, while you're setting there fishing around for topics to think about, won't you give a little study to how sweet it could be, the two of us living in that white cottage on the water?"

Miss Erna was busy with her own thoughts, tales she'd heard of the island's earlier days, in which proud and gallant men like her father and Grandfather Wilton had protected their women and their young against every manner of nuisance from wild Indians to drunken pirates.

"Some people don't shoot to kill," she said aloud, "they shoot to maim. That might be something to consider." Then she raised the gun to her eye and drew a bead on the moon, just for practice. "Mr. Evil, you think you run this world. Well, you know what Miss Erna says to that? Miss Erna says *tut-tut!*"

ERNA WILTON got through that first night just fine. The second night was all right, too. She was proud of her ability to remain awake and alert with nothing to look at but the moonlit jungle under the window, nothing to listen to but the occasional scurrying sounds of wild things that had come to live there, raccoons and birds and homeless cats.

But on the third night she began to feel imprisoned by the whole damn mess. It didn't look like there'd ever be any prowler to shoot at. And yet she'd told it all over town, vowed everywhere that Miss Erna Wilton would not again close her eyes after dark until she'd nailed her man with a bullet. The poor woman was hemmed in on all sides: by the night, by the endless boredom of waiting, and by her own pride.

The next morning she was irritable. Her daytime naps in the humid and motionless summer air failed to restore her energies. Miss Dolores offered to fan her, but she was too stubborn to allow it. By the end of the week, a terrible melancholy had descended upon her.

Miss Dolores grew worried: her sister was not even irritable any more. She simply wasn't *there*, seemed no longer to see or hear or even feel. Miss Dolores herself developed a dreadful new fear: what if she should awaken one morning to find her sister slumped dead over the windowsill from heart failure or fatigue? She even went so far as to suggest calling in a doctor: "A soldier has to look after his health, doesn't he?" But Miss Erna answered this with such a savage snarl of contempt that it seemed best to drop the matter.

At length, Miss Dolores became so concerned that she no longer said her bedtime prayers lying down but knelt right on the bare hardwood floor. Nor did she continue to beg for the little white cottage with yellow curtains. "Just please keep us from getting *too* peculiar," she implored. "That's all."

By the end of the second week, Miss Erna had passed

through melancholy into a state of angry despair that had
about it some of the qualities of actual madness. She had
taken to mumbling through the night, speaking her thoughts
aloud. And Miss Dolores, resting none too soundly herself,
heard some of these thoughts and more than once they'd sent
a chill all through her bloodstream.

One night, for instance, Miss Dolores awakened to find her
sister sitting on the edge of the bed talking at a salesman's
pace about some kind of a "plan" that made no sense at all.
The gist of it was that they run away to Chicago together
"before Papa gets back."

Oh God, thought Miss Dolores, *Sister's mind has come loose
at the hinges!* Miss Erna seemed to think the Captain was
away on a long trip, that before leaving he had assigned to her
the task of protecting the place; and somehow she had come
to believe this was all part of some freakish stratagem he had
devised to trap her on the property forever.

"He hates this place worse'n we do; else why is he always
going off on trips to get away from it?"

"Erna?" Miss Dolores questioned softly. "Do you hate this
house, too?"

"Like devils and snakes, I hate it. Like poison and death
and big, hairy spiders."

Miss Dolores was so taken aback at this admission that for
a moment she failed to consider that it had been spoken by an
old lady almost deranged from sleeplessness and exhaustion.
"Well, since you feel so strongly," she said, seizing her opportunity, "I wouldn't mind if we just moved out altogether!
Who knows but what we might even find a little cottage
somewhere! A white one would be nice! On the water! . . .
Now let's just put our heads together and *think!*"

At this point, however, Miss Erna's conversation went
from the strange to the incoherent, and then petered out altogether. The next morning at breakfast when Miss Dolores
broached the subject, the old woman insisted it was Miss Dolores who was given to having nightmares, not herself.

And on the Friday night, Miss Dolores awakened just after
midnight in time to hear this fearsome extension of that same

nightmare conversation: "When Papa comes home, I'm gonna kill him."

Miss Dolores sat up in bed, goose-pimpled with fright. When she could use her voice, she said, "You what?"

"Gonna kill him," Erna said.

"But you know you love our papa!" Miss Dolores said.

"Then how come him to leave us alone like this?"

Miss Dolores forced her own mind back some forty-odd years. "Erna, honey, our papa has gone to fight the Spanish. Teddy Roosevelt has picked all his bravest men to go and help the Cubans. Aren't you proud enough to burst?" And then, to the heavens, she added, "Help me, sweet Jesus."

Miss Dolores got out of bed and went barefooted to the window. She placed her arm around Miss Erna's shoulder, squeezed her gently and looked into her eyes. "Our papa got killed, honey. Don't you remember the lovely memorial parade?"

Then a perplexing thing happened. Miss Erna looked at her and said, "Why of course I remember, precious! Is my little sweet having bad dreams again?"

"Me?" said Miss Dolores.

Miss Erna got to her feet. "Come on, let me tuck you in." Miss Dolores was confused. She climbed into bed, permitted her sister to stroke her brow for a few moments, and made no further reference to their eerie conversation.

When she had closed her eyes for what seemed no longer than a few seconds, a sudden racket at the window brought her rapidly to a sitting position.

"Haaaaiee!" shouted Erna Wilton. Then the shotgun crashed like thunder, followed by another Indian-like war cry.

Miss Dolores screamed and pulled the sheet up over her eyes.

"It's jammed, goddammit, it's jammed!" mumbled Erna Wilton. Holding the shotgun like a big stick, she took quick aim and threw the weapon itself. And then she let fly with some of the most sinful language she knew, hurling the ugly words out the window like big rocks. "He's tripped and fell; I believe I've winged the dirty devil! Gimme that slop jar, I'll finish him off!"

"AND THEN I grabbed up the slop jar," she said next day, telling the story, it seemed to Miss Dolores, for the hundredth time. At this moment, which was early in the afternoon, the sisters were standing at the notions counter at Woolworth's surrounded by their audience of salesgirls.

"I held it just as dainty as you please, right by the handles, like so"—all this with gestures—"and I said to him, 'Mr. Tom, you down there, Mr. Peeping Tom, can I have your attention? I got something here with your name on it. I got a potful of pee for you. Don't go 'way!' And then I let her fly."

"Did you hit him?" one of her listeners asked.

"Well now, honey," said Miss Erna, rolling the moment around on her tongue like a swallow of cream, "what would be your guess? Would you say I hit him, or would you say I missed?"

"What I mean, did you *kill* him?"

"Naw. What I want to do that for?" Miss Erna had all the modesty of a boxer being interviewed after a first-round knockout. "I was only out to do him a little damage is all."

Miss Dolores was annoyed. At noon, she and her sister had set forth from Cocoa Lane to do some shopping. At each store, Miss Erna told her story of the night before. Miss Dolores had begun by nodding agreement to each detail. ("Oh yes, saw the entire thing with m'own eyes.") But as the tale grew, and Miss Erna's language became more and more explicit, her attention began to wander. She was bored and embarrassed. ("Erna Wilton, you're behaving something awful, saying pee in front of men. I warn you, quit!")

But Miss Erna would not quit, and her punishment was this: while they were standing there at Woolworth's, Miss Dolores, having got hold of about forty dollars in rent money, slipped away from the old woman altogether.

More than fifteen minutes had elapsed before Miss Erna, deeply engaged in telling her story all over again to the janitor, even noticed her sister was missing.

The hunt started at the Palace Theater. Miss Erna checked

her sister's regular seat (back row on the lefthand aisle), the ladies' room and the candy counter. Then she went up and down Duval Street asking everyone she knew if they'd seen Miss Dolores. Clues gathered in this way indicated there had been an extensive shopping spree, but no one knew where to find the missing woman.

Miss Erna grew frantic. She began giving out a description to perfect strangers: "Pretty little thing? Gold patch on her eye? About so high? Are you sure? Now *think!*"

At one point, when the search had been going on for more than two hours, Miss Erna became aware that dark clouds had moved in over the island. She took this as a sign that life would never again be the same for either of them, not after today. And this thought filled her heart with a dreadful foreboding: "Oh, what if I never find her again?"

And then the old lady found herself standing in, of all places, a saloon, tapping on the counter with a fifty-cent piece. The bartender set a shot glass full of rum before her. Miss Erna picked it up, raised it toward the ceiling, closed her eyes and made a wish: *Come on now, You give her back to me, hear?* She swallowed the rum, left a ten-cent tip for the bartender (believing that God upon occasion had been known to accept bribes) and hurried back into the street.

Her glance fell once more on a marquee of the Palace Theater:

ELEANOR POWELL IN
BORN TO DANCE

SUDDENLY Miss Erna knew that her sister was indeed hiding somewhere in that movie house; the shrewd little creature had no doubt avoided her usual seat on purpose, just to throw her off the scent.

The usher, assisting Erna Wilton with his flashlight, found Miss Dolores way down in front eating a box of chocolates. Most of the money was gone. She'd given some of it away and had made a few purchases: a bolt of yellow chintz, a box of

Whitman's Samplers, and a lifetime supply of Tangee Red-Red. Miss Dolores made no excuses. Her only comment in fact as they passed through the lobby pertained to the quality of the candy: "The bottom layer is *never* as good as the top!" And Miss Erna, giddy with relief, was in no mood to scold. She chose instead to admire each purchase, and it was then she proposed a fish supper in the fanciest restaurant in town.

BEFORE THE SUN had set, word got around on Duval Street that Miss Erna Wilton had not only shot somebody the night before, but was, at that very moment, sitting with her sister in Diego's Sea Food Palace at a table right next to the window, drinking rum like a sailor on payday.

Nor was this too far from the truth.

For at ten minutes after seven, when the sheriff arrived at Diego's to tell the sisters their house had just burned to the ground and a man with a bandaged thigh had been appre-hended on the spot and charged with arson, Miss Erna gaily announced that it'd take more than a few flames to spoil her day—and went right on blowing smoke rings for the benefit of anyone who chose to watch.

Miss Dolores, however, did frown. But only for a moment. And then she filled their glasses and said she thought it'd be wasteful to buy another sewing machine: why not just hire a seamstress to make up the lovely new curtains?

Zora Neale Hurston

(1901?–1960) was born and grew up in Eatonville, a small town near Orlando, and took much of her material for her books from the area. The daughter of a local minister and frequently in the audience at story-telling sessions at the town's general store, she came to love words and stories, some of which she later collected in book form. She attended Howard University, earned a bachelor's degree from Barnard College in 1928, became a writer in the Harlem Renaissance, researched folklore in Haiti and Florida, and wrote such well-known works as *Mules and Men* (1935), *Their Eyes Were Watching God* (1937), *Dust Tracks on a Road* (1942), and *Seraph on the Suwanee* (1948). Toward the end of her life she returned to Florida, where she worked as a maid, rather like the woman in the story included here. She

died in 1960 in Fort Pierce, where she is buried and where novelist Alice Walker has placed a grave marker that reads ZORA NEALE HURSTON / "A GENIUS OF THE SOUTH" / 1901–1960 / NOVELIST, FOLKLORIST / ANTHROPOLOGIST.

Hurston's story, "Conscience of the Court" (1950), takes place in a Jacksonville courtroom. A black servant woman is being tried for assaulting a loan shark who had tried to collect a debt from her mistress. The story was partly autobiographical in that the author had been falsely charged in a court of law and had also worked as a maid. At the end of the story the white judge speaks at length about the rights of the individual and delivers his verdict.

Some have judged this story to be inferior to her longer fiction and a mere potboiler written for money. Critics point out that the subservient maid is a far cry from Hurston's characteristically strong women characters. The critics' uncertainty as to the author's motives and goals in the story illustrates what an enigma

Hurston has been. Those who have studied her fiction for many years still have questions about when she was born, whom she married, how many times she married, and where she was at certain times. While such biographical details can add to a full picture of a person, in the case of someone like Hurston, who gave different answers to these questions at different times, one has to judge her from her work. And that work, while fluctuating in popularity and attention from scholars and the reading public, has stood up well over the years.

Hurston and another distinguished Florida writer of the time, Marjorie Kinnan Rawlings, became friends in the 1940s, and they corresponded over the years. In one letter Rawlings described Hurston as having "a most ingratiating personality, a brilliant mind, and a fundamental wisdom that shames most whites." A recent play by Barbara Speisman entitled *A Tea with Zora and Marjorie* explores their friendship.

Zora Neale Hurston

The Conscience of the Court

HE CLERK of the court took a good look at the tall brown-skinned woman with the head rag on. She sat on the third bench back with a husky officer beside her. "The People versus Laura Lee Kimble!"

The policeman nudged the woman to get to her feet and led her up to the broad rail. She stood there, looking straight ahead. The hostility in the room reached her without her seeking to find it.

Unpleasant things were ahead of Laura Lee Kimble, but she was ready for this moment. It might be the electric chair or the rest of her life in some big lonesome jail house, or even torn to pieces by a mob, but she had passed three long weeks in jail. She had come to the place where she could turn her face to the wall and feel neither fear nor anguish. So this here so-called trial was nothing to her but a form and a fashion and an outside show to the world. She could stand apart and look on calmly. She stood erect and looked up at the judge.

"Charged with felonious and aggravated assault. Mayhem. Premeditated attempted murder on the person of one Clement Beasley. Obscene and abusive language. Laura Lee Kimble, how do you plead?"

Laura Lee was so fascinated by the long-named things that they were accusing her of that she stood there tasting over the words. *Lawdy me!* she mused inside herself. *Look like I done every crime excepting habeas corpus and stealing a mule.*

"Answer the clerk!" The officer nudged Laura Lee. "Tell him how you plead."

"Plead? Don't reckon I make out just what you all mean by that." She looked from face to face and at last up at the judge, with bewilderment in her eyes. She found him looking her over studiously.

The judge understood the look in her face, but he did not interfere so promptly as he ordinarily would have. This was the man-killing bear cat of a woman that he had heard so much about. Though spare of fat, she was built strongly enough, all right. An odd Negro type. Gray-green eyes, large and striking, looking out of a chestnut-brown face. A great abundance of almost straight hair only partially hidden by the high-knotted colored kerchief about her head. Somehow this woman did not look fierce to him at all. Yet she had beaten a man within an inch of his life. Here was a riddle to solve. With the proud, erect way she held herself, she might be some savage queen. The shabby housedress she had on detracted nothing from this impression. She was a challenge to him somehow or other.

"Perhaps you don't understand what the clerk means, Laura," the judge found himself saying to her in a gentle voice. "He wants you to say whether you are guilty of the charges or not."

"Oh, I didn't know. Didn't even know if he was talking to me or not. Much obliged to you, sir." Laura Lee sent His Honor a shy smile. "'Deed I don't know if I'm guilty or not. I hit the man after he hit me, to be sure, Mister Judge, but if I'm guilty I don't know for sure. All them big words and all."

The clerk shook his head in exasperation and quickly wrote something down. Laura Lee turned her head and saw the man on the hospital cot swaddled all up in bandage rags. Yes, that was the very man who caused her to be here where she was.

"All right, Laura Lee," the judge said. "You can take your seat now until you are called on."

The prosecutor looked a question at the judge and said,

"We can proceed." The judge nodded, then halted things as he looked down at Laura Lee.

"The defendant seems to have no lawyer to represent her." Now he leaned forward and spoke to Laura Lee directly. "If you have no money to hire yourself a lawyer to look out for your interests, the court will appoint one for you."

There was a pause, during which Laura Lee covered a lot of ground. Then she smiled faintly at the judge and answered him. "Naw sir, I thank you, Mister Judge. Not to turn you no short answer, but I don't reckon it would do me a bit of good. I'm mighty much obliged to you just the same."

The implications penetrated instantly and the judge flushed. This unlettered woman had called up something that he had not thought about for quite some time. The campus of the University of Virginia and himself as a very young man there, filled with a reverence for his profession amounting to an almost holy dedication. His fascination and awe as a professor traced the more than two thousand years of growth of the concepts of human rights and justice. That brought him to his greatest hero, John Marshall, and his inner resolve to follow in the great man's steps, and even add to interpretations of human rights if his abilities allowed. No, he had not thought about all this for quite some time. The judge flushed slowly and deeply.

Below him there, the prosecutor was moving swiftly, but somehow his brisk cynicism offended the judge. He heard twelve names called, and just like that the jury box was filled and sworn in.

Rapidly now, witnesses took the stand, and their testimony was all damaging to Laura Lee. The doctor who told how terribly Clement Beasley had been hurt. Left arm broken above the elbow, compound fracture of the forearm, two ribs cracked, concussion of the brain and various internal injuries. Two neighbors who had heard the commotion and arrived before the house in time to see Laura Lee fling the plaintiff over the gate into the street. The six arresting officers all got up and had their say, and it was very bad for Laura Lee. A two-legged she-devil no less.

Clement Beasley was borne from his cot to the witness stand, and he made things look a hundred times blacker. His very appearance aroused a bumble of pity, and anger against the defendant. The judge had to demand quiet repeatedly. Beasley's testimony blew strongly on the hot coals.

His story was that he had come in conflict with this defendant by loaning a sizable sum of money to her employer. The money was to be repaid at his office. When the date was long past due, he had gone to the house near the river, just off Riverside Drive, to inquire why Mrs. Clairborne had not paid him, nor even come to see him and explain. Imagine his shock when he wormed it out of the defendant that Mrs. Clairborne had left Jacksonville. Further, he detected evidence that the defendant was packing up the things in the house. The loan had been made, six hundred dollars, on the furnishings of the entire house. He had doubted that the furnishings were worth enough for the amount loaned, but he had wanted to be generous to a widow lady. Seeing the defendant packing away the silver, he was naturally alarmed, and the next morning went to the house with a moving van to seize the furniture and protect the loan. The defendant, surprised, attacked him as soon as he appeared at the front door, injured him as he was, and would have killed him if help had not arrived in time.

Laura Lee was no longer a spectator at her own trial. Now she was in a flaming rage. She would have leaped to her feet as the man pictured Miz' Celestine as a cheat and a crook, and again as he sat up there and calmly lied about the worth of the furniture. All of those wonderful antiques, this man making out that they did not equal his minching six hundred dollars! That lie was a sin and a shame! The People was a meddlesome and unfriendly passel and had no use for the truth. It brought back to her in a taunting way what her husband, Tom, had told her over and over again. This world had no use for the love and friending that she was ever trying to give.

It looked now that Tom could be right. Even Miz' Celestine had turnt her back on her. She was here in this place, the house of The People, all by herself. She had ever disbelieved

Tom and had to get to be forty-nine before she found out the truth. Well, just as the old folks said, "It's never too long for a bull frog to wear a stiff-bosom shirt. He's bound to get it dirtied some time or other."

"You have testified," Laura Lee heard the judge talking, "that you came in contact with the defendant through a loan to Mrs. J. Stuart Clairborne, her employer, did you not?"

"Yes, Your Honor," Beasley answered promptly and glibly.

"That being true, the court cannot understand why that note was not offered in evidence."

Beasley glanced quickly at the prosecutor and lowered his eyes. "I—I just didn't see why it was necessary, Your Honor. I have it, but —"

"It is not only pertinent, it is of the utmost importance to this case. I order it sent for immediately and placed in evidence."

The tall, lean, black-haired prosecutor hurled a surprised and betrayed look at the bench, then, after a pause, said in a flat voice, "The State rests."

What was in the atmosphere crawled all over Laura Lee like reptiles. The silence shouted that her goose was cooked. But even if the sentence was death, she didn't mind. Celestine Beaufort Clairborne had failed her. Her husband and all her folks had gone on before. What was there to be so happy to live for any more? She had writ that letter to Miz' Celestine the very first day that she had been placed in jail. Three weeks had gone by on their rusty ankles, and never one word from her Celestine. Laura Lee choked back a sob and gritted her teeth. You had to bear what was placed on your back for you to tote.

"Laura Lee Kimble," the judge was saying, "you are charged with serious felonies, and the law must take its course according to the evidence. You refused the lawyer that the court offered to provide for you, and that was a mistake on your part. However, you have a right to be sworn and tell the jury your side of the story. Tell them anything that might help you, so long as you tell the truth."

Laura Lee made no move to get to her feet and nearly a minute passed. Then the judge leaned forward.

"Believe it or not, Laura Lee, this is a court of law. It is needful to hear both sides of every question before the court can reach a conclusion and know what to do. Now, you don't strike me as a person that is unobliging at all. I believe if you knew you would be helping me out a great deal by telling your side of the story, you would do it."

Involuntarily Laura Lee smiled. She stood up. "Yes, sir, Mister Judge. If I can be of some help to you, I sure will. And I thank you for asking me."

Being duly sworn, Laura Lee sat in the chair to face the jury as she had been told to do.

"You jury-gentlemens, they asked me if I was guilty or no, and I still don't know whether I is or not. I am a unlearnt woman and common-clad. It don't surprise me to find out I'm ignorant about a whole heap of things. I ain't never rubbed the hair off of my head against no college walls and schooled out nowhere at all. All I'm able to do is to tell you gentlemens how it was and then you can tell me if I'm guilty or no.

"I would not wish to set up here and lie and make out that I never hit this plaintive back. Gentlemens, I ain't had no malice in my heart against the plaintive. I seen him only one time before he come there and commenced that fracas with me. That was three months ago, the day after Tom, my husband, died. Miz' Celestine called up the funeral home and they come and got Tom to fix him up so we could take him back to Georgia to lay him to rest. That's where us all come from, Chatham County—Savannah, that is.

"Then now, Miz' Celestine done something I have never knowed her to do be-fore. She put on her things and went off from home without letting me know where she was bound for. She come back afterwhile with this plaintive, which I had never seen before in all my borned days. I glimpsed him good from the kitchen where I was at, walking all over the dining room and the living room with Miz' Celestine and looking at things, but they was talking sort of low like, and I couldn't make out a word what they was talking about. I figgered that

Miz' Celestine must of been kind of beside herself, showing somebody look like this plaintive all her fine things like that. Her things is fine and very scarce old antiques, and I know that she have been offered vast sums of money for 'em, but she would never agree to part with none. Things that been handed down in both the Beaufort and the Clairborne families from way back. That little old minching six hundred dollars that the plaintive mentioned wouldn't even be worth one piece of her things, not to mention her silver. After a while they went off and when Miz' Celestine come back, she told me that everything had been taken care of and she had the tickets to Savannah in her purse.

"Bright and soon next morning we boarded the train for Savannah to bury Tom. Miz' Celestine done even more than she had promised Tom. She took him back like she had promised, so that he could be buried in our family lot, and he was covered with flowers, and his church and his lodges turned out with him, and he was put away like some big mogul of a king. Miz' Celestine was there sitting right along by my side all the time. Then me and Miz' Celestine come on back down here to Jacksonville by ourselves.

"And Mrs. Clairborne didn't run off to keep from paying nobody. She's a Clairborne, and before that, she was born a Beaufort. They don't owe nobody, and they don't run away. That ain't the kind of raising they gets. Miz' Clairborne's got money of her own, and lives off of the interest which she receives regular every six months. She went off down there to Miami Beach to sort of refresh herself and rest up her nerves. What with being off down here in Florida, away from all the folks she used to know, for three whole years, and cooped up there in her house, and remembering her dear husband being dead, and now Tom gone, and nobody left of the old family around excepting her and me, she was nervous and peaked like. It wasn't her, it was me that put her up to going off down there for a couple of months so maybe she would come back to herself. She never cheeped to me about borrowing no money from nobody, and I sure wasn't packing nothing up to move off when this plaintive come to the door. I was just

gleaming up the silver to kill time whilst I was there by myself.

"And, gentlemens, I never tackled the plaintive just as
soon as he mounted the porch like he said. The day before
that, he had come there and asked-ed me if Miz' Clairborne
was at home. I told him no, and then he asked-ed me just
when I expected her back. I told him she was down at Miami
Beach, and got the letter that she had sent me so he could get
her right address. He thanked me and went off. Then the next
morning, here he was back with a great big moving wagon,
rapped on the door and didn't use a bit of manners and polite-
ness this time. Without even a 'Good morning' he says for me
to git out of his way because he come to haul off all the furniture and things in the house and he is short for time.

"You jury-gentlemens, I told him in the nicest way that I
knowed how that he must of been crazy. Miz' Celestine was
off from home and she had left me there as a kind of guardeen
to look after her house and things, and I sure couldn't so
handy leave nobody touch a thing in Mrs. Clairborne's house
unlessen she was there and said so.

"He just looked at me like I was something that the
buzzards laid and the sun hatched out, and told me to move
out of his way so he could come on in and get his property. I
propped myself and braced one arm across the doorway to
bar him out, reckoning he would have manners enough to go
on off. But, no! He flew just as hot as Tucker when the mule
kicked his mammy and begun to cuss and double-cuss me,
and call me all out of my name, something nobody had never
done be-fore in all my borned days. I took it to keep from tearing up peace and agreement. Then he balled up his fistes and
demanded me to move 'cause he was coming in.

"'Aw, naw you aint,' I told him. 'You might think that
you's going to grow horns, but I'm here to tell you you'll die
butt-headed.'

"His mouth slewed one-sided and he hauled off and hit
me in my chest with his fist two times. Hollered that nothing
in the drugstore would kill me no quicker than he would if I
didn't git out of his way. I didn't, and then he upped and

kicked me.

"I jumped as salty as the 'gator when the pond went dry. I stretched out my arm and he hit the floor on a prone. Then, that truck with the two men on it took off from there in a big hurry. All I did next was to grab him by his heels and frail the pillar of the porch with him a few times. I let him go, but he just laid there like a log.

"'Don't you lay there, making out you's dead, sir!' I told him. 'Git up from there, even if you is dead, and git on off this place!'

"The contrary scamp laid right there, so I reached down and muscled him up on acrost my shoulder and toted him to the gate, and heaved him over the fence out into the street. None of my business what become of him and his dirty mouth after that.

"I figgered I done right not to leave him come in there and haul off Miz' Celestine's things which she had left there under my trust and care. But Tom, my husband, would have said I was wrong for taking too much on myself. Tom claimed that he ever loved me harder than the thunder could bump a stump, but I had one habit that he ever wished he could break me of. Claimed that I always placed other folks's cares in front of my own, and more expecially Miz' Celestine. Said that I made out of myself a wishbone shining in the sun. Just something for folks to come along and pick up and rub and pull and get their wishes and good luck on. Never looked out for nothing for my ownself.

"I never took a bit of stock in what Tom said like that until I come to be in this trouble. I felt right and good, looking out for Miz' Celestine's interest and standing true and strong, till they took me off to jail and I writ Miz' Celestine a letter to please come see 'bout me and help me out, and give it to the folks there at the jail to mail off for me."

A sob wrestled inside Laura Lee and she struck silence for a full minute before she could go on.

"Maybe it reached her, and then maybe again it didn't. Anyhow, I ain't had a single scratch from Miz' Celestine, and here I is. But I love her so hard, and I reckon I can't help myself. Look, gentlemens, Celestine was give to me when I was going on five—"

The prosecutor shot up like a striking trout and waved his long arm. "If the court please, this is not a street corner. This is a court of law. The witness cannot be allowed to ramble—"

The judge started as if he had been shaken out of a dream. He looked at the prosecutor and shook his head. "The object of a trial, I need not remind you, is to get at the whole truth of a case. The defendant is unlearned, as she has said. She has no counsel to guide her along the lines of procedure. It is important to find out why an act was committed, as you well know. Please humor the court by allowing the witness to tell her story in her own way." The judge looked at Laura Lee and told her to go ahead. A murmur of approval followed this from all over the room.

"I don't mean that her mama and papa throwed her away. You know how it used to be the style when a baby was born to place it under the special care of a older brother or sister, or somebody that had worked on the place for a long time and was apt to stay. That's what I mean by Celestine was give to me.

"Just going on five, I wasn't yet old enough to have no baby give to me, but that I didn't understand. All I did know that some way I loved babies. I had me a old rag doll-baby that my mama had made for me, and I loved it better'n anything I can mention.

"Never will forget the morning mama said she was going to take me upstairs to Miz' Beaufort's bedroom to lemme see the new baby. Mama was borned on the Beaufort place just like I was. She was the cook, and everything around the place was sort of under her care. Papa was the houseman and drove for the family when they went out anywhere.

"Well, I seen that tee-ninchy baby laying there in a pink crib all trimmed with a lot of ribbons. Gentlemens, it was the prettiest thing I had ever laid my eyes on. I thought that it was a big-size doll-baby laying there, and right away I wanted it. I carried on so till afterwhile Miz' Beaufort said that I could have it for mine if I wanted it. I was so took with it that I went plumb crazy with joy. I ask-ed her again, and she still said that she was giving it to me. My mama said so too. So, for fear they might change they minds, I said right off that I better take my baby home with me so that I could feed it my ownself and make it something to put on and do for it in general.

"I cried and carried on something terrible when they wouldn't leave me take it on out to the little house where we lived on the place. They pacified me by telling me I better leave it with Miz' Beaufort until it was weaned.

"That couldn't keep me from being around Celestine every chance I got. Later on I found out how they all took my carrying-on for jokes. Made out they was serious to my face, but laughing fit to kill behind my back. They wouldn't of done it if they had knowed how I felt inside. I lived just to see and touch Celestine—my baby, I thought. And she took to me right away.

"When Celestine was two, going on three, I found out that they had been funning with me, and that Celestine was not my child at all. I was too little to have a baby, and then again, how could a colored child be the mother of a white child? Celestine belonged to her papa and mama. It was all right for me to play with her all I wanted to, but forget the notion that she was mine.

"Jury-gentlemens, it was mighty hard, but as I growed on and understood more things I knowed what they was talking about. But Celestine wouldn't allow me to quit loving her. She ever leaned on me, and cried after me, and run to me first for every little thing.

"When I was going on sixteen, papa died and Tom Kimble, a young man, got the job that papa used to have. Right off he put in to court me, even though he was twelve years older than me. But lots of fellows around Savannah was pulling after me too. One wanted to marry me that I liked extra fine, but he was settling in Birmingham, and mama was aginst me marrying and settling way off somewhere. She ruthered for me to marry Tom. When Celestine begin to hang on me and beg and beg me not to leave her, I give in and said that I would have Tom, but for the sake of my feelings, I put the marriage off for a whole year. That was my first good chance to break off from Celestine, but I couldn't.

"General Beaufort, the old gentleman, was so proud for me to stay and pacify Celestine, that he built us a nice house on the place and made it over to us for life. Miz' Beaufort give me the finest wedding that any colored folks had ever seen around Savannah. We stood on the floor in the Beaufort parlor with all the trimmings.

"Celestine, the baby, was a young lady by then, and real pretty with reddish-gold hair and blue eyes. The young bloods was hanging after her in swarms. It was me that propped her up when she wanted to marry young J. Stuart Clairborne, a lawyer just out of school, with a heap of good looks, a smiling disposition, a fine family name and no money to mention. He did have some noble old family furniture and silver. So Celestine had her heart's desire, but little money. They was so happy together that it was like a play.

"Then things begin to change. Mama and Miz' Beaufort passed on in a year of each other. The old gentleman lingered around kind of lonesome, then one night he passed away in his sleep, leaving all he had to Celestine and her husband. Things went on fine for five years like that. He was building up a fine practice and things went lovely.

"Then, it seemed all of a sudden, he took to coughing, and soon he was too tired all the time to go to his office and do around like he used to. Celestine spent her money like water, sending her husband and taking him to different places from one end of the nation to the other, and keeping him under every kind of a doctor's care.

"Four years of trying and doing like that, and then even Celestine had to acknowledge that it never did a bit of good. Come a night when Clairborne laid his dark curly head in her lap like a trusting child and breathed his last.

"Inside our own house of nights, Tom would rear and pitch like a mule in a tin stable, trying to get me to consent to pull out with him and find us better-paying jobs elsewhere. I wouldn't hear to that kind of a talk at all. We had been there when times was extra good, and I didn't aim to tear out and leave Miz' Celestine by herself at low water. This was another time I passed up my chance to cut aloose.

"The third chance wasn't too long a-coming. A year after her husband died, Miz' Celestine come to me and told me that the big Beaufort place was too much for her to keep up with the money she had on hand now. She had been seeking around, and she had found a lovely smaller house down at Jacksonville, Florida. No big grounds to keep up and all. She choosed that instead of a smaller place around Savannah because she could not bear to sing small where she had always led off. An' now she had got hold of a family who was willing to buy the Beaufort estate at a very good price.

"Then she told me that she wanted me to move to Florida with her. She realized that she had no right to ask me no such a thing, but she just could not bear to go off down there with none of her family with her. Would I please consent to go? If I would not go with her, she would give Tom and me the worth of our property in cash money and we could do as we pleased. She had no call to ask us to go with her at all, excepting for old-time love and affection.

"Right then, jury-gentlemens, I knowed that I was going. But Tom had ever been a good husband to me, and I wanted him to feel that he was considered, so I told her that I must consult my pillow. Give her my word one way or another the next day.

"Tom pitched a acre of fits the moment that it was mentioned in his hearing. Hollered that we ought to grab the cash and, with what we had put away, buy us a nice home of our own. What was wrong with me nohow? Did I aim to be a wishbone all my days? Didn't I see that he was getting old? He craved to end his days among his old friends, his lodges and his churches. We had a fine cemetery lot, and there was where he aimed to rest.

"Miz' Celestine cried when he told her. Then she put in to meet all of Tom's complaints. Sure, we was all getting on in years, but that was the very reason why we ought not to part now. Cling together and share and lean and depend on one another. Then when Tom still helt out, she made a oath. If

Tom died before she did, she would fetch him back and put him away right at her own expense. And if she died before either of us, we was to do the same for her. Anything she left was willed to me to do with as I saw fit.

"So we put in to pack up all the finest pieces, enough and plenty to furnish up our new home in Florida, and moved on down here to live. We passed three peaceful years like that, then Tom died."

Laura Lee paused, shifted so that she faced the jury more directly, then summed up.

"Maybe I is guilty sure enough. I could be wrong for staying all them years and making Miz' Celestine's cares my own. You gentlemens is got more book-learning than me, so you would know more than I do. So far as this fracas is concerned, yeah, I hurted this plaintive, but with him acting the way he was, it just couldn't be helped. And 'taint nary one of you gentlemens but what wouldn't of done the same."

There was a minute of dead silence. Then the judge sent the prosecutor a cut-eye look and asked, "Care to cross-examine?"

"That's all!" the prosecutor mumbled, and waved Laura Lee to her seat.

"I have here," the judge began with great deliberation, "the note made by Mrs. J. Stuart Clairborne with the plaintiff. It specifies that the purpose of the loan was to finance the burial of Thomas Kimble." The judge paused and looked directly at Laura Lee to call her attention to this point. "The importance to this trial, however, is the due date, which is still more than three months away."

The court officers silenced the gasps and mumbles that followed this announcement.

"It is therefore obvious why the plaintiff has suppressed this valuable piece of evidence. It is equally clear to the court that the plaintiff knew that he had no justification whatsoever for being upon the premises of Mrs. Clairborne."

His Honor folded the paper and put it aside, and regarded the plaintiff with cold gray eyes.

"This is the most insulting instance in the memory of the

court of an attempt to prostitute the very machinery of justice for an individual's own nefarious ends. The plaintiff first attempts burglary with forceful entry and violence and, when thoroughly beaten for his pains, brazenly calls upon the law to punish the faithful watch-dog who bit him while he was attempting his trespass. Further, it seems apparent that he has taken steps to prevent any word from the defendant reaching Mrs. Clairborne, who certainly would have moved heaven and earth in the defendant's behalf, and rightfully so."

The judge laced the fingers of his hands and rested them on the polished wood before him and went on.

The protection of women and children, he said, was inherent, implicit in Anglo-Saxon civilization, and here in these United States it had become a sacred trust. He reviewed the long, slow climb of humanity from the rule of the club and the stone hatchet to the Constitution of the United States. The English-speaking people had given the world its highest concepts of the rights of the individual, and they were not going to be made a mock of, and nullified by this court.

"The defendant did no more than resist the plaintiff's attempted burglary. Valuable assets of her employer were trusted in her care, and she placed her very life in jeopardy in defending that trust, setting an example which no decent citizen need blush to follow. The jury is directed to find for the defendant."

Laura Lee made her way diffidently to the judge and thanked him over and over again.

"That will do, Laura Lee. I am the one who should be thanking you."

Laura Lee could see no reason why, and wandered off, bewildered. She was instantly surrounded by smiling, congratulating strangers, many of whom made her ever so welcome if ever she needed a home. She was rubbed and polished to a high glow.

Back at the house, Laura Lee did not enter at once. Like a pilgrim before a shrine, she stood and bowed her head. "I ain't fitten to enter. For a time, I allowed myself to doubt my Celestine. But maybe nobody ain't as pure in heart as they aim to be. The cock crowed on Apostle Peter. Old Maker, please take my guilt away and cast it into the sea of forgetfulness where it won't never rise to accuse me in this world, nor condemn me in the next."

Laura Lee entered and opened all the windows with a ceremonial air. She was hungry, but before she would eat, she made a ritual of atonement by serving. She took a finely wrought silver platter from the massive old sideboard and gleamed it to perfection. So the platter, so she wanted her love to shine.

Sarah Orne Jewett

(1849–1909) was born in Maine and spent most of her life there. She often accompanied her physician father on his daily rounds in southern Maine, an experience that provided her rural values and the idea that women are closer than men are to reality.

The latter theme informs her selection, "Jim's Little Woman" (1893). It is one of her few stories

St. Augustine

with much material for her writing. Her fictional works like *A Marsh Island* (1885), *Tales of New England* (1890), *The Life of Nancy* (1895), and *The Country of the Pointed Firs* (1896) dealt with tensions between urban and that takes place outside New England. Set in St. Augustine, it contrasts the wandering, alcoholic, but good-hearted sailor Jim and his faithful, hard-working wife from New England. The woman is clearly the center and strongest member of the family; having left family, friends, and home in New England, she faces the uncertainties of life on the foreign frontier of East Florida.

The scenes of St. Augustine show the varied life of the town and include mention of one group of people unknown to most Americans, the Minorcans. That group, to which Jim's grandmother belonged, was from the Spanish island of Minorca in the Mediterranean and had been brought to New Smyrna, Florida, by the British in the eighteenth century to produce Mediterranean-style products and to make the new colony profitable. The Spanish-speaking, Catholic Minorcans had a difficult time working the land and complained to the authorities in St. Augustine of harsh conditions under their overseer, Dr. Andrew Turnbull. When the colony at New Smyrna broke up, many Minorcans fled to St. Augustine, where they settled and prospered and have assumed positions of leadership.

Sarah Orne Jewett

Jim's Little Woman

HERE WAS laughter in the lanes of St. Augustine when Jim returned from a Northern voyage with a Northern wife. He had sailed on the schooner Dawn of Day, one hundred and ninety-two tons burden, with a full cargo of yellow pine and conch-shells. Not that the conch-shells were mentioned in the bill of lading, any more than five handsome tortoise-shells that were securely lashed to the beams in the captain's cabin. These were a private venture of the captain's and Jim's. The Dawn of Day did a great deal of trading with the islands, and it was only when the season of Northern tourists was over that her owners found it more profitable to charter her in the lumber business. It was too hot for bringing any more bananas from Jamaica, the last were half spoiled in the hold; and those Northerners who came excitedly after corals and sprouted cocoanuts and Jamaica baskets, who would gladly pay thirty cents apiece for the best of the conch-shells, brought primarily by way of ballast, —those enthusiastic, money-squandering Northerners had all flown homeward at the first hints of unmistakable summer heat, and market was over for that spring.

St. Augustine is a city of bright sunshine and of cool sea winds, a different place from the steaming-hot, listless-aired Southern ports which Jim knew well,—Kingston and Nassau and the rest. He had sailed between the islands and St. Augustine and Savannah, and made trading voyages round into the Gulf, ever since he ran away to sea on an ancient brigantine bound for Havana, in his early youth. Jim's grandfather was a

Northern man by birth, a New-Englander, who had married a
Minorcan woman, and settled down in St. Augustine to spend
the rest of his days. Their old coquina house near the sea-wall
faced one of the narrow lanes that ran up from the water, but
it had a wide window in the seaward end, and here Jim remembered that the intemperate old sailor sat and watched the
harbor, and criticised the rigging of vessels, and defended his
pet orange-tree from the ravages of boys. His wife died long
before he did, and the daughter, Jim's mother, was married,
and her husband ran away and never was heard from, and
Jim himself was ten years old when he walked at the head of
the funeral procession, dimly imagining that the old man had
gone up North, and that he was to live again there among the
scenes of his youth. There were a few old shipmates walking
two by two, who had known the captain in his active life, but
they held no definite views about his permanent location in
high latitudes. Still, there was a long procession and a handsome funeral; and after a few years Jim's mother died too, a
friendly, sad-faced little creature whom everybody lamented.
Jim came into port one day after a long absence, expecting to
be kissed and cried over and coaxed to church and mended
up, to find the old coquina house locked and empty. He
shipped again gloomily; there was nothing for him to do
ashore; and that year the boys took all the oranges, and people
said that the old captain's ghost lived in the house. The bishop
stopped Jim one day on the plaza, and told him that he must
come to church sometimes for his mother's sake; she was a
good little woman, and had said many a prayer for her boy.
Did Jim ever say a prayer for himself? It was a hard life, going
to sea, and he must not let it be too hard for his soul. "Marry
you a good wife soon," said the kind bishop. "Be a good man
in your own town; you will be tired of roving and will want a
home. God have pity on you, my boy!"

Jim took off his hat reverently, and his frank, bold eyes
met the bishop's sad, kind eyes, and fell. He had never really
thought what a shocking sort of fellow he was until that
moment. He had grown used to his mother's crying, but it
was two or three years now since she died. The fellows on

board ship were afraid of him when he was surly, and owned him for king when he was pleased to turn life into a joke. He was Northern and Southern by turns, this Southern-born young sailor. He could talk in Yankee fashion like his grandfather until the crew shook the ship's timbers with their laughter. But in all his roving sea-life he had never been to the coast of Maine until this story begins.

The Dawn of Day was a slow sailer, and what wind she had was only a light southwesterly breeze. Every other day was a dead calm, and so they drifted up the Northern coast as if the Gulf Stream alone impelled them, making for the island of Mount Desert with their yellow pine for house-finishing; and somewhere near Boothbay Harbor their provisions got low, and the drinking-water was too bad altogether, and there was nothing else left to drink, so the captain put in for supplies. They could not get up to the inner harbor next the town, but came to anchor near a little village when the wind fell at sundown. There were some houses in sight, dotted along the shore, and a long, low building at the water's edge, close to the little bay. Jim and the captain and another man pulled ashore to see what could be done about the water-casks, and the old water-tank, which had been rusty, was leaky and good for nothing when they first put to sea.

Jim went ashore, and presently put his head into a window of the long, low building; there were a dozen young people there, and two or three men, with heaps of lobster shells and long rows of shining cans. It was a lobster-canning establishment, and work was going on after hours. Somebody screamed when Jim's shaggy head and broad shoulders shut out the little daylight that was left, and a bevy of girls laughed provokingly; but one of them— Jim thought she was a child until she came quite close to him—asked what he wanted, and listened with intelligent patience until he had quite explained his errand. It proved easy to get somebody to solder up the water-tank, and in spite of the other girls this little red-haired, white-faced creature caught her hat from a nail by the door, and went off with Jim to find the solderer, who lived a quarter of a mile down the shore.

Jim thought of the old bishop many times as he walked decently along by the little woman's side. He thought of his mother, too, and how she used to cry over him; he never pitied her for it before. He remembered his cross old grandfather and those stories about the North, and by a strange turn of memory he mentally cursed the boys who came to steal the old man's oranges, there in the garden of his own empty little coquina house. What a thing to have a good little warmhearted wife of his own! Jim felt as if he had been set on fire; as if something hindered him from ever feeling like himself again; as if he must forever belong to this little bit of a woman, who almost ran, trying to keep up with his great rolling sea strides along the road. She had a clear, pleasant little voice, and kept looking up at him, asking now and then something about the voyage as if she were used to voyages, and seemed pleased with his gruff, shy answers. He heaved a great sigh when they came to the solderer's door.

The solderer came out and walked back with them, saying that his tools were all at the factory. He told Jim that there was the best cold spring on the coast convenient to the schooner, just beyond the factory, and a good grocery store near by. There was no reason for going up to Boothbay Harbor and losing all that time in the morning, and Jim's heart grew light at the news. He sent the solderer off to the schooner, and stayed ashore himself. The captain had already heard about the grocery, and had gone there. The grumbling member of the crew, who was left in the boat, looked back with heart-felt astonishment to see Jim sit down on a piece of ship timber beside that strange little woman, and begin to talk with her as if they were old friends. It was a clear June evening, the sky was pale yellow in the west, and on the high land above the shore a small jangling bell rang in its white steeple. A salt breath of sea wind ruffled the smooth water. The lights went out in the canning factory and twinkled with bright reflections from the schooner. The solderer finished his work on board, and was put ashore close to his own house; as for the captain, he remained with some new-made friends at the grocery.

They wondered on the deck of the Dawn of Day what had

come over Jim; they laughed and joked, and thought that he might have found one of his relations about whom he had told the Yankee stories. As long as there was any light to see, there he sat, an erect, great fellow, with the timid-looking little woman like a child by his side. The captain came off late, and in a state unbefitting the laws of Maine, and Jim came with him, sober, pleasant, but holding his head in that high, proud way which forbade any craven soul from putting an unwelcome question.

The next morning, when the wind rose, the Dawn of Day put out to sea again. Somebody besides Jim may have noticed that a white handkerchief fluttered at one of the canning-factory windows, but nobody knew that it meant so much to Jim as this: the little woman was going to marry him, and promised by that signal to come to Mount Desert to meet him. They had no more time for courtship; it was now or never with the quick-tempered fellow. Little Martha did not dare to promise until she had thought it over that night; but she was a lonely orphan, and had no ties to keep her there. Jim had told her about his home and his orange-tree in the South, and when morning came she had thought it over and said yes, and then even cried a little to see the old schooner go out to sea. She said yes because she loved him; because she had never thought that anybody would fall in love with her, she was so small and queer, and not like the rest of the girls. Jim had certainly waved his handkerchief in reply; and as Marty remembered that, she felt in her pocket for a queer smooth shell to make herself sure that she was not dreaming. Jim had carried this shell in his pocket for good luck, as his strange old seafaring grandfather had done before him, and by it he plighted his faith and troth. Before they sighted Monhegan, running far out to catch the wind, he told the skipper that he was going to be married, and expected to carry his wife down to St. Augustine in the Dawn of Day. The skipper swore roundly, but Jim was the ablest man aboard, and had been shipped that voyage as first mate. They were short-handed, and he was in Jim's power in many ways. There was a wedding, before the week was out, at a minister's house, and Jim

gave the minister's wife a pretty basket of shells besides what
Marty considered to be a generous wedding fee. He had
bought a suit of ready-made clothes before he went to the
cousin's house where the little woman had promised to wait
for him. Marty did not explain to this cousin that she had only
seen her lover once in the twilight. She wondered if people
would think Jim rough and strange, that was all; but Jim for
once was in possession of small savings, and when he came,
so tall and dark, shaven and shorn and dressed like other people, she fell to crying with joy and excitement, and had much
difficulty in explaining to her lover that it was nothing but
happiness and love that had brought such tears. And after the
yellow pine was on the wharf, and the conch-shells sold at
unexpected rates to a dealer in curiosities at Bar Harbor, who
got news of them, and after much dickering gave but a
meagre price for the tortoises also, the Dawn of Day set forth
again southward with dried fish and flour from Portland,
where, with his share of the conch-shell gains, Jim had given
his wife such a pleasuring as he thought a lord who had an
earldom at his back might give his fair lady.

When the crew first caught sight of Jim's small, red-
headed, and pale-faced wife, the discrepancy in the size of the
happy couple was more than could be silently borne. Jim always spoke of her as his little woman, and Jim's little woman
she was to the world in general. She was as proud-spirited as
he. She seldom scolded, but she could grow pale in the face
and keep silence if things went wrong. The schooner was a
different place on that return voyage. They had the captain's
cabin, and she made it look pretty with her girlish arts. She
mended everybody's clothes, and took care of the schooner's
boy when he was sick with a fever turn,—a hard-faced little
chap, who had run about from ship to ship, just as Jim had;
and though the wind failed them most of the time going
south, they were all sorry when they reached St. Augustine
bar. The last Sunday night of all, Jim's little woman got out
her Moody and Sankey song-book for the last time, and sang
every tune she knew in her sweet, old-fashioned voice. She
was rough in her way sometimes, but the crew of the Dawn of

Day kept to the level of its best manners in her hearing all the time she was on board. As they lay out beyond the bar, waiting for enough water to get in, she strained her eyes to see her future home. There was the queer striped lighthouse, with its corkscrew pattern of black and white, and far beyond were the tall, slender towers of a town that looked beautiful against the sunset, and a long, low shore, white with sand and green here and there with a new greenness which she believed to be orange-trees. She may have had a pang of homesickness for the high ledgy pasture shores at home, but nobody ever guessed it. If ever anybody in this world married for love, it was Jim's little woman.

II

It was not long before the dismal little, boarded-up, spidery coquina house was as clean as a whistle, with new glass windows, and fresh whitewash inside and yellow wash outside; with curtains and rugs and calico cushions, and a shining cooking-stove, on which such meals were concocted as Jim never dreamed of having for his own. The little woman had a small inheritance of housekeeping goods, which had been packed into the schooner's hold; luckily these had been in charge of the Northeast Harbor cousin; as Jim said, they had to get married, for everything came right and there was nothing else to do. He seemed as happy as the day was long, and for once was glad to be ashore. They went together to do their marketing, and he showed her the gray old fort one afternoon and the great hotels with the towers. In narrow St. George Street, under the high flower-lined balconies, everybody seemed to know Jim, and they had to spend much time in doing a trifling errand. Go into St. George Street when she would, the narrow thoroughfare was filled with people, and dark-eyed men and women leaned from the balconies and talked to passers-by in a strange lingo which Jim seemed to know. People laughed a good deal as they passed, and the little woman feared that they might think that she was queer-looking. She hated to be so little when Jim himself was so big;

but somehow the laughter all stopped after one day, when a man with an evil face said something in a mocking voice, and Jim, blazing with wrath, caught him by the waist and threw him over the fence into a garden.

"They laugh to think o' me getting so small a wife," said Jim frankly one day, in one of his best moods. "One o' the boys thought I'd raised me a fambly while we was gone, and said I'd done well for a little gal, but where was the old lady. I promised I'd bring him round to supper some night, too; he's a good fellow," added Jim. "We'll have some o' your clam fritters, and near about stuff him to death."

The summer days flew by, and to everybody's surprise Jim lived the life of a sober man. He went to work on one of the new harbor jetties at his wife's recommendation, and did good service. He gave Marty his pay, and was amused and astonished to see how far she made it go. With plenty of good food, he seemed to have lost his craving for drink in great measure; and they had two boarders, steady men and Jim's mates, for there was plenty of room; and the little woman was endlessly busy and happy. Jim had his dark Spanish days with a black scowl, and Marty had her own hot tempers, that came, as she said, of the color of her hair. Like other people, they had their great and small trials and troubles, but these always ended in Marty's stealing into her husband's lap as he sat by the window in his grandfather's old chair. The months went by, and winter came, and spring and their baby came, and then they were happier than ever. Jim, for his mother's sake, carried him to the old bishop to be christened, and all the neighbors flocked in afterward and were feasted. But there was no mistake about it, Jim drank more than was good for him that day in his pride and joy, and had an out and out spree while the baby's mother was helpless in bed; it was the first great worry and sorrow of their married life. The neighbors came and sat with Marty and told her all about him; and she got well as fast as she could, and went out, pale and weak, after him, and found Jim in a horrid den and brought him home. But he was sorry, and said it was all the other fellows' fault, and a fellow must have his fling. The little woman

sighed, and cried too when there was nobody to see her. She
had never believed, though she had had warnings enough,
that there was any need of being anxious about Jim. Men were
different from women. Yet anybody so strong and masterful
ought surely to master himself. But things grew worse and
worse; and at last, when the old schooner, with a rougher-
looking crew than usual, came into the harbor, the baby's
father drank with them all one night, and shipped with them
next morning, and sailed away, in spite of tears and coaxing,
on a four months' voyage. Marty had only three cents in her
thrifty little purse at the time. It was a purse that her mate at
the canning factory gave her the Christmas before she was
married. All the simple, fearless old life came up before her as
she looked at it. The giver had cried when they parted, and
had written once or twice, but the last letter had been long unanswered. Marty had lost all her heart now about writing; she
must wait until Jim was at home and steady again. Alas, the
months went by, and it seemed as if that time would never
come.

Jim came home at last, drunk and scolding, and when he
went away again with the schooner it would have been a
relief to be rid of him, if it were not for the worry. He did not
look so strong and well as he used. Under the tropic skies his
habits were murdering him slowly. The only comfort Marty
could take in him was when he lay asleep, with the black hair
curling about his smooth white forehead, and that pleasant
boyish look coming out on his face instead of the Spanish
scowl. The little woman lost her patience at last, and began to
wear a scowl too. She was a peppery little body, and sometimes Jim felt himself aggrieved and called her sharp names in
foreign tongues. He had a way of bringing his cronies home
to supper when she was tired, and ordering her about contemptuously before the low-faced men. At last, one night,
they made such a racket that a group of idle negroes clustered
about the house, laughing and jeering at the company within.
Marty's Northern fury rose like a winter gale; she was vexed
by the taunts of a woman who lived up the lane, who used to
come out and sit on her high blue balcony and spy all their

goings on, and call the baby *poor child* so that his mother
could hear. Jim's little woman drove the ribald company out
of doors that night, and they quailed, drunk as they were, before her angry eyes. They chased the negroes in their turn,
and went off shouting and swearing down the bayside. They
tried to walk on the sea-wall, and one man fell over and was
too drunk to find his way ashore, and lay down on the wet,
shelly mud. The tide came up and covered Joe Black, and that
was the last of him, which was not without its comfort, for Jim
stayed humbly at home, and tried to make his wife think
better of him, for days together. He had won an out and out
bad name in the last year. Nobody would give him a good job
ashore now, so that he had to go to sea. He was apt to lead his
companions astray, and go off on a frolic with too many followers. Yet everybody liked Jim, and greeted him warmly
when he came ashore; and he could walk as proudly as ever
through the town when he had had just drink enough to make
him think well of himself and everybody else. He dodged
round many a corner to avoid meeting the bishop, that good,
gray-haired man with the kind, straightforward eyes.

Marty made a good bit of money in the season. She liked
to work, and was always ready to do anything there was to
do,—scrubbing or washing and ironing or sewing,—and she
came to be known in the town for her quickness and power of
work. While Jim was away she always got on well and saved
something; but when he came in from his voyages things
went from bad to worse; and after a while there was news of
another baby, and the first one was cross and masterful; and
the woman up the lane, in her rickety blue balcony, did nothing but spy discomforts with her mocking eyes.

Jim was more like himself that last week before he went to
sea than for a long time before. He seemed sorry to go, and
kept astonishingly sober all the last few days, and picked the
oranges and planted their little vegetable garden without being asked, and made Marty a new bench for her tubs that she
had only complained of needing once or twice. He worked at
loading the schooner down at the sawmill, and came home
early in the evening, and Marty began to believe she had at

last teased him and shamed him into being decent. She even thought of writing to her friend in Boothbay after two years' silence, she had such new hopes about being happy and prosperous again. She talked to Jim about that night when they first saw each other, and Jim was not displeased when she got the lucky shell out of a safe hiding-place and showed him that she had kept it. They looked each other in the face as they seldom did now, and each knew that the other thought the shell had brought little luck of late. Jim sat down by the window and pulled Marty into his lap, and she began to cry the minute her head was on his shoulder. Life had been so hard. What had come over Jim?

"That old bishop o' my mother's," faltered Jim. "He's been givin' it to me; he catched me out by the old gates, and he says, 'Jim, you're goin' to break your little woman's heart.' Was that so, Marty?"

Marty said nothing; she only nodded her head against his shoulder and cried like a child. She could feel his warm shoulder through his coat, and in a minute he asked her again, "Was that so, Marty?" And Marty, for answer, only cried a little less. It was night, and Jim was going away in the morning. The crickets were chirping in the garden. Somebody went along the sea-wall singing, and Jim and his little woman sat there by the window.

"The devil gets me," said Jim at last, in a sober-minded Northern way that he had sometimes. "There's an awful wild streak in me. I ain't goin' to have you cry like mother always done. I'm goin' to settle down an' git a steady job ashore, after this one v'y'ge to the islands. I'm goin' to fetch ye home the handsomest basketful of shells that ever you see, an' then I'm done with shipping, I am so."

" 'T ain't me only; 't is them poor little babies," said Marty, in a tired, hopeful little voice. She had done crying now. She felt somehow as if the reward for all her patience and misery was coming.

"I would n't go off an' leave ye now, as things be with ye," said Jim, "but you see we need the money; an' then I've shipped, and the old man's got my word. I'm stout to work

aboard ship, an' he knows it, the cap'n does. The old bishop
he warned me against the cap'n; he said if 't wa'n't for him I'd
be master o' a better vessel myself. He works me hard an'
keeps me under. I do believe the bishop's right about him,
and I'd kept clear from drink often if 't wa'n't for the old
man."

"*You've* kep' you under," said honest Marty. "Nobody
ain't master over you when it comes to that. *You've* got to set
your mind right against drink an' the cap'n, Jim."

"It's so cursed hot in them islands," Jim explained. "You
get spent, and have to work right through everything; but I
give you my honest word I'll bring you home my pay this
trip."

At which promise the little woman gave a pleased sigh,
and moved her head as if for sheer comfort. She tried to think
whether there was anything else she could have done to the
poor clothes in his battered sea-chest; then she fell asleep.
When she waked in the morning, Jim had laid her on the bed
like a child, and spread an old shawl over her, and had gone.
At high tide in the early morning the schooner Dawn of Day
had come up from the sawmill wharf with a tug, and sent a
boat ashore for Jim. Marty had never missed him as she did
that morning; she had never felt so sure of his loving her, and
had waked thinking to find herself still in his arms as she had
fallen asleep. There stood the empty chair by the window; and
through the window, over beyond the marshes, she could see
the gray sails of the schooner standing out to sea. Oh, Jim!
Jim! and their little child was crying in the crib, like a hungry
bird in its nest—the poor little fellow!—and calling his father
with pleading confidence. Jim liked the brave little lad. When
he was sober, he always dressed up on Sundays and took little
Jim and his mother for a walk. Sometimes they went to the old
Spanish burying-ground, and Jim used to put the baby on his
grandfather's great tombstone, built strong over his grave like
a little house, and pick the moss from the epitaph with his
great sea jack-knife. His mother had paid for the tomb. She
was laid at one side of it, but Jim had never built any tomb for
her. He meant to do it, some time, and Marty always picked

some flowers and green sprigs and laid them on the grave
with its bits of crumbling coquina at the head and foot.

In spite of a pain at her heart, and a foreboding that Jim
would never come back from his unwilling voyage, the little
woman went up the lane boldly that late morning after he
sailed; she no longer feared the mocking smile and salutation
of the neighbor in the balcony. She went to her work cheer-
fully, and sang over it one of her Moody and Sankey hymns.
She made a pleasure for the other women who were washing
too, with her song and her cheerful face. She was such a little
woman that she had a box to stand on while she washed, but
there never was such a brisk little creature for work.

III

Somehow everything prospered in the next two
months until the new baby came. Some young women hired
all her spare rooms, and paid well for their lodging, besides
being compassionate and ready to give a little lift with the
housework when they had the time. Marty had never laid by
so much money before, and often spoke with pride of her
handsome husband to the lodgers, who had never seen him;
they were girls from the North, and one of them had once
worked in a canning factory. One day Marty wrote to her own
old friend, and asked her to come down by the steamer to Savannah, and then the rest of the way by rail, to make her a
long visit. There was plenty of hotel work in the town; her
lodgers themselves got good wages on George Street.

Jim was not skilled with his pen; he never wrote to her
when he went away, but ever since they were married Marty
always had a dream one of the nights while he was gone, in
which she saw the schooner's white sails against a blue sky,
and Jim himself walking the deck to and fro, holding his head
high, as he did when he was pleased. She always saw the
Dawn of Day coming safe into harbor in this dream; but one
day she thought with a sudden chill that for this voyage the
good omen was lacking. Jim had taken the lucky shell along;
at any rate, she could not find it after he went away; that was

a little thing, to be sure, but it gave some comfort until one
morning, in shaking and brushing the old chair by the seaward window, out dropped the smooth white shell. The luck
had stayed with her instead of going with poor Jim, and the
time was drawing near for his return. The new baby was a
dear little girl; she knew that Jim wanted a girl baby, and now,
with the girl baby in her arms, she began her weary watch for
white sails beyond the marshes.

The winter days dawned with blue skies and white clouds
sailing over; the town began to fill with strangers. As she got
strong enough there was plenty of work waiting for her. The
two babies were a great deal too large and heavy for their little
mother to tend; they seemed to take after Jim in size, and to
grow apace, and Marty took the proud step of hiring help.
There was a quiet little colored girl, an efficient midget of a
creature, who had minded babies for a white woman in Baya
Lane, and was not without sage experience. Marty had bought
a perambulator the year before from a woman at one of the
boarding-houses, who did not care to carry it North. When
she left the hired help in charge that first morning, and hurried away to her own work, the neighbor of the blue balcony
stood in her lower doorway and bade her a polite good-morn-
ing. But Jim's little woman's eyes glittered with strange light
as she hurried on in the shadow of the high wall, where the
orange boughs hung over, and beyond these, great branches
laden with golden clusters of ripening loquats. She had not
looked out of the seaward window, as she always liked to do
before she left the house, and she was sorry, but there was no
time to go back.

The old city of St. Augustine had never been more picturesque and full of color than it was that morning. Its narrow
thoroughfares, with the wide, overhanging upper balconies
that shaded them, were busy and gay. Strangers strolled
along, stopping in groups before the open fronts of the fruit
shops, or were detained by eager venders of flowers and
orange-wood walking-sticks. There were shining shop windows full of photographs and trinkets of pink shell-work and
palmetto. There were pink feather fans, and birds in cages,

and strange shapes and colors of flowers and fruits, and stuffed alligators. The narrow street was full of laughter and the sound of voices. Lumbering carriages clattered along the palmetto pavement, and boys and men rode by on quick, wild little horses as if for dear life, and to the frequent peril of persons on foot. Sometimes these small dun or cream-colored marsh tackeys needed only a cropped mane to prove their suspected descent from the little steeds of the Northmen, or their cousinship to those of the Greek friezes; they were, indeed, a part of the picturesqueness of the city.

The high gray towers of the beautiful Ponce de Leon Hotel, with their pointed red roofs, were crowned with ornaments like the berries of the chinaberry-trees, and Marty looked up at them as she walked along, and at the trees themselves, hung with delicate green leaves like a veil. Spring seemed to come into the middle of summer in that country; it was the middle of February, but the season was very early. There was a mocking-bird trying its voice here and there in the gardens. The wind-tattered bananas, like wrecked windmills, were putting out fresh green leaves among their ragged ones. There were roses and oranges in bloom, and the country carts were bringing in new vegetables from beyond the old city gates; green lettuces and baskets of pease and strawberries, and trails of golden jasmine were everywhere about the gray town. Down at the foot of the narrow lanes the bay looked smooth and blue, and white sails flitted by as you stood and looked. The great bell of the old cathedral had struck twelve, and as Marty entered the plaza, busy little soul that she was and in a hurry as usual, she stopped, full of a never outgrown Northern wonder at the foreign sights and sounds,—the tall palmettoes; the riders with their clinking spurs; the gay strangers; the three Sisters of St. Joseph, in their quaint garb of black and white, who came soberly from their parish school close by. Jim's little woman looked more childlike than ever. She always wore a short dress about her work, and her short crop of red curly hair stood out about her pale face under the round palmetto hat. She had been thinking of Jim, and of her afternoon's affairs, and of a strange little old negro woman who had been looking out of a doorway on George Street, as she passed. It seemed to Marty as if this old withered creature could see ghosts in the street instead of the live passers-by. She never looked at anybody who passed, but sometimes she stood there for an hour looking down the street and mumbling strange words to herself. Jim's little woman was not without her own superstitions; she had been very miserable of late about Jim, and especially since she found his lucky shell. If she could only see him coming home in her dream; she had always dreamed of him before!

Suddenly she became aware that all the little black boys were running through the streets like ants, with single bananas, or limp, over-ripe bunches of a dozen; and she turned quickly, running a few steps in her eagerness to see the bay. Why had she not looked that way before? There at the pier were the tall masts and the black and green hull of the Dawn of Day. She had come in that morning. Marty felt dizzy, and had to lean for a minute against the old cathedral doorway. There was a drone of music inside; she heard it and lost it; then it came again as her faintness passed, and she ran like a child down the street. Her hat blew off and she caught it with one hand, but did not stop to put it on again. The long pier was black with people down at the end next the schooner, and they were swarming up over the side and from the deck. There were red and white parasols from the hotel in the middle of the crowd, and a general hurry and excitement. Everybody but Marty seemed to have known hours before that the schooner was in. Perhaps she ought to go home first; Jim might be there. Now she could see the pretty Jamaica baskets heaped on the top of the cabin, and the shining colors of shells, and green plumes of sprouted cocoanuts for planting, and the great white branches and heads of coral; she could smell the ripe fruit in the hold, and catch sight of some of the crew. At last she was on the gangway, and somebody on deck swore a great oath under his breath. "Boys," he said, in a loud whisper, "here's Jim's little woman!" and two or three of them dropped quickly between decks and down into the hold rather than face her. When she came on board, there was nobody to be seen but the hard-faced cabin-boy whom she had taken care of in a fever as they came down from Boothbay. He had been driving a brisk trade with some ladies down in the captain's cabin.

"Where's Jim gone?" said Marty, looking at him fiercely with her suspicious gray eyes.

"You'd better go ask the cap'n," said the boy. He was two years older than when she first knew him, but he looked much the same, only a little harder. Then he remembered how good Marty had been to him, and that the "old man" was in a horrid temper. He took hold of Marty's thin, freckled, hard-worked little hand, and got her away aft into the shadow and behind the schooner's large boat. "Look here," he faltered, "I'm awful sorry, Marty; it's too bad, but—Jim's dead."

Jim's wife looked the young fellow straight in the face, as if she were thinking about something else, and had not heard him.

"Here, sit right down on this box," said the boy. But Marty would not sit down; she had a dull sense that she must not stay any longer, and that the sun was hot, and that she could not walk home along the sea-wall alone.

"I'll go home with you," said the boy, giving her a little push; but she took hold of his hand and did not move.

"Say it over again what you said," she insisted, looking more and more strange; her short red hair was blowing in the wind all about her face, and her eyes had faded and faded until they looked almost white.

"Jim's dead," said the hard-looking boy, who thought he should cry himself, and wished that he were out of such a piece of business. The people who had come to chaffer for shells began to look at them and to whisper. "He's dead. He—well, he was as steady as a gig 'most all the time we was laying off o' Kingston, and the ol' man could n't master him to go an' drink by night; and Jim he would n't let me go ashore; told me he'd 'bout kill me; an' I sassed him up an' down for bossin', and he never hit me a clip back nor nothin'; he was queer this voyage. I never see him drunk but once,—when we first put into Nassau,— and then he was a-cryin' afterwards;

and into Kingston he got dizzy turns, and was took sick and laid in his bunk while we was unloadin'. 'T was blazin' hot. *You* never see it so hot; an' the ol' man told how 't was his drinkin' the water that give him a fever; an' when he went off his head, the old man got the hospit'l folks, an' they lugged him ashore a-ravin; an' he was just breathin' his last the day we sailed. We see his funeral as we come out o' harbor; they was goin' out buryin' of him right off. I ain't seen it myself, but Jim Peet was the last ashore, an' he asked if 't was our Jim, an' they said 't was. They'd sent word in the mornin' he was 'bout gone, and we might 's well sail 'f we was ready."

"Jim Peet saw his funeril?" gasped the little woman. "He felt sure 't was *Jim?*"

"Yes 'm. You come home 'long o' me; folks is lookin'," said the boy. "Come, now; I'll tell you some more goin' along."

Marty came with him through the crowd. She held her hat in her hand, and she went feeling her way, as if she were blind, down the gangway plank. When they reached the shore and had gone a short distance, she turned, and told the lad that he need not come any farther; if he would bring his clothes over before the schooner sailed, she would mend them all up nice for him. Then she crept slowly along Bay Street bareheaded; the sun on the water at the right blinded her a little. Sometimes she stopped and leaned against the fence or a house front, and so at last got home. It was midday, there was not a soul in the house, and Jim was dead.

That night she dreamed of a blue sky, and white sails, and Jim, with his head up, walking the deck, as he came into harbor.

IV

All the townsfolk who lived by the waterside and up and down the lanes, and many of the strangers at the hotels, heard of poor Marty's trouble. Her poorest neighbors were the first to send a little purse that they had spared out of their small savings and earnings; then by and by some of the hotel people and those who were well to do in the town made her presents of money and of clothes for the children; and even the spying neighbor of the balcony brought a cake, and some figs, all she had on her tree, the night the news was known, and put them on the table, and was going away without a word, but Marty ran after her and kissed her, for the poor soul's husband had been lost at sea, and so they could weep together. But after the dream everybody said that Marty was hurt in her mind by the shock. She could not cry for her own loss when she was told over and over about her neighbor's man; she only said to the people who came that they were very kind, and she was seeing trouble, but she was sure that Jim would come back; she knew it by her dream. They must wait and see. She could not force them to take their money back, and when she grew too tired and unstrung to plead about it any longer, she put it together in a little box, and hid it on a high cupboard shelf in the chimney. There was a wonderful light of hope in her face in these days; she kept the little black girl to tend the two babies, and kept on with her own work. Everybody said that she was not quite right in the brain. She was often pointed out to strangers in that spring season, a quaint figure, so small, so wan, and battling against the world for her secret certainty and hope.

Never a man's footstep came by the house at night that she did not rouse and start with her heart beating wildly; but one, two, three months went by, and still she was alone. Once she went across the bay to the lighthouse island,— babies, baby-carriage, the small hired help, and all,—and took the railway that leads down to the south beach. It was a holiday, and she hoped that from this southern point she might look far seaward, and catch sight of the returning sails of the old schooner. She would not listen to her own warnings that Jim had plenty of ways of getting home besides waiting for the Dawn of Day. Those who saw the little company strike out across the sand to the beach laughed at the sight. The hired help pushed the empty perambulator with all the strength she could muster through the deep white sand, and over the huge green, serpent-like vines that wound among the low dunes. Marty carried the baby and tugged the little boy by the other

hand, and sat down at the edge of the beach all alone, while
the children played in the sand or were pushed to and fro. She
strained her eyes after sails, but only a bark was in sight to the
northward beyond the bar, and a brigantine was beating
southward, and far beyond that was a schooner going steadily
north, and it was not the Dawn of Day. All the time Jim's little
woman kept saying to herself: "I had the dream; I had the
dream. Jim will come home." But as this miserable holiday
ended, and they left the great sand desert and the roar of the
sea behind them, she felt a new dread make her heart heavier
than ever it had been before; perhaps even the dream was
mocking her, and he was dead indeed.

Then Marty had need of comfort. She believed that as long
as she kept faith in her omen it would come true, and yet her
faith slowly ebbed in spite of everything. It was a cruel test,
and she could not work as she used; she felt the summer heat
as she never had before. All her old associations with the cool
Northern sea-coast began to call her to come home. She wondered if it would not do to go North for a while and wait for
Jim there. The old friend had written that next winter she
would come down for a visit, and somehow Marty longed to
get home for a while, and then they could come South together; but at last she felt too tired and weak, and gave up the
thought. If it were not for the children, she could go to Jamaica and find out all about Jim. She had sent him more than
one letter to Kingston, but no answer came. Perhaps she
would wait now until next summer, and then go North with
Lizzie.

In midsummer the streets are often empty at midday, and
the old city seems deserted. Marty sometimes took the children and sat with them in the plaza, where it was shady.
Often in the spring they all wandered up the white pavement
of the street by the great hotel to see the gay Spanish flags,
and to hear the band play in the gardens of the Ponce de Leon;
but the band did not play as it used. Marty used to tell the
eldest of the children that when his father came home he
would take him sailing in the bay, and the little fellow got a
touching fashion of asking every morning if his father were

coming that day. It was a sad summer,—a sad summer. Marty knew that her neighbors thought her a little crazed; at last she wondered if they were not right. She began to be homesick, and at last she had to give up work altogether. She hated the glare of the sun and the gay laughter of the black people; when she heard the sunset gun from the barracks it startled her terribly. She almost doubted sometimes whether she had really dreamed the dream.

One afternoon when the cars stopped at the St. Augustine station, Marty was sitting in the old chair by the seaward window, looking out and thinking of her sorrow. There was a vine about the window that flickered a pretty shadow over the floor in the morning, and it was dancing and waving in the light breeze that blows like a long, soft breath, and then stops at sundown. She saw nothing in the bay but a few small pleasure-boats, and there was nothing beyond the bar. News had come some time before that the Dawn of Day had gone North again with yellow pine, and the few other schooners that came now and then to the port were away on the sea, nobody knew where. They came in as if they dropped out of the sky, as far as Marty was concerned. She thought about Jim as she sat there; how good he was before he sailed that last time, and had really tried to keep his promise on board ship, according to the cabin-boy's story. Somehow Jim was like the moon to her at first; his Spanish blood and the Church gave an unknown side to his character that was always turned away; but another side shone fair through his Northern traits, and of late she had understood him as she never had before. She used to be too smart-spoken and too quick with him; she saw it all now; a quick man ought to have a wife with head enough to keep her own temper for his sake. "I could n't help being born red-headed," thought Marty with a wistful smile, and then she was dreaming and dozing, and fell fast asleep.

The train had stopped in the station, and among the strangers who got out was a very dark young man, with broad shoulders, and of uncommon height. He was smartly dressed in a sort of uniform, and looked about him with a familiar smile as he strolled among the idlers on the platform.

Suddenly somebody caught him by the hand, with a shout, and there was an eager crowd about him in a minute. "Jim! Here's dead Jim!" cried some one, with a shrill laugh, and there was a great excitement.

"No," said Jim, "I ain't dead. What's the matter with you all? I've been up North with the best yacht you ever see; first we went cruisin' in the Gulf an' over to Martinique. Why, my wife know'd I was goin'. I had a fellow write her from Kingston, an' not to expect me till I come. I give him a quarter to do it."

"*She* thinks you're dead. No; other folks says so, an' she won't. Word come by the schooner that you was dead in hospit'l, of a Jamaica fever," somebody explained in the racket and chatter.

"They always was a pack o' fools on that leaky old Dawn o' Day," said Jim contemptuously, looking down the steep, well-clothed precipice of himself to the platform. "I don't sail with those kind o' horse-marines any more."

Then he thought of Marty with sudden intensity. "She never had got his letter!" He shouldered his great valise and strode away; there was something queer about his behavior; nobody could keep up with his long steps and his quick runs, and away he went toward home.

Jim's steps grew softer and slower as he went down the narrow lane; he saw the little house, and its door wide open. The woman in the blue balcony saw him, and gave a little scream, as if he were a ghost. The minute his foot touched the deep-worn coquina step, Marty in her sleep heard it and opened her eyes. She had dreamed again at last of the blue sky and white sails; she opened her eyes to see him standing there, with his head up, in the door. Jim not dead! not dead! but Jim looking sober, and dressed like a gentleman, come home at last!

That evening they walked up Bay Street to King Street, and round the plaza, and home again through George Street, making a royal progress, and being stopped by everybody. They told the story over and over of its having been another sailor from a schooner, poor fellow! who had died in Kingston that day, alone in hospital. Jim himself had gone down to the gates of death and turned back. There was a yacht in harbor that had lost a hand, and the owner saw handsome Jim on the pier, looking pale and unfriended, and took a liking to him, and found how well he knew the Gulf and the islands, so they struck a bargain at once. They had cruised far south and then north again, and Jim only had leave to come home for a few days to bring away his little woman and the children, because he was to keep with the yacht, and spend the summer cruising in Northern waters. Marty had always been wishing to make a visit up in Maine, where she came from. Jim fingered his bright buttons and held his head higher than ever, as if he had been told that she felt proud to show him to her friends. He looked down at little Marty affectionately; it was very queer about that dream and other people's saying he was dead. He must buy her a famous new rig before they started to go North; she looked worn out and shabby. It seemed all a miracle to Marty; but her dream was her dream, and she felt as tall as Jim himself as she remembered it. As they went home at sunset, they met the bishop, who stopped before them and looked down at the little woman, and then up at Jim.

"So you're doing well now, my boy?" he said good humoredly, to the great, smiling fellow. "Ah, Jim, many's the prayer your pious mother said for you, and I myself not a few. Come to Mass and be a Christian man for the sake of her. God bless you, my children!" and the good man went his wise and kindly way, not knowing all their story either, but knowing well and compassionately the sorrows and temptations of poor humanity.

It seemed to Marty as if she had had time to grow old since the night Jim went away and left her sleeping, but the long misery was quickly fading out of her mind, now that he was safe at home again. In a few days more, the old coquina house was carefully shut and locked for the summer, and they gave the key to the woman of the blue balcony. The morning that they started northward, Marty caught a glimpse of the Dawn of Day coming in through the mist over the harbor bar.

She wisely said nothing to Jim; she thought with apprehension of the captain's usual revelry the night he came into port. She took a last look at the tall lighthouse, and remembered how it had companioned her with its clear ray through many a dark and anxious night. Then she thought joyfully how soon she should see the far-away spark on Monhegan, and the bright light of Seguin, and presently the towers of St. Augustine were left out of sight behind the level country and the Southern pines.

Donald Justice

(1925–) is a Florida-born writer who has spent the early and current stages of his career working in the state. He was born in Miami and earned his B.A. from the University of University of Iowa, and the University of Florida. His books include *The Summer Anniversaries* (1960), *The Collected Poems of Weldon Kees* (1960), *Night Light* (1967), *Sixteen*

Miami, his M.A. from the University of North Carolina, and his Ph.D. from the University of Iowa. He has taught at the University of Missouri, Reed College, Syracuse, Princeton, the *Poems* (1970), *Departures* (1973), *Platonic Scripts* (1984), and *The Sunset Maker* (1987). He won the Pulitzer Prize for poetry in 1980.

"The Artificial Moonlight" (1983) is based on an incident Justice experienced in Miami.

The character of Jack in the story represents the author. The framework is built on a group of friends at a party who go to an island late at night. More important than the trip are the interactions among friends and spouses that reveal the sadness and doubts in their lives. The epilogue shows that they have gone in different directions over twenty-two years and that few of them have found any real happiness. The story reflects both the passing of the old in Miami in favor of the new—progress in one sense, but a real loss in another—and the change in relationships among even the best of friends over a period of time.

Loss, a theme in much of Justice's poetry, pervades this story: loss of innocence, loss of youth, loss of friends. As the title promises, much of the story deals with artificiality, but there is also a feeling that one can come to terms with life and can find a niche in it. The sense of place in the story is most prevalent on the isolated island, which is peaceful and quiet in the midst of busy Miami, just as several of the individuals are introspective and reticent in the midst of party-goers.

The Miami setting is symbolic of the great mixture of peoples in the city—northern transplants, Cuban and Haitian immigrants, disaffected blacks, even Seminole Indians. The great turmoil of that international city, which is a part of North America but looks to Latin America and the Caribbean for much of its commerce and tourism, makes it easier to understand the search for tranquility that plays an important part in the story. Whether it is Jack's peaceful aloneness in the midst of the party or his being stranded on the island alone overnight or his loneliness twenty years later, there is a sense of the necessity of finding strength from within oneself rather than depending on others.

Donald Justice

The Artificial Moonlight

Coconut Grove, 1958

HE LANGS, Hal and his wife Julie, were giving a party.

From the screen porch of their apartment you could see, strung out across the bay, the colored lights of the neighborhood sailing club—the Langs did not belong—and, farther out, the bulky shadows of the members' boats riding at anchor. Almost always, with nightfall, there would be a breeze. It came from the bay and across the bayshore road past the shaggy royal palms bordering the driveway, cooling the porch like a large and efficient fan.

But tonight was one of those rare end-of-summer nights without any saving breeze. It was past midnight, and still the apartment felt oppressive and close. The heat was spoiling the party. It was a going-away party for an old friend of the Langs', Jack Felton, whom they saw now only when he came home from graduate school to visit his parents, and in a day or two, with summer over, he would be taking off for Europe on a Fulbright. But it was not only the heat. Some vague melancholy of departure and change seemed to have settled over everyone and everything.

In the back room a record player was turning, unattended. Sounds of the jazz of a dozen years ago, early Sarah Vaughan, drifted out to the porch. The casual guests, the friends of friends, had all departed. The few who remained looked settled in, as though they might stay forever, listless and bored, some on the sagging wicker chair and settee, and some on the floor cushions brought out from the stuffy back rooms. They looked as though they might never move again, not even to flip the stack of records when the music ended.

IF ANYONE did, it would probably be Julie herself. Of the Langs, Julie was the dependable one. Five afternoons a week she worked as a legal stenographer, while her husband kept up appearances by giving occasional painting lessons to the daughters of tourists. Yet except for a shortage of money from time to time they lived with as much freedom from care and nearly as much leisure as the well-to-do. Approaching their thirties, they seemed as perpetually youthful as movie stars.

The odd hours they kept could be hard on Julie, and occasionally she retired early. She would be so wound up that she could not sleep and would have to read for a long time before her eyes closed. It was an intense sort of reading, beyond simple pleasure. One wall of their bedroom was filled with books, and sometimes when they made love without turning the lights off she caught herself innocently letting her eyes rove across the titles on the spines of the larger books. Once or twice Hal had complained of this publicly, to her embarrassment, but she seemed unable to change.

Alone in their bedroom, reading or not, she liked the sound of conversation floating back late at night from the porch. It was soothing, like the quiet, washing sound of an ocean. It was hot back there, and there was a little fan she could reach out for and turn on, but she did not often use it. She liked the warm weather; she could not imagine living anywhere but Miami.

Still, there were nights when Julie felt left out of things. Their friends all drank, and, except on the most ceremonial occasions, Julie did not. Of course the feeling went beyond that. She would suspect them of planning something incalculably exciting from which she was to be excluded. Unreasonable, but there was nothing she could do about the feeling. Julie gazed with half-closed eyes across the porch at her husband, where he sat perched on an arm of the old wicker settee, bending down to speak to a tall blond woman in slacks. She wondered if she would ever be able to trace this feeling of hers back to its source. How far back would she have to go? She was an orphan, adopted by a couple old enough to be her grandparents, long ago dead. Could it be as simple as that? She thought, sometimes, that she might have Spanish blood. That would account for her dark coloring, for her thick black eyebrows, her almost blue-black hair, which only a few days before she had cut short, despite Hal's protests.

In the back room now the record stopped and another dropped down from the stack—Duke Ellington, slow and bluesy. Shutting her eyes, Julie took a sip of the plain orange juice in her glass and, leaning back, crossed her legs. One tiny sandaled foot, the nails that afternoon painted a deep blood-red for the party, commenced to swing nervously back and forth, back and forth, to some inner rhythm of her own.

HOWEVER SERIOUS his life elsewhere might have become, Jack had kept his old reputation locally for stirring things up. He wondered if the others were waiting for him to take some initiative now. After all, the party was for him.

But he was not the same person they remembered, not really. Whenever he came back home now it was as if the curtain had risen on a new act, with the same actors, but the playwright had without notice shifted the course of the action. It was impossible to point to a time when everything had been as it should be, but that time must have existed once. They all felt it. And lately, to Jack, every change—the divorce of one couple, the moving away of another—came as an unwelcome change.

As for himself, Jack knew that he seemed quieter than he used to seem. In fact, he was. He had no wish to pretend otherwise, but in a very small way, just as he could imagine his friends doing, he missed his old self. He sat now very quietly, stretched out on his floor cushion, leaning back against the wall, his long legs folded in a lazy tangle before him. He looked half asleep. But behind his glasses his eyes were still open. It might have seemed that he was listening to the music, except that it had stopped.

He had intended to listen. He had stacked the records himself, some of his favorites. Then, just as the unforgotten sounds had begun to bear him back towards his own adolescence, it had struck him suddenly why the girl sitting beside him, to whom he had been talking desultorily for the last twenty minutes or so, was wearing so loose and unbecoming a blouse—tardily, for she was, if not very far along, nevertheless visibly pregnant. To Jack, who had known her all his life, the realization came like a blow. When those very records were being cut, this girl, Susan, who was almost certainly the youngest person in the room, had been listening obediently to the nuns of her grammar school, wearing the blue-and-white uniform Jack still remembered. The summer before, when he had last seen her, Susan had not even been married. And already her husband, Robert or Bob, the sallow, sleepy-looking fellow in the corner who never had much to say, had got her pregnant.

For the time being Jack could concentrate on nothing but this, this fact that to him seemed so irremediably, if obscurely, wrong.

HAL WAS bending down, whispering into the blond woman's ear. Not that there was anything important to be said, but there was a pleasure in merely leaning towards her in that way, some momentary illusion of intimacy. What he had to say was only that soon they would be out of vodka.

And then he sighed. There was a sort of perfume coming, apparently, from a spot just behind her ear. Green was her married name, Karen Green, and Hal had known her longer than he had known his wife. As far back as high school he had had a hopeless crush on her, but never before had he noticed how peculiarly large and yet shapely her left ear was, from which the hair was drawn back, and how many little whorls it contained, impossible to count. Was she wearing her hair some new way?

Hal leaned closer and whispered, "Of course we could always go out to Fox's for more. More vodka."

It was half a question. It was the tone he always adopted with Karen, the tone of casual flirtation, just as though they were in school together still.

A RUSTLING stirred in the palms outside, the first sign of something like a breeze. For a moment the wind rose, the rolled tarpaulins high up on the screen seemed to catch their breath.

All at once, borne to them on the faint edge of wind, they heard a dance band playing, not very far away, a rhumba band—snarling trumpet, bongo drums, maracas. Had it been playing all this time? Everyone listened. Jack straightened up and peered about the room, somewhat crossly, like a person roused from an interesting dream.

"The Legion dance," someone called out.

The large, good-looking man, who from his cushion beside Julie Lang's chair had also been watching Hal and the blond woman, climbed to his feet. This was Sid Green, Karen's husband. Standing, he loomed larger than anyone else in the group.

Normally unassertive, Sid heard his own voice calling across the porch, "Hey, Hal, you by any chance a member?" To himself his voice sounded unexpectedly loud, as if it contained some challenge he did not wish to issue more directly.

"For Christ's sake, Sid, the *Foreign* Legion maybe, not the American."

"If somebody was a member we could go to the dance," Sid said. "I mean if anybody wanted to."

"Crash it?" the pregnant girl asked.

"Oh, maybe not," Sid said, looking around, and even his flash of enthusiasm was fading.

"I don't know," Hal said, with a glance at Sid's wife beside him.

"Oh, let's do go!" Julie cried out suddenly from across the porch. "For God's sake, let's do something! Just wait a minute till I change my shoes." And kicking her sandals off, fluffing her short crop of hair out as she went, she hurried back through the dark apartment towards the bedroom.

BUT WHEN she returned it was apparent that something
was wrong. Hal and Karen were missing, and Jack as well.
Julie peered into the corner where the other women were sitting—Susan and a girl named Annabelle, who appeared to be
sound asleep.

"Aren't you coming?" Julie asked nervously.

"Not me," Susan said, placing one hand on her stomach.
"Not in my condition." Her silent husband beamed, as if
Susan had said something witty or perhaps flattering to him.

Julie felt more uncomfortable than ever. She had never
been a mother, and she was a good deal older than Susan,
seven or eight years at least, but she did not think that Susan
and her husband would intentionally try to embarrass her.
Everyone knew that she had never wanted children, that she
preferred her freedom.

Julie turned to Sid; their eyes met. He was quiet, too quiet
to be amusing in the way that Hal and even Jack could sometimes be, but really quite good-looking in his athletic fashion,
dark and mysterious, withheld. They knew very little about
Sid. Was it true that his family had money? If only, Julie
thought, he would volunteer himself more, like Hal. But at
least Sid could be managed.

"Come on, you," she said, taking him by the hand and
pulling. "Let's catch up with the others."

Meekly, Sid allowed himself to be led out the door.

ON THE DOCK it was very quiet. Only stray phrases of the
Cuban trumpet carried out that far.

As they had walked out onto the dock, which was floated
on an arrangement of great, slowly rusting oil drums, it had
bobbed and swayed with every step. By now it had settled
down. The three of them—Hal and Karen and Jack—sat dang-
ling their legs over the end, looking out at the anchored boats
which the water rocked as gently as cradles. Above the water,
very bright, as if left over from some festivity, were strung the
lights of the sailing club. All of the lights together cast a
strange glow on the dark waters of the bay, a thin swath of
artificial moonlight which reached out perhaps halfway

towards the long, indistinct blur of the nearest island.

Jack wanted to touch the water, see how cold it was. Carefully he set the drink he had brought with him down upon the planking and removed his loafers. Not that he meant to swim. But as he thrust one leg down, and his toes touched water, which was not as cold as expected, he found himself thinking of a woman they all knew, a woman named Roberta, who had once lived in the apartment above the Langs, and how she sometimes used to swim out to the island, which was no more than a dark, low line on the horizon. There was nothing to do out there; it was a mere piny arm of sand. She would wait just long enough to catch her breath and then swim back. That was all. It would not have been, if you were a swimmer, very dangerous. There were plenty of boats along the way to catch hold of if you tired.

Perhaps they were all thinking of Roberta just then, for when Hal asked, out of the blue, if they knew that Roberta was in San Francisco, Karen said, "Funny, I was just thinking of that time she drove her car into the bay."

"Well, not quite all the way in," Hall said. "It stalled, you know."

Hal was the authority on the stories they told about people they used to know. There was a good-sized collection of them, recounted so often the identities of the participants tended to blur, and the facts themselves were subject to endless small revisions and adjustments.

"I thought it was a palm tree that stopped her," Jack commented, rather sourly. He had never been one of Roberta's admirers. At the time, she had seemed a silly romantic girl, mad for attention. He tried to recall her face but could not. Had it been pretty? He seemed to remember it as pale, rather moon-shaped, but perhaps that was someone else's, someone more elusive still.

"You're right," Hal agreed. "There was a palm tree somewhere, but where?" He began to reconstruct. "The car must have caromed off the palm and gone on into the bay. Yes, part way in. I seem to picture it hanging over the edge sort of."

"I always thought she did it on purpose," Karen said.

"No, it was an accident." On that point Hal was definite.

Gradually a deeper melancholy settled over them. All around, the small dinghies tied up at the dock nosed familiarly against the wood. One was painted a vivid orange and white, the colors of the sailing club. A car passed behind them along the bayshore road, swiftly, heading for Miami proper.

Karen looked out across the bay. "Well, she should have done it on purpose. That would have made sense. It would have been—oh, I don't know . . . "

OFF AND ON all evening Jack had been wondering what, if anything, was on between Hal and Karen. Karen was very beautiful, more beautiful than she had been ten years ago, just out of high school, when everyone, himself and Hal too, as he remembered, was buzzing around her. Experience had only ripened her; she made him think of some night-blooming flower the neighbors call you out to see. Probably just then —at that very minute, Jack would have liked to believe—she was at the absolute peak of her beauty. The next summer, surely by the summer after, she would have crossed the invisible line they were all approaching. On the other side of that line strangers would no longer find her quite so remarkable to look at, only old friends like Hal and himself, who would remember her face as it had been lit momentarily by the driftwood fire of some otherwise forgotten beach picnic, or more likely as it was now, shaped by the glow of the lights strung out from the dock over the water.

He recalled a story of Hal's, a story he did not much like to think of, of how Hal and a girl Jack didn't know had rowed out to the island one night and stayed till dawn. Thinking about the story now, with the island itself so near, Jack began to feel curiously giddy, as if the dock were starting to bob again.

"What about the island?" he asked.

"What about it?" Karen said.

"What about going out to the island?"

"I couldn't swim that far," she said. "Not nearly."

"Not swim. We borrow one of these dinghy things. Ask

Hal. He's done it before."

Hal grinned. "Right. The night watchman, he sleeps back in that little shack. Besides, he doesn't really give a damn."

In a moment they were climbing down into the orange-and-white dinghy, a trickier operation than it looked. Whenever one of them put a foot down, exploring, the boat seemed to totter almost to the point of capsizing. Jack could not hold back a snort of laughter.

"Shh," Hal said.

"I thought he didn't give a damn," Karen said, tittering.

"Shh," Jack said. "Shh."

Once they were all seated, Hal took up the oars. They were just casting off, Jack had just managed to slip the rope free, when they heard footsteps coming up the walk. The rope dropped with a thick splash.

"Hey, we see you down there," a voice called, and Karen recognized it as her husband's. Just behind him stood Julie, their shadows bent out over the water.

"Shh," Karen hissed. Already the current was bearing them out, and there was a wide dark patch between boat and dock.

"Come on back."

"Can't. Current's got us."

But Hal was able to plant one oar firmly in the water and with that the boat began to turn in a slow circle.

"How was the dance?" Hal called politely.

For reply Julie stamped her foot on the dock. "Come on back," she called.

"Tell me, Julie, I sincerely want to know how it was."

"Oh, Hal, stop it."

"Actually they were very nice about it," Sid said, "but we felt kind of out of place."

"I feel kind of out of place right here," said Jack, dizzy with the motion of the boat.

"Oh, you're all drunk," Julie said. "Every one of you is hopelessly drunk and besotted."

It ENDED with Sid and Julie untying another dinghy and

climbing into it. Quietly then the two boats glided out with the mild current through the lighted water.

Under the lights Jack felt like an escaping prisoner caught in the beam of a spotlight, and he closed his eyes, distinctly giddy now. When he looked again, they were already emerging from the shadows of the anchored boats into the clear space beyond, where it was dark. The other boat was no longer in sight. Hal feathered the oars, and they drifted with the flow, letting Sid and Julie catch up. It was very still. They could hear Sid grunting over the oars before they saw his dinghy coming up, gaining fast. In the dark his bent-over shape looked like part of the ghostly, gliding boat. Their eyes had become used to the dark by now, and they were near enough to make out ahead the narrow strip of sand edged with stunted pines that marked the shore of the island. A moment later the outline of a landing pier with several large nets spread out to dry on skeletal frames came into sight. Hal pointed the boat that way and resumed rowing.

The pier was rickety but apparently safe. When Hal leaped out, the others followed.

KAREN LIVED with the vaguely troubling impression that someone, some man, had all her life been leaning towards her, about to touch her. It was like a dream. Instinctively she wished to draw back but could not. Moments ago, on the island, lying on the little beach, with Hal leaning towards her, whispering something about exploring the island a little farther down, around the point, she had consented without a thought, without strict attention to the words. Tomorrow, thinking back over it, excusing herself, she might suppose that she had thought Hal meant for the others to come too, but now, with that little moment still round and clear in her mind, she could admit that she had come away under no such illusion. She could not understand why she had come. Karen was not in any way angry with her husband, and she had never felt the least tremor of desire for Hal, who was simply an old friend.

Her earliest recollection of Hal was of a brash, rebellious

boy in high school, a loud talker, but solitary, whom she had seen once standing alone after classes at the end of a long corridor puffing away at—strange!—a cigar, much too advanced for his years. Perhaps that was why she had been tempted to come with him now, that fragment of memory. Hal had looked up from the end of the corridor and seen her watching him puff away at the forbidden cigar, though neither had spoken at the time, nor, for that matter, had either brought the incident up since. Karen was not certain that Hal would remember it. Even if he did not, Karen believed that out of that moment, in some not-to-be-explained way, this moment had come, and that it was in some way inevitable that the two of them should be standing together now, around the point from the beach where the others were lying, though not yet so far off as to keep an occasional murmur of voices from drifting their way.

Hal was no longer leaning towards her. He had taken her hand to lead her across one stretch of slippery rocks, but he had not otherwise touched her. He was talking softly and at incredible length about a book he was reading, a novel about some boys marooned on an island. Of all things! Karen thought, slightly indignant. Of all things! She had failed at the outset to catch the novelist's name, and the conversation by now was too far advanced to ask. Hal seemed to have reached the point of criticizing the style of the writer. Seemed—she could not really say. Her attention was failing, fading. She was overcome by a feeling of surrender, a sense of division that was almost physical, in which she stood watching herself disappear over the water, which was dark, of a deep gemlike hue, and astonishingly calm.

In the distance she could hear Sid's laughter. She had the most vivid sensation of his anxiety and of Julie's as well. She wished she might do something to alleviate it, but it was as if Hal's voice going on and on endlessly about the novel she would never read were fixing her, or a part of her, to a certain point, pinning her there, draining her of all power, while the rest of her drifted out, out. . . . If only Sid would raise his voice and call her! She remembered the after-supper games of hide-

and-seek as a child with her large family of sisters and a brother. One game in particular was among her most persistent memories, one that recurred even in her dreams. She was crouching behind a prickly bush—for years afterwards she could go to that same bush and point it out; she knew exactly where it stood on the lawn of her parents' house. She was the last one of all the sisters not yet found by her brother, who was "It," and she could hear her brother's footsteps coming through the dusk and then his soft voice calling, almost whispering, "Karen? Karen? Karen?" And she ran to him and threw her arms around him, whereupon her brother, who was quite a few years older and much larger than she—he was only playing the game as a favor to his sisters—lifted her from the ground and swung her around and around until they both fell to the grass, overcome with laughter and relief.

How tired she was! She wanted Hal to stop talking. She was ready. She wanted him to touch her; she wanted whatever was going to happen to begin. Love! And yet she could not bring herself to say to him that it would be all right, that whatever he did or did not do scarcely mattered any longer.

JACK WOKE from a sound sleep feeling cold. He was alone.

He sat up and listened, a little apprehensively, for some sound to indicate where the others might be. Except for the water that was licking up along the sand almost to his feet and out again, the silence was complete. Where had they gone? He took it for granted that they were off exploring the island, two by two probably, but by what pairs and for what purpose he hardly considered. His curiosity, brimming not long before, had gone flat.

Somewhere he had misplaced his glasses. Groping in the sand near where he had been sleeping, failing to find them, he blinked out across the water into the sky. The first faint streaks and patches of light were beginning to show. For a long time he sat, reluctant to get up and start looking for the others. He did not like the idea of stumbling across them in the dark, especially half-blind as he was. For the time being he did not care if he never saw any of them again. His stomach felt a little queasy, but he was not sure if it was from drinking. It might have been from emotion. In any case, he had been through worse.

Only after he had made his way back along the path to the landing pier and seen that the boats were missing did he realize what had happened. They had left him behind; they had abandoned him on the island.

At first he was simply angry. He peered as well as he could towards land. The sailing-club lights were still burning over the water. That he could see, but no farther. It was beginning to get light, and soon, he knew, the night watchman would wake up and turn the lights off. Already the lights were beginning to look superfluous. What a stupid joke this was, he thought. He imagined the story they would make out of it—the night they marooned Jack on the island! For a moment he considered the chance of swimming back, like Roberta. If he could make seventy or eighty yards on his own, there would be plenty of boats to hang on to. But the water looked cold, and his stomach was too unsettled.

Cold after the warmth of the night, he wrapped his arms around his shoulders. He felt as alone as he could ever remember having felt, and in an unfamiliar place, a place he could not even, without his glasses, see clearly, all fuzzy and vague—the last absurd touch. Any minute his teeth would start chattering. Standing there like that, realizing how foolish and pointless it was, for he must have been very nearly sober by then, he began to call their names out as loud as he could, one after the other—a kind of roll call—whether out of annoyance or affection he did not pause to consider. *Hal, Sid, Karen, Julie!* He had no idea how far his voice carried over the water, and in any case there was no answer.

At last he sat down on the little rickety pier and began to wait for someone to come and rescue him. And gradually, siting there, beginning to shiver with the morning cool, Jack reflected, absurdly enough, that he was to be the hero of whatever story came to be told of the night. A curious form of flattery, but flattery of a sort. He had been singled out. At once he felt better about the evening. The party—it had not been a dead loss, after all. He almost found himself forgiving them for having abandoned him; eventually perhaps he would forgive them, forgive them everything, whatever they had done or not done. Without him, whatever had happened—and he did not want to know yet what that was, afraid that his new and still fragile sense of the uniqueness of the evening might evaporate once he knew—would not have happened. In some way, he was responsible. In any case, he would have forgiven them a great deal—laughter, humiliation, even perhaps betrayal —as they would forgive him practically anything. He saw all that now. Well, it was a sentimental time of night—the very end of it—and he had had a lot to drink, but he was willing to believe that the future would indeed be bleak and awful without such friends, willing to take their chance with you, ready even to abandon you on a chunk of sand at four A.M. for nothing but the sheer hell of it. And he was, for the moment, remarkably contented.

Brighton, 1980

THE APARTMENT building the Langs had lived in had been gone since the late sixties. There had been a boom. The fine old house—one of the oldest in the area, one to which Indians just before the turn of the century had come up across the bay in their canoes to trade—had lasted as long as any, but it had succumbed in the end to time and money. In any case, it would have been quickly dwarfed by the new high-rises looming around it. On its site stood one of the poshest of the latest generation of high-rises, expensive and grand, with glass and impractical little tilted balconies painted in three bold colors. Admittedly, it had been and was still a grand site, with a marvelous sweeping view of the bay, the little masted boats thick on the water, like blown leaves.

But it was the people who concerned Jack. And he knew none of the new people. In his own place, when he went there now, he felt uncomfortable and alien.

One day—twenty years and more had passed—sitting in a flat in Brighton, England, looking idly out over the gray, dis-

turbed sea in a direction he thought must be towards home,
Jack began making a sort of mental catalogue of all his friends
from that period. He had not thought it out in advance. The
idea just came to him, and he began. He was trying to remember everyone who was together at a certain time in the old life,
at a precise moment even, and the night of his going-away
party came back to him.

The list began with Susan's son, the one she had been
pregnant with at the time, and Jack was pleased with himself
for having thought to include her child-to-be in his recollection. She never had another. The son, he had heard, was a
fine, intelligent boy, off at college somewhere, no trouble to
anybody. Jack had not seen him since the boy started grammar school. The boy's name slipped his memory, but he did
remember, if not very clearly, curls and a sort of general shy-
ing away from the presence of grown-ups.

The sallow husband—Robert or Bob—had been some
trouble or had some trouble. Drinking? Whatever in the past
had caused his silence, he was to sink deeper and deeper into
it over the years. Eventually he had found his way back north
to Philadelphia, into his father's business, a chain of liquor
stores. Just the thing, Jack thought ruefully, just the thing.

Susan herself was another story, though not much of one.
She owned a small stucco house in the Grove, almost hidden
by shrubs and palms and jacarandas. Her time seemed to go
into nothing at all, unless it was a little gardening, but it
surely went. She had no time for anything, certainly not for
friends, and never or very rarely ventured out. She kept a few
cats, quite a few. Their number grew.

The great surprise was Sid, the only one to have become
famous. Not exactly famous, Jack acknowledged, but well-
known. No one had sensed the power and ambition hidden so
quietly in Sid back then, certainly not Karen. From small
starts, from short sailing trips down into the Keys, later out to
the Bahamas, Sid had taken the great dare of a long solo sail
across the Atlantic, kept a journal, and published an account
of the voyage. Modestly popular. Later, other adventures,
other books. He was married now to a minor movie actress,

past her prime but still quite beautiful—a brunette, not at all
like Karen in appearance—and they lived most of the year,
predictably somehow, in southern France. (It was true—his
family had had some money.) Jack had recently had occasion
to call on them on the continent and found that he enjoyed his
visit immensely. Sid had become voluble, a great smiler—of
all of them, the most thoroughly and happily changed.

Karen, on the other hand, had been through three more
husbands. Two daughters, one of them married, with a
daughter of her own. It seemed incredible to Jack that Karen,
of all people, should have become a grandmother. It was like
a magic trick, seen but not believed. Sometimes, of an evening, as they sat talking over a drink beside the current husband's pool, the bug light sending out its intermittent little
zap, he had caught a sidelong glimpse of the former Karen, a
Karen absolute and undiminished, still slender, seemingly remote, cool if not cold, not to be found out. Some secret she
had, and it had kept her beautiful. Her present husband was
often ill, and there was a bad look around her own eyes. She
looked away from you much of the time. She had never done
anything of any importance in her life, and everybody had always loved her for herself alone. What happiness!

Julie, as she had wished, never had had any children. Over
the years she had gone a little to corpulence, but her foot, sur-
prisingly tiny still, still swung back and forth to some nervous
rhythm of her own. She, who had always abhorred and fled
from the cold, ran a bookstore now in Boston. She had become
an expert on books. The way Jack had of explaining this to
himself—he had browsed in her shop once or twice when in
the city—was simply that she had liked to read, always. Those
nights Hal had been out catting around she had read. She had
read and read and she had always loved books and, in the
end, it had come to this. She seemed satisfied.

Nor was Hal—the great romantic, Hal—a totally lost
cause, even though he had, in his maturity, held down a
steady job, the same job now, for ten or eleven years, easily a
record for him. He managed a gallery. He was perfect for it, a
gallery in the Grove popular with everyone, wealthy tourists

especially. It also provided him the contacts with women he seemed to need—wives, daughters, perhaps even a youthful grandmother or two. Women, young and old, some beautiful, some rich, pursuing Hal, who was not getting any younger. He let his colorful shirts hang out usually, over a slight belly, wore dark glasses much of the time, rode out his hangovers with good grace and considerable experience. He still painted, excellent miniatures, obsessively detailed, with the clear jeweled colors of Byzantine work. He sold everything he made and never set too high a price, though it was certain he could demand more if he chose. But no, he was as happy as he deserved, perhaps happier. Not married—it was easier that way. Some nights he liked being alone.

Several of his friends, Jack realized, were actually happy. The shape of their futures must always have been there, somehow, just as eye color is built into the chromosomes before birth. Impossible to read, all the same, except backwards, as with some obscure Eastern language. Or perhaps the night of the party had been a sort of key, and it had been clear, or should have been clear then, that the Langs would never last, not as a couple, and if the Langs went, then the Greens constituted a doubtful case; and something in the way her husband had cast his silent, wary, unfathomable glances at the pregnant Susan might have hinted at some future division between them as well. Now no one was married to the right person. No one, as Jack would have it, would ever be married to the right person again. The time when everything was as it should be was always really some other time, but back then, that summer, it had seemed near.

From the window of the flat he could see only a little corner of the sea, and he wanted, for some reason, to be closer to the water. Dressing warmly, Jack walked down to the parade, braced himself against the baby gale and walked and walked, for forty minutes or so. He found himself down on the shingle, almost alone there. It was too nasty a day for there to be much company. A big boat hung on the horizon. Jack thought back to the beach of the little sandy bay island and he guessed that what had happened that night must be why he had ventured down to the sand now, to which he almost never descended. Here in this foreign place he felt again that he was on a little island, isolated, the last civilized speck, himself against a faceless and unpredictable world—unknowable, really. Jack felt like calling out the names again, the names of his friends, but of course he did not. He could not even remember how he had been rescued that other time, who it was that had come out in a dinghy for him, risking the wrath of the sleepy night watchman. Probably Sid. Julie had cooked a nice breakfast—he remembered that. No one would be coming to rescue him now, not that he needed rescuing or wanted rescuing, even in the sort of half-dreaming state he had fallen into. But the thought did occur to him, in passing.

MacKinlay Kantor

(1904–1977) is one of the most prolific writers in this collection: he wrote over thirty novels, several collections of short stories, and a number of nonfiction works. Born in Iowa,

Union soldiers in Georgia. From 1936 on, the great story-teller lived on Siesta Key, near Sarasota.

"No Storm on Galilee" (1941) takes place on Lake Okeechobee

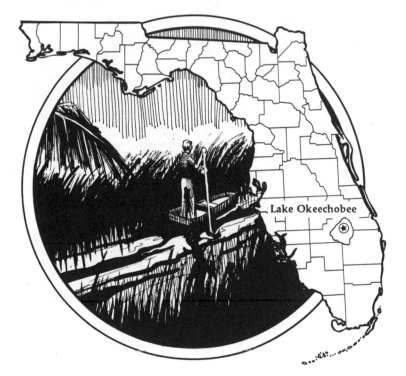

Lake Okeechobee

he worked in Chicago, Cedar Rapids, and Des Moines while writing the novels that would later make him famous, especially *Andersonville* (1955), the Pulitzer Prize–winning novel about a Confederate prison for

in southern Florida. Although stories about people in the area usually deal with the farmers who work the rich, deep muck around the lake, as in Richard Powell's *I Take This Land*, Kantor's story describes the fishermen who ply its waters. A blood feud has erupted between two families over the trapping of fish on the lake, a feud that may have begun in misunderstanding but has been kept alive by stubbornness. In the end it is the girlfriend of the man sent to prison for his part in the feud who solves the problem between the two families and gets them to think about reconciliation rather than revenge. Under the surface of a story about professional fishermen who fish Florida's inland waters for a livelihood, Kantor describes interrelationships among these strong-willed people.

What is not mentioned in the story but what had to take place to enable such fishermen as described here to make their livelihood from Lake Okeechobee was control of its flooding. The "storm" in the title may allude to the disastrous hurricanes that devastated the area, first in 1926, killing some 300 people, and then in 1928, killing 2,000 people. Because the state was unable to afford the extensive work needed to control flooding around the lake, the federal government did the job by dredging deeper channels and building bigger dikes and levees around the lake. Such water control did much to make the area livable and the lake more fishable.

The title of the story might also refer to the storm on Galilee mentioned in the New Testament (Matthew 8:23–27). The disciples of Jesus panicked when a storm came up quickly on the lake and Jesus was asleep in the boat, supposedly unaware of the danger. They woke him and he calmed the sea, but then he rebuked them for their lack of faith. Kantor may have been using the biblical reference to comment on the lack of faith and trust between the two feuding families and on the fear that had fueled it all those years.

MacKinlay Kantor

No Storm on Galilee

UMOR had been running like a fox along
the shore. Rumor had left its tracks in
every dooryard, and many people stood
at Galilee Landing that morning; but they
lost their powers of speech when they actually saw Weaver
Pray before them.

Probably the suspicions about his homecoming started
when Weaver's grandfather, old Judah P.B. Millis, kept driving to town on ostensibly routine errands, but always bringing home a roll or two of heavy, triple-dipped, galvanized
poultry wire in the back of his truck. There was only one
common use for such wire on the western flats of Lake
Okeechobee.

People spied around the Peebee Millis place; they made
excuses to drop in at odd hours. None of them saw hide nor
hair of Weaver Pray, and nobody wanted to mention his
name, or his dead father's name, or the name of any of the
Booths. Nobody had dared to say those names out loud in
front of Peebee Millis during the past three and a half years.

The Booths were more nervous than anyone else. They
burned a light in their house, right through every night, after
the whispers started. The youngest Booth boy made a great
show of wandering up and down the road with a shotgun
evenings, and booming away at any frog or snake or mud hen

that crossed his path.

Neighbors grimaced at all this gunfire; no Booth was ever born who could handle a gun like Weaver Pray. One had been born who could handle a knife more adequately than Weaver Pray's father. Now he was dead, and quite unable to defend his progeny if it came to gunplay or knifeplay again.

Vaguely, the whispers had the word "Monday" mixed up in them, which explains the crowd at Galilee Landing that morning.

Men bunched together when they heard the sound of an unfamiliar motor far out beyond the skinning bench. They conjectured as to whose motor it could be. They quit conjecturing when a green-painted launch and a towed skiff came into view and they saw who was bringing them.

Blaze Digby, who ran the fish market at Pretty Point, was at Galilee too; it was unusual for him to be there on a Monday. But a heavy rain on the previous Saturday had drowned out his car when he started to drive to the Landing to pay off the trappers; only a few men had been able to come down to Pretty Point for their money over the week end.

Digby didn't want to hold out on his neighbors. Bright and early that morning he climbed into his coupé and drove the fifteen miles up to Galilee. He was handing out money to the trappers and checking his tally slips against theirs before Weaver Pray came into sight.

The assemblage left Mr. Digby standing by the open door of his car, with a little ledger on the seat before him; they drifted across solid ground until the bare feet of the foremost were buried in the warm brown mud. They looked at Weave and let their money go for a while.

Weaver shut off his motor when he reached the shallows. He nosed the launch among weeds until it was solid at the bow; then he drew up his skiff, unhitched the hawser and climbed aboard. He poled steadily across the last hundred yards, and when the skiff grounded he sank his push pole through the pipe and stepped overboard and waded ashore.

His face was expressionless. Black eyebrows grew close together above his long flat nose, just the way everyone remembered; it was the way Millis eyebrows—Weave's dead mother was Martha Millis—always grew.

Folks had expected that he might be pale. Weave was the first resident of the neighborhood who had ever served a sentence for murder. In the old days there had been a moderate amount of killing, but in the old days the Law didn't bother you. Murder was promptly avenged if the circumstances demanded it, and promptly forgotten if they didn't.

Nowadays it was different. They sent you up the state, and you wore stripes, and the hard labor was said to be hard labor indeed. Maybe that was the reason folks expected Weaver Pray to be as pale as paper. But he wasn't. His skin was the color of an old penny; he had grown an extra half inch or so, and had put on a good fifteen pounds.

There was a chorus; people said, "Hello, Weave.... Howdy, Weaver....Morning, boy," and things like that. Nobody ventured to remark upon the weather, or to suggest that it was a fit day to do any good with the traps. They just stood there until Weave spoke to them.

He said, "Morning." His eyes went over them speedily —the hard black eyes they had known so well. Timid people shrank a little from his gaze, and that was odd; plenty of them remembered the time when he was a shirttail kid not big enough to hold an oar. He wasn't much more than a kid now, despite his size and his hardihood. He was only twenty-two or twenty-three.

They all wondered whether he was looking for Booths. But there weren't any such around—the Booths had seen to that. Distressed by fearful rumors about Monday morning, the Booths had gone out on the lake two hours early.

Weaver went up onto the green turf. The feet of others made a smothered sound as they hastened along behind.

Blaze Digby was waiting beside his coupé. He still held white tally slips in his hand.

"Morning, Weave."

"Morning."

"How are things?"

"Things are all right."

"How's your grandma?"

"She's keeping good enough."

"How's your Grandpa Judah P.B. Millis? You tell him I wish he'd go out and get me some fish."

The other people stopped about ten feet behind Weaver Pray; that was as close as they wanted to come.

Weave said, "Well, I'll tell you, Mr. Blaze. You know Grandpa Peebee keeps himself mighty busy with his bass-fishing camp. He's got him four cabins in the yard for tourists, and he's finishing another one, up on the ridge behind the cypress."

People had heard about a new fishermen's cabin on the Millis place, but that was the first time they reckoned just who the initial tenant might be.

Mr. Digby said casually, "Been around very long, son?"

"Nigh onto two weeks. My grandpa and grandma are mighty crowded for room these days, what with cooking and fishermen and all. I've been sleeping up in that new cabin." He folded his arms across his wide chest. "Mr. Blaze."

"What's on your mind, son?" Digby was beginning to guess just what was on Weaver Pray's mind.

"You want I should trap fish for you?"

Digby squinted across the green-and-brown wilderness — that wilderness of water and plant growth which was delft blue on any map, but the color of old palmetto scrub when you saw it.

"I'm always buying fish, Weave." Blaze lowered his voice, hoping to spare the embarrassment of talking business in public. "I stand ready to advance you the wire for your traps. What about a boat?"

"I don't need any boat," said Weaver. "I've done made a deal with Grandpa Peebee, and I cleaned up the engine on that old boat of his lying next to the canal. I got her painted too. There she is out there. The skiff was mine before—"

"About the wire—"

"I don't need wire, captain. I've done bought my wire already. I got me out a hundred and two traps. I'll make that a hundred fifty soon."

Blaze Digby let his face turn bright red, as he always did in moments of interest or excitement. "You sure been working. You mean you got your trails cut and everything?"

"Yes, sir. What I want to know is, do I sell to you or to Cushman Brothers? What I want to know is, have you got too many people trapping for you already? Because I can't afford to take a chance on trucks being late or full up, or on my being delayed, and maybe having to ship all the way over through Moore Haven."

Digby told him earnestly, "Don't you fret yourself about those little items, Weave. People still eat fish and I still ship plenty, and stand ready to ship more. I'm giving three cents a pound for the regular run, anything above six-seven inches, undressed. Seven cents for dressed catfish; you're privileged to use my skinning bench for the dressing."

At this moment another car came out of the timber road behind the growth of elderberry; it bumped forward across the soft ground until it stopped in line with the cars already parked there. It was an old high-wheeled roadster with the top down. A girl slid from behind the steering wheel.

Slowly she approached the crowd of men beside the fish dealer's car. She was small and slender, with bright yellow hair bleached to an even paler gold by the Florida sun, and this hair she had combed and brushed carefully, and had tied with a tiny bow of purple ribbon. She wore a short-sleeved khaki blouse and newly pressed khaki trousers, faded, but stiff and clean. Her slim wiry feet were bare. Perhaps she was eighteen years old.

The girl edged around the group until she could rest her hand on the left front fender of Blaze Digby's car.

If Weaver Pray saw her he made no sign. But Blaze took his eyes away from Weave's. He turned, lifting his brows a little; he smiled and removed his straw hat. "Miss Gracious," he said. "Glad to see you, honey."

Gracious Shipley murmured a greeting that seemed to catch in her throat and leave her strangled.

All the time, her big gray eyes were not watching Digby: they were watching Weaver Pray, and seemed pleading with him to turn his face toward her.

"Catfish, seven cents, dressed?" said Weave. "You only used to pay six."

"Paying seven cents now, son. I reckon you'll have to bait you some of your traps and get some of that seven cents a pound."

As soon as Mr. Digby spoke that sentence about baiting traps, he could have kicked himself over the sward of Galilee Landing. All day his bunglesome remark came back to haunt him, and he shook his head whenever he thought of it. That noon he would tell his wife that he was still upset.

"Imagine me saying such a thing to the son of Seminole Pray! I remember how Seminole looked, there in that trap, when they dragged him ashore. He was all doubled up; his hide was squeezed tight into the meshes. Only a damn fool would say a thing like I said."

The sole recognition which Weave gave to Blaze Digby's damn-foolery was a quick blinking of his black eyes. His voice was studiously calm. "Who all you said you had trapping for you, Mr. Blaze?"

"Oh, same fellows. I take it you know that Jick Lasher is dead of pneumonia. Ab Jones is trapping for me now. Then I got a new fellow named Ryder, moved up here from Clewiston. That's about all. Just the same fellows."

"I reckon the Booth boys are trapping for you, Mr. Blaze?"

The crowd moved. Mr. Digby saw two limpkins fly out of the grass near at hand, and seemed astonished to witness this very ordinary spectacle.

He managed to say, "I reckon the Booth boys are out there on the lake somewhere. Probably they went out early, so's to get through. I guess they went out early."

Men looked to see whether Weave's right hand had slid down to the sheathed knife which was fastened on his belt. No, he still kept his arms folded across his chest. Men thought about Weaver's gun. Of course, it had been confiscated when the officers came to pick up Weave, the night of the murder, but there were plenty of places where Weave could get another gun. Old Peebee Millis had guns around his place. It was unlikely that a Millis revolver was not resting now, oily and sweaty, under the hollow of Weave's left arm.

There was nothing more to say; everything was known. Weave was back. He had been back two weeks. He had been working like a dog. He had built a hundred and two traps, and it took an hour to build one. In addition to that, he had cut his trails and sunk his traps; and in further addition he had repaired the motorboat which now beckoned in the shallows.

Mr. Digby closed his plump hand on Weaver Pray's right shoulder. "I'll be expecting you to bring me a lot of fish." Forthwith he congratulated himself that he did not declare, "I expect you to make a big killing," which was what he usually told his trappers.

"Thank you, Mr. Blaze." Weave turned, gave a short nod to the men behind him, and walked to the lake.

He was fairly in the water, and his feet were crushing the loose warm weeds, when Gracious Shipley caught her breath and whispered something—a kind of prayer, perhaps, and to herself entirely.

She started after him. Gracious couldn't seem to make her legs go fast enough. Weave had left his skiff and was loosening his push pole from its anchorage in the mud, when Gracious came splashing up to him.

They were far enough offshore for the others to fail to hear their words, although the mutter of their voices could be heard.

Gracious said, "Weave."

His somber gaze was on her. "What?"

"You didn't even say hello."

"I was busy. I was busy talking business."

"Weave, look at me. I was always your girl, wasn't I?"

Weave said, "We were just kids."

"Weave, wait." And she climbed into the skiff and stood in the stern facing him. "It isn't fair nor right for you to come back home and stay up there two weeks at your grandma's, and not come near our place, or anything like that."

"You heard me," said Weave. "A hundred and two traps

don't just build themselves."

"You're going after the Booth boys!"

He said nothing, but the limpkins screamed in reaches beyond, as if horrified at the idea.

"You know you are," the girl repeated miserably.

"I just said I was going to look at my traps."

The girl sobbed, "Oh, I don't trust you!"

"All right," he said, "you're privileged to get out and wade ashore, same way you came."

"No, I'm going out with you in the boat. Look, Weave; I brought lunch for both of us." She exhibited a fat paper sack, neatly folded and tied.

Weaver rested his push pole in the mud and clutched it with both hands. He looked at Gracious suspiciously, and his brows were closer together every minute. "How did you know I was back? How did you know I planned to speak to Mr. Blaze, and then go out on the lake this morning?"

"It was just talked around, that's all."

"Sure. Talked around! Every soul and body in this end of creation was standing on that grass when I poled in. People had been guessing and wondering, and I suppose you had to do your wondering too!"

She tried to laugh. "No. I heard the rumors. A little bird told me."

"I'll bet that little bird was Grandma Millis."

"I won't tell you."

"I'll break her neck," he said savagely.

This time Gracious Shipley could really laugh. "Oh, no, you won't! You wouldn't harm a hair of her old head, and you know it. She's been mother to you from the time you were little. I remember well enough."

He snarled, "You remember! You can't remember anything. You're a good four years younger than me."

"Never mind; I'm going out on the lake with you. If you don't want me you can throw me overboard." Her chin quivered with the desperation of her appeal. "Weave, I know well enough what you've been thinking. You know that the Booth boys are out here looking after their traps, and you think you're going to meet them, and you think—Weave, you've got to promise me— "

He watched the painted minnows speeding back and forth among the reeds.

"You're not talking to a boy, Gracious," he said. "I may have been a boy then. But that was three and a half years ago. I've been on the road gang. I've been truck-driving with a lot of jailbirds. I've been with a mighty tough crowd. I've had time to do my thinking. Nobody on Okeechobee nor anyplace else can keep me from doing what I've set my mind to do. If I want to meet the Booth boys out here, that's my own business. Now you get out of this boat."

"I won't get out." She sat there looking at her bare feet, feeling cold perspiration in her palms. She kept wondering whether, if there hadn't been that crowd of people watching on the sod, Weaver Pray might not have thrown her overboard as she challenged him to do.

More smoothly than the ripple of silk, the skiff began to move. It glided through rushes and weed-dotted water; the surface rubbed beneath the bow like oil and silver.

For a moment everything turned dusky before the girl's eyes. Her hands slid down and gripped the thwart beneath her. This much of her battle she had won. He was taking her out on the lake. The rest of the battle would come later.

WEAVE HAD cut his trails three miles up the shore from Galilee Landing, and offshore a mile and a half, near the flat patch of lilies and lotus which for some reason was called High Grass. He had worked late, from five o'clock until dark on many days, dragging a v-shaped cutter behind his skiff and poling stubbornly through the weeds.

The young people reached the first trap twenty minutes after they passed Digby's skinning bench. A red cork, freshly painted, floated among some flowers of tiny blue; though the trap had been there only two or three days, curly tendrils of wild water celery had already closed around the marker.

"How come you painted your corks, Weave? Nobody ever painted corks before."

"So's there wouldn't be a mistake."

"I wonder folks around here never thought of that. If everybody had a different color— "

Weave said flatly, "There wouldn't be enough colors to go around. People have got to be honest, but a lot of them ain't."

He drew up the trap; a hollow barrel of chicken wire, five feet long, with concave funnels at either end. Two bluegills, two crappies, a sun perch and a fair-sized bass flopped inside.

The sun perch wasn't big enough to keep; Weave threw it overboard, and the bass after it. Together, Weave and Gracious watched the bronzed back speed to vanishment behind the grasses.

Weaver dropped the other fish into a tub, and reset his trap carefully with the outermost funnel blocking the open trail through the rushes.

"I wish we could keep bass, Weave."

"It's against the law."

"So's shooting. Shooting folks, I mean. That's against the law."

No one else on those flats would have dared to say that to him; his brows crawled together as he looked at her.

She whispered bravely, "Tell me about Seminole, Weave —about your father. I only heard what other people told."

His hands played with the lanyard on the motor's wheel, and she thought that he was going to ignore her. "Oh, daddy pulled up a trap to look at it—just when he was going past, not when he was collecting fish—and he happened to see a grass pickerel caught halfway through the mesh, with scales rubbed off the middle of its belly. When he came back next day, taking up fish, that trap and a lot of others was empty. He'd been having many empty traps."

"The fish don't always run just right," said Gracious.

"That night when the boats came in to Galilee, on top of the Booth tub there was that same grass pickerel. Daddy, he accused Charley Booth about it. Of course Big Charley wouldn't go admitting anything. He was an awful liar anyway."

"Grass pickerel's a mighty slim fish," said Gracious. "There might also have been one of them belly-strangled in a

Booth trap."

"Never you mind!" cried Weaver. "It was the same fish! They had words about it, and Charley Booth threatened to carve daddy with his skinning knife, and daddy he said that if any of the Booths pulled knife on him, he'd make catfish bait out of them. It was next night that he was found."

The girl cried, "That part you don't need to tell!"

"I thought you asked me to tell you," said Weave brutally. "Reckon he met all the Booths at once, and they were more than a match for him. Even Big Charley Booth alone would have been, for daddy was ailing. Well, men found him stabbed to death, right in his own trap. Charley had taken out the funnel and put daddy inside. I reckon they met in their skiffs, and they had their fight, and it was Booth hands that sunk him there."

Gracious sat chewing her little lip.

"I was working ashore," Weave told her. "It was Saturday, and folks had been paid, and I figured the Booths would hit for the store at Pretty Point that night. But only Charley came in. He had an arm cut, where daddy had raked him. I shot him then. I started hunting for the boys then, but the law officers they got me first."

The girl watched a ponderous flight of white pelicans overhead, and Weaver turned up his face to see them too.

"Weave, what will you do to the Booth boys?"

"I aim to try to keep from killing them. I reckon it depends on how I'm feeling when we meet."

He started the motor. The girl wanted to shriek that it was all a mistake; wanted to insist that, after all, there might have been two grass pickerel caught and rubbed in the narrow meshes. Perhaps old Charley Booth had some right on his side—a right that grew from false accusation—though doubtless he had killed Seminole Pray in the end, just as Weaver told.

Yet she could say nothing. The ominous persistence with which Weaver clung to his feud seemed to stifle the very breath in her body.

Gracious could not have spoken to Weaver Pray then,

even if the motor had been silent.

She had loved him since she was capable of loving a boy; he had always been tall and black-browed, a forbidding figure on her horizon, and still a figure entrancing her. She remembered times when she was smaller, before she went to high school. She remembered hunting for tadpoles in the one-inch shallows; how speedily his long brown hands could scoop the tadpoles and put them in an old pop bottle for her.

Those same hands, grown wider and thicker now ... she imagined them pressing the trigger of a revolver, or clasped on the hilt of a razor-edged knife. Gracious thought of the Booth boys—round-shouldered, dull, helpless as mud hens before a hunter. She prayed at the sky; her eyes were hard with fear.

By NOON they had visited forty traps. One tub in the launch was overflowing with shiny, mottled spoils—sun perch, grass perch, bluegills and other bream, pickerel—even a few stray catfish which had swum inside to feast on the bodies of strangled victims.

Gracious eyed the catch. She smiled a little as Weaver lifted another tub out of the skiff. They had over a hundred pounds already, she was sure; if the run kept up like this, Weaver ought to have six or seven dollars for his day's work. Such days would never build a phenomenal three-thousand-pound and ninety-dollar week; but at least Weaver could begin to pay his grandfather for the wire.

Twice Weaver had fastened the motorboat in the rushes and climbed into the skiff; Gracious followed him without bidding. That was the way most of the trappers worked; that was the way they saved gas. You'd leave your power boat and pole your skiff down the weedy side alleys where you had fastened your snares, where you had dragged your weighted saw blade long before.

With the sun high and hot, they sat eating their meal. There was no ice aboard the launch; still, the slices of papaya which Gracious had wrapped in waxed paper—as she had been taught in her domestic-science course—the papaya still retained its native coolness and flavor of pepsin. Weaver ate it without a word, pausing only to sprinkle salt upon his slice.

The sandwiches were better than anything he had eaten in a long time.

"Where'd you learn to make sandwiches like this?"

"In high school. I've done graduated from high school now, Weave. I went every day on the bus. We studied domestic science, among other things."

"What kind of sandwich do you call this?"

She smiled. "I guess you'd call that Gracious's Special. I sort of mingled it together, just what we happened to have on the shelf at home."

He finished the sandwich; it was the last one left in the sack. Weave took an empty pop bottle and held it overboard, submerging the neck until the bottle was filled with lake water. They both drank, and Weaver flung out the drops that remained.

"Now I got to get on with my work," he said.

Gracious stood up and stretched herself luxuriously. A bird whistled past, laboring in mighty flight above the feathery bull grass. She thought the bird was a curlew. . . . No. . . . Now it was gone far beyond those brooding pelicans that clustered like sheep on the pale and lonely water.

The girl mounted to a thwart, that she might follow the bird's flight with her eyes.

She stepped down abruptly—too abruptly. The boat rocked crazily. Weave glowered.

"I'm sorry." Gracious' voice was suddenly stiff and squeaky. "Don't know what makes me so blame unhandy in a boat." She pointed to a fresh-cut sluice that twisted east through the rushes. "Is that one of your trails?"

"Yes. See my red corks down that way? This other path off to the left, inshore—that's mine too."

Gracious took a deep breath. "Weave, I tell you what let's do. You take this motorboat; I'll take the skiff. I can pole as good as you can. Let me travel this road due ahead and I'll empty all the traps along there, same time you're emptying the others. We can save a lot of time that way."

He muttered, "I didn't figure on your doing heavy work for me."

She cried, "My family have been putting out traps since the first white folks came to Okeechobee. I got traps in my blood, I guess. You want to bet I bring back fifty pounds?"

Before he could accept her challenge, she had gone shoving away. Weaver sat watching her thin brown body as it leaned and bent and straightened against the push pole, with birds and snakes speeding from her path. Gracious halted at the first red cork; Weave saw the wire come up when she pulled—fresh wire gleaming, unfouled as yet by mossy accumulation. He saw her hold some fish triumphantly aloft; the eagerness and excitement of her manner seemed to tighten a coil within him. When Weaver looked again, Gracious was out of sight around a curve in the brush-lined corridor.

After he had visited the sixteen traps which rested in the left-hand channel, he came pressing back through the reeds. Gracious was nowhere in sight. He was minded to go in search of her, but presently she came, squeezing out of grass that grew as high as her head and sometimes taller.

"Why didn't you hold to the trail?"

"There was a steelhead ibis," Gracious told him. Her face was pale, her eyes were exceedingly large and black and bright; it was odd that gray eyes could turn so dark, almost as dark as his. "I thought the steelhead had a busted wing and I tried to get her, but she disappeared. Where's your next trail, Weave?"

He pointed due east. "Over yonder. There's another up against it; I don't know whose. We'll have to go around this patch and on the outside, to get there."

He tied the hawser of the skiff, and Gracious crawled up to join him. Before they had rounded the next clump of bulrushes and had driven into the wide, unruffled space beyond, the hum of an outboard motor came to their ears.

Weave bent his head toward the sound. He had heard from his grandparents of several outboard motors that were now kicking their boats around that end of the lake; he had heard of one outboard motor in particular; he didn't like the name attached to it.

The outboard hum rose high and bold within their hearing; its note changed quickly to a scream. The sound was shorn off. There was no further disturbance in the region, except for the brisk winging of a dozen ducks that came flapping overhead. Weaver guided along the boundaries of grass and entered a cover that arched toward the shallows.

He stiffened suddenly. He felt the girl's glance upon him, but he couldn't turn to face her. The boat plowed ahead; Weaver had eyes only for that other boat which huddled like a fugitive in grass across the bay.

Gracious was speaking to him above the song of his own motor, but Weaver Pray would not turn. "Red-handed," he said coldly to himself. "I see them plain." His hand bent the throttle across its arc; the prow of his launch stood higher above the torn surface of the bay. Over against the mat of grass, that other boat and the three figures in it were painted clearly.

Gracious Shipley came piling forward over the thwarts. Her trouser leg touched the whirling flywheel, and Weaver lifted his left arm to hold her back. Over and over, she was calling his name, she was saying things to him; he swore that he would not care what she said; he would not listen.

His motorboat trailed close, and now he could see the Booths staring in their terror. The Booth boys were thin and small and Chinesey-looking, like their mother. None of them boasted the physical might or the swagger with which their father had been endowed.

Weave silenced his motor and coasted forward. Harrison Booth was at the stern of the other boat; Cracklin' Booth crouched beside him. That was Billy, up toward the bow. Billy was just a kid—too small to have been of much account at trapping in the days before Weaver went away.

Gracious whispered steadily, "You won't do anything, Weave. I won't let you."

He thought of crying "The hell you won't!" but he only flashed his hot eyes at her. His shirt was open—unbuttoned halfway down the middle. The fingers of his right hand began to bend.

He had known what he would see, all along—one of his own traps, the wire fresh and silvery in the sun, the telltale red cork bobbing as the Booth boys struggled with it. There were fish within the mesh; he could see them dancing. The Booth boys fumbled; their hands were agonized; constantly they turned their sad faces toward him.

The green prow kissed the rail of the Booth boat amidships. Now they were all together; the Booth boys were dreading him; they had Weaver's trap; they were robbing it, just as he had hoped and feared that they might.

His trap. He had set it among the weeds. His red cork—

Gracious said sharply, "You got yourselves some trouble, boys?"

Cracklin' Booth's thin jaw twisted, but it would not move enough to let him open his mouth.

Weaver's fingers were far inside his own shirt.

"That's a shame," said Gracious, far away and up in the air, as if a curlew had spoken from the blueness above. "It's wrapped clean around your propeller, isn't it?"

Harrison Booth made a sound. He nodded quickly.

"For goodness' sake," said Gracious, her voice still birdlike behind Weaver Pray. "Looky, Weave, your red cork was all twisted up in the wire and fastened deep in that trap. Those boys couldn't see it any way they looked."

Cracklin' Booth's face was like white-flag flowers under his tan. "That's just how it happened, Miss Gracious. We were driving along here, and all of a sudden we were purely twisted up. We didn't know what we'd hit, at first. Our own trap line runs mighty close; comes in just the other side of those weeds."

The next older brother, Harrison, said, "Mighty sorry your trap is spoilt, Weave! We couldn't help it. Accidental."

"Did you do yourselves any damage?" asked the girl mildly.

The Booth boys nodded, bobbing their heads as if they were downright happy to have damaged their motor. "Sheared off a pin," explained Cracklin'. "We can fix that all right. I guess it was our fault one way or another. We'll be glad to pay you for the trap, Weave."

Weaver swallowed. He had his hand outside his shirt now. He was plucking at the lanyard, unraveling it; which was silly of him, because he'd need that lanyard to start his motor again.

"Not necessary," he said sharply.

"We couldn't see a thing," said the Booth boys.

Weave began to coil the little rope around his flywheel. The three boys in the other boat had all bunched together. Finally Cracklin' could say what was on his mind, "We want you to know one thing, Weave. We had no hand in—in that other business. We were away off in the launch that day, and our pappy had the skiff. We didn't know that he—that your own father—"

"Pappy was mean to us, Weave," said Harrison Booth. "He was purely mean to ma too."

Gracious told them briskly, with all the air of an owner, "Weave's trap isn't good for anything now, with the wire torn. When you get it off your propeller just sink it out in deep water somewhere."

"Yes, ma'am," the Booth boys said.

Weaver started his motor. Gracious lay back and closed her eyes.

THAT NIGHT they went frogging, far down the black road past the Brighton turn-off. They walked slowly, skulking amid fireflies at the ditch side; and Weaver had a gunny sack and club in his hands, and Gracious wore the frogging light on her head.

Somewhere near the Parker Etheridge place, Gracious began to laugh.

Weaver shifted his club to the gunny-sack hand. "What's ailing you, Gracious? You turned foolish?"

"No! But you have. Oh, Weave, you were mighty foolish."

"Don't see what about."

"The Booth boys, I mean."

He gazed at her through the singing darkness.

Gracious said, "I knew for a certain that everything would be all right if you'd only give those Booths a chance to talk, and say what they wanted to say. Otherwise, Weave, I was afraid—"

He croaked in chorus with the frogs behind him, "Gracious, you mean you—"

"Sure, I did it! When I stood up in our boat, I saw the Booth boys working along their own trail, and it was right next to yours. I poled up that way, and I twisted the cork wires on four of your traps and sank the corks down under. I concluded that if the Booth boys came close they'd surely hit a trap with their outboard. You could talk to them. You could see how innocent—how almighty harmless—"

Weaver stood, silent, wondering at what she had told him. Then Gracious began to love him, to smother his lips with her own.

Ring Lardner

(1885–1933) spent only a little time in Florida but nevertheless used his knowledge of one part of the state to write a memorable short story. Born in Michigan, Lardner spent most of

of newspaper columns.

While staying at Belleair in 1922, he visited St. Petersburg to gather material for a short story and wrote "The Golden Honeymoon" on the train back to New

his adult life in New York as a sports writer for newspapers and as a short story writer. By the time he died in 1933 at the age of forty-eight, he had written over one hundred short stories, nine plays, and hundreds

York. The *Saturday Evening Post* turned it down because it was too unlike Lardner's previous stories, but *Cosmopolitan* saw its merits and published it. The story's many reprintings and its television dramatization testify to its universal appeal to readers of several generations.

"The Golden Honeymoon" is a monologue by a man who has brought his wife to St. Petersburg to celebrate their fiftieth wedding anniversary. There they meet his wife's former suitor and the woman he married. The two couples spend some time together, find themselves squabbling over cards and horseshoes, and finally break off the strained friendship. In the end the jealousy and nitpicking of the protagonists threaten to disrupt the golden honeymoon and perhaps their long marriage.

The train plays an important role in the story, as indeed it did in the history of Florida's development and tourism industry. In the story the beginning and the end of the trip deal with the train timetable, the details of which may seem strange or irrelevant in today's world, but which reassure the protagonist of a sense of the predictable progression of time. The train was the most common means of travel in the early part of this century, when the story takes place, and as workers laid tracks farther and farther south in Florida the entrepreneurs and tourists soon followed. What Henry Plant on the west coast and Henry Flagler on the east coast did was to open up Florida to such people as the golden honeymooners. St. Petersburg, in fact, was named after the native city of the Russian-born president of the Orange Belt Railway as the line was being extended down the west coast. The newspaper that the protagonist refers to in the story, the *St. Petersburg Times*, was given away free on any day that the sun did not shine by press time. St. Petersburg, nicknamed "The Sunshine City," prided itself on its weather and on its facilities for elderly travelers, as it still does.

Ring Lardner

The Golden Honeymoon

OTHER SAYS that when I start talking I never know when to stop. But I tell her the only time I get a chance is when she ain't around, so I have to make the most of it. I guess the fact is neither one of us would be welcome in a Quaker meeting, but as I tell Mother, what did God give us tongues for if He didn't want we should use them? Only she says He didn't give them to us to say the same thing over and over again, like I do, and repeat myself. But I say:

"Well, Mother," I say, "when people is like you and I and been married fifty years, do you expect everything I say will be something you ain't heard me say before? But it may be new to others, as they ain't nobody else lived with me as long as you have."

So she says:

"You can bet they ain't, as they couldn't nobody else stand you that long."

"Well," I tell her, "you look pretty healthy."

"Maybe I do," she will say, "but I looked even healthier before I married you."

You can't get ahead of Mother.

Yes, sir, we was married just fifty years ago the seventeenth day of last December and my daughter and son-in-law was over from Trenton to help us celebrate the Golden Wedding. My son-in-law is John H. Kramer, the real estate

man. He made $12,000 one year and is pretty well thought of
around Trenton; a good, steady, hard worker. The Rotarians
was after him a long time to join, but he kept telling them his
home was his club. But Edie finally made him join. That's my
daughter.

Well, anyway, they come over to help us celebrate the
Golden Wedding and it was pretty crimpy weather and the
furnace don't seem to heat up no more like it used to and
Mother made the remark that she hoped this winter wouldn't
be as cold as the last, referring to the winter previous. So Edie
said if she was us, and nothing to keep us home, she certainly
wouldn't spend no more winters up here and why didn't we
just shut off the water and close up the house and go down to
Tampa, Florida? You know we was there four winters ago
and staid five weeks, but it cost us over three hundred and
fifty dollars for hotel bill alone. So Mother said we wasn't
going no place to be robbed. So my son-in-law spoke up and
said that Tampa wasn't the only place in the South, and besides we didn't have to stop at no high price hotel but could
rent us a couple of rooms and board out somewheres, and he
had heard that St. Petersburg, Florida, was *the* spot and if we
said the word he would write down there and make inquiries.

Well, to make a long story short, we decided to do it and
Edie said it would be our Golden Honeymoon and for a present my son-in-law paid the difference between a section and a
compartment so as we could have a compartment and have
more privatecy. In a compartment you have an upper and
lower berth just like the regular sleeper, but it is a shut in
room by itself and got a wash bowl. The car we went in was
all compartments and no regular berths at all. It was all compartments.

We went to Trenton the night before and staid at my
daughter and son-in-law and we left Trenton the next
afternoon at 3.23 P.M.

This was the twelfth day of January. Mother set facing the
front of the train, as it makes her giddy to ride backwards. I
set facing her, which does not affect me. We reached North
Philadelphia at 4.03 P.M. and we reached West Philadelphia at

4.14, but did not go into Broad Street. We reached Baltimore at 6.30 and Washington, D.C., at 7.25. Our train laid over in Washington two hours till another train come along to pick us up and I got out and strolled up the platform and into the Union Station. When I come back, our car had been switched on to another track, but I remembered the name of it, the La Belle, as I had once visited my aunt out in Oconomowoc, Wisconsin, where there was a lake of that name, so I had no difficulty in getting located. But Mother had nearly fretted herself sick for fear I would be left.

"Well," I said, "I would of followed you on the next train."

"You could of," said Mother, and she pointed out that she had the money.

"Well," I said, "we are in Washington and I could of borrowed from the United States Treasury. I would of pretended I was an Englishman."

Mother caught the point and laughed heartily.

Our train pulled out of Washington at 9.40 P.M. and Mother and I turned in early, I taking the upper. During the night we passed through the green fields of old Virginia, though it was too dark to tell if they was green or what color. When we got up in the morning, we was at Fayetteville, North Carolina. We had breakfast in the dining car and after breakfast I got in conversation with the man in the next compartment to ours. He was from Lebanon, New Hampshire, and a man about eighty years of age. His wife was with him, and two unmarried daughters and I made the remark that I should think the four of them would be crowded in one compartment, but he said they had made the trip every winter for fifteen years and knowed how to keep out of each other's way. He said they was bound for Tarpon Springs.

We reached Charleston, South Carolina, at 12.50 P.M. and arrived at Savannah, Georgia, at 4.20. We reached Jacksonville, Florida, at 8.45 P.M. and had an hour and a quarter to lay over there, but Mother made a fuss about me getting off the train, so we had the darky make up our berths and retired before we left Jacksonville. I didn't sleep good as the train done a lot of hemming and hawing, and Mother never sleeps good on a train as she says she is always worrying that I will fall out. She says she would rather have the upper herself, as then she would not have to worry about me, but I tell her I can't take the risk of having it get out that I allowed my wife to sleep in an upper berth. It would make talk.

We was up in the morning in time to see our friends from New Hampshire get off at Tarpon Springs, which we reached at 6.53 A.M.

Several of our fellow passengers got off at Clearwater and some at Belleair, where the train backs right up to the door of the mammoth hotel. Belleair is the winter headquarters for the golf dudes and everybody that got off there had their bag of sticks, as many as ten and twelve in a bag. Women and all. When I was a young man we called it shinny and only needed one club to play with and about one game of it would of been a-plenty for some of these dudes, the way we played it.

The train pulled into St. Petersburg at 8.20 and when we got off the train you would think they was a riot, what with all the darkies barking for the different hotels.

I said to Mother, I said:

"It is a good thing we have got a place picked out to go to and don't have to choose a hotel, as it would be hard to choose amongst them if every one of them is the best."

She laughed.

We found a jitney and I give him the address of the room my son-in-law had got for us and soon we was there and introduced ourselves to the lady that owns the house, a young widow about forty-eight years of age. She showed us our room, which was light and airy with a comfortable bed and bureau and washstand. It was twelve dollars a week, but the location was good, only three blocks from Williams Park.

St. Pete is what folks call the town, though they also call it the Sunshine City, as they claim they's no other place in the country where they's fewer days when Old Sol don't smile down on Mother Earth, and one of the newspapers gives away all their copies free every day when the sun don't shine. They claim to of only give them away some sixty-odd times in the last eleven years. Another nickname they have got for the town is "the Poor Man's Palm Beach," but I guess they's men that comes there that could borrow as much from the bank as some of the Willie boys over to the other Palm Beach.

During our stay we paid a visit to the Lewis Tent City, which is the headquarters for the Tin Can Tourists. But maybe you ain't heard about them. Well, they are an organization that takes their vacation trips by auto and carries everything with them. That is, they bring along their tents to sleep in and cook in and they don't patronize no hotels or cafeterias, but they have got to be bona fide auto campers or they can't belong to the organization.

They tell me they's over 200,000 members to it and they call themselves the Tin Canners on account of most of their food being put up in tin cans. One couple we seen in the Tent City was a couple from Brady, Texas, named Mr. and Mrs. Pence, which the old man is over eighty years of age and they had come in their auto all the way from home, a distance of 1,641 miles. They took five weeks for the trip, Mr. Pence driving the entire distance.

The Tin Canners hails from every State in the Union and in the summer time they visit places like New England and the Great Lakes region, but in the winter the most of them comes to Florida and scatters all over the State. While we was down there, they was a national convention of them at Gainesville, Florida, and they elected a Fredonia, New York, man as their president. His title is Royal Tin Can Opener of the World. They have got a song wrote up which everybody has got to learn it before they are a member:

> *"The tin can forever! Hurrah, boys! Hurrah!*
> *Up with the tin can! Down with the foe!*
> *We will rally round the campfire, we'll rally once*
> *   again,*
> *Shouting, 'We auto camp forever!'"*

That is something like it. And the members has also got to have a tin can fastened on to the front of their machine.

I asked Mother how she would like to travel around that way and she said:

"Fine, but not with an old rattle brain like you driving."

"Well," I said, "I am eight years younger than this Mr. Pence who drove here from Texas."

"Yes," she said, "but he is old enough to not be skittish."

You can't get ahead of Mother.

Well, one of the first things we done in St. Petersburg was to go to the Chamber of Commerce and register our names and where we was from as they's a great rivalry amongst the different States in regards to the number of their citizens visiting in town and of course our little State don't stand much of a show, but still every little bit helps, as the fella says. All and all, the man told us, they was eleven thousand names registered, Ohio leading with some fifteen hundred-odd and New York State next with twelve hundred. Then come Michigan, Pennsylvania and so on down, with one man each from Cuba and Nevada.

The first night we was there, they was a meeting of the New York–New Jersey Society at the Congregational Church and a man from Ogdensburg, New York State, made the talk. His subject was Rainbow Chasing. He is a Rotarian and a very convicting speaker, though I forget his name.

Our first business, of course, was to find a place to eat and after trying several places we run on to a cafeteria on Central Avenue that suited us up and down. We eat pretty near all our meals there and it averaged about two dollars per day for the two of us, but the food was well cooked and everything nice and clean. A man don't mind paying the price if things is clean and well cooked.

On the third day of February, which is Mother's birthday, we spread ourselves and eat supper at the Poinsettia Hotel and they charged us seventy-five cents for a sirloin steak that wasn't hardly big enough for one.

I said to Mother: "Well," I said, "I guess it's a good thing every day ain't your birthday or we would be in the poorhouse."

"No," says Mother, "because if every day was my birthday, I would be old enough by this time to of been in my grave long ago."

You can't get ahead of Mother.

In the hotel they had a card-room where they was several men and ladies playing five hundred and this new fangled whist bridge. We also seen a place where they was dancing, so I asked Mother would she like to trip the light fantastic toe and she said no, she was too old to squirm like you have got to do now days. We watched some of the young folks at it awhile till Mother got disgusted and said we would have to see a good movie to take the taste out of our mouth. Mother is a great movie heroyne and we go twice a week here at home.

But I want to tell you about the Park. The second day we was there we visited the Park, which is a good deal like the one in Tampa, only bigger, and they's more fun goes on here every day than you could shake a stick at. In the middle they's a big bandstand and chairs for the folks to set and listen to the concerts, which they give you music for all tastes, from Dixie up to classical pieces like Hearts and Flowers.

Then all around they's places marked off for different sports and games—chess and checkers and dominoes for folks that enjoys those kind of games, and roque and horse-shoes for the nimbler ones. I used to pitch a pretty fair shoe myself, but ain't done much of it in the last twenty years.

Well, anyway, we bought a membership ticket in the club which costs one dollar for the season, and they tell me that up to a couple years ago it was fifty cents, but they had to raise it to keep out the riffraff.

Well, Mother and I put in a great day watching the pitchers and she wanted I should get in the game, but I told her I was all out of practice and would make a fool of myself, though I seen several men pitching who I guess I could take their measure without no practice. However, they was some good pitchers, too, and one boy from Akron, Ohio, who could certainly throw a pretty shoe. They told me it looked like he would win the championship of the United States in the February tournament. We come away a few days before they held that and I never did hear if he win. I forget his name, but he was a clean cut young fella and he has got a brother in Cleveland that's a Rotarian.

Well, we just stood around and watched the different games for two or three days and finally I set down in a checker game with a man named Weaver from Danville, Illinois. He was a pretty fair checker player, but he wasn't no match for me, and I hope that don't sound like bragging. But I always could hold my own on a checker-board and the folks around here will tell you the same thing. I played with this Weaver pretty near all morning for two or three mornings and he beat me one game and the only other time it looked like he had a chance, the noon whistle blowed and we had to quit and go to dinner.

While I was playing checkers, Mother would set and listen to the band, as she loves music, classical or no matter what kind, but anyway she was setting there one day and between selections the woman next to her opened up a conversation. She was a woman about Mother's own age, seventy or seventy-one, and finally she asked Mother's name and Mother told her her name and where she was from and Mother asked her the same question, and who do you think the woman was?

Well, sir, it was the wife of Frank M. Hartsell, the man who was engaged to Mother till I stepped in and cut him out, fifty-two years ago!

Yes, sir!

You can imagine Mother's surprise! And Mrs. Hartsell was surprised, too, when Mother told her she had once been friends with her husband, though Mother didn't say how close friends they had been, or that Mother and I was the cause of Hartsell going out West. But that's what we was. Hartsell left his town a month after the engagement was broke off and ain't never been back since. He had went out to Michigan and become a veterinary, and that is where he had settled down, in Hillsdale, Michigan, and finally married his wife.

Well, Mother screwed up her courage to ask if Frank was still living and Mrs. Hartsell took her over to where they was pitching horse-shoes and there was old Frank, waiting his turn. And he knowed Mother as soon as he seen her, though it was over fifty years. He said he knowed her by her eyes.

"Why, it's Lucy Frost!" he says, and he throwed down his shoes and quit the game.

Then they come over and hunted me up and I will confess I wouldn't of knowed him. Him and I is the same age to the month, but he seems to show it more, some way. He is balder for one thing. And his beard is all white, where mine has still got a streak of brown in it. The very first thing I said to him, I said:

"Well, Frank, that beard of yours makes me feel like I was back north. It looks like a regular blizzard."

"Well," he said, "I guess yourn would be just as white if you had it dry cleaned."

But Mother wouldn't stand that.

"Is that so!" she said to Frank. "Well, Charley ain't had no tobacco in his mouth for over ten years."

And I ain't!

Well, I excused myself from the checker game and it was pretty close to noon, so we decided to all have dinner together and they was nothing for it only we must try their cafeteria on Third Avenue. It was a little more expensive than ours and not near as good, I thought. I and Mother had about the same dinner we had been having every day and our bill was $1.10. Frank's check was $1.20 for he and his wife. The same meal wouldn't of cost them more than a dollar at our place.

After dinner we made them come up to our house and we all set in the parlor, which the young woman had give us the use of to entertain company. We begun talking over old times and Mother said she was a-scared Mrs. Hartsell would find it tiresome listening to we three talk over old times, but as it turned out they wasn't much chance for nobody else to talk with Mrs. Hartsell in the company. I have heard lots of women that could go it, but Hartsell's wife takes the cake of all the women I ever seen. She told us the family history of everybody in the State of Michigan and bragged for a half hour about her son, who she said is in the drug business in

Grand Rapids, and a Rotarian.

When I and Hartsell could get a word in edgeways we joked one another back and forth and I chafed him about being a horse doctor.

"Well, Frank," I said, "you look pretty prosperous, so I suppose they's been plenty of glanders around Hillsdale."

"Well," he said, "I've managed to make more than a fair living. But I've worked pretty hard."

"Yes," I said, "and I suppose you get called out all hours of the night to attend births and so on."

Mother made me shut up.

Well, I thought they wouldn't never go home and I and Mother was in misery trying to keep awake, as the both of us generally always take a nap after dinner. Finally they went, after we had made an engagement to meet them in the Park the next morning, and Mrs. Hartsell also invited us to come to their place the next night and play five hundred. But she had forgot that they was a meeting of the Michigan Society that evening, so it was not till two evenings later that we had our first card game.

Hartsell and his wife lived in a house on Third Avenue North and had a private setting room besides their bedroom. Mrs. Hartsell couldn't quit talking about their private setting room like it was something wonderful. We played cards with them, with Mother and Hartsell partners against his wife and I. Mrs. Hartsell is a miserable card player and we certainly got the worst of it.

After the game she brought out a dish of oranges and we had to pretend it was just what we wanted, though oranges down there is like a young man's whiskers; you enjoy them at first, but they get to be a pesky nuisance.

We played cards again the next night at our place with the same partners and I and Mrs. Hartsell was beat again. Mother and Hartsell was full of compliments for each other on what a good team they made, but the both of them knowed well enough where the secret of their success laid. I guess all and all we must of played ten different evenings and they was only one night when Mrs. Hartsell and I come out ahead. And that one night wasn't no fault of hern.

When we had been down there about two weeks, we spent one evening as their guest in the Congregational Church, at a social give by the Michigan Society. A talk was made by a man named Bitting of Detroit, Michigan, on How I was Cured of Story Telling. He is a big man in the Rotarians and give a witty talk.

A woman named Mrs. Oxford rendered some selections which Mrs. Hartsell said was grand opera music, but whatever they was my daughter Edie could of give her cards and spades and not made such a hullaballoo about it neither.

Then they was a ventriloquist from Grand Rapids and a young woman about forty-five years of age that mimicked different kinds of birds. I whispered to Mother that they all sounded like a chicken, but she nudged me to shut up.

After the show we stopped in a drug store and I set up the refreshments and it was pretty close to ten o'clock before we finally turned in. Mother and I would of preferred tending the movies, but Mother said we mustn't offend Mrs. Hartsell, though I asked her had we came to Florida to enjoy ourselves or to just not offend an old chatter-box from Michigan.

I felt sorry for Hartsell one morning. The women folks both had an engagement down to the chiropodist's and I run across Hartsell in the Park and he foolishly offered to play me checkers.

It was him that suggested it, not me, and I guess he repented himself before we had played one game. But he was too stubborn to give up and set there while I beat him game after game and the worst part of it was that a crowd of folks had got in the habit of watching me play and there they all was, looking on, and finally they seen what a fool Frank was making of himself, and they began to chafe him and pass remarks. Like one of them said:

"Who ever told you you was a checker player!"

And:

"You might maybe be good for tiddle-de-winks, but not checkers!"

I almost felt like letting him beat me a couple games. But

the crowd would of knowed it was a put up job.

Well, the women folks joined us in the Park and I wasn't going to mention our little game, but Hartsell told about it himself and admitted he wasn't no match for me.

"Well," said Mrs. Hartsell, "checkers ain't much of a game anyway, is it?" She said: "It's more of a children's game, ain't it? At least, I know my boy's children used to play it a good deal."

"Yes, ma'am," I said. "It's a children's game the way your husband plays it, too."

Mother wanted to smooth things over, so she said:

"Maybe they's other games where Frank can beat you."

"Yes," said Mrs. Hartsell, "and I bet he could beat you pitching horse-shoes."

"Well," I said, "I would give him a chance to try, only I ain't pitched a shoe in over sixteen years."

"Well," said Hartsell, "I ain't played checkers in twenty years."

"You ain't never played it," I said.

"Anyway," says Frank, "Lucy and I is your master at five hundred."

Well, I could of told him why that was, but had decency enough to hold my tongue.

It had got so now that he wanted to play cards every night and when I or Mother wanted to go to a movie, any one of us would have to pretend we had a headache and then trust to goodness that they wouldn't see us sneak into the theater. I don't mind playing cards when my partner keeps their mind on the game, but you take a woman like Hartsell's wife and how can they play cards when they have got to stop every couple seconds and brag about their son in Grand Rapids?

Well, the New York–New Jersey Society announced that they was goin to give a social evening too and I said to Mother, I said:

"Well, that is one evening when we will have an excuse not to play five hundred."

"Yes," she said, "but we will have to ask Frank and his wife to go to the social with us as they asked us to go to the only done it to humor Hartsell.

Before we started, Mother patted me on the back and told me to do my best, so we started in and I seen right off that I was in for it, as I hadn't pitched a shoe in sixteen years and didn't have my distance. And besides, the plating had wore off the shoes so that they was points right where they stuck into my thumb and I hadn't throwed more than two or three times when my thumb was raw and it pretty near killed me to hang on to the shoe, let alone pitch it.

Well, Hartsell throws the awkwardest shoe I ever seen pitched and to see him pitch you wouldn't think he would ever come nowheres near, but he is also the luckiest pitcher I ever seen and he made some pitches where the shoe lit five and six feet short and then schoonered up and was a ringer. They's no use trying to beat that kind of luck.

They was a pretty fair size crowd watching us and four or five other ladies besides Mother, and it seems like, when Hartsell pitches, he has got to chew and it kept the ladies on the anxious seat as he don't seem to care which way he is facing when he leaves go.

You would think a man as old as him would of learnt more manners.

Well, to make a long story short, I was just beginning to get my distance when I had to give up on account of my thumb, which I showed it to Hartsell and he seen I couldn't go on, as it was raw and bleeding. Even if I could of stood it to go on myself, Mother wouldn't of allowed it after she seen my thumb. So anyway I quit and Hartsell said the score was nineteen to six, but I don't know what it was. Or don't care, neither.

Well, Mother and I went home and I said I hoped we was through with the Hartsells and I was sick and tired of them, but it seemed like she had promised we would go over to their house that evening for another game of their everlasting cards.

Well, my thumb was giving me considerable pain and I felt kind of out of sorts and I guess maybe I forgot myself, but anyway, when we was about through playing Hartsell made

Michigan social."

"Well," I said, "I had rather stay home than drag that chatter-box everywheres we go."

So Mother said:

"You are getting too cranky. Maybe she does talk a little too much but she is good hearted. And Frank is always good company."

So I said:

"I suppose if he is such good company you wished you had of married him."

Mother laughed and said I sounded like I was jealous. Jealous of a cow doctor!

Anyway we had to drag them along to the social and I will say that we give them a much better entertainment than they had given us.

Judge Lane of Paterson made a fine talk on business conditions and a Mrs. Newell of Westfield imitated birds, only you could really tell what they was the way she done it. Two young women from Red Bank sung a choral selection and we clapped them back and they gave us Home to Our Mountains and Mother and Mrs. Hartsell both had tears in their eyes. And Hartsell, too.

Well, some way or another the chairman got wind that I was there and asked me to make a talk and I wasn't even going to get up, but Mother made me, so I got up and said:

"Ladies and gentlemen," I said. "I didn't expect to be called on for a speech on an occasion like this or no other occasion as I do not set myself up as a speech maker, so will have to do the best I can, which I often say is the best anybody can do."

Then I told them the story about Pat and the motorcycle, using the brogue, and it seemed to tickle them and I told them one or two other stories, but altogether I wasn't on my feet more than twenty or twenty-five minutes and you ought to of heard the clapping and hollering when I set down. Even Mrs. Hartsell admitted that I am quite a speechifier and said if I ever went to Grand Rapids, Michigan, her son would make me talk to the Rotarians.

When it was over, Hartsell wanted we should go to their house and play cards, but his wife reminded him that it was after 9.30 P.M., rather a late hour to start a card game, but he had went crazy on the subject of cards, probably because he didn't have to play partners with his wife. Anyway, we got rid of them and went home to bed.

It was the next morning, when we met over to the Park, that Mrs. Hartsell made the remark that she wasn't getting no exercise so I suggested that why didn't she take part in the roque game.

She said she had not played a game of roque in twenty years, but if Mother would play she would play. Well, at first Mother wouldn't hear of it, but finally consented, more to please Mrs. Hartsell than anything else.

Well, they had a game with a Mrs. Ryan from Eagle, Nebraska, and a young Mrs. Morse from Rutland, Vermont, who Mother had met down to the chiropodist's. Well, Mother couldn't hit a flea and they all laughed at her and I couldn't help from laughing at her myself and finally she quit and said her back was too lame to stoop over. So they got another lady and kept on playing and soon Mrs. Hartsell was the one everybody was laughing at, as she had a long shot to hit the black ball, and as she made the effort her teeth fell out on to the court. I never seen a woman so flustered in my life. And I never heard so much laughing, only Mrs. Hartsell didn't join in and she was madder than a hornet and wouldn't play no more, so the game broke up.

Mrs. Hartsell went home without speaking to nobody, but Hartsell stayed around and finally he said to me, he said:

"Well, I played you checkers the other day and you beat me bad and now what do you say if you and me play a game of horseshoes?"

I told him I hadn't pitched a shoe in sixteen years, but Mother said:

"Go ahead and play. You used to be good at it and maybe it will come back to you."

Well, to make a long story short, I give in. I oughtn't to of never tried it, as I hadn't pitched a shoe in sixteen years, and I

the remark that he wouldn't never lose a game of cards if he could always have Mother for a partner.

So I said:

"Well, you had a chance fifty years ago to always have her for a partner, but you wasn't man enough to keep her."

I was sorry the minute I had said it and Hartsell didn't know what to say and for once his wife couldn't say nothing. Mother tried to smooth things over by making the remark that I must of had something stronger than tea or I wouldn't talk so silly. But Mrs. Hartsell had froze up like an iceberg and hardly said good night to us and I bet her and Frank put in a pleasant hour after we was gone.

As we was leaving, Mother said to him: "Never mind Charley's nonsense, Frank. He is just mad because you beat him all hollow pitching horseshoes and playing cards."

She said that to make up for my slip, but at the same time she certainly riled me. I tried to keep ahold of myself, but as soon as we was out of the house she had to open up the subject and begun to scold me for the break I had made.

Well, I wasn't in no mood to be scolded. So I said:

"I guess he is such a wonderful pitcher and card player that you wished you had married him."

"Well," she said, "at least he ain't a baby to give up pitching because his thumb has got a few scratches."

"And how about you," I said, "making a fool of yourself on the roque court and then pretending your back is lame and you can't play no more!"

"Yes," she said, "but when you hurt your thumb I didn't laugh at you, and why did you laugh at me when I sprained my back?"

"Who could help from laughing!" I said.

"Well," she said, "Frank Hartsell didn't laugh."

"Well," I said, "why didn't you marry him?"

"Well," said Mother, "I almost wished I had!"

"And I wished so, too!" I said.

"I'll remember that!" said Mother, and that's the last word she said to me for two days.

We seen the Hartsells the next day in the Park and I was

willing to apologize, but they just nodded to us. And a couple days later we heard they had left for Orlando, where they have got relatives.

I wished they had went there in the first place.

Mother and I made it up setting on a bench.

"Listen, Charley," she said. "This is our Golden Honeymoon and we don't want the whole thing spoilt with a silly old quarrel."

"Well," I said, "did you mean that about wishing you had married Hartsell?"

"Of course not," she said, "that is, if you didn't mean that you wished I had, too."

So I said:

"I was just tired and all wrought up. I thank God you chose me instead of him as they's no other woman in the world who I could of lived with all these years."

"How about Mrs. Hartsell?" says Mother.

"Good gracious!" I said. "Imagine being married to a woman that plays five hundred like she does and drops her teeth on the roque court!"

"Well," said Mother, "it wouldn't be no worse than being married to a man that expectorates towards ladies and is such a fool in a checker game."

So I put my arm around her shoulder and she stroked my hand and I guess we got kind of spoony.

They was two days left of our stay in St. Petersburg and the next to the last day Mother introduced me to a Mrs. Kendall from Kingston, Rhode Island, who she had met at the chiropodist's.

Mrs. Kendall made us acquainted with her husband, who is in the grocery business. They have got two sons and five grandchildren and one great-grandchild. One of their sons lives in Providence and is way up in the Elks as well as a Rotarian.

We found them very congenial people and we played cards with them the last two nights we was there. They was both experts and I only wished we had met them sooner instead of running into the Hartsells. But the Kendalls will be there again next winter and we will see more of them, that is, if we decide to make the trip again.

We left the Sunshine City on the eleventh of February, at 11 A.M. This give us a day trip through Florida and we seen all the country we had passed through at night on the way down.

We reached Jacksonville at 7 P.M. and pulled out of there at 8.10 P.M. We reached Fayetteville, North Carolina, at nine o'clock the following morning, and reached Washington, D.C., at 6:30 P.M., laying over there half an hour.

We reached Trenton at 11.01 P.M. and had wired ahead to my daughter and son-in-law and they met us at the train and we went to their house and they put us up for the night. John would of made us stay up all night, telling about our trip, but Edie said we must be tired and made us go to bed. That's my daughter.

The next day we took our train for home and arrived safe and sound, having been gone just one month and a day.

Here comes Mother, so I guess I better shut up.

Andrew Lytle

(1902–) was born in Murfreesboro, Tennessee, and educated at Sewanee Military Academy, Exeter College in England, and Vanderbilt University. He became editor of Vanderbilt University. He has published four novels, a Civil War biography, and a collection of essays.

"Ortiz's Mass" (1935) recreates a historical incident

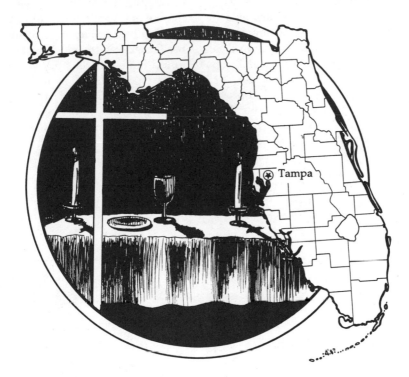

the *The Sewanee Review*, professor in the creative writing program at the University of Florida (1948–61), and professor at Southwestern College, the University of the South, the University of Iowa, and that happened when the Spanish were exploring the area around Tampa in the sixteenth century. In 1528, Spanish explorer Panfilo de Narváez and his soldiers landed near Tampa, marched north, and seemingly disappeared. Another group of Spanish explorers later set out from Cuba to look for them. When one of them, Juan Ortiz of Seville, went ashore near Tampa to seek news of Narváez, he was captured by hostile Indians but was saved from death by the chief's daughter.

For eleven years, Ortiz worked for the Indians as a menial laborer, learning their language and customs and learning the area around Tampa Bay. In 1539 the Spanish explorer Hernando de Soto landed there and eventually rescued him. Ortiz accompanied de Soto as an interpreter as de Soto explored Florida and other lands in the years from 1539 to 1542. De Soto died in the area of the Mississippi River, and Ortiz also died on the way.

Ortiz's true story is similiar to that of Pocahontas, which appeared seventy years later in Virginia. The seventeenth-century Indian princess saved the life of Captain John Smith by holding him in her arms when her father's warriors were about to kill him. Ortiz's story was probably the basis of the Pocahontas story, one that Captain John Smith liked so much that he included it in his own history of Virginia.

Andrew Lytle

Ortiz's Mass

F ATHER FRANCISCO of the Rock tied the cords
of the amice, dropped the flowing alb over
his head and quickly, with deft and accustomed fingers, fastened the girdle about his
middle. His server handed him the stole. The cords of the girdle were brought up, looped, the maniple slipped on his arm,
and then with care he put on the rich and stiffly embroidered
chasuble. Abstractedly he looked through the door of the hut.
The altar stone was in place upon the cypress log, the crucifix
stood up, slim and pure, before the great dirt wall of the
mound. Upon the corporal the Sacred Vessels waited. The
flames of the two candles, he noticed, twisted and curled before the morning breeze. He should have ordered some kind
of screen. He turned to his server to bid him find something,
changed his mind. The army had already gathered, the entire
army. They had never shown themselves so eager for worship
before. He would speak to them on the vice of curiosity. He
continued to look abstractedly at his server. That Cacho was a
worthless lad, slothful and he feared already marked with
every sin. Assisting at Mass in spurs. Perhaps, though, there
was nothing vain in this. It was only the way the boy wore
them. "Cacho, take off those spurs." The acolyte looked as if
he would disobey; then leaned over and reluctantly
unbuckled the straps. The spurs dropped to the ground with a
clink.

He must perform well this morning. The Governor had asked Mass to be said especially for this Ortiz. For twelve years the Christian had gone without hearing God's Word. Twelve years . . . the man had forgotten how long it had been. He had had to ask the time he was cast away. It was fearful to contemplate, this loss of the knowledge of time. Day following dark day, time hurrying him to death and judgment, when time would be no more, and he so deep in savage sloth as not to know or care. One had only to look to see that he had been wholly lost. There in the presidio rubbing the Governor's shoulders for greeting like any heathen until even the Governor had mistaken him for an Indian. "No, no, Ortiz, greet your lord in a civil way," the Constable had said and laughed.

It was not a thing to laugh about. There was too great levity in certain quarters of this armament. Ah, Holy Mary, ever Virgin, is it not enough that Your Son has died once so bitterly for man? Is the spirit so weak, so ready to fall into forgetfulness, that each morning He must be sacrificed afresh? Must He each day cross the brook of Kedron and climb the Mount of Olives, climb anew to his agony, to the kiss of betrayal? Must He stand by the Roman Pilate's couch as he laves his hands and hear, Crucify Him! Crucify Him! from the lips of those who when He went down into the city sang hosannas and cast palm branches at the feet of his ass? *Ah! Jerusalem! Jerusalem! Thou that stonest the prophets! How often would I have gathered ye under my wings as a hen doth her chicks, and ye would not! Ye would not!*

"Look, Father," Cacho said. "Juan Ortiz dressed in the black velvet the Governor gave him. . . .How strangely he walks."

Father Francisco raised his eyes.

Beside de Soto's brisk step Ortiz swung wide his legs and set each foot down in place after the other. He twisted his neck as though the collar choked him. He scratched himself. It was a cool morning, but sweat gathered in beads on his forehead.

"—besides he gave him his second best coat of mail, a

breastplate of silver gilt and . . . "

"Peace, boy," the priest said sharply.

Ortiz paused uncertainly. The Governor was sinking to his knees and crossing himself. For an instant Ortiz watched his superior; then quickly followed him to the ground. Father Francisco sighed. At least he has not forgotten to do reverence before the altar. . . .

"Did you speak, Father?"

Perhaps after all the Church is wise to make daily the Sacrifice of Our Lord, the Sacrifice which consecrates, the Consecration which is the Sacrifice—Christ Himself offering Himself.

"It is time, Father. The Governor looks this way."

The priest nodded his head and followed the acolyte out of the hut.

In nomine Patris, et Filii, et Spiritus Sancti.

He had come to the foot of the altar.

An object came between Ortiz and the crucifix. He ran his hand over his eyes, removed it: the priest was bowing and striking his breast—through my fault, through my fault, through my most grievous fault. Standing at a distance, contrite, the concealing heart punished, bruised, and humbled; the human race fallen and driven from Paradise: four thousand years of misery, sickness, and death, four thousand years of repentance for sin and hope in the promised Redeemer.

Again that promise was about to be fulfilled. If only he could quiet his body. Spasms had seized it the moment he sank to his knees, all trembling, before the Presence on the altar. Out of the forest at his back the light which flows before the sun fell upon the silver cross and, as he watched, it ran with blood. For him it ran. He beat his breast in a frenzy of remorse and fear and hope, and then he grew very quiet, his head thrown slightly back as though transfixed suddenly by a blinding light. In that instant he felt the darkness of his purgatory slip from his eyes . . .

He was pulling towards the shore, he and González, dipping their oars in the limpid water, pulling towards the letter held up on the stick by the Indians. Surely there was no treachery. The companions they had left on the brigantine were overcautious. Obviously it was a letter left by de Nar-váez telling where he had gone, and to find him they had been sent out from Cuba. It was their service to look into so plain a clue. And then some impulsion had made him look back. The brigantine was riding at anchor and it seemed that all on board were dead. The tiny men hung, motionless, over the gunwales; the sails drooped; at the water line the small craft leaned on the sea. In that moment he knew that he and González were lost. He turned to González to speak of his forewarning, but González was bending over the oar. And what could he say to him? The Indians ran down into the water and pulled them ashore. Others came whooping from the forest. González drew his sword. Once he heard him cry out, only once so quickly was it done . . . on the sand the flat and naked trunk quivering and spurting blood, the dark sponge of sand, an arm, a leg, the hair, the very privates of his companion swinging in the air. Cries and whoo-whoo-whoops. He shut his eyes and then he felt a stinging at his shoulders. He was being pulled along a path through the forest.

The priest ascended to the altar, bent over it.
Oramus te, Domine . . .

A short distance from the gulf, but deep in the forest, the Indians halted and built a fire. All but two scouts who went off to stand watch gathered around in silence as the war leader stretched González' scalp on a hoop, tied it with gut, and carefully, so as not to burn the hair, dried it over the coals. This done, the savage took a red paint from his pouch and painted the scalp and the hoop. His server brought a branch of the green-leaved pine, and to this the hair was tied. Then calling the scouts, the leader set out again on the path. As he, Ortiz, followed in file, his eyes would not turn away from the

arms and legs of González scattered in the hands of his
captors. "He was here. He is gone—gone." He repeated the
word as if by repetition he might surprise the meaning, but
the words were like the sounds of a foreign tongue. He began
again. "An hour ago he was alive and pulling at the oar." He
tried to see him, but just as González' form was about to appear an arm or the hoop of hair swung before his eyes. Then
the leader whooped and answering whoops came back
through the trees. He turned cold: they had reached the
Indian town.

The trees gave out at an open ground on one side of the
town. As they came in view, the Indians spread out in single
file, each a few yards behind the other, whooping and insulting the prisoner. They entered the yard singing the death
song, raising at intervals the shrill whoo-whoo-whoop.
Women and children, young warriors and old men came out
to meet them. In the center of the yard stood a pole. To this his
captors tied him and then carried the hair and González'
members into the town. His turn would come soon, he
thought, and as he began to envy the fate of his friend, the
crowd gave way. An Indian of great dignity was coming
towards him, at his side an old man with an owl-skin head-
dress and claws through his ears. Seven tattooed warriors
followed close behind. Ortiz looked narrowly at the Indian
but something made him avoid his face. He was crowned
with eagle feathers. From his shoulders fell a skin held up by
an attendant. About his ankles loops of shells tinkled as he
walked. Upon his arms he wore bracelets of shell. Upon his
breast hung a copper plate. And then, as he drew nearer, Ortiz
saw the face. Below the feathered head, below the malevolent
eyes, two holes gaped for nostrils. Through a lipless mouth
teeth parted in a perpetual snarl.

Slowly the Indian approached. Like doom he bore down
on the Christian. On he came to within a foot of the pole. Ortiz
pressed his back to the wood but the Indian had stopped. He
tried to look away but the cold red eyes sank into his and held
them fast. Strands of flesh about the death-like holes trembled
as the breath sucked in and out. A long time the two men

confronted each other; then slowly large tears gathered under the flaming lids and rolled down the tattooed face. Suddenly the cacique threw back his head and gave a wail of despair. The cries were taken up and rose through the crowded yard. At the height of the wailing the cacique fell upon Ortiz with his hands. The long nails scratched at his eyes, tore the flesh from his face. As suddenly the cacique turned and walked away.

From where he was tied, Ortiz could see the war leader's house. In front of it, on either side of the doorway, two rows of women faced each other, singing in their soft shrill voices a solemn, moving air. They would sing for a minute and then keep perfectly silent for a long interval, when they began again. And as they sang, they gave their legs a small muscular motion without lifting their feet or bending a joint. All night they kept this up. Every two or three hours the war leader came out and danced about his war pole facing the door. Three times he went around it, against the sun, whooping and singing.

Towards dawn Ortiz fell asleep. He had scarcely closed his eyes when he was aroused. His guards were stripping him of his clothes. Half-dazed, he leaped up and kicked out about him. They struck him with a club and he came to his senses. Overhead he heard a hissing and popping noise. He looked up. A burning brand had been tied to the pole. Moccasins were being put on his feet, bear skin with the black fur turned out. At one corner of the yard women were piling brush and sticks under a low scaffold. Black on his feet; fire over his head. He had received his sentence. Black is the sign for death.

Around the corner of the yard the Indians gathered. Between him and the scaffold women were forming in two lines. He saw them go to the leader of the party who had taken him and give into his hands an herb. Suddenly he saw he was naked. He began to shiver and shame overwhelmed him. The cacique passed with his family and nobles and sat himself on a bench covered by brush. At a signal from the cacique the guards unbound Ortiz' hands. The women began to jeer and shake their sticks. At the head of a line an old woman, her thin gray hair falling over her face, danced, her long, dry paps flapping at her sides. Feebly she raised a stone hoe and shook it. A girl turned about, lifted the moss over her rear and thrust it towards him. His guards pushed him forward. He held back. They jabbed him with the ends of their clubs. Not until then did he understand what they meant him to do. He took in his breath and began to run down the lane. The sticks and hoes fell upon his back and shoulders. He dodged and struck out at faces which came too close. Behind he heard the clatter of sticks beating together. Half way through he stumbled. As he was going down, a blow across the eyes blinded him and he lay for a full half minute and took his punishment. A fat leg came down by his ear. He grabbed and bit it, jumped up and butted his way clear, caught two women off balance and rammed their heads together. Gales of laughter greeted this stratagem.

When he came to, he was tied to a wooden frame. The frame was raised in the air and two old men were putting clay on his hair. He looked at his feet and his hands. They began to throb. "I am a Saint Andrew's cross," he said. And then four men lifted him and carried him across the yard to the scaffold. He began to notice the sounds, the death whoops and shaking of rattles, but most of all he noticed the high, shrill yelps of the women. He got a whiff of smoke, a crackling persistently travelling, like a lone man running through brush. So would the last man run on the day when the graves open and give up their dead. . . . A yellow flame leapt up at his side. It was thin and without heat. Under him he felt a round spot of heat. He squirmed out of its way. The cords cut into his flesh. A hot awl bored at his ribs, melting and spreading. He raised up. It still bored. Another struck his backbone. He began to scream. His screams were drowned by the laughter of the Indians. . . .

The priest returned to the center of the altar.
Kyrie, eleison.
    Lord, have mercy upon us.
Christe, eleison.

Christ, have mercy upon us.

Mercy, mercy, mercy. He was lying on the floor of a cabin, his dry lips moving in supplication. Soft hands were spreading a cool paste over his blisters. He closed his eyes not to see for fear it would cease, in fear that it was not true but an illusion of pain. The hands continued to soothe, and where they passed the sharp throbbing grew duller and he could feel the heat of the fever. He tried to remember what it was to suffer from fire but his senses were dull and blank. Pain cannot be heard or seen or touched or smelt. It lacks a taste. It has no memory. Under the cool hands his mind wandered, grew drowsy.

When he awoke splinters of light fell through the cane walls. He had slept into doom and out again or was this another station in his progress? He sat up, but the motion twisted his wounds so that, leaning on his arms, he made a low moan. It was then he saw the girl. She was standing by him and words came out of her mouth, and she pointed to the couch. The skins were damp and his own odor was mixed with the stronger smell of cat. Watching the girl, he let himself carefully down on his side. She did not come nearer or move away. Her hair hung loose over her shoulders and the moss skirt hung loose about her thighs and as they looked at each other he understood it was she who had saved him from the frame. And then an old woman passed between them and gave him a cool, slimy drink out of a conch shell.

He did not count the days, but quickly, so it seemed, quickly, his body mended, although there must have been a time when the flesh under his blisters had mortified. By bending and straining his neck he could see the track of worms. How close, he thought, the worms had come to the full measure of their feast but for his luck, the unaccountable, the against-all-odds luck. Or was it luck? What had she seen in him, scratched and bleeding beyond any comeliness? Had it been pity or had it . . . The old woman, her mother, the first wife of the lipless, earless, gaping cacique, had said, moons later—when he had come to be held in some esteem—had said that it seemed to them—to them—a pity for one so young, without war honors, a boy with smooth and unpricked skin, to be burned like a fighter who has brought in much hair. And when the girl had begged his life of her father, the cacique saw only the child he loved. He forgot the dishonor the Christians had done him, forgot his mother thrown to the dogs. Her he could forget now that the hair of González had released her spirit from haunting the eaves of the lodge. Little did he, Ortiz, think that comfort would ever come from seeing the hair of his friend waving at the end of a pole. This scalp had saved his life, for once the dead are at peace the living do not recall them to mind lest memory renew their sorrow. But Ucita, though he could forget his mother, found always fresh cause to remember his shame and his grief. Dipping a shell into the great jar of water, he would see the two holes where his nose should be, the fangy teeth, the clipped ears such as adulterers have. And he would hurl the shell into the jug, raise the whoop of grief.

Ortiz would hear and flee to the woods and there he would stay until the girl, coming upon him like silence, would tell him it had passed. He might return to the town, not to the lodge but to the hut of the wind clan whom the skunk, Ucita's clan, called nephew. Then quietly one day he would sit down with the uncles of his master, dip into the same pot with him and them, first throwing a choice piece of fat into the fire to make it merry. But as the days passed and he grew strong and well, the cacique's anger returned. The Indian would not look at him or in any way recognize his presence, but once by chance Ortiz turned and saw him watching, and he knew that some evil was preparing in the cacique's mind.

But those days he was too weary for thinking or fear. The women set him to menial tasks but mostly he brought in the wood. They gave him a stone axe and thongs to tie the sticks and all day he must pass through thick woods to be torn by thorns and brush and worn away lifting and carrying. How simple one good Biscayan axe would have made his task! The sun brought sores to his shoulders and chest; the wind parched them; the heavy loads tore them afresh, made them bleed. And then he would lie down by the wood, too weak from weariness and bleeding to drag it or lift it. In those moments his comfort was the Lord Jesus who had suffered and bled for him.

One morning a man of the potato clan ran out of his house with a lighted brand and waved it over his head, lamenting and crying out; then he dipped the brand into water and watched it sink down. The cacique's wife came out of the lodge and stood by Ortiz and all the people came out and watched the Indian. "What happens, old woman?" Ortiz asked. She replied, "The spirit of his son has left its body." When he returned that night, green boughs of mourning hung all about. For four days the child's kin, at morning and evening, whooped and cried around the house where it had dwelt so that its spirit would not linger to haunt them. The morning of the fifth day the cacique spoke to Ortiz, "You will watch the bones of the dead," he said.

Stepping in their tracks, he followed the two old beloved men. At first he had been pleased at his change of occupation but now that he was on his way to watch the dead his thoughts turned sober. Instinctively he felt that his position was more precarious than at any other time since he had been condemned to burn on the frame. He had begun to understand the beloved speech but more than that, he had learned somewhat the things the Indians held taboo, especially of the dangers to the sacred fire in polluted people. He had watched the women at their time of the moon slip into the woods to stay until their uncleanness had passed, and in that time he knew how careful they were never to let the wind blow by them to others or wash in water that would flow by the town. He had seen war parties withdraw into the lodge of their leader and fast for three days, with a Knower watching the youngest to make sure they drank the white drink and kept away from their women, so that no pollution could damage the ark of war and bring disaster upon the war party. It was indeed serious to watch the dead, or he would not be so carefully escorted. Four times they had made him wash in the stream and chew green tobacco until he had retched and

vomited. And the girl had slipped him a sabbia to keep him
from harm. It was wrapped tight in white deer skin and tied
to his flap. Very carefully she had taught him the song to sing
and what to do to make him see well at night. She had tried to
steal a true male sabbia, for that had many powers. It could
charm a deer within range of the arrow and what could charm
a deer would charm a woman. She had said this openly and
frankly, coming close so that the moss about her middle
teased his thighs and he reached out to take her but she shook
her head. They could not have love with him as he was, a boy
set down among women. So the cacique had planned, although it was known to all when she saved him from the
frame that she had seen he was good and without blemishes.
Perhaps soon now, if he guarded well the bones. But there
were many perils—the wolves that would come stealing the
breath of the bodies they loved and the ghosts of the dead
who were like wolves of the air. And then she gave him some
hilis hatki to chew. This would drive away the ghosts, but he
must watch the old beloved men as they approached and do
as they did. And then she slipped away, for he would be
called to purify himself and she must not be seen. . . .

The priest finished the Collect. He placed both hands upon
the Missal and faced the east. *O Orient, splendor of light
eternal, thou Sun of Justice, come and enlighten those who are
sitting in darkness and in the shadow of death*—Ortiz watched
his lips, moving swiftly and soundlessly, as he read the
Epistle. He could not hear but through the priest's lips passed
all the prophets, soundlessly to the ear but crying in the heart,
out of the wilderness smelling of goats, in the streets where
the stench of the market rose with the words. . . . And that one
man sent from God who is not the Light but is sent to bear
witness of the Light, the Light born not of blood, nor of the
will, nor of the will of the flesh. . . .

The old beloved men were no longer moving. He stopped
at their heels. He was not abrupt and yet his motions beside
theirs seemed violent and clumsy. Their very stillness was

motion, the motion of sap hidden under the bark, their walking a kind of flowing, an unobtrusive extension, an integral
part, of the wilderness which enclosed them and him. Not a
leaf shook as they passed, but where he went vines and thorns
leaped to bind him. An overwhelming feeling of strangeness
oppressed him. He would never discover the mystery of this
absolute oneness between the Indians and their world. And
yet to live he must do more than understand it.

They were taking hilis hatki out of their pouches. Quickly
he put some into his mouth and began to chew it. He tasted
the earth which still clung to the herb and his spit ran bitter,
and into his nose crept an odor, sweet and faintly nauseous, a
thin cool odor which stuck like glue. He chewed and watched.
The old men spat out of one corner of the mouth, then out of
the other. Turning slowly and with slow dignity they spat
four times each way; and as they moved, the stuffed horned
owls on their heads turned and bowed, turned and bowed,
and their red eyes watched him as he followed the ritual, step
by step. Then his mouth grew dry and silently he dropped the
root at his feet. The old men had faced about and were
viewing him gravely.

The oldest put two darts into his hand and pointed to the
green thickets to the right; then, stepping around him, the
Indians departed. Not more than a hundred paces away he
saw through the trees what looked like great eagle nests, but
eagles do not build in the low forked limbs. "They build in the
tops of the highest and the deadest trees," he said aloud. All at
once he felt an acute nostalgia for his wood-gathering, the
buffets of the old women and all the contempt which had
been heaped upon him since he had cried out at the frame. He
looked at the darts. They were good ones, flint-pointed and
balanced well. He gripped them tight and began walking
towards the burial ground, and then drifting through the air
he smelled the same cool sweet odor, invisible, resistant,
clinging yet penetrating, surrounding him yet passing, and
suddenly thick with nausea. He reached up to brush it from
his face. It had saturated his hands. He leaned over and wiped
them on the ground. It rose in waves from the ground.

Holding his breath, he pulled moss out of the trees and stuffed it in his nose. The moss was corrupt. He tore it out, drew in his breath. His stomach heaved but he held it down and ran into the center of the burial ground. There surrounded by the rough log coffins caught haphazardly in trees or resting on frames, he slowly freed his lungs, tried the air. One short gasp and the full force of afterdeath, streaming in viscid flow from the adipose substance of the dead, tightened like a vise about his middle and threw him to the ground.

With lips clenched he thought the borders of purgatory must be like this, and hunted for those bones which were driest, for he knew that when the bones were utterly clean Ucita's people gathered them into the house with the owl on its roof, the owl with the red bead eyes. He found a tree and sat down by it, burying his face in his arms, and waited for the retching to cease. He must have dozed, for when he looked up it was dark. A slight wind was at his back and the air had blown almost clean. Across the yard he could see the glow of the expiring fire which had burned at the foot of the child's coffin. Not trusting the wind, he held his breath and brought away on a piece of bark enough live coals to make a fire of his own. This was a serious business, his fire, for in this coastal country when the sun went under, the air grew chill and damp. He had awakened shivering. He fed the coals with moss and twigs and blew them into a blaze. He broke off dead limbs, picked up what down wood he could find and soon had the flames leaping. He warmed himself on all sides. Once through the yellow swerving light he thought he saw the coffins shift and swell. He smiled at this, so much better did he feel now that he was warmed and cheered. He was even beginning to have some liking for what he had to do. He was alone, in a disagreeable place, but he was alone and that was something he had not known for months. Sleeping in the round lodge with Indians of all ages and sexes where the air was never free of smoke nor the room of smells, he had not realized how much he had missed the privacy of Christendom. Even in the woods gathering sticks he had felt eyes spying from behind every bush, and in the town the Indians went freely about and strangers would walk into a dwelling as if they were come to their own house with an "I am come." And the only reply, "Good, you are come." They would leave as suddenly. "I go now." "What, you go?"

But when the fire fell into its coals and the night settled thick and close about, to guard the dead did not seem so good a thing. He reached into his pouch and took out the sabbia and rubbed it vertically over his eyes; then horizontally. This would help him, she had said, to see the wolves and other scavengers who were now his enemies. Yet it was not the wolves but the lids of his eyes which troubled him. They grew rough and dry and his head rolled heavy as a stone. It was a long straining to keep awake. At first he had been able to follow the sharp soft snap of a twig, hear the soft pads, he thought he could hear them, as the animal trotted away. Perhaps it was a fox or a mink, or even a rat. And once he had seen shining the still eyes of a cat. Many of the grandfathers of Ucita's people are out tonight, he said softly to himself, but I shall waste no darts on them or else I shall have to pay forfeit to their kin. But the time came when he no longer heard. The time came when there was no time, only the heavy slow effort of the will to stiffen his neck and shake out the heavy fog which settled over his eyes, which blew thick and slow through his eyes, into his head, weighting it, pulling it down, down, and a down . . . down . . .

Dominus vobiscum
Et cum spiritu tuo
Oremus . . .

He sat up, his eyes all awake and his heart beating: it was broad light. Voices wailed, low and then high. He leapt to his feet and in a glance took in the coffins. They were all intact. Where the child lay, two women sat before it wailing. Their white mulberry bark mantles they had drawn over their heads. He could not see who they were. Obviously the child's mother and grandmother or two old aunts. He wondered if they had seen him lying asleep by the dead fire. If they had, they would surely report it. Perhaps their grief had saved him. His luck rather. Suddenly he remembered that malevolent look on Ucita's face and knew why he had set him to watching the dead. The cacique had foreseen the trap of the long vigil, that almost irresistible drowsiness that comes to all who watch without relief, that comes just before dawn.

Carefully he walked towards the women. They did not hear him approach. Overnight, he repeated it, overnight he had come to walk like an Indian. He moved into the sound of their voices. "Why did you leave us, Little One? Did your bow not please you, the one your uncle gave you to make war on the rats and flies?" The woman paused as though listening for an answer and the older one's wails fell into a low, an almost voiceless moan. The woman continued, "Did your playboys displease you? Perhaps you feared the gartooth's scratch? It was but to make you manly. The Dog-cacique told you he would not kill you. Had you not enough to eat? Long did I let you suck—Why did you leave us?"

Very quietly he slipped away and when he came near the town, he washed in the stream four times and then went to the sofki pot to eat, without fear of polluting the holy fire. Afterwards he lay down on a skin. He lay under a great water oak, and the hanging moss stirred the gray air over his face. He had thought to sleep all day and prepare himself for the night's vigil, but sleep he could not. To stretch at his ease without any to bother him was so great a freedom that he lay in a kind of stimulated doze, awake and yet with all the ease of sleep. The old women no longer abused him and the old men, the young warriors, saluted him respectfully and called him Ispani. He knew he was still a slave but at last he had a name. Idly he thought that to be free among Christians is to have a place, but to be free among Indians you must have a name and a name must be won. You must bring in hair or do some great feat on the hunt or pass the examinations set by the Knowers and learn to read the secrets of nature. None of these proofs did he have to his credit and yet they had given him a name. The fighter receives his after he shows the scalp. What had he, Ortiz, shown? Nothing, for to move among dangers is not enough with Indians. And then it came to him: they had given him a name because they considered him as one lost, and bravely lost.

Accept, O Holy Father, Almighty and Eternal God, this unspotted Host which I, Thine unworthy servant, offer unto Thee.

Back in the burial ground towards the close of day, his hours of rest, unrest, gone, for who is cunning enough to forfend the many ghosts that wander the caverns of the wilderness or upside down walk the roads most used by men, wandering in search of their substantial kin, crying blood for blood that they may travel west; or when their own kin fail them, take blood, any blood, to speed them on their way to the land of the Breath-Holder. This was what the Indians were thinking when they called him Ispani. Nor did they forget that he must watch in darkness when wolves see and man is blind.

—grant that by the Mystery of this water and wine . . .

He heaped wood onto his fire. This night he would not fall asleep, nor any other night. Ucita should not pay off his score with him. It would be hard at first but in time he would learn to turn night into day. He would escape. The chance would come. There was the cacique of the Mocoços. He had asked for him. The two tribes were at peace but they would not always be at peace. Some fine day a boy would covet to sit with the men or he would ask a girl to lie with him and she would jeer and say she was unworthy to lie with one who has brought in so much hair. And the boy would hide where the Mocoço people went to fish and get his hair. And the path would run red. Then he would get his chance. Until then he must wait and keep his watch.

We offer unto Thee, O Lord, the chalice of salvation . . .

Waiting would not be too bad. A man could be put to hard

measures and still find life bearable. It would be more than bearable if he could persuade the girl to lie with him. She had made it plain that she had saved him for this very purpose. The cacique had thwarted them by setting him down among the women, but that was over. Nothing now stood in the way but his occupation. Just how that interfered he was uncertain. She probably feared to follow him into so many known and unknown dangers. Perhaps it was taboo in a burial place. He must find out. Certainly the odor of corruption did not make for love. But there were other ways, there must be other ways. The days were long and the woods deep, but how the nights would pass if she would spend them with him, if not actually here, then close by, near enough for him to be at hand if anything should go amiss. There was a fine retreat near the spring, where the moss made of the ground a bed, deep and soft and cool . . .

He rose from before the fire lighter than a deer. Out of the darkness she came walking towards him. Everywhere it was dark but she walked in an even light. And then he was beside her, close enough to touch but he did not touch her. He called her name yet no sound came from his lips. He reached to draw her to him but without moving she evaded him, smiling and shaking her head. Not now, she seemed to say. When we have passed the dangers on our way, but not now. She took his hand and they began to walk up the air. Strange, he thought, that one can walk the air, and yet it is no different from a path. He could have fled had he known. She was smiling and holding his hand. She was smiling when they reached a broad way strewn with stones shining of milky light. Why, this is the spirits' road, he said and she replied, Yes, of course. Then I must be . . . You are, she replied.

How easy it is to die in Heathendom, he thought. No purgatory, no hell, no sins to account for. Only to travel without tiring, without hunger or thirst, across the sky to the land of the Breath-Holder. What is it like in that land, he thought. Lacking breath, he had only to think to speak and she, thinking, replied, It is a warm pleasant country where maize grows all the year and springs never dry up. In that land the nuts drop of their own accord near the cracking stone, the bear jars overflow with grease, and on the fire pots of sofki and venison forever simmer, for in any moon the hunter may hunt knowing he shall never lack for game.

It's a good land, he said. Let us make haste.

—There are no red towns but all are white and the people dance and play ball and feast without interruption, and that place which the fighter has loved most on earth he shall find again and raise his lodge.

—Let us be off.

I have loved, O Lord, the beauty of Thy house and the place where Thy glory dwelleth.

She had scarcely ceased to speak when the broad way they were travelling ran into a body of water. As far as he could see there was nothing but water, and his heart fell within him. Not one piragua lay on its bank.

This is the first danger, she said. If a woman has sold herself to a man and then sleeps with another, even though her ears are not cropped or her nose cut off, the water will not part for her. And if a man has spilled his own blood, he must swim, if he can swim it.

I have killed no man, he replied, and looked hard at the girl. She returned his look.

Like others, she said, I have had my pleasure at the time of the busk dances, but to no man have I sold my freedom, to no man until now.

Without pausing she walked down upon the water and he followed her. Before his eyes the water parted to right and left and the path of milky stones rolled through it. The winds blew down and stood up like mounds of dirt, and they passed through without hurt.

But I have walked in my innocence; redeem me and have mercy.

The path rose through curving hills, the ways grew rough and full of stones, and the stones made caves. In these caves and along the ledges before them he saw where tribes of snakes had raised their towns. And on the path they danced and rolled the chunghe stone. Some shook their rattles, the big bull snakes beat the drum and around the fire, coiling and uncoiling, the Highland Moccasins danced the death dance. Slowly and cautiously they raised their heads and struck the air, and out of the rocks there came a noise as of a thousand pots hissing and singing.

Let us find some other way, he said to the girl. We cannot pass here.

There is no other way, she replied and pulled baksha branches, wrapping them close about his body. These will stop their fangs, she added and took his hand and led him through the stamping ground, and as they passed the fangs struck the baksha like hail.

The priest turned to the people:
Orate, fratres . . .

They climbed to the top of a mountain, a mountain so high that, standing on its very top, they could see the underside of the sky. Below lay a plain and beyond another mountain. There our journey ends, she said, where the sky ends. Between those two peaks we leave the path, passing out under the sky to the land we seek, but first we must overcome two other dangers.

What are they?

Without replying she led the way down into the plain. As they approached, he could hear from afar the whoops of death and the noise of men fighting. At the foot the path curved about a rock so high the sun never reached its base and, as he went around it, he could smell, rising from the slimy floor, the odor of the dead.

Let us hurry on, he said and, stooping beneath an escarpment, came out of the mountain onto the plain. She was beside him. He heard her say: Take this pipe and blow the smoke, first to the north, then to the east, and to the south, lastly towards the west where we go.

But he did not hear, watching the battle as it moved from side to side across the valley's floor. From above the valley had seemed a wide plain, but now he saw it for what it was, a basin with neither inlet nor egress except by way of the mountain they had come down and the one yet to climb. Eagerly he looked towards the last barrier, but it lay hidden in mist. And as he looked, the battle spread out before him. At the same instant he saw it in part and as a whole: each Indian who behind a tree pulled his bow, each separately and all together as they crept through the grass; each insult and whoop of defiance; each axe that fell and split a skull; each knife that took its hair—and those farthest away seemed of a size with those who fought near by. In between the two parties lay the path they must travel and over it the arrows so sped that they made a flickering darkness, and so fast the air whistled one shrill never-ceasing moan. And out of this clearly he heard a bell ringing three times and a voice saying *Sanctus, Sanctus, Sanctus*.

Who are these who fight and never die? he asked.

—They are those who walk the path without pipe or tobacco. Outcasts. Hunters and fighters who have died without proper burial.

—And must they fight forever thus?

She nodded her head. —Once struck by an arrow you may never leave this plain. But take this pipe and smoke it as I have directed and we shall pass invisibly by.

Very carefully he blew the smoke to the north, to the east, the south, the west and, as the smoke rose and disappeared, the sound of fighting died away, the warriors vanished, and the path ran unblocked over the stilled grass to the forest which circled the mountain at the other end of the basin.

We may now walk without fear, she said.

Be mindful, O Lord, of thy servant, Ortiz . . .

—Be mindful of your step, Ispani, as you climb. All our dangers are past but one and that one you alone must overcome.

—What is it?

—You will see.

He did not press her further, for suddenly he began to shiver. This chill is strange, he thought, and then he saw that frost lay heavy on the ground. The forest stood out in a clear cold light, bare of leaves. Brown shrivelled clusters hung in scattered patches to the oaks. The bark was tight and gray and dead. The sun fell to the ground in broad slick strips. Tree shadows lay athwart the strips flat and black and sharply lined. Where am I, he wondered, that a glance may bring winter where all was green and pleasant?

Hurry on, she said.

Walking faster, he came out of the forest to the foot of the mountain. Ice covered the path. A frozen river winding among the blue-white slopes fell motionless into a gorge. Out of the gorge a wind blew, driving the snow, piling it in heaps, and bringing to the upper air an endless blizzard.

—So this is the danger each faces alone, with no mantle to cover us, no sticks for a fire.

—Not yet. Climb.

—Climb to our death.

The dead cannot die; climb, she said and, speeding before him, disappeared into a flurry of snow.

Wait, he called and leapt after her.

Almost losing but never quite losing her, he followed running up the frozen path. The snow blinded his eyes, his feet drew tight with pain. They burned, they throbbed, they lost all feeling. He ran clumsily like a man in heavy shoes. He ran until he came to a place swept by winds. The ground turned soft. Not ten paces away he saw the girl. Bent slightly forward, she pulled along the path. Her hair and the most of her skirt stood out behind her, streaming through the air. As he watched, she jerked forward and stopped and the hair settled about her shoulders. She motioned to him and he came up beside her. The wind fell away, the air grew mild and all about them the sides of the mountain turned yellow green, buds swelled on the trees and underfoot strange herbs were in flower.

How is this? he asked.

Big winter, little winter and the wind moon . . . all have we passed. Now we are come to the planting moon. Look before you, she said.

He looked and saw that the mountain was no longer steep but sloped gently upwards into summer. From tender shoots to the full-grown stalks fields of maize followed the slopes. In the distance thunder storms passed, twisting and shaking the fields. In the very distance there was the brown look of drought.

There are still other moons, she said. The mulberry, the blackberry, the big ripening moon, and after them the black water and the whip-poor-will. There are many moons but only the four sacred seasons. Of all things they are the last.

Then all now is simple, he said.

—You carry your darts?

He held them up.

—Then let us be on our way.

Into winter, out of it; into, out of, spring; through summer, summer's heat, summer the ripening time, out of it and into autumn. And at last they came to a place where no seasons were. Time they had left where the path began. Now they stood in No-place, the last station. All the way they had walked, through every danger but the last, out of time, out of the seasons, out of space. They saw the sun's bed, where he slept with the moon. They saw night and day.

There, she cried.

—Where?

—There.

Two stones no taller than a man enclosed a passage. On either side the sky came down. Straining his eyes, he saw at the passage end a point of light, clear and bright and of such a blue that it struck pain at the back of his head.

Now, she said.

—Now?

—Throw well your darts, or we are lost.

As she spoke, down the passage a great wind rushed. Strike this with a dart? he shouted, but the words blew back into his mouth . . . he was being sucked towards the entrance, the point of light went out, he stumbled and fell to his knees; then darkness bolted from the mouth of the cave. It passed over him and pinned his back to the ground. It screamed as it passed and overhead he heard a noise as of the mainsails of a ship popping in a storm.

Up, before it dives, she cried.

Then he saw the eagle curving on the air, its wings outspread and its talons drawn up against the smooth white breast. From the tip of each tail feather hung the hair of a hundred scalps. The bird soared like a thing of down, curved into a spiral, and for one long instant held itself poised in space; then it reached down its open beak, folded its wings and, like a ball, dropped from the sky.

He sighted along the dart, flung it. With a side sweep the bird caught the shaft in its beak and broke it.

Too soon, the girl cried.

He waited until he saw the two small nostrils in the beak. He raised his arm and let the last dart fly. It went straight and upward. The eagle screamed and caught itself in its flight.

Now run for the cave, she shouted.

—Where is it?

Here! Here!

A dull heavy thud struck and the dark fell between them. Where? he shouted. Where? returned his voice, high and strained, and then he felt himself standing alone in a vast silence, then in a tight, close, too familiar place. His body was taut, his arm raised, and his hand clasping the darts. At his feet spread a soft red glow. Even before he looked, he knew that he had leapt up out of a dream before the ashes of his fire and in that instant he received the full impact of the world. And then out of the woods beyond the burial ground he heard a thing being dragged through the brush, haltingly, unresisting. . . .

He did not wait to think but ran where the corpse of the child rested on its frame. The frame was empty. The overturned coffin lay on the ground. He turned it over with his foot—it was empty. His body was cold and running with sweat. He held his breath and listened. No sound. Perhaps he had never heard it. Perhaps he had heard it in his dreaming and, like his voice, it had persisted into consciousness. There was no time to lose. Quickly, instinctively, he entered the woods. Creeping, listening, alert and calm, he moved swiftly through the undergrowth, and yet carefully he broke apart the brush and set his foot down as though he stalked the unquiet ghost of the dead. The night air was cool and heavy. He had gone a short distance when, cooler, heavier, throat-stopping, the odor familiar above all others drifted across his path. The trail was now plain. He followed it.

The priest spread his hands over the oblation.

His foot came to sand and scattering palmettos. His nose gave him warning and then his ears. Somewhere to the front he heard a crunching and suddenly a low growl. He stiffened. Near the ground, within casting distance, the darkness shifted. It shifted in silence. As he waited, his eyes explored the distance, measuring, isolating. . . . The darkness moved again, the crunching began again. Slowly he raised his arm: the dart swished, the blood rushed to his ears. He heard no muffled growl, no slipping away, but his hand was salty. He threw again. The second dart went wide of its aim, and he realized the spot of darkness which had been his target had vanished into the general darkness the moment the first dart left his hand. Suddenly he was shaking, all his nerve gone; yet he forced himself, unarmed as he was, to stumble about the palmettos hunting what he feared to find and yet must find. Suppose he had not struck the beast? Suppose it was lying in wait, wounded and cornered? Had it done away with the corpse of the child? Had the corpse, even, been stolen while he slept and he now pursued some other beast?

Chilled and disheartened, empty of courage, he returned to the burial yard. He threw twigs and sticks on the fire, and it popped and blazed. He looked at the flames, leaping with cheer and warmth. They brought him no comfort. And then before the heat the scars on his back began to twinge and

draw. With a start he drew away. Slowly, as a man turns upon
his doom, he turned to the fire. His gaze was still fixed upon it
long after the flames had fallen away when, hours later, the
dawn came and time returned quietly to the forest. So was he
standing when he heard the Indians file into the burial yard.

Take and eat ye of this, for this is My Body.
The bell rang three times and the priest, kneeling, adored
the Sacred Host and, rising, elevated it before the altar.

He waited for the discovery, waited, waited . . . a woman
cried out in a high shrill wail. . . .

*Take and drink ye all of this, for this is the Chalice of My Blood
of the new and eternal Testament. . . .*
The bell rang, the priest knelt and, rising, elevated the
Chalice.

In a moment they would see him standing apart . . .

Striking his breast and raising his voice, the priest:
To us sinners also . . .

They seized him and led him, bound, before Ucita. They
did not tie him when they brought him to the slave post. His
two guards, Big-Handsome-Child and Two-Fell-Together,
motioned to him to sit down and they sat on either side of
him. He took this to mean that at least he would not be condemned until the scouts who had been sent on the trail of the
missing body returned. Ucita would want to deliver him up to
the frame. Such had been his plan in giving him the bone yard
watch. But the Indians would hold a council on him and even
Ucita would not go against its expressed judgment. At least it
was not customary, but then he was not sure whether a
custom had been established in a case such as his. Big-
Handsome-Child and Two-Fell-Together belonged to the
White Deer hasomi. This was encouraging. If his death had
been predetermined, they would have put guards of the Fish

hasomi over him, since the mother of the child belonged to the
Fish people.

Holding the Sacred Host, three times the priest made the
sign of the Cross over the Chalice—three hours of agony
—and twice away from it—the flesh and spirit are parted. The
Host and the Chalice are slightly raised:
It is ended.

The Indians were gathering before the long council house.
They entered according to rank. First Ucita with Him-Who-
Leads-the-Cacique-by-the-Hand on one side and Mocoço-
Killer, the war leader, on the other. After them the beloved old
men. Their flesh was like rotting wood, and the bracelets of
fish teeth and pearls hung loose on their arms, but they held
themselves erect and walked slowly up to the open piazza
where gradually they faded into the cool shadows of the
house. Then came the inihama, the second men. They passed
through the town yard, haughtily, indifferently; then more
quickly the ibitano and after them, the toponole. He saw them
all out of the corner of his eye, for decorum ordered that he
must show no interest in anything that bore upon his
dangerous position.

Father . . . Thy will be done.
Over the Chalice hovered the body of Christ. The priest
broke it and, holding the fragment in his hand, three times
made the sign; then the fragment fell; the blood and the flesh
were joined.
*May this mixture and consecration of the body and blood of
our Lord Jesus Christ be to us that receive it eternal life.*

He must show no fear, either now or at the time of
judging. Nor too much insolence. Insolence on the part of a
prisoner is expectation of death. His guards would be watching to report his slightest movement. Even though they sat
with averted heads, he was not fooled. He must show the
same supposed indifference.

Lamb of God who taketh away the sins of the world, have mercy on us.

Outcries announced the return of the scouts. They filed across the yard towards the long house. What did they carry? If only he could look. He could feel the tension of his guards and hear the low sounds of the Indians who were not allowed in council. And then he listened to the slow beat of his heart.

I will take the bread of Heaven and call upon the name of the Lord.

He was standing. The guards pressed his arms against their bodies. He walked between them. The bear grease on their bodies was hot and slick. On the piazza two beloved old women were brewing cassena. One fanned the fire with turkey feathers. The other stirred the drink with a gourd until the dark liquid frothed, and out of the handle he heard the talk of the brew. He passed with his guards into the house. *Lord, I am not worthy. . . .* Ucita's skull-like face confronted him from the royal bed, impassive under its perpetual grin. Arranged according to their castes the Indians sat in council. He felt their eyes upon him as he moved between the beds, but his own he kept at Ucita's feet. And then when they had reached a certain distance, Big-Handsome-Child and Two-Fell-Together raised their hands twice to their faces, saying, Hah, he, hah, hah, hah! From all the beds came the response, Hah, Hah! And then his guards went to the warriors' bed, and he was left alone. He did not move, or move his eyes. The silence grew.

To his lips the priest raised the Bread of Angels, laid it upon his tongue. And drank of the precious Blood. It was no longer the priest who lived. Jesus Christ lived in him.

Ucita pointed to the floor. Slowly he dropped his eyes. There at his feet lay a wolf and out of its breast, running along the gray sandy floor, was the handle of the dart. He took in his breath and held it.

At last Ucita spoke. "The little child is found and not far away the thief is found—dead." From all the beds came grunts of approval. He almost dared to hope. Behind him he heard a low humming, and a Waiter, bowing and singing in a low tone, went by him to Ucita, holding before him the conch shell of cassena. Ucita took it and drank and the Waiter sang, and when his breath was out, Ucita lowered the shell and handed it to the first councillor. The Waiter sang as before. As it passed from mouth to mouth, Ucita broke into a sweat and with great composure leaned over to vomit, spewing the liquid onto the floor at his feet. When all the first and second men had drunk, the Waiter came to him.

His hand shook as he reached for the shell. He drank deep of the bitter stuff.

May Thy Body, O Lord, which I have received, and Thy Blood which I have drunk, cleave to my bowels; and grant that no stain of sin may remain in me . . .

He began to sweat, a nausea seized him. He leaned over and the warm bitter liquid spewed out of his mouth.

Ite missa est.

There was the murmur of a great throng moving and a voice said, "You may rise now. It is over." And then he felt a jerk at his arm. He turned his head, his eyes focused. De Soto was smiling and his hand was on his sleeve. "You live again as a Christian, Señor. Among Christians."

John D. MacDonald

(1916–1986) was a successful writer long associated with Florida because of his Travis McGee series, set in Fort Lauderdale, and because of his novel *Condominium*, which wrote seventy novels, including the famous Travis McGee series, and six hundred short stories. Always popular, his works were translated into at least eighteen languages and sold more than 80

lambasted Florida's plan boards. He was born in Pennsylvania, educated at Syracuse University, the University of Pennsylvania, and the Harvard Graduate School of Business, and served in the army in World War II. He million copies. He lived on Siesta Key near Sarasota for many years and set some of his stories in southern Florida; one of these is "Kitten on a Trampoline" (1961).

This story takes place in

Sarasota, a town known as the winter headquarters for circus companies. A harried salesman who is passing through Sarasota becomes fascinated by a beautiful circus aerialist and gives up a successful job to join the traveling performers. There is no "happily-ever-after" ending; rather, MacDonald stresses, as he does in much of his writing, the peace that comes from doing a job as well as possible and living in harmony with inner feelings. While the question of whether the narrator will find peace with his circus friends is unanswered, it is more important to MacDonald that the protagonist made the difficult decision to follow his instincts and leave the rat race.

Unlike much of MacDonald's later writing, in this story the narrator is a participant but not the protagonist of the story. He can only interact with the girl, the "Kitten on a Trampoline," and hope he can find a place with her. The fact that this story takes place in Florida—the mythical land of opportunity—is significant because of the choices that the narrator must make about his own future. The girl clearly espouses much of what MacDonald believed in over the years—for example that ruining the environment, or in this case ruining one's health, is wrong.

This story was published three years before Travis McGee appeared on the scene and, like much of MacDonald's writing up to that time, has been overshadowed by the McGee novels and their American detective/folk hero.

John D. MacDonald

Kitten on a Trampoline

O N A WARM and bright and shining day of a brand-new year I was driving a company car from Naples, Florida, north to Tampa. I was slamming it through traffic, irritable and edgy. The back end was stowed with samples, literature and display materials. I'd kept myself in top gear for three years, ever since I'd been graduated from Florida State. I'd turned myself into the best road man the Owen Drug Company had ever seen. I was making twenty thousand a year. I was buying Owen stock with every dime I could hoard after taxes and bachelor living expenses. I'd won all kinds of awards by working ninety-hour weeks at a dead run. I was on my way to a brilliant career.

But I was chronically hoarse from giving my spiel to doctors and druggists, and I tried not to notice that I was going through three packs of cigarettes a day, or notice the persistent tremor in my hands or the deepening frown wrinkles between my brows. I hadn't been sleeping well of late, and I was bothered by nervous indigestion. My weight was down, and my temper was too easily lost.

But you have to keep pushing and churning if you are going to get anywhere in this world.

I came roaring up Route 41 into the south end of Sarasota. I would have made the light by a big shopping center if a dawdling cluck in a quarter acre of Ohio Cadillac hadn't drifted over into my lane and blocked me out of the play. I was running behind schedule, and so I sat, cursing him, holding my steering wheel so tightly my knuckles ached.

I happened to glance over toward a part of the big shopping-section parking lot which had been fenced off. A crowd of people were clustered with their backs toward the highway, watching something.

I saw a girl burst up into the air, higher than their heads. With her body straight out, she made a turn so slow and so elegant it seemed that I was watching it in slow motion, and then fell back out of sight and reappeared again in a slight variation of the first turn. I knew that the girl in the sunlight was the most astonishingly beautiful thing I had ever seen. I watched her until an indignant horn blatted behind me, and I saw the Ohio Cadillac so far ahead I knew the light had changed long ago.

I charged ahead, but somehow I couldn't get back into the strain-and-scurry frame of mind. I suddenly had the horrible realization that I was close to breaking into tears. I now know it was a clue to the extent of my nervous exhaustion. Something so precious had occurred that I couldn't even put a name to it. And here I was, running away from it. I drifted over to the curb, found a place to turn around and went back and parked, locked the car and joined the people.

It was one of those Trampoline layouts which are suddenly appearing all over the country. Seventy-five cents for thirty minutes of bouncing up and down. I had seen it being done, but not like this. Neither had the other people, I guess. Except for some squealing kids, the other customers inside the fence had stopped to watch her also, in a hypnotic silence. It was like a wild strange dance she was improvising as she went along, with a complete grace and total control in spite of the tremendous height she was achieving. She was young, she had a burnished tan and she was sweetly and strongly constructed. Her hair was a tousled brown-red mass. She wore a sleeveless yellow-print blouse and little chocolate-colored shorts. I could see her face clearly only at the apex of those leaps when she was turning slowly. It was one of those wide-cheeked Slavic faces of a totally deceptive placidity. She had a dreaming look, a contentment, a half smile. She drifted and spun in a better world than any of us could know.

Suddenly she smothered the next leap with a deft flex of brown knees and stepped off the Trampoline. We gave an audible group sigh because it was over, and then we all began clapping. She looked startled, but smiled with a professional brilliance, bowed with professional aplomb and bent to put her shoes back on as the applause died and the people began drifting away.

I moved toward the gate where she would come out. I heard the proprietor telling her to stop there at any time and be his guest. It was a smart business gambit for him. She came out, moving slowly, earthbound after soaring, carrying a yellow purse. She was sturdy and smaller than I would have guessed. But as she neared me I could detect none of the residual puffing and damp sweatiness of great athletic effort.

"There should have been music with that," I told her. She gave me that single cool glance of dismissal all girls that pretty must learn. I walked beside her. She pretended I was not there.

"I have to tell you something," I said. "I don't loaf around bothering pretty girls. I was driving through. I had to stop for that light. Then I saw you over the heads of those people, way up in the middle of the air. I drove on because I'm supposed to be in Tampa by four o'clock for a sales meeting, but I found out I had to come back and find you and tell you how beautiful it was. That's all."

She stopped and looked up at me. "So you've told me. Now go to Tampa." It was an urchin voice, unmannered and with a faraway spice of accent. She was affecting an elaborate boredom.

We were near a drugstore. "I could buy you a coffee or a soda."

She shrugged. "I'm thirsty," she said.

We went in and sat at the counter. She ordered limeade. I ordered coffee. I put my business card on the counter top.

"Paul Fox," she read. "Short name."

"I'm twenty-five. I'm not married. I cover the whole southern half of the state. I'm based in Tampa. I spend four days a month there. I drive fifty thousand miles a year."

"Enchanting," she said tonelessly.

"I had the ridiculous feeling you might tell me your name."

"For one limeade? Why not? Wanda Markava."

I looked at my watch. I spotted the phone booths. "Wanda, I have to make a phone call. Promise you won't leave before I get back."

"If you don't get back before I feel like leaving, I won't be here. How much do you expect out of one limeade?"

I called Harry Fletcher in Tampa and told him I was held up in Sarasota by car trouble, and I couldn't make the meeting. He told me to pick up a rental car. I said it was tire trouble, and I'd wrenched my back changing the wheel and I didn't feel like driving. He believed my every word. It was my first lapse from total dependability. I saw Wanda get off the stool and stroll toward the door. I cut Harry off by saying loudly, "Hello? Hello? Hello? Damn it!" and hanging up.

I caught up with her a hundred feet from the store. "Where are you going?"

"Home."

"Can I walk with you?"

"I don't own the sidewalks. It's a long way. You'll miss your meeting."

"I phoned Tampa and told them I would."

"You're wasting your time, Paul Fox."

"Kindly let me be the judge of what is a waste of time and what isn't."

She gave me an oblique glance and said, "I have to go home to take care of my three babies and start cooking a big hot dinner for my husband."

I stopped dead in my tracks. My heart rolled over and died. She walked on and turned back and looked at me curiously. Suddenly she threw her head back and gave a curiously abrupt bark of rather harsh laughter. "No husband. No babies. Come along. It was a good way to get rid of you,

Paul Pest Fox, but you looked too sad. There's a hundred other ways."

We walked together in January sunlight. I stole careful glances at her. Only the most perfect physical conditioning can produce a walk like hers, as lithe and unself-conscious as a tan panther on a jungle path. There was a childish look about the blandness of forehead, the snubbed nose and the placid symmetry of her cheek. And there was a small-boy appeal in the squareness and sturdiness of her hands. But the impact of the total creature was vividly, uncompromisingly female.

She seemed placidly content with our silence, and I knew I would have to initiate any new topic. We were passing a suburban bank. "You were terrific on that Trampoline, Wanda. And you look so very trim. I was wondering if you—if you're on some sort of gymnastic team."

The bank lawn looked green and soft. Without breaking her stride she stepped off onto the grass and went into a series of three limber flip-flaps which ended with a complete front flip with a half turn so that she ended the series facing me. Again she gave that bark of laughter. "Gym team!" she said with complete derision. "Circus," she said haughtily as she fell in step with me again.

I felt like thumping myself in the head. This was Sarasota. It explained some of the strangenesses of her. These were the most clannish people in the world. "Which circus?" I asked.

She seemed truly astonished. "With my name, which one would it be? Rossoni and Markava. It isn't big, but we are known. I am a flier. You should know that too. I can do many things, but flying is best. I was on the rings when I was five years old." She held her arm out. "Look at this arm! Tell me what you think of this arm, Paul Fox."

We stopped and I looked at it carefully, wondering what I was supposed to be looking for. It was round, firm and brown, and gracefully proportioned. The skin texture was silken. I had the dizzy wish to kiss the hollow of the elbow. "It's a lovely arm, Wanda."

"Yes it is," she said with a wonderfully innocent pride.

"My mother, my grandmother, they are both the same. It is good luck for a woman to be this way. With either arm I can lift more than you can with two. But we Markava women get no ugly bulging muscles. With my uncle sitting on my shoulders, I can do very slow deep-knee bends. He weighs over two hundred. I weigh one hundred and eighteen. The muscles show a little bit more in the legs, but it is still not ugly, is it?" She moved away from me to pose for inspection and looked back over her shoulder at me with a rather anxious expression.

"They're lovely legs, Wanda."

"No. The arms are better, as arms. The legs are too short. I am just five feet two and a half, and I am too long in the waist to have a really good figure. If I were five feet six, the legs would be just right, with the same length from the hips up. I'd look better when I fly. But I might not be so strong. Here. Press with your knuckle here, against the calf." I saw her tense her leg. It became like sleek brown marble. A passing tourist boggled at us and nearly ran up over the curbing.

We walked on. I searched my memory for a properly circusy question and finally dredged one up. "Can you do the triple?" I asked politely.

"Out of the last hundred practice tries, I got forty-one. When I can get to sixty out of a hundred, we'll put it in, Uncle Charley says. He's my catcher on the triple. After we practice, our hands are so swollen we have to soak them."

I had run out of questions. It seemed to me we had walked a very long distance. I could feel a blister beginning to form on my right heel.

"You smoke too much," she said abruptly.

"I know I do."

"So why don't you smoke less?"

"There's a lot of strain connected with my job, Wanda."

"Strain? Selling pills?" she asked with such surprise that it irritated me.

"They set a quota for me, and I have to meet it."

"So what happens when you meet it? The strain is over?"

"Well, no. They set a new quota."

She snorted and said, "Even in the seal act, a seal always gets a fish after every trick. They don't make her work harder each time for the fish. That quota thing is ridiculous."

I thought about it, and I saw that it was. I was being treated with less dignity than a seal. But I had to salvage something. "I make darn good money."

"How much?" she demanded.

"Uh—twenty thousand dollars."

"What do you spend it all on?"

"Taxes take a big bite because I'm single. After I pay living expenses, I invest what's left in stock in the company I work for."

"Ha."

"What's this ha?"

"Nothing. It just sounds like a crummy way to live, Paul Fox."

"I'm considered very successful for my age."

"Ha," she said again, and I didn't feel like contesting that one. I didn't know what she was calling me in her mind. A townie, perhaps. Or a mark. It was an odd experience to be scorned and pitied by this delicious little flier.

"We turn here," she said. "Five more blocks. Are you sick?"

The question startled me. "Why do you ask me that?"

"You are pale, and I saw your hand shaking when you picked up your coffee cup. You look thin and stringy, and when somebody squealed their brakes a little while ago you went right up in the air."

"I don't get a chance to get much sun, Wanda. I've been working hard without a break for a long time. No, I'm not sick."

"You don't look healthy."

"Compared to you I've never been healthy, I guess."

"You look older than twenty-five."

"I like what you do for my morale, friend."

"I'm not doing it. You've been doing it to yourself—for that twenty thousand dollars."

"You don't mind saying exactly what you think, do you?"

"I wouldn't say it if you really were sick."

So I used up a couple of blocks of silence thinking that over. I was scowling at the sidewalk when she said, "Here it is."

The paving and sidewalks and small, careful houses ended. The Markava domain was beyond the end of the street, and it seemed to have been spilled across several scrubby acres. I stood and looked at the cars parked at complete random, at several house trailers and at haphazard sheds and outbuildings. The original house had been a cottage. It looked as if it had been enlarged through a dreamy process of buying abandoned garages and affixing them to the house and to each other in the quickest possible manner. There was a big new front porch of raw wood across the front of it. I looked at all the kids racing around.

"Is there a party going on?"

"Oh, no. It's mostly all family. But there are people always coming and going. Come on."

The children ignored us. As we went up onto the porch, a huge man pushed the screen door open and came out. "Charley, this is Paulfox," she said, turning me into one word.

"Hahya," he said to me. "Go change and we'll work some, Wan."

"You could watch," she said to me and went into the house. Charley was eating some sort of stew out of a yellow bowl with his fingers. He looked like a television version of a Siberian bandit. He was bare to the waist, and his magnificently-muscled torso was hairless. After each chunk of stew meat he would lick his thumb and finger and then wipe them on a dish towel tucked into the waistband of his baggy trousers. He looked at me with distant amusement.

"That Wanda," he said finally. "I wanted to build up an army, know what I'd do? Send her out six or ten times a day. Make a big circle. Come back here. One guy following every time. Clunk his head and swear him in. Sure. She talks to you, though. You're ahead. One guy in twenty she even says hello. The others just follow. A big one last week got out of line. Fritz was here. He's only so big, and maybe he's sixty, who can tell? Does a wire act. The big guy got on Fritz's nerves. He bent down, picked up the guy's right foot and put it behind the big guy's right ear. After he found out he could walk, he didn't stay long."

Wanda came out in a faded gray-blue leotard. Charley put his bowl down on the porch floor and stepped out of his pants. He was wearing patched maroon tights. I followed them around the house. The big practice rigging was there with the safety net slung in position. All the chrome was shiny, and the whites were very white. Such flying rigs look smaller outdoors. I learned one thing the Markavas weren't casual about. Charley and Wanda went to work, and they checked every line, every guy wire and every fastening—patiently, thoroughly and without haste. Then they went up hand over hand to opposite platforms and used the lead strings to pull their traps up to their platforms. Several persons had appeared from nowhere to watch. I didn't know then that a couple of the men had positioned themselves in the only places where there was any chance she might miss the net on a partial catch and a slip.

Charley swung out and built the swing higher with two hard strokes, then settled himself into the leg-twined upside-down posture of the catcher and established a stately, predictable rhythm. Charley started the count for her. She swung out and high. At the apex of her second swing she released the trap and did a full slow layout and seemed to float into the catch. All four hands catch wrists. They caught with an audible smack. It was so beautiful I wanted to hear 10,000 persons applauding. I watched several more catches.

"You that Paulfox, hah?" a heavily accented female voice said at my elbow.

I looked down into the leathery face of a stocky woman with bright yellow hair. She wore black denim pants and a sweat shirt that was stenciled with the curious legend, SARASOTA JUNGLE GARDENS. She stared at me with great intensity and repeated her question.

"Yes, that's my name."

"I'm her mamma, Jenny Markava."

"How do you do?"

"I was top flier one time. Sixteen years. Longer than you tink, hah? Was damn good. But not so good as her. You watch. Wan has special ting. How you say? Floating. A slowness, like a magic. Hang in air. Nijinsky had. In ballet is called *ballon*, hah? A jeté lasting like forever. She is one of the great ones." Her mouth twisted into a curious smirk. "But you tink is foolish nonsense, jumping around in the air, hah? Somebody gets hurt, hah?"

I looked up to see Wanda rise high in a blurred spin and, just as she started to fall, snap open for the wrist smack of the precision catch.

I turned back to Jenny Markava. "It is one of the most beautiful things in the world," I said. "Anything that beautiful is very important, Mrs. Markava. It could never be nonsense."

She gave me a stevedore grin, and such a backhanded crack across the middle that it nearly dropped me. "You stay and eat good, hah? You too tin and weak."

I watched all of the practice session. At the end Wanda wanted to try the triple. Charley wouldn't let her. He told her she was a little bit off in her timing. She had fallen into the net twice. They both dropped, bounded, came to the edge of the net in that curious, wide wading walk and dropped lightly to the ground. She was sweaty and winded, and there was a net burn on the outside of her right leg.

"You eating here?" she asked me.

"Your mother invited me."

"Don't get close to me. I smell like a horse. I'll see you in a little while."

It was the most confusing house I've ever been in. There seemed to be four or five tiny living rooms, each with its own group. In one room three old ladies were gabbling at each other in a foreign tongue while they sewed sequins to heavy new material with a dazzling speed. People were singing, some were arguing, some were cooking and some were eating. Two television sets and a radio were going with the volume turned high. I estimate I met about one out of every four of them, and usually it was only the first name. They all had muscles, vitality and violent opinions. The children seemed able to run up the walls and across the ceiling, but I suspect that was an illusion. I remember one dreamlike sequence in particular. I was still waiting for Wanda to appear. Somebody had put an opened can of beer in my hand. I found a chair in a corner. A tired skinny little dog with ancient gray on his muzzle came trudging over and stared at me. Suddenly, as if arriving at a decision, he hoisted himself up onto his hind legs and jumped up and down a half dozen times. Then, with great elderly care, he rocked himself up onto his front legs and stood balanced there, looking sideways at me. "Nice doggie," I said weakly. He stayed as he was, looking at me with sad, expectant patience.

"He wants you to clap," said a very tall and wonderfully beautiful girl in a thin little voice. I clapped. The dog dropped back to all fours, sighed, yawned and walked away.

"That's Captain Bligh," she explained.

"Oh."

"He's retired, but he wants strangers to know he's been with it."

"I see his point."

Soon Wanda joined me. She was in a full crisp white skirt and a black trim blouse. Her eyes and her smile were shiny in the dusk. She brought us two bowls of an ominous-looking stew and two bowls of salad. We took them out on the porch, away from the confusion, and sat in a band of light that came through one of the windows. The stew was superb; so was the salad. Later we joined some singing in foreign tongues, and I smiled in a strained way at jokes I couldn't understand which sent powerful men into helpless falling-down laughter. At a little after eleven, a morose boy drove me in an old pickup back to my car. I finally found a vacancy in a rather dreary motel. There was a handsome blister on my heel.

At eleven the next morning, when four of them came swinging down over the edge of the big safety net, Wanda walked over to me, scowling, and said, "How many meetings can you miss?"

"I've got vacation time piled up that I didn't use. My boss didn't want me to take it now because we're bringing out new products. I told him on the phone this morning that I have to take it now."

She put a big beach towel around her shoulders like a cape, and we strolled over and sat on a plank-and-sawhorse table in the shade.

"So will you just be—around here?" she asked.

"If nobody minds too much."

She looked at me with a tolerant amusement. "We leave in March for the season on the road, Paulfox. There is always work to do at this time. Without cheap labor the small circuses would die. Over there is the bunkhouse for single men. You would eat fine, you know. Maybe you are too important. No? I can ask then and see if it is all right with everybody."

I took the two weeks, and then I demanded a third week. Harry Fletcher was very sour about it, but he couldn't afford to get too nasty. Other firms had been after me, and he knew it.

I drove up to Tampa on a Monday morning. When I walked into his office I knew he had decided to be jolly. He's a pasty little man with steel-wool hair and a lot of nervous mannerisms.

"Paul!" he said. "You look absolutely marvelous! Got that weight back. Got a tan. My, my, my."

I sat by his desk and said, "I appreciate all you've done for me, Harry. I know I should give you more warning. But just as soon as you can line up a guy for my territory, I'll spend a week taking him around and introducing him."

All the cheer slid out of his face. He tugged his ear, shifted some pencils around, and said, "I get pressure coming down from the top and up from underneath. You can't appreciate what it's like. I can get into a serious hypertension situation. One thing I thought I could rely on. Loyalty!" He stared fiercely at me and then sighed with resignation. "So if I have to buy your loyalty, Paul, I can face that too. Tell me what you've been offered. We'll match it."

"It isn't like that, Harry."

"You're taking another job, aren't you?"

"Sort of."

He began to tear a memo into strips. "What is this 'sort of'?"

"Harry, I'm joining a circus."

I saw him take it the way a good fighter takes a surprise right lead. He kept moving until his world came back into focus. "You're making a mistake. An advance man for a show is more like press-agent work. It isn't your kind of selling, Paul, believe me. You're a repeat business salesman, not one-shot promotions."

"No, Harry. I'm unloading my Owen stock and I'm buying a concession. The man who owns it wants to get off the road. He says I can make out. He'll go along for the first month and get me going right. He's got arthritis."

"Have you lost your mind!"

"I'm just going into business for myself."

He jumped up and began to pace. "What a business! Why don't you get into buggy whips? How about the big new field that's opening up making hoops for hoop skirts, kiddo? Circuses are in trouble! Haven't you heard?"

I'd had no intention of explaining it all to him. But he was very agitated and, according to his own lights, he'd been fair to me. "That's why I'm doing this, Harry."

He sat down heavily and stared at me. "You're suicidal. You need help."

"Harry, listen to me. Two years from now, five years from now or ten years from now, could I make a good living as a salesman?"

"Yes. Any time. When you go broke, come back here."

"Harry, there is an old circus clan named Markava. They've been performers for generations. Now they have a twenty-year-old girl who might turn out to be the best they've ever had. But she has come along at the end of an era. The whole clan is proud of her. They want her to have the best possible life. Suppose she married another performer, and in three or four years there's no more circus left. They'd be untrained for anything else. It might become a mean and squalid life for her, Harry."

"What's this got to do with you?"

"They're a practical clan. They've been thinking about hedging their beautiful bet by finding her a civilian. She'd have no part of it until I happened along."

"And she fell madly in love with you?" Harry said with great sarcasm.

"They're practical people. She seems to like me. They have the old-world idea that you arrange a practical marriage, and then you fall in love afterward. I jumped the gun on that theory."

He shook his head sadly. "A circus girl! Holy Maroney! When does the marriage get arranged anyhow?"

"We'll go on the road. They've got to know if I can take that kind of a life. Some people can't. If I can—and I can handle the concession—then we'll get married, and they'll set us up with our own deal, one of those house-trailer layouts on a flat-bed truck. It's a truck show."

"Very romantic," he said. "Say, have you thought of this? If she's real beautiful, it would be a slick way for them to unload sick concessions on suckers like you, Paul."

"I thought of that. Maybe they're all kidding me. I don't think so."

"You've got wonderful promise, Paul, and I hate to see you do this to your life. If the circuses don't all fold, then you're stuck in a nickle-dime operation all your life."

I couldn't avoid a smile of contentment. "With no quotas, no sales meetings and no expense accounts."

"O.K., so what if it goes the other way? You get back into harness, and you've got a wife who won't do you much good in a business-contact way."

"Harry, she has absolutely no interest in functional kitchens, gracious living or social standings. She says that if it turns out that way, she wants to raise horses and kids."

Harry had to make one last sly try. "Don't those circus people have a kind of a loose moral way of living, boy?"

"I've spent three weeks with them, Harry. I've been learning all about one of the lost arts. It's called self-respect."

He found a man, and I broke him in, drew my final check and went back to Sarasota with all my worldly goods. The tempo of work was increasing. Wan was up to a comfortable three out of five on the triple. They never had any trouble thinking of things I could do.

One day, a week before we left, I was out behind the house on a chilly afternoon, all by myself, unbolting rows of folding seats, painting them and repairing them, bolting them back together and stenciling the numbers back on.

I didn't know Wan was behind me until I heard her abrupt laugh. I stood up, straightening a weary back, and said, "What's so hilarious?"

She sat on a stack of seats and looked blandly at me. "I was thinking that we never had such a rich man working for us."

I put one foot up on the seats and looked down at her upturned face. "Does it give you a sense of power, Miss Markava?"

"I don't think I like that, Paulfox. Anything we do, it is because we are willing to do it. Because the reasons are good, don't you think?"

"I'm sorry. The reasons are very good. But—I don't want *you* to feel trapped into anything."

"How do you mean?"

"We have an arrangement. But if any time you should want to get out of it—"

I was stopped by the expression on her face. It had turned into a stubborn mask of contempt, her eyes narrow, dangerous and oddly Oriental.

"So sweet," she purred. "So unselfish you are. So honorable. All I have to do is change my mind, eh, and you give me a nice little hurt smile and then perhaps we can shake hands or something like that?"

Never have I felt such a quick hot bursting of rage within myself. Forgetting that even after all my manual labor she could very probably toss me up into a pine tree, I snatched her wrist and yanked her up onto her feet and dug my hands into her shoulders and shook her until her face blurred.

"You can't get out of it!" I yelled at her. "You made a deal! I sat up all one night yelling at all your weird relatives and drinking that plum brandy, and we made the arrangement, see? So don't even think of trying to get out of it!"

I was suddenly aware of her complete lack of resistance. I let go of her. She looked up at me with an odd half-smile, docile, respectful, but with a kind of pride and gladness showing through. "O.K., Paul," she said. "O.K., sweetie."

I finished the folding seats in the late afternoon and went back to where they were practicing. I sat cross-legged on top of a gear box. Jenny brought me a cold beer. I lit my second cigarette of the day. I felt like a king as I watched her up there, my sweet sailing lady, my flying woman poised against the blue, blue sky, way up in the middle of the air.

THE END

Theodore Pratt

(1901–1969) wrote extensively and in varied formats about Florida: fourteen books, three movie scripts, one Broadway play, and numerous stories and essays. Born in Minneapolis, describe the state between 1880 and 1924 and give him the unofficial title of "the literary laureate of Florida."

"Five to Seven, Palm Beach" (1959) pokes fun at the Palm

West Palm Beach
Palm Beach

he studied at Colgate and Columbia universities but spent much of his life in Delray Beach. He is best known for a trilogy of Florida books—*The Barefoot Mailman*, *The Flame Tree*, and *The Big Bubble*—that

Beach set he knew well, though more as an outsider than as a member. The protagonist of his story—also an outsider—arrives on time at a party, but the host arrives an hour late; couples arrive with spouses other than their own; the host and hostess leave before their guests do. A parody of high-society parties and stereotypical characters, Pratt's story is typical of his treatment of the "haves" of Florida society.

The story is appropriately set in one of the many grandiose mansions for which Palm Beach is famous, mansions associated with Henry Flagler, Marjorie Merriweather Post, and the Kennedys. Unlike other Florida towns that are known for their topography or history or people, Palm Beach is known for its buildings. It has two of Florida's most magnificent hotels: the Royal Poinciana, a thousand-room building used by the rich and famous from 1894 to 1930; and the Breakers, a huge structure modeled after Rome's Villa Medici that has catered to the wealthy since 1925. Architect Addison Mizner designed many of the homes built in the town in the first quarter of this century, using the Spanish Mediterranean style that was fashionable at the time.

Pratt knew Palm Beach well and wrote about it in *That Was Palm Beach* (1968), his historical novel *The Flame Tree* (1950), and part of his most famous novel, *The Barefoot Mailman* (1943). The main post office in West Palm Beach has a series of six large murals depicting scenes from *The Barefoot Mailman*, and Highway U.S. 1 south of there is dotted with motels and stores whose names commemorate the men who carried the mail barefoot along the seashore in the late 1800s from Palm Beach to Miami. None of that history would seem to interest the characters in Pratt's short story. They see only the concentration of wealthy individuals in this small area.

Theodore Pratt

Five to Seven, Palm Beach

RACE BRANTLEY got out of the taxi, paid the driver, and then faced the wide arched doorway of the Palm Beach mansion. As she walked to it, rather tall and somewhat ungainly, she realized, aghast, that she was the first guest to arrive. Over the phone, after Grace explained she was spending a few days in West Palm Beach during mid-winter vacation from her New York schoolteaching job, Felice, her college sorority sister, now become the socially prominent Mrs. Richard Northampton, Jr., had said her cocktail party would be from five to seven. Grace, after being persuaded by Felice to come without an escort, had made the terrible mistake of arriving on time.

Feeling gauche, she entered the vast marble hall, brilliantly lighted from two gorgeous and glittering chandeliers. A wide, curved stairway led to upper regions. Great bursts of tall flowers exploded from large vases. At one side of the room a long bar with three men standing behind it had been set up. Near it stood a broad round table laden with fancy foods, including bowls of caviar, all surrounding a centerpiece of a huge grave lion carved out of a block of ice.

In one corner, with her back to Grace, stood an exquisitely gowned woman giving directions to a man clad in green uniform with dickey. The man started for the front door, passing Grace, at the same time the woman turned. It was Felice, whose too-blond head went to one side with a quick quizzical expression at the sight of Grace. Then recognition broke into her evaluation of the other woman, a smile came to her face, and she strode forward, both hands outstretched, crying, "Grace! How good to see you again after all these years!"

They embraced, and Grace murmured sincerely but awkwardly, "It's been a long time."

"Too long!" Felice exclaimed. "But it's wonderful to see you now."

Her friend's manner and voice had become brittle, in the way of many people with too much money and assured social position. Grace said admiringly, "Your house is beautiful."

"It's a shack."

"It was good of you to ask me to your party."

"Nonsense! We're delighted to have you. Dick isn't home yet from polo practice, but—"

"I'm afraid I've come too early," Grace apologized, "but you said—"

"My dear! I meant it was my husband's bad manners, not yours."

"I can't wait to meet him."

"Now an extra man or two will be along soon. Do you mind if we put off talking until later, while I attend to a few things? Make yourself at home; if you want a drink or anything to chew on ..." She waved toward the formidable bar and the array of rich food guarded by the glacial lion, and then went busily off to another part of the house.

To escape the eyes of the servitors watching her Grace wandered, as nonchalantly as she could, toward the rear of the big room where, through high open doors, she had glimpsed a view of broad garden. She went out into it, entering a world of tropical plants and flowers and colorful bushes and trees lighted by small flood lamps set on the ground or fastened to the building and even in the heads of slender, tall, gracefully waving coconut palms which were mostly lighted in blue. It was a bewitching place.

She stayed there for some time, walking about, or just standing and drinking it in. She thought of the social personages, including perhaps Mrs. Forsyth Callader, her favorite, who might be here, so that she could see them at close hand, and even meet them. She went back inside the house to discover that a seven-piece orchestra had appeared, which now struck up, quietly, softly, with muted cadences. Also now three men had arrived.

Two were handsome young men, very nearly pretty, who stood by the doorway, watching it as though expectantly. The third was an older, rather tall, sharp-faced man with long, flowing dark hair; he looked just a bit seedy. All three glanced at Grace. The almost pretty men's faces remained impassive and uninterested and they turned away at once. Grace fancied that across the face of the third a grimace passed, but she was sure she must be mistaken when he came over to her, bowed slightly, and was extremely gracious when he said, "Felice told me all about you. I'm Harold Devin, the artist. Would you care to dance?"

Grace regarded the empty bare spaces. "I—no, thank you, not just yet at least."

"Would you like a drink?"

"I think I need—That is, yes, thank you."

"Scotch and soda?"

"That will be fine."

Grace was grateful to Mr. Devin for his attentions and flattered by them; he seemed to be very charming. She sat on a soft couch and in a a moment he joined her, carrying two drinks. After they sipped for the first time Grace inquired, "What sort of things do you paint, Mr. Devin?"

"Well, for one thing, that." He pointed to a large portrait above the Gargantuan fireplace.

Grace had not previously noticed the huge portrait of Felice; she saw now that it was an almost outrageously glamorized one; though Felice was still an attractive woman, she had not retained the extent of youth or ever was as beautiful as the artist had made her out to be. Lamely in spirit, but injecting as much conviction as she could in her tone, Grace said, "It's very nice."

The artist regarded her. He smiled slightly and said bitterly, "There are many forms of prostitution, some worse than selling your body."

She could find nothing to say to that shocking statement. She glanced at her watch and saw it was now a quarter to six. The sound of car doors being snapped shut and then that of voices came from outside. The man at the door strode to a side room, from which Felice then emerged swiftly, to go to the door; there was no sign yet of her husband. She received two couples, who greeted her gaily, one of the women gushing. The younger was more reserved and dignified, being so beautifully gowned that she looked like a posed model.

Grace recognized her, but only faintly. "Why," she said, "that's—that's—"

"Deborah Glenridge," Mr. Devin supplied.

"Yes!" Grace almost gasped. "She led the cotillion ball last year in New York."

"Then you know her?"

"Oh, no! I've just read about her."

"Would you like to meet her?"

"I—why—oh, yes, Mr. Devin."

The artist went over to Deborah Glenridge and her escort and brought them back. Grace, who got to her feet to be introduced, said she was glad to meet them, while she took in, with acute pleasure, the girl's startling beauty as set off by her gown and jewels.

Deborah Glenridge appraised Grace coolly, as if instantly and instinctively placing a value on her. She murmured in an affected tone, "How do you do?" Then, abruptly, she turned away with her escort and went to the bar.

Grace flushed. The girl might have said in so many words that she had accurately gauged her importance in the scale of things here and found it to be worthless. She heard the artist speaking at her side. "The trouble with her," he said, "is that she doesn't need her portrait painted right now." He mused. "But after a few more affairs and a couple of marriages and still more affairs and another marriage, she will, she will."

Grace stared at him. She did not think he could be serious; his cynical statement, surely, was meant to be a joke. She laughed nervously, and said, "It's a wonderful party."

He gave her a look and excused himself, leaving her alone. People were now arriving fast, in bunches. Grace saw the two pretty boys hovering over and talking with animation, or listening with grave intensity, to two old women, one of whom was deeply wrinkled. Grace wondered if they had come alone, like her, without escorts.

There was no sign of the host, and it was now a little after six. A buzz of conversation began to rise in the room. The orchestra played more loudly so that it could be heard by the few people dancing. Grace felt apart, out of things, and foreign to the easy, glib, accentuated talk about the Everglades Club and its orange garden and golf terrace and tombola luncheons, the Bath and Tennis, Ta-Boo, the Continental, and last night's parties.

There was a shout from the crowd. At the top of the broad stairs a figure had appeared, a tall, athletic-looking man. It was the host, who had slipped in the back way, to change. Derisively hilarious hoots greeted him as he bounded down the stairway; to those giving these he thumbed his nose, to others he apologized as he went about greeting people he had not been on hand to receive. It was treated as being highly amusing. His glance passed over Grace, not knowing who she was, and then he joined Felice at the door to receive more people. Because there were so many of these Grace excused Felice for not bringing her husband to her, telling herself that she would met him later.

Grace's drink had long been consumed. Mr. Devin did not come back. She felt hungry and went, defiantly alone, to the food table and partook of the delicious offerings there. No one paid any attention to her or offered to speak to her. She looked about for Mr. Devin but could not see him in the crowd, which she estimated now to consist of more than a hundred and fifty people, with more continually arriving. The heat generated in the room was beginning to melt the ice lion.

She accepted a second drink from a serviceman who appeared before her even though she knew she should not, for it was apt to make her squiffy. But she had to have something to occupy herself with. She stood alone, surrounded by a lively sea of expensive people who spoke dynamically and in a supercilious manner, and who laughed loudly. A man recounted a story at which his group broke into uproarious laughter. It took Grace a long moment to understand the point of the story; when she did, her face flushed with shame.

In confusion she turned, to look at the front door. In it was standing a woman whose identity she could not mistake. Mrs. Forsyth Callader, groomed and gowned and jeweled to be the most regal figure Grace had ever seen, surveyed the room as though considering if it was worthy of her presence. Grace thrilled at the sight of the great social leader who, in spite of certain things people said about her—mere malicious gossip —would certainly never listen to an off-color story.

Even Felice and her husband greeted her deferentially, and escorted her into the room, where she was surrounded by an attentive group whose voices lifted unnaturally high when they addressed her. Mrs. Callader paid little attention, but looked about as though searching for a particular person. Grace did not hope to meet her; it was enough to be in the same room with her, at the same party, merely to be able to see her. Grace looked at her watch and saw that Mrs. Callader had arrived at the party at seven thirty, half an hour after it was supposed to end; that certainly was the way to do things.

She witnessed at close hand the arrival of two couples, neither sober, who drew the attention of all those near the doorway. From remarks not whispered, but sharply and audibly expressed, often in deep voices by women, Grace gathered that the first couple were not man and wife, but each was the mate of another. The other couple, arriving right on top of the first, caused the immediate sensation, for they comprised the true mates of the first couple; some time ago they had exchanged wives and husbands. The second sensation came when one of the wives saw her husband and, with a tipsy shriek, threw her arms passionately about him, crying out how much she loved him. The second wife, not to be outdone, followed suit with her husband, so that the correctly mated couples stood there embracing and tearfully and publicly deciding to go back to each other.

The event caused ripples of comment to sweep over the entire party. "Shocking!" Grace heard, and "Scandalous!" and to both she vehemently agreed, glad for this support of a high moral standard. But then it penetrated to her that the people uttering these comments did not seem to take them seriously, and with a start Grace realized that the words were applied, not censoriously to the vicious lack of decency so blatantly displayed, but mockingly to the readjustment.

Confused and troubled, Grace went out into the garden again. There she would find sanctuary for her disturbed thoughts. The peaceful beauty of the garden was now rather well occupied. Groups stood about holding glasses and drinking from them, and taking other glasses from servingmen passing with trays. One couple stood closely embraced, quite frankly, and Grace hurried away from them when the man's hand, on the woman's back, slipped down below her waist.

She stopped, her heart beating fast with apprehension she did not entirely understand. Her ears caught what a woman was saying in a group nearby. The story had only just begun, and Grace was drawn, as though compelled, to follow it to its dreadful conclusion, which was greeted with wild laughter.

The garden seemed desecrated. She could no longer stay there. She went back into the house. Even though now well after eight, the party continued to grow. The room was so crowded that there was hardly space to move. It was nearly impossible to hear the orchestra, which could be seen to be playing furiously, above the shrill cacophony of talk, cries, extravagant exclamations, and shrieking laughter. Grace looked about again for Mr. Devin, but still could not see him; apparently he had deserted her entirely.

A medium-sized, extremely good-looking man, faultlessly dressed, came up to her and without preliminary of any kind boldly demanded, "Who are you?"

She thought he might be a detective who was questioning her presence at the party. She faltered, "Why, I—I'm Grace Brantley."

He thought over her name while he regarded her with

piercing dark eyes. "Of the Hobe Sound Brantleys?"

"Oh, no. I'm just a schoolteacher."

He stated unequivocably, "You're funning me."

"'Funning' you?" she repeated, not understanding at once, and then realizing he thought she was not serious. "I'm really a teacher."

He stared at her as though she had said something indecent. In a tone of ultimate disgust he exclaimed, "*School-teacher!*" and then stomped away.

More confused than ever, Grace felt a hand on her elbow. Mr. Devin stood there. Grace blurted, "I thought you'd left."

"I don't dare leave yet."

She didn't comment on that surprising statement, but indicated the man who had just departed and asked, "Who is that?"

"Are you sure you want to know?"

"I—yes."

Mr. Devin peered at her. He looked as if, since she saw him last, he had been doing quite a bit of drinking. He seemed to consider something, made his decision about it, and then he said, "Why, he's this season's leading stud."

"'Stud'?"

"You don't know what I mean?"

"Why . . . " In a low voice she murmured, "I guess I do. It—it's really like that?"

"Really."

Grace put down her drink, not finishing it, not wanting to risk it affecting the slight dizziness she already felt. She asked, "What did you mean by saying you didn't dare leave yet?"

Again he considered before making the decision to tell her. He took a deep draught of his drink. It seemed to help him to say, "I'm still earning my prostitute's fee for the atrocity above the fireplace."

Grace glanced, above the heads of the milling throng, at the too highly glamorized portrait of Felice. Perception stabbed into her. She realized it had been a grimace she saw on the artist's face when he first came to her. "You mean she makes you come to these parties and be an extra man, the way she told you to look after me?"

"Oh, I get something out of it, too, by being here," he explained candidly. "The chance to pick up new commissions. There hasn't been anything doing tonight and now everybody's so drunk they couldn't be sucked into a miniature—or at least remember it afterward."

That, then, was why he had come back to her. Grace looked away from him and murmured miserably, "How late do you have to stay?"

"Until she gives me the word. This will go on here until about eleven, with people from other parties dropping in with their house guests. Then what's left go to the various late bistros for supper. There some will choose partners who they'll spend the rest of the night with."

Even in the depths of her shock Grace noted and disapproved of his bad grammar. She pleaded, "Please don't say things like that to me."

"You mean you still like the party?"

Valiantly, still wanting to believe in something, Grace replied stiffly, "It's all right."

Mr. Devin addressed her crossly and firmly. "Look around you."

Grace looked.

She saw one of the old women, the wrinkled one, leaving with one of the pretty boys; she could not fathom what their association meant until she wondered how such a young man could have anything to do with an old woman like that. Then she knew that the woman sought it and undoubtedly—Grace could hardly use the term even in her mind—paid him.

In a corner of the room the beauteous and glamorous Deborah Glenridge was executing a dance for a highly entertained audience of both men and women. One shoulder strap had fallen down, her hair was mussed, her eyes were glazed in her head thrown far back, and her gown was hiked up to the bare brown thighs to give her limbs freedom as she thrust out and in with her body and ground her hips like a burlesque stripper.

Recoiling, Grace closed her eyes, turning her head, not

wanting to see this. She opened them to a worse sight.

Mrs. Forsyth Callader did not have youth to excuse her in small part. She was sprawled on a couch in greater disarray than Deborah Glenridge, with nothing regal about her now. Her hair was actually down over one eye. She had lost a slipper and her foot, in her wrinkled stocking, waved in the air as though looking for it. Her face showed all its deep lines in a pasty complexion; she looked ugly and mean. She held a glass to her lips, drained it, and then lifted it high, bawling for another drink.

Most ghastly of all, at her side, taking the glass from her to get her another drink, and obviously her chosen companion, was this season's leading stud. Mrs. Callader had found what she had been looking for.

Grace shuddered, barely able to credit her senses. Now she believed, horribly, the gossip about the social leader. She felt cruelly betrayed. For an instant she thought she was going to faint. Filled with revulsion, she was actually nauseated and feared she might be ill right there before all these people.

She turned to Mr. Devin as though he, no matter if she was now repelled by him as well as by the others, might help her. She gasped, "I must say good-by to Felice and Mr. Northampton, and thank them."

"You can't," Mr. Devin replied.

"Can't?" Grace repeated blankly.

"They've gone to another party," Mr. Devin explained.

"Left their own party?"

"They'll be back later. It's supposed to be a joke. You're supposed to laugh because it's supposed to be funny."

Grace laughed, but not because it was funny. This, the final indignity, included the fact that she had not even met Felice's husband and host of the party. And Felice, obviously, had forgotten her, or, even worse, took this means of snubbing her.

Grace turned from Mr. Devin, and started for the door, pushing between people, rudely, until she was outside. Her only thought was to get away, quickly, and she kept on going, past groups of chauffeurs standing around parked cars. She was sure that if this was what Felice's life had become she did not want to see her friend again, ever. Outside the gates, when she reached the road, a brown-uniformed policeman on duty there asked her, "Can I help you?"

Distraught, hardly knowing what she was saying, Grace cried in reply, "The house, it's so beautiful! And the garden and all—but the people, the people!"

He stared at her as she went off down the road, fleeing.

Belatedly Grace remembered seeing that the ice lion, which had once—it seemed long ago—symbolized the grandness of the party, had melted to an unrecognizable shape.

Marjorie Kinnan Rawlings

(1896–1953) emphasized place and its strong effect on people's lives in her writing. Half her life had passed in Maryland, Washington, D.C., Wisconsin, and upper New York state new home in fond terms: "From my first moment here, I have felt more at home than since my childhood days on my father's farm in Maryland." She made thousands of her readers aware

before she settled in 1928 in Cross Creek, where she bought an orange grove that she tried unsuccessfully to harvest; then she began writing her famous stories of the "cracker" people around her. She described her of the area of central Florida that she described so well in *South Moon Under* (1933); *The Yearling* (1938), which won the Pulitzer Prize; a collection of short stories entitled *When the Whippoorwill* (1940), from which "A Plumb

Clare Conscience" is taken; the autobiographical *Cross Creek* (1942); and *Cross Creek Cookery* (1942).

Before she discovered her talent for writing about the people around her, she had tried to write English gothic romances—without success. Only when she began to write about the experiences of living in the scrub country east of Ocala and southeast of Gainesville did she find her true subject. By the time she left there to live in St. Augustine, she had produced some of the finest and most authentic regional literature of this century.

"A Plumb Clare Conscience" is typical of her realistic treatment of the people she came to know so well and whose speech and habits she captured so successfully. In it she recounts the chase of a moonshiner by a revenuer through the palmetto bushes and the long night when the agent tries to outwait his quarry. Having made moonshine herself, she could empathize with the quarry. She once wrote her editor and friend Maxwell Perkins, "The federal agents have been very active lately, so don't be too surprised if your correspondent has the misfortune to be run in! If it should happen please don't bail me out, because the jailhouse would be a splendid place for quiet work!"

Marjorie Kinnan Rawlings

A Plumb Clare Conscience

HINER TIM was missing.

He had left his cabin in the piney-woods, without food, without money, without a gun, and he had not returned.

Fifteen years of 'shining have scraped his Cracker ribs through tight places. Revenue agents have found and destroyed his still time and again. But a few hours after, he is usually home, personally undamaged, ready to set another mash when the horizon shall be clear of the federal storm. This he attributes to his far ancestry of Carolina Irish. He is "mostly Irish," he says.

"Like a bird-dog. Times, he's brown and white; times, he's black and white, or mixed-like; times, he's got a leetle collie in him, or a leetle hound. But that's what he is, mostly bird-dog."

He has clung zestfully to his 'shining. It is his destiny to make low-bush corn liquor. His removal, by death or incarceration, would be a loss to the county, for his liquor is as sound as the best Kentucky Bourbon. It is made of pure running branch water, corn, and cane-sugar. He has a fierce contempt for 'shiners who cut the mash with lye, color the liquor with tobacco-juice, or hurry the fermentation with stable manure. Ocklawaha River 'shine ranks next after Tim's, but it is vitriol in comparison.

During the forty-eight hours of his disappearance it seemed that he must have made his last run. He was trapped in the swamp. His new partner, a Georgia boy, showed up at the cabin at the end of the first twenty-four hours to report the catastrophe to Tim's wife. They had mixed the mash by moonlight the previous night, and had been trailed to the still early that morning. Two agents had taken them by surprise, had smashed the still and seized Tim's battered old car. The Georgia boy escaped. Tim was hemmed in.

"Cooter" in person must have been tipped off to the still's location. The federal agent has the long, leathery brown neck, the beaked nose, and glittering pop-eyes of that variety of turtle, and it was only logical that the Florida 'shiners should give him its name. "Cooter" surely, said the Georgian, had shot Tim if he did not soon bring him in.

The morning of the second day Tim had not been brought in. He must therefore be lying in the swamp, dead or mortally wounded. He could not be there alive, voluntarily. We drove over to his cabin. Tim's wife was there, the Georgia boy, and two Cracker friends who, like us, had received word of his plight. The Georgian described the lay of the country where Tim was caught.

The still, against Tim's better judgment, was located in black-jack. Black-jack, for Florida, is open country. Scraggly black-jack oaks, an inch or two in thickness, are scattered loosely. The sandy soil is spotted with scrub palmettos, sweet myrtle, and low-bush huckleberries. The still lay here, in a thicket. The land sloped down to a leaf-brown branch which widened into something of a pond. Beyond the branch was a loathsome stretch of marsh, mucky of water, a-stink with decaying lily-pads, swarming with frogs, mosquitoes, and moccasins. Next came a fringe of impenetrably dense palmetto scrub, and then the lush jungle of virgin hammock.

Proximity to running water is the first requisite for 'shining, but the need of good cover runs it a close second. It was in hammock that Tim was most at home and there he would have preferred to locate the still. He had yielded to his partner's dislike of crossing the swamp to get to water. The Georgian admitted they had been on the right side for comfort but the wrong for safety. He had last seen Tim at the edge of the swamp, about to cross, with Cooter close on his heels and Cooter's henchman heading him off from the safe refuge of the hammock.

"He's shore drowned or shot, one," the boy lamented.

Tim's wife said: "Give him 'til late evenin' afore you raises up a fuss, lookin' for him."

At two o'clock in the afternoon Tim walked in.

He was scarcely recognizable. His face and hands were swollen out of shape. The Mongolian cast of his heavy-lidded eyes was accentuated, and he looked like a puffy scarlet Chinaman. He was soaked with sweat from his long walk. The front of his blue shirt and blue pin-check pants was stained with dark muck.

"Hi-yah!" he said and went to the water-bucket.

He drained the gourd dipper several times. He looked at the last empty bottom.

"I drinkt more water then," he remarked, "than I've drinkt ary week."

He picked up a slab of corn bread and a piece of white bacon from the remains on the table and sat down in a cowhide-bottomed chair by the clay fireplace. He looked around with interest to see who was present. He ignored all questions and remarks as he ate, concentratedly but without greed. When he had finished he opened the snuff-box on the pine mantel and rolled a generous pinch inside his lips. He leaned forward, his hands on his knees. The two Cracker friends hitched closer and spat in the fireplace.

Tim nodded at us severally.

"I orter allus let my conscience be my guide," he announced solemnly.

The Georgia boy fidgeted, scuffling his feet on the deerskin rug.

"Didn't I say I was oneasy, yestiddy mornin' afore we sets out for the still?"

The boy nodded.

"That was my conscience a-tellin' me to lay low!

"We'd done set the mash that night and gone back to git us a piece o' sleep," he explained for the general benefit.

"When I walked up at crack o' day I felt kind o' froggy. Not scairt, jest froggy. And I says to myself, iffen I still feels that-a-way when we gits there, I ain't goin' to turn into no still.

"My conscience had tol' me 'twa'n't no place for a still. No trees around the water, jest a plumb naked pond." He frowned sternly at his partner. "I've had me a ground-hog still like that one, in open country, but I've had me some watchment."

"I should of give in to you," agreed the Georgia boy. "I thought you was kilt dead. Last time I seed you, you was shore surrounded. What the devil did you do with Cooter?"

Tim pondered. Then he slapped his knees and broke into cat-sneezes of laughter.

"Well, I cain't say I've outrunned Cooter. I can't exactly say I've outsmarted him. But I shore kin say I've done out-waited him!"

"Tim!" said his wife. "Where at?"

He ignored her and addressed the boy.

"Remember jest afore we turns in to the dirt road yestiddy mornin'? A car passes us, a Chivvolay? A couple o' quarelookin' sap-suckers in it?"

"I shore remember that thing."

"And recolleck, I says my conscience done tol' me to keep right on a-goin'? Well, I shore orter allus foller my conscience. That was Cooter hisself, a-trackin' us. And we pottered around a piece, and was fixin' to take out, when we heerd a pistol shoot? Well, right then we'd orter done been gone!

"But we stops to look, like dogged cur'ous deer—and into the black-jack comes the Chivvolay. And I says to you, 'Yonder's them scoundrels now!'"

The Georgian shivered. Tim jerked a thumb in his direction.

"He's a noble-timid boy," he remarked to the rest of us. "So I tells him, 'You walk down to the branch and squat. I'll see kin I mislead 'em into the hammock.'"

"But when I sees one o' them fellers nosin' along behind me," interrupted the Georgian, "I lights out for the hard road and I'm long gone. I looks back and sees you headed for the swamp."

Tim nodded.

"I seed you had a fair chanct," he said, "so I threw over the ol' barrel thumper, and the whole works took after me."

"Well," he chuckled, "hit's a pore set o' heels cain't save a scairt body. I reckon I could outrun ary one o' them rascals myself, jest runnin'. Me and Cooter done some runnin', too.

"And while we was runnin', I had about half a mile to study in. We was crowdin' on toward the swamp, not makin' as much time as we was at first, when I looks back and notices hit's jest only Cooter after me. T'other of them catbirds, the one that took after you, had done cut in the short way from the side, like, and was makin' the hammock ahead o' me.

"We splashed thu the swamp and hit the palmeeters.

"If I'd had thirty more yards, I'd done been safe in the hammock. I'd done been in the clare. I'd been home yestiddy for a hot dinner."

He nodded to his wife.

"But I couldn't make the hammock."

He lipped snuff again and lowered his voice confidentially.

"So I plays the rabbit on them. I jumps into the palmeeters. I gits down hog-style and crawls off. I plumb snaked into those palmeeter clumps and takes me a palmeeter root for a pillow.

"That was yestiddy mornin'," he said, "and I ain't so much as moved my jawbones until this mornin'."

The Georgian puzzled. "Cain't them fellers foller ary track?" he asked.

"Cooter's a prime bloodhound." Tim winked broadly. "But I was hittin' the ground too fur apart!

"Well," he went on, "they was shore I hadn't made the hammock without they'd of seed me. So they beats around and tracks here and yonder, and pokes in the palmeeters, scairt as chickens they'd fall on snakeses, and they sits down to wait for me.

"I says to myself, 'I hope you scoundrels does squat there.'

"I could hear them talkin' plain as this room. Cooter says:

'I know that feller in the blue pants squatted in here in the palmeeters, but say, that son of a bitch in the striped shirt that runned to the hard road, he didn't even go around the stumps, he jest tossed over 'em!'

"We was jest out of the swamp, like, and I was all buried up in the mud. Hit shore was cold, wet muck, black as a nigger's gizzard. When the sun gits high and beats down thu these palmeeter fans, one side o' me was a-freezin' and t'other was a-burnin' up.

"Along toward noon I was so half froze and half scorched I thinks I've been there long enough. And then I studies, and I says, 'Hit'll be a heap longer thirty days in the county jail.' So I settles down to enjoy myself. There's times a palmeeter root's shore a soft pillow. If my wife was to put me a thing like that in the bed, I'd shore chunk it at her, but me and that palmeeter root got real fondlike.

"The antses got to me and got a-stingin', but Cooter must a plumb set in some, for I heerd him a-slappin' and a-cussin'. I begins to get thirsty and my tongue shore swole up when the other catbird goes back to the Chivvolay and brings 'em a jar o' water. But I thinks: 'Let 'em drink.'

"Cooter sends his man back to smash up the still, but he done a mighty sorry job. I can git it together again in no great whiles.

"Then I hears 'em crank up the Chivvolay and my ol' fliv-ver and go off. I studies some and I figgers they mought not o'gone no further than the hard road, a trap, like. So I lays quiet a piece longer.

"'Long in the evenin' 'bout three o'clock I could smell my shirt smokin' in the heat. I heerd the mosquitoes makin' that fuss they makes when they's so full o' blood they cain't fly. I says to 'em, 'Git your rations, you scoundrels. I'll get mine to-morrer.' I don't even slap 'em. You kin hear a feller slappin'.

"I thought of liftin' my head to look. But I've done turkey-hunted. You know, when you're sittin' quiet, waitin' for a gobbler to fly in? And a squirrel comes down a tree and comes on you sudden-like? That squirrel is goin' to run up and chatter. And over yonder in the black-jack I heerd a squirrel run up and chatter. So I knowed Cooter was there right on.

"'Long about good-dark he starts hisself a skeeter smudge and I could smell it a-smokin'. I says: 'Well, you rascal, hit's a question who fust gits a bait o' waitin', you or me, one.' The mosquitoes was crowdin' so on me they was fightin' for standin'- room. A big ol' moccasin slides by so clost I could o' spit on him, but I figgers 'twa'n't no use to budge. I could smell rattlesnake musk along in the night. Lyin' there in the dark, dogged iffen hit didn't make me kind o' faintified. I says: 'Go give Cooter a smell of you.'"

Tim chuckled deeply.

"I don't reckon Cooter nor me would study none on spendin' another day and another night in jest that pertickler fashion. But anyways, I shore outwaited him.

"Come crack o' day, t'other feller comes back. They comes to the edge o' the palmeeters.

"'They ain't nary mortal in there,' says the other.

"'I reckon not,' says Cooter. 'If they is, hit ain't no human being. Hit's half rabbit or half snake or half wildcat, but hit ain't human.'

"And then they goes off. I mean, they' good gone."

Tim yawned sleepily.

"Well, hit serves me dogged right," he admitted. "I shore knowed better. It proves I orter allus let my conscience be my guide."

"I mean!" agreed the Georgia boy. "You kin put that ol' still on top of a alligator and I ain't got ary word to say. How soon kin we fix to git to work again?"

"To-morrer. Them scoundrels done the carelessest smash-in'."

"Reckon they'll be traipsin' back again?"

Tim shook his head.

"No. We ain't in ary danger a whiles yet. Cooter'll be crowdin' on to Marion County. I reckon——"

He rose and streched.

"I reckon for about thirty days I'd orter have a plumb clare conscience."

Isaac Bashevis Singer

(1904–   ) differs from the other authors included here because he was born in Europe (he moved to Miami Beach late in life) and writes primarily in Yiddish. He grew up in Goray, was published, and he continued to write and translate Yiddish stories, one of which was turned into the movie *Yentl*. Among his other books are *Gimpel the Fool and Other Stories*

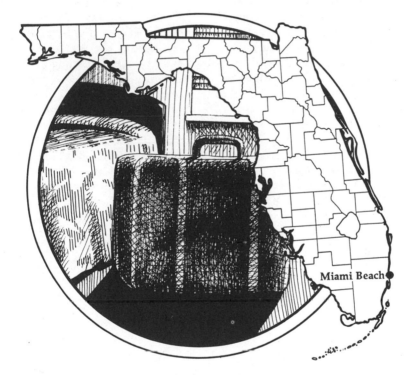

Miami Beach

Warsaw, where he learned the art of story-telling from his relatives and eked out a hard life as a proofreader and literary translator. He came to the United States in 1934, the same year his first book, *Satan in* (1957), *The Magician of Lublin* (1960), and *Enemies, a Love Story* (1972). His great talent was finally recognized when he was awarded the 1978 Nobel Prize for Literature and two National Book Awards. Many of his stories, published in Yiddish in New York's *Jewish Daily Forward*, take place in Poland.

His story "Alone" (1962) takes place in Miami Beach, where Singer bought a condominium in 1973. A lonely man rents a room in a hotel that suddenly closes. He moves into another seedy hotel run by a deformed Cuban girl, wanders by bus through the city, then returns to his room during a storm. After rejecting the seductive overtures of the girl, he ponders some philosophical questions dealing with the world of appearance and superior beings.

The story contains several elements familiar to those who know Miami Beach: Cuban and Jewish residents, sudden changes in weather, shabby hotels. The story shows a different side of sunny Miami Beach and touches on deep issues that Singer has wrestled with since his early days in Poland: good and evil, dreams and reality. Significantly, Miami Beach has confronted similar issues, for example, how to stop the influx of drugs and how to accommodate refugees. The standoff of dreams and reality can also be seen in the Art Deco revival.

The two hotels that the narrator stayed in might have been part of the Art Deco District around Flamingo Park. Its eighty blocks have eight hundred buildings, many built during the 1930s in a style that emphasized glass-block construction, porthole windows, ribbon windows, and bands of pastel decoration. Politicians and developers who want to raze the buildings and build more high-rise apartments have been confronted by preservationists who have begun to renovate the buildings, found nowhere else in such numbers.

Isaac Bashevis Singer

Alone

ANY TIMES in the past I have wished the impossible to happen—and then it happened. But though my wish came true, it was in such a topsy-turvy way that it appeared the Hidden Powers were trying to show me I didn't understand my own needs. That's what occurred that summer in Miami Beach. I had been living in a large hotel full of South American tourists who had come to Miami to cool off, as well as with people like myself who suffered from hay fever. I was fed up with the whole business—splashing about in the ocean with those noisy guests; hearing Spanish all day long; eating heavy meals twice each day. If I read a Yiddish newspaper or book, the others looked at me with astonishment. So it happened that taking a walk one day, I said out loud: "I wish I were alone in a hotel." An imp must have overheard me, for immediately he began to set a trap.

When I came down to breakfast the next morning, I found the hotel lobby in confusion. Guests stood about in small groups, their voices louder than usual. Valises were piled all over. Bellboys were running about pushing carts loaded with clothing. I asked someone what was the matter. "Didn't you hear the announcement over the public-address system? They've closed the hotel." "Why?" I asked. "They're bankrupt." The man moved away, annoyed at my ignorance. Here was a riddle: the hotel was closing! Yet so far as I knew, it did a good business. And how could you suddenly close a hotel with hundreds of guests? But in America I had decided it was better not to ask too many questions.

The air conditioning had already been shut off and the air in the lobby was musty. A long line of guests stood at the cashier's desk to pay their bills. Everywhere there was turmoil. People crushed out cigarettes on the marble floor. Children tore leaves and flowers off the potted tropical plants. Some South Americans, who only yesterday had pretended to be full-blooded Latins, were now talking loudly in Yiddish. I myself had very little to pack, only one valise. Taking it, I went in search of another hotel. Outside, the burning sun reminded me of the Talmudic story of how, on the plains of Mamre, God had removed the sun from its case so that no strangers would bother Abraham. I felt a little giddy. The days of my bachelorhood came back when, carefree, I used to pack all my belongings in one valise, leave, and within five minutes find myself another room. Passing a small hotel, which looked somewhat run-down, I read the sign: "Off-Season Rates from $2 a Day." What could be cheaper? I went inside. There was no air conditioning. A hunchbacked girl with black piercing eyes stood behind the desk. I asked her if I could have a room.

"The whole hotel," she answered.

"No one is here?"

"Nobody." The girl laughed, displaying a broken row of teeth with large gaps between. She spoke with a Spanish accent.

She had come from Cuba, she told me. I took a room. The hunchback led me into a narrow elevator, which took us up to the third floor. There we walked down a long, dark corridor meagerly lit by a single bulb. She opened a door and let me into my room, like a prisoner into his cell. The window, covered by mosquito netting, looked out over the Atlantic. On the walls the paint was peeling, and the rug on the floor was threadbare and colorless. The bathroom smelled of mildew, the closet of moth repellent. The bed linen, though clean, was damp. I unpacked my things and went downstairs. Everything was mine alone: the swimming pool, the beach, the ocean. In the patio stood a group of dilapidated canvas chairs. All around the sun beat down. The sea was yellow, the waves low and lazy, barely moving, as if they too were fatigued by the stifling heat. Only occasionally, out of duty, they tossed up a few specks of foam. A single sea gull stood on the water trying to decide whether or not to catch a fish. Here before me, drenched in sunlight, was a summer melancholy—odd, since melancholy usually suggests autumn. Mankind, it seemed, had perished in some catastrophe, and I was left, like Noah—but in an empty ark, without sons, without a wife, without any animals. I could have swum naked, nevertheless I put on my bathing suit. The water was so warm, the ocean might have been a bathtub. Loose bunches of seaweed floated about. Shyness had held me back in the first hotel—here it was solitude. Who can play games in an empty world? I could swim a little, but who would rescue me if something went wrong? The Hidden Powers had provided me with an empty hotel—but they could just as easily provide me with an undertow, a deep hole, a shark, or a sea serpent. Those who toy with the unknown must be doubly careful.

After a while I came out of the water and lay down on one of the limp canvas beach chairs. My body was pale, my skull bare, and though my eyes were protected by tinted glasses, the sun's rays glared through. The light-blue sky was cloudless. The air smelled of salt, fish, and mangoes. There was no division, I felt, between the organic and the inorganic. Everything around me, each grain of sand, each pebble, was breathing, growing, lusting. Through the heavenly channels, which, says the Cabala, control the flow of Divine Mercy, came truths impossible to grasp in a northern climate. I had lost all ambition; I felt lazy; my few wants were petty and material—a glass of lemonade or orange juice. In my fancy a hot-eyed woman moved into the hotel for a few nights. I hadn't meant I wanted a hotel completely to myself. The imp had either misunderstood or was pretending to. Like all forms of life, I, too, wanted to be fruitful, wanted to multiply—or at least to go through the motions. I was prepared to forget any moral or aesthetic demands. I was ready to cover my guilt with a sheet and to give way wholly, like a blind man, to the sense of touch. At the same time the eternal question tapped in my brain: Who is behind the world of appearance? Is it Substance with its Infinite Attributes? Is it the Monad of all Monads? Is it the Absolute, Blind Will, the Unconscious? Some kind of superior being has to be hidden in back of all these illusions.

On the sea, oily-yellow near the shore, glassy-green farther out, a sail walked over the water like a shrouded corpse. Bent forward, it looked as if it were trying to call something up from the depths. Overhead flew a small airplane trailing a sign: MARGOLIES' RESTAURANT—KOSHER, 7 COURSES, $1.75. So the Creation had not yet returned to primeval chaos. They still served soup with kasha and kneidlach, knishes and stuffed derma at Margolies' restaurant. In that case perhaps tomorrow I would receive a letter. I had been promised my mail would be forwarded. It was my only link, in Miami, with the outside world. I'm always amazed that someone has written me, taken the trouble to stamp and mail the envelope. I look for cryptic meanings, even on the blank side of the paper.

II

WHEN YOU are alone, how long the day can be! I read a book and two newspapers, drank a cup of coffee in a cafeteria, worked a crossword puzzle. I stopped at a store that auctioned Oriental rugs, went into another where Wall Street stocks were sold. True, I was on Collins Avenue in Miami Beach, but I felt like a ghost, cut off from everything. I went into the library and asked a question—the librarian grew frightened. I was like a man who had died, whose space had already been filled. I passed many hotels, each with its special decorations and attractions. The palm trees were topped by half-wilted fans of leaves, and their coconuts hung like heavy testicles. Everything seemed motionless, even the shiny new automobiles gliding over the asphalt. Every object continued its existence with that effortless force which is, perhaps, the essence of all being.

I bought a magazine, but was unable to read past the first

few lines. Getting on a bus, I let myself be taken aimlessly over causeways, islands with ponds, streets lined with villas. The inhabitants, building on a wasteland, had planted trees and flowering plants from all parts of the world; they had filled up shallow inlets along the shore; they had created architectural wonders and had worked out elaborate schemes for pleasure. A planned hedonism. But the boredom of the desert remained. No loud music could dispel it, no garishness wipe it out. We passed a cactus plant whose blades and dusty needles had brought forth a red flower. We rode near a lake surrounded by groups of flamingos airing their wings, and the water mirrored their long beaks and pink feathers. An assembly of birds. Wild ducks flew about, quacking—the swampland refused to give way.

I looked out the open window of the bus. All that I saw was new, yet it appeared old and weary: grandmothers with dyed hair and rouged cheeks, girls in bikinis barely covering their shame, tanned young men guzzling Coca-Cola on water skis.

An old man lay sprawled on the deck of a yacht, warming his rheumatic legs, his white-haired chest open to the sun. He smiled wanly. Nearby, the mistress to whom he had willed his fortune picked at her toes with red fingernails, as certain of her charms as that the sun would rise tomorrow. A dog stood at the stern, gazing haughtily at the yacht's wake, yawning.

It took a long time to reach the end of the line. Once there, I got on another bus. We rode past a pier where freshly caught fish were being weighed. Their bizarre colors, gory skin wounds, glassy eyes, mouths full of congealed blood, sharp-pointed teeth—all were evidence of a wickedness as deep as the abyss. Men gutted the fishes with an unholy joy. The bus passed a snake farm, a monkey colony. I saw houses eaten up by termites and a pond of brackish water in which the descendants of the primeval snake crawled and slithered. Parrots screeched with strident voices. At times, strange smells blew in through the bus window, stenches so dense they made my head throb.

Thank God the summer day is shorter in the South than in
the North. Evening fell suddenly, without any dusk. Over the
lagoons and highways, so thick no light could penetrate,
hovered a jungle darkness. Automobiles, headlamps on, slid
forward. The moon emerged extraordinarily large and red; it
hung in the sky like a geographer's globe bearing a map not
of this world. The night had an aura of miracle and cosmic
change. A hope I had never forsaken awoke in me: Was I
destined to witness an upheaval in the solar system? Perhaps
the moon was about to fall down. Perhaps the earth, tearing itself out of its orbit around the sun, would wander into new
constellations.

The bus meandered through unknown regions until it
returned to Lincoln Road and the fancy stores, half-empty in
summer but still stocked with whatever a rich tourist might
desire—an ermine wrap, a chinchilla collar, a twelve-carat
diamond, an original Picasso drawing. The dandified
salesmen, sure in their knowledge that beyond nirvana pulses
karma, conversed among themselves in their air-conditioned
interiors. I wasn't hungry; nevertheless, I went into a
restaurant where a waitress with a newly bleached permanent
served me a full meal, quietly and without fuss. I gave her a
half-dollar. When I left, my stomach ached and my head was
heavy. The late-evening air, baked by the sun, choked me as I
came out. On a nearby building a neon sign flashed the
temperature—it was ninety-six, and the humidity almost as
much! I didn't need a weatherman. Already, lightning flared
in the glowing sky, although I didn't hear thunder. A huge
cloud was descending from above, thick as a mountain, full of
fire and of water. Single drops of rain hit my bald head. The
palm trees looked petrified, expecting the onslaught. I hurried
back toward my empty hotel, wanting to get there before the
rain; besides, I hoped some mail had come for me. But I had
covered barely half the distance when the storm broke. One
gush and I was drenched as if by a huge wave. A fiery rod lit
up the sky and, the same moment, I heard the thunder
crack—a sign the lightning was near me. I wanted to run
inside somewhere, but chairs blown from nearby porches

somersaulted in front of me, blocking my way. Signs were falling down. The top of a palm tree, torn off by the wind, careened past my feet. I saw a second palm tree sheathed in sackcloth, bent to the wind, ready to kneel. In my confusion I kept on running. Sinking into puddles so deep I almost drowned, I rushed forward with the lightness of boyhood. The danger had made me daring, and I screamed and sang, shouting to the storm in its own key. By this time all traffic had stopped, even the automobiles had been abandoned. But I ran on, determined to escape such madness or else go under. I had to get that special-delivery letter, which no one had written and I never received.

I still don't know how I recognized my hotel. I entered the lobby and stood motionless for a few moments, dripping water on the rug. In the mirror across the room, my half-dissolved image reflected itself like a figure in a cubist painting. I managed to get to the elevator and ride up to the third floor. The door of my room stood ajar: inside, mosquitoes, moths, fireflies, and gnats fluttered and buzzed about, sheltering from the storm. The wind had torn down the mosquito net and scattered the papers I had left on the table. The rugs were soaked. I walked over to the window and looked at the ocean. The waves rose like mountains in the middle of seas—monstrous billows ready once and for all to overflow the shores and float the land away. The waters roared with spite and sprayed white foam into the darkness of the night. The waves were barking at the Creator like packs of hounds. With all the strength I had left, I pulled the window down and lowered the blind. I squatted to put my wet books and manuscripts in order. I was hot. Sweat poured from my body, mingling with rivulets of rain water. I peeled off my clothes and they lay near my feet like shells. I felt like a creature who has just emerged from a cocoon.

III

THE STORM had still not reached its climax. The howling wind knocked and banged as if with mighty hammers. The hotel seemed like a ship floating on the ocean. Something came off and crashed down—the roof, a balcony, part of the foundation. Iron bars broke. Metal groaned. Windows tore loose from their casements. The windowpanes rattled. The heavy blind on my window billowed up as easily as a curtain. The room was lit with the glare of a great conflagration. Then came a clap of thunder so strong I laughed in fear. A white figure materialized from the darkness. My heart plummeted, my brain trembled in its socket. I always knew that sooner or later one of that brood would show himself to me bodily, full of horrors that are never told because no one who has seen them has survived to tell the story. I lay there silently, ready for the end.

Then I heard a voice: "Excuse please, señor, I am much afraid. You are asleep?" It was the Cuban hunchback.

"No, come in," I answered her.

"I shake. I think I die with fear," the woman said. "A hurricane like this never come before. You are the only one in this hotel. Please excuse that I disturb you."

"You aren't disturbing me. I would put on the light but I'm not dressed."

"No, no. It is not necessary....I am afraid to be alone. Please let me stay here until the storm is over."

"Certainly. You can lie down if you want. I'll sit on the chair."

"No, I will sit on the chair. Where is the chair, señor? I do not see it."

I got up, found the woman in the darkness, and led her to the armchair. She dragged herself after me, trembling. I wanted to go to the closet and get some clothing. But I stumbled into the bed and fell on top of it. I covered myself quickly with the sheet so that the stranger would not see me naked when the lightning flashed. Soon after, there was another bolt and I saw her sitting in the chair, a deformed creature in an overlarge nightgown, with a hunched back, disheveled hair, long hairy arms, and crooked legs, like a tubercular monkey. Her eyes were wide with an animal's fear.

"Don't be afraid," I said. "The storm will soon be over."

"Yes, yes."

I rested my head on the pillow and lay still with the eerie feeling that the mocking imp was fulfilling my last wish. I had wanted a hotel to myself—and I had it. I had dreamed of a woman coming, like Ruth to Boaz, to my room—a woman had come. Each time the lightning flashed, my eyes met hers. She stared at me intently, as silent as a witch casting a spell. I feared the woman more than I did the hurricane. I had visited Havana once and, there, found the forces of darkness still in possession of their ancient powers. Not even the dead were left in peace—their bones were dug up. At night I had heard the screams of cannibals and the cries of maidens whose blood was sprinkled on the altars of idolaters. She came from there. I wanted to pronounce an incantation against the evil eye and pray to the spirits who have the final word not to let this hag overpower me. Something in me cried out: *Shaddai*, destroy Satan. Meanwhile, the thunder crashed, the seas roared and broke with watery laughter. The walls of my room turned scarlet. In the hellish glare the Cuban witch crouched low like an animal ready to seize its prey—mouth open, showing rotted teeth; matted hair, black on her arms and legs; and feet covered with carbuncles and bunions. Her nightgown had slipped down, and her wrinkled breasts sagged weightlessly. Only the snout and tail were missing.

I must have slept. In my dream I entered a town of steep, narrow streets and barred shutters, under the murky light of an eclipse, in the silence of a Black Sabbath. Catholic funeral processions followed one after the other endlessly, with crosses and coffins, halberds and burning torches. Not one but many corpses were being carried to the graveyard—a complete tribe annihilated. Incense burned. Moaning voices cried a song of utter grief. Swiftly, the coffins changed and took on the form of phylacteries, black and shiny, with knots and thongs. They divided into many compartments—coffins for twins, quadruplets, quintuplets . . .

I opened my eyes. Somebody was sitting on my bed—the Cuban woman. She began to talk thickly in her broken English.

"Do not fear. I won't hurt you. I am a human being, not a beast. My back is broken. But I was not born this way. I fell off a table when I was a child. My mother was too poor to take me to the doctor. My father, he no good, always drunk. He go with bad women, and my mother, she work in a tobacco factory. She cough out her lungs. Why do you shake? A hunchback is not contagious. You will not catch it from me. I have a soul like anyone else—men desire me. Even my boss. He trust me and leave me here in the hotel alone. You are a Jew, eh? He is also a Jew ... from Turkey. He can speak—how do you say it?—Arabic. He marry a German señora, but she is a Nazi. Her first husband was a Nazi. She curse the boss and try to poison him. He sue her but the judge is on her side. I think she bribe him—or give him something else. The boss, he has to pay her—how do you call it?—alimony."

"Why did he marry her in the first place?" I asked, just to say something.

"Well, he love her. He is very much a man, red blood, you know. You have been in love?"

"Yes."

"Where is the señora? Did you marry her?"

"No. They shot her."

"Who?"

"Those same Nazis."

"Uh-huh ... and you were left alone?"

"No, I have a wife."

"Where is your wife?"

"In New York."

"And you are true to her, eh?"

"Yes, I'm faithful."

"Always?"

"Always."

"One time to have fun is all right."

"No, my dear, I want to live out my life honestly."

"Who cares what you do? No one see."

"God sees."

"Well, if you speak of God, I go. But you are a liar. If I not a cripple, you no speak of God. He punish such lies, you pig!"

She spat on me, then got off the bed, and slammed the door behind her. I wiped myself off immediately, but her spittle burned me as if it were hot. I felt my forehead puffing up in the darkness, and my skin itched with a drawing sensation, as if leeches were sucking my blood. I went into the bathroom to wash myself. I wet a towel for a compress and wrapped it around my forehead. I had forgotten about the hurricane. It had stopped without my noticing. I went to sleep, and when I woke up again it was almost noon. My nose was stopped up, my throat was tight, my knees ached. My lower lip was swollen and had broken out in a large cold sore. My clothes were still on the floor, soaking in a huge puddle. The insects that had come in for refuge the night before were clamped to the wall, dead. I opened the window. The air blowing in was cool, though still humid. The sky was an autumn gray and the sea leaden, barely rocking under its own heaviness. I managed to dress and go downstairs. Behind the desk stood the hunchback, pale, thin, with her hair drawn back, and a glint in her black eyes. She wore an old-fashioned blouse edged with yellowed lace. She glanced at me mockingly. "You have to move out," she said. "The boss call and tell me to lock up the hotel."

"Isn't there a letter for me?"

"No letter."

"Please give me my bill."

"No bill."

The Cuban woman looked at me crookedly—a witch who had failed in her witchcraft, a silent partner of the demons surrounding me and of their cunning tricks.

Gore Vidal

(1925–   ), a writer not usually associated with Florida, found in Key West the appropriate setting for a short story about the revenge of a black dwarf on a prejudiced white woman.

and political candidate, often appearing on television. He has written novels about war (*Williwaw*, 1946), lawyers (*In a Yellow Wood*, 1947), homo-sexuality (*The City and the Pillar*,

Key West

Born in West Point, New York, and growing up near Washington, D.C., he was greatly influenced by his grandfather, Senator Thomas P. Gore of Oklahoma. Vidal became a playwright, essayist, novelist

1948 and 1965), the sexual revolution (*Myra Breckinridge*, 1968), and American politics (*Burr*, 1973, and *1876*, 1976).

"Erlinda and Mr. Coffin," first published in 1952, represents one of his few short stories, a genre he abandoned for the novel. Told in the first-person narrative that Vidal likes, it is about a woman in Key West who rents out a room to two people who she thinks are Mr. Coffin and his child ward, Erlinda. When Erlinda, in reality a forty-one-year-old black dwarf, is replaced in a local theatrical production by a prominent woman from the town, she plots and carries out a revenge that seems out of character for such a meek person. It is a tale full of humor and tragedy, and it presents Key Westers unknown in Hemingway's fiction.

Except for St. Augustine, Key West has been the setting for more stories than any other Florida city, partly because it has been the home for so many writers but also because its history offers so many possibilities: sunken treasure, pirates, Indians, deep-sea fishing, hurricanes, and tourists. It is also the end of the line, whether for Highway U.S. 1 or

for persons trying to get as far away as possible but still remain connected to the mainland by bridges. Landlady Craig is such a person, long removed from her South Carolina upbringing but comfortable in her clique of bigoted blue bloods. It is ironic that she mentions President Truman's visits to Key West since he was responsible for desegregating the armed forces.

Mrs. Craig exemplifies a theme found in several of the stories in this collection, that of appearance versus reality. She appears to be open-minded and unbiased, but her real feelings surface when she is presented with Erlinda. And the black girl, who appears to be eight years old, turns out to be someone else. If what happened that night in the theater were really true and if Tennessee Williams were really in the audience, as the narrator claims, one wonders what he would have thought of the tragically dramatic moment at the play's end.

Gore Vidal

Erlinda and Mr. Coffin

I AM A GENTLEWOMAN in middle life and I have resided for a number of years at Key West, Florida, in a house which is a mere stone's throw from the naval station where President Truman visits.

Before I recount, as nearly as I am able, what happened that terrible night at the Theater-in-the-Egg, I feel that I should first give you some idea of myself and the circumstances to which Providence has seen fit to reduce me. I came originally from a Carolina family not much blessed with this world's goods but whose lineage, if I may make the boast in all modesty, is of the highest. There is a saying that no legislature of the state could ever convene without the presence of a Slocum (my family name) in the Lower House, a lofty heritage you must concede and one which has done much to sustain me in my widowhood.

In olden times my social activities in this island city were multifarious, but since 1929 I have drawn in my horns, as it were, surrendering all my high offices in the various organizations with which our city abounds to one Marina Henderson, wife of our local shrimp magnate and a cultural force to be reckoned with in these parts not only because her means are ample but because our celebrated Theater-in-the-Egg is the child of her teeming imagination: she is its Managing Directress, Star and sometime Authoress. Her productions have been uniformly well regarded since the proceeds go to charity. Then, too, the unorthodox arrangement of the theater's interior has occasioned much interested comment, for the action, such as it is, takes place on an oval platform ("the yolk") about which the audience sits restively in camp chairs. There is no curtain, of course, and so the actors are forced to rush in and out, from lobby to yolk, traversing the aisles at a great rate.

Marina and I are good friends, however, even though we do not foregather as often as we once did: she now goes with a somewhat faster set than I, seeking out those of the winter residents who share her advanced views, while I keep to the small circle that I have known lo! these many years, since 1910, in fact, when I came to Key West from South Carolina, accompanied by my new husband Mr. Bellamy Craig, who had accepted a position of some trust earlier that year with a bank which was to fail in '29, the year of his decease. But of course no such premonition marred our happiness when we set out, bag and baggage, to make our way in Key West.

I do not need to say that Mr. Craig was in every sense a gentleman, a devoted husband, and though our union was never fulfilled by the longed-for arrival of little ones we managed, nonetheless, to have a happy home, one which was to end all too soon as I have intimated, for when he passed on in '29 I was left with but the tiniest of incomes, a mere pittance from my maternal grandmother in Carolina, and the house. Mr. Craig had unfortunately been forced, shortly before his death, to jettison his insurance policy, so I could not even clutch at that straw when my hour came.

I debated whether to go into business, or to establish a refined luncheon room, or to seek a position with some established business house. I was not long in doubt, however, as to what course I should pursue. For, not being desirous of living anywhere but in my own home, I determined with some success, financially at least, to reorganize the house so that it might afford me an income through the distasteful but necessary expediency of giving shelter to paying guests.

Since the house is a commodious one, I have not done

badly through the years and, in time, I have accustomed myself to this humiliating situation; then, too, I was sustained
secretly by the vivid memory of my grandmother Arabella
Stuart Slocum of Wayne County who, when reduced from
great wealth to penury by the war, maintained herself and
children, widow that she was, by taking in laundry, mostly
flat work, but still laundry. I will confess to you that there
were times at night when I sat alone in my room, hearkening
to the heavy breathing of my guests, and saw myself as a
modern Arabella, living, as did she, in the face of adversity,
inspired still by those high ideals we, she and I and all the Slo-
cums, have held in common reverence since time immemorial
in Wayne County.

And yet, in spite of every adversity, I should have said until recently that I had won through, that in twenty years as
innkeeper I had not once been faced with any ugliness, that I
had been remarkably fortunate in my selection of paying
guests, recruiting them, as I did, from the ranks of those who
have reached the age of discretion, as we used to say. But all
of this must now be in the past tense, alas.

Late one Sunday morning, three months ago, I was in the
parlor attempting with very little success to tune the piano. I
used to be quite expert at tuning but my ear is no longer true
and I was, I confess, experiencing a certain frustration when
the ringing of the doorbell interrupted my labors. Expecting
certain of my late husband's relatives who had promised to
break bread with me that day, I hastened to answer the door.
It was not they, however; instead a tall thin gentleman in middle life, wearing the long short trousers affected over in Ber-
muda, stood upon my threshold and begged admittance.

As was my wont, I ushered him into the parlor where we
sat down on the two Victorian plush chairs Grandmother
Craig left me in her will. I asked him in what way I might be
of service to him and he intimated that rumor had it I entertained guests on a paying basis. I told him that he had not
been misinformed and that, by chance, I had one empty room
left, which he asked to see.

The room pleased him and, if I say so myself, it is attractively furnished with original copies of Chippendale and Regency, bought many years ago when, in the full flush of our prosperity, Mr. Craig and I furnished our nest with objects not only useful but ornamental. There are two big windows in this room: one on the south and the other on the west. From the south window there is a fine view of the ocean, only partly obliterated by a structure of pink stucco called the "New Arcadia Motel."

"This will do very well," said Mr. Coffin (he had very soon confided his name to me). But then he paused and I did not dare meet his gaze for I thought that he was about to mention the root of all evil and, as always, I was ill at ease for I have never been able to enact the role of businesswoman without a certain shame, a distress which oftentimes communicates itself to the person with whom I must deal, causing no end of confusion for us both. But it was not of money that he wished to speak. If only it had been! If only we had gone no further in our dealings with one another. To call back yesterday, as the poet observed, bid time return! But it was not to be and wishing cannot change the past. He spoke then of *her*.

"You see, Mrs. Craig, I must tell you that I am not alone." Was it his English accent which gave me a sense of false security? created a fool's paradise wherein I was to dwell blissfully until the rude awakening? I cannot tell. Suffice it to say I trusted him.

"Not alone?" I queried. "Have you some companion who travels with you? a gentleman?"

"No, Mrs. Craig, a young lady, my ward ... a Miss Lopez."

"But I fear, Mr. Coffin, that I have only the one room free at the moment."

"Oh, she can stay with me, Mrs. Craig, in this room. You see, she is only eight." Both of us had a good laugh and my suspicions, such as they had been, were instantly allayed. He asked me if I could find him a cot and I said of course, nothing could be more simple, and then, correctly estimating the value of the room from the sign on the door, he gave me a week's rent in cash, demonstrating such delicacy of feeling by

his silence at this juncture that I found myself much prejudiced in his favor. We parted then on excellent terms and I
instructed my girl-of-all-work to place a cot in the room and
to dust carefully. I even had her supply him with the better
bath towels, after which I went in to dinner with my cousins
who had meanwhile arrived, ravenously hungry.

NOT UNTIL the next morning did I see Mr. Coffin's ward.
She was seated in the parlor looking at an old copy of *Vogue.*
"Good morning," she said and, when I entered the room, she
rose and curtsied, very prettily I must admit. "I am Erlinda
Lopez, the ward of Mr. Coffin."

"I am Mrs. Bellamy Craig, your hostess," I answered with
equal ceremony.

"Do you mind if I look at your magazines?"

"Certainly not," I said, containing all the while my surprise not only at her good manners and grown-up ways, but
also at the unexpected fact that Miss Lopez was of an unmistakable dusky hue, in short a Dark Latin. Now I must say that
although I am in many ways typical of my age and class I
have no great prejudice on the subject of race. Our family,
even in their slave-holding days, were always good to their
people and once as a child when I allowed the forbidden
word "nigger" to pass my lips I was forced to submit to a
thorough oral cleansing by my mother, with a cake of strong
soap. Yet I am, after all, a Southern woman and I do not
choose to receive people of color in my own home, call it in-
tolerant, old-fashioned or what have you, it is the way I am.
Imagine then what thoughts coursed through my startled
brain! What was I to do? Having accepted a week's rent, was I
not morally obligated to maintain both Mr. Coffin and his
ward in my house? At least until the week was up? In an
agony of indecision, I left the parlor and went straight to Mr.
Coffin. He received me cordially.

"Have you met Erlinda yet, Mrs. Craig?"

"I have indeed, Mr. Coffin."

"I think her quite intelligent. She speaks French, Spanish
and English fluently and she has a reading knowledge of Ital-

ian."

"A gifted child I am sure but *really*, Mr. Coffin . . . "

"Really what, Mrs. Craig?"

"I mean I am *not* blind. How can she be your ward? She is . . . colored!" I had said it and I was relieved; the fat was in the fire; there was no turning back.

"Many people are, Mrs. Craig."

"I am aware of that, Mr. Coffin, but I had not assumed that your ward was to be counted among that number."

"Then, Mrs. Craig, if it offends your sensibilities, we will seek lodgings elsewhere." Oh, what insane impulse made me reject this gesture of his? What flurry of *noblesse oblige* in my breast caused me suddenly to refuse even to entertain such a contingency! I do not know; suffice it to say I ended by bidding him remain with his ward as long as he should care to reside beneath my roof, on a paying basis.

When the first week was up I must confess that I was more pleased than not with my reckless decision for, although I did not mention to my friends that I was giving shelter to a person of color, I found Erlinda, nonetheless, to be possessed of considerable charm and personality and I spent at least an hour every day in her company, at first from a sense of duty but, finally, from a very real pleasure in her conversation which, when I recall it now (the pleasure, I mean), causes my cheeks to burn with shame.

I discovered in our talks that she was, as I had suspected, an orphan and that she had traveled extensively in Europe and Latin America, wintering in Amalfi, summering in Venice, and so on. Not of course that I for one moment believed these stories but they were so charming and indicated such a fund of information that I was only too pleased to listen to her descriptions of the Lido, and her recitations from Dante, in flawless Italian or what I took to be Italian since I have never studied other tongues. But, as I have said, I took her tales with the proverbial grain of salt and, from time to time, I chatted with Mr. Coffin, gleaning from him—as much as I was able without appearing to pry—the story of Erlinda's life.

She was the child of a Cuban prize-fighter who had toured

Europe many times, taking Erlinda with him on his trips, showering her with every luxury and engaging tutors for her instruction, with a particular emphasis on languages, world literature and deportment. Her mother had died of an infected kneecap, a few months after Erlinda was born. Mr. Coffin, it seems, had known the prize-fighter for several years and since he, Mr. Coffin, was English, a friendship between them was possible. They were, I gathered, very close and since Mr. Coffin had independent means they were able to travel together about Europe, Mr. Coffin gradually becoming responsible for Erlinda's education.

This idyllic existence ended abruptly a year ago when Lopez was killed in the ring by a Sicilian named Balbo. It appears that this Balbo was not a sportsman and that shortly before the fight he had contrived to secrete a section of lead pipe in his right boxing glove, enabling him to crush Lopez's skull in the first round. Needless to say the scandal which ensued was great. Balbo was declared middleweight champion of Sicily and Mr. Coffin, after protesting to the authorities who turned a deaf ear to him, departed, taking Erlinda with him.

As my friends will testify, I am easily moved by a tale of misfortune and, for a time, I took this motherless tyke to my heart. I taught her portions of the Bible which she had not studied before (Mr. Coffin, I gather, was a free-thinker), and she showed me the scrapbooks she and Mr. Coffin had kept of her father's career as a pugilist ... and a handsome young man he was, if photographs are to be believed.

Consequently, when a new week rolled around and the period of probation, as it were, was up, I extended them the hospitality of my home indefinitely, and soon a pattern of existence took shape. Mr. Coffin would spend most of his days looking for shells (he was a collector and, I am assured by certain authorities, the discoverer of a new type of pink-lipped conch), while Erlinda would remain indoors, reading, playing the piano or chatting with me about one thing or the other. She won my heart and not only mine but those of my friends who had soon discovered, as friends will, the unusual combination I was, with some initial misgiving I must confess, sheltering. But my fears were proved to be groundless, a little to my surprise for the ladies of my acquaintance are not noted for their tolerance: yet Erlinda enchanted them all with her conversation and saucy ways. Especially Marina Henderson, who was not only immediately attracted to Erlinda personally but, and this I must say startled me, professed to see in the child thespian qualities of the highest order.

"Mark my words, Louise Craig," she said to me one afternoon when we were sitting in the parlor and Erlinda had gone upstairs to fetch one of the scrapbooks, "that child will be a magnificent actress. Have you listened to her voice?"

"Since I have been constantly in her company for nearly three weeks I could hardly *not* have heard it," I responded drily.

"I mean its timbre. The inflection ... it's like velvet, I tell you!"

"But how can she be an actress in this country when ... well, let us say the opportunities open to one of her ... *characteristics* are limited to occasional brief appearances as a lady's maid?"

"That's beside the point," said Marina, and she rattled on as she always does when something new has hit her fancy, ignoring all difficulties, courting disaster with a commendable show of high spirits and bad judgment.

"Perhaps the child has no intention of exploiting her dramatic gifts?" I suggested, unconsciously wishing to avert disaster.

"Nonsense," said Marina, staring at herself in the tilted Victorian mirror over the fireplace, admiring that remarkable red hair of hers which changes its shade from season to season, from decade to decade, like the leaves in autumn. "I shall talk to her about it this afternoon."

"You have something in mind, then? some role?"

"I have," said Marina slyly.

"Not ... ?"

"Yes!" Needless to say I was astonished. For several months our island city had been agog with rumors concerning Marina's latest work, an adaptation of that fine old classic *Ca-*

mille, executed in blank verse and containing easily the finest part for an actress within memory, the title role. Competition for this magnificent part had been keen but the demands of the role were so great that Marina had hesitated to entrust it to any of the regular stars, including herself.

"But this will never do!" I exclaimed; my objections were cut short, however, by the appearance of Erlinda and when next I spoke the deed was done and Erlinda Lopez had been assigned the stellar role in Marina Henderson's "Camille," based on the novel by Dumas and the screenplay by Miss Zöe Akins.

IT IS CURIOUS, now that I think of it, how everyone accepted as a matter of course that Erlinda should interpret an adult Caucasian woman from Paris whose private life was not what it should have been. I can only say, in this regard, that those who heard her read for the part, and I was one of them, were absolutely stunned by the emotion she brought to those risqué lines, as well as by the thrilling quality of her voice which, in the word of Mr. Hamish the newspaperman, was "golden." That she was only eight and not much over three feet tall disturbed no one for, as Marina said, it is *presence* which matters on the stage, even in the "Theater-in-the-Egg": make-up and lighting would do the rest. The only difficulty, as we saw it, was the somewhat ticklish problem of race, but since this is a small community with certain recognized social arbiters, good form prevents the majority from questioning too finely the decisions of our leaders, and as Marina occupies a position of peculiar eminence among us there was, as far as I know, no grumbling against her bold choice. Marina herself, by far our most accomplished actress, certainly our most indefatigable one, assigned herself the minor role of Camille's confidante Cecile. Knowing Marina as I do, I was somewhat startled that she had allowed the stellar role to go to someone else, but then recalling that she was, after all, directress and authoress, I could see that she would undoubtedly have been forced to spread herself thin had she undertaken such an arduous task.

Now I do not know precisely what went on during the rehearsals. I was never invited to attend them and although I felt I had some connection with the production, Erlinda having been my discovery in the first place, I made no demur and sought in no way to interfere. Word came to me, however, that Erlinda was magnificent.

I was seated in the parlor one afternoon with Mr. Coffin, sewing some lace on a tea gown our young star was to wear in the first scene, when Erlinda burst into the room.

"What is the matter, child?" I asked as she hastened to bury her head in her guardian's lap, great sobs racking her tiny frame.

"Marina!" came the muffled complaint. "Marina Henderson is a ——!" Shocked as I was by the child's cruel observation, I could not but, in my heart of hearts, agree that there was some truth to this crushing estimate of my old friend's character. Nonetheless, it was my duty to defend her and I did, as best I could, recounting relevant episodes from her life to substantiate my defense. But before I could even get to the quite interesting story of how she happened to marry Mr. Henderson I was cut short by a tirade of abuse against my oldest friend, an attack inspired, it soon developed, by a quarrel they had had over Erlinda's interpretation of her part, a quarrel which had ended in Marina's assumption of the role of Camille while presenting Erlinda with the terrible choice of either withdrawing from the company entirely or else accepting the role of Cecile, hitherto played by the authoress herself.

Needless to say we were all in a state of uproar for twenty-four hours. Erlinda would neither eat nor sleep. According to Mr. Coffin she paced the floor all night, or at least when he had slipped off to the Land of Nod she was still pacing and when he awakened early the next morning she was seated bitterly by the window, haggard and exhausted, the bedclothes on her cot undisturbed.

I counseled caution, knowing the influence Marina has in this town, and my advice was duly followed when, with broken heart but proud step, Erlinda returned to the boards in the part of Cecile. Had I but known the fruit of my counsel I would have torn my tongue out by the roots rather than advise Erlinda as I did. But what is done is done. In my defense, I can only say that I acted from ignorance and not from malice.

The opening night saw as brilliant an assemblage as you could hope to see in Key West. The cream of our local society was there as well as several of Mr. Truman's retinue and a real playwright from New York named Tennessee Williams. You have probably heard many conflicting stories about that night. Everyone in the state of Florida now claims to have been present and, to hear the stories some of the people who were there tell, you would think they had been a hundred miles away from the theater that fateful night. In any event, *I* was there in my white mesh over peacock blue foundation, and carrying the imitation egret fan that I have had for twenty years, an anniversary gift from Mr. Craig.

Mr. Coffin and I sat together and chatted pleasantly, both of us excited to fever-pitch by the long-awaited debut of our young star. The audience too seemed to have sensed that something remarkable was about to happen for when, in the middle of the first scene, Erlinda appeared in a gown of orchid-colored tulle, they applauded loudly.

As WE TOOK our seats for the fifth and final act we were both aware that Erlinda had triumphed. Not even in the movies have I ever seen such a performance! Or heard such a magnificent voice! Poor Marina sounded like a Memphis frump by comparison and it was obvious to all who knew our authoress that she was in a rage at being outshone in her own production.

Now in the last act of Marina's "Camille" there is a particularly beautiful and touching scene where Camille is lying on a chaise longue, wearing a flowing negligee of white rayon. There is a table beside her on which is set a silver candelabra, containing six lighted tapers, a bowl of paper camellias and some Kleenex. The scene began something like this.

"Oh, will he never come? Tell me, sweet Cecile, do you not

see his carriage approaching from the window?" Cecile (Erlinda) pretends to look out a window and answers, "There is no one in the street but a little old man selling the evening newspapers." The language as you see is poetic and much the best writing Marina has done to date. Then there is a point in the action, the great moment of the play, when Camille (that's not the character's real name I understand but Marina called her that so as not to confuse the audience) after a realistic fit of coughing, rises up on her elbow and exclaims, "Cecile! It grows dark. He has not come. Light more tapers, do you hear me? I need more light!"

Then it happened. Erlinda picked up the candelabra and held it aloft for a moment, a superhuman effort since it was larger than she was; then, taking aim, she hurled it at Marina who was instantly ignited. Pandemonium broke loose in the theater! Marina, a pillar of fire, streaked down the aisle and into the night, where she was subdued at last in the street by two policemen who managed to put out the blaze, after which they removed her to the hospital where she now resides, undergoing at this moment her twenty-fourth skin graft.

Erlinda remained on the stage long enough to give *her* reading of Camille's great scene which, according to those few who were close enough to hear it, was indeed splendid. Then, the scene finished, she left the theater and, before either Mr. Coffin or I could get to her, she was arrested on a charge of assault and battery, and incarcerated.

My story, however, is not yet ended. Had this been all I might have said: let bygones be bygones. The miscreant is only a child and Marina did do her an injury, but during the subsequent investigation it was revealed to a shocked public that Erlinda had been legally married to Mr. Coffin in the Reformed Eritrean Church of Cuba several months before and a medical examination proved, or so the defense claims, that Erlinda is actually forty-one years old, a dwarf, the mother and not the daughter of the pugilist Lopez. To date the attendant legal complications have not yet been unraveled to the court's satisfaction.

Fortunately, at this time, I was able to avail myself of a

much needed vacation in Carolina, where I resided with kin in Wayne County until the trouble in Key West had abated somewhat.

I now visit Marina regularly and she is beginning to look more or less like her old self, even though her hair and eyebrows are gone for good and she will have to wear a wig when she finally rises from her bed of pain. Only once has she made any reference to Erlinda in my presence and that was shortly after my return from the north when she remarked that the child had been all wrong for the part of Camille and that if she had it to do over again, everything considered, she would still have fired her.

Philip Wylie

(1902–1971), now best remembered as a writer of the outdoors, gave modern American literature two of its best-loved characters, Crunch Adams and Desperate Smith. but left before obtaining a degree. He went to work at *The New Yorker* and later became a full-time freelance writer, publishing over fifty novels and hundreds of short stories.

Born in Massachusetts, the son of a Presbyterian minister who loved the outdoors and disliked religion (two traits handed on to his son) and a mother who wrote fiction but died when Philip was five, Wylie attended Princeton

Among his best-know works were *When Worlds Collide* (1932), *Finnley Wren* (1934), *Generation of Vipers* (1942), *Opus 21* (1949), and *Triumph* (1963). He settled in Miami in 1937 for reasons of health and set many of his stories there, including the Crunch and Des stories that became so popular.

"Widow Voyage" (1939) is one of the stories about those two Miami charter fishermen who, in this story, are determined to launch an independent business by fixing up a recently acquired dilapidated boat. It is the first of fifty-nine tales about the two likable fishermen who overcome adversity, usually in the form of large, volatile bullies, to triumph in the end. Patient and tenacious in the face of difficulties but subject to human weaknesses, Crunch and Des are appealing and believable characters. Wylie's stories reveal his knowledge of the sport fishing business and his empathy for the underdog.

One point in which the times depicted in the story differ from today's world concerns the sailfish that Mr. Taylor catches and takes home to mount. The waters off southern Florida are famous for their sailfish, especially abundant in the cold months of November through March. The fish, called spindlebeaks by many anglers, arrive when the seas are rough and the northeast winds are strong. Because today's fishermen want to keep the supply plentiful and worry that greater numbers of participants in sailfish tournaments might deplete the fish population, more people have adopted catch-and-release fishing, and tournaments today award points for the release and not the killing of the fish. Charter fishermen now hoist flags for sailfish caught and released, thus prolonging the sport for descendants of the clients of Crunch and Des.

Philip Wylie

Widow Voyage

C RUNCH WHISTLED lovingly. "A beauty," he said, balancing himself on the riverbank by grabbing a palm frond. "A sheer, pure beauty!"

"She'll do," his companion answered. He wiped sweat from his forehead with a bandanna and nodded to himself. "Only a real sea boat has lines like that! She's a duzie!"

The object of their affection scarcely merited such praise. Indeed to give it any, required imagination and hardihood. Before them lay the hull of the *Evangeline IV*.

A mere glance would have revealed that it had been under the water for some days, another that it had been partially burned, and a third that it was holed and plugged in the stern. The cabin was a carbonized melee. The engines had been lifted out and sold to some other optimists. So had her twin screws, her steering gear, her compass and her chromed fittings; even her name was partly missing, so that it spread on her forward bulwark in quasi-Esperanto: *Ev ng l ne IV*.

"We'll clear that stuff out this afternoon—"

Crunch nodded. "Then cut the stern out, put in a sliding door to haul the big ones through, build a new cabin—a trunk cabin, by golly!"

"Get an engine!"

The mention of an engine silenced them. A good engine would cost six or seven hundred dollars. They had put their

savings—two hundred dollars—in the hull. They had signed
a note for two hundred more—a note due in six months. And
Crunch's wife was going to have a baby sooner than that.
Only, it was she who had taken the money from the bank.

"Buy that bottom," Sari had said. "You may never get
another chance. It's worth a thousand, easy." She'd thrust her
chin out nearly an inch, and Crunch had argued for three
days, but he had known by the chin that all argument was
simply vanity.

So now they jumped silently aboard the *Ev ng l ne IV* and
through the hot afternoon they wrenched loose and poured
upon the oily bosom of the Miami River an aquacade of damaged jetsam—cushions and window frames, linoleum, parti-
tions, shelves, bedsprings, rudder cable, rope, bent brass,
planks, canvas, and even broken dishes. But everything that
might be usable was carefully transported to the bank.

When the light failed, they straightened up. The demoli-
tion had largely cleared the hull, but what remained looked
more like the archaeological residue of a Viking longboat than
the foundation for a successful business—the business of
scouring the open sea, under charter, in quest of sailfish, marlin, broadbill, dolphin, grunts.

Crunch rubbed his arms and, in the omniprevailing screen
of twilight, changed his shirt and pants. So did his companion, who would serve as mate aboard the fishing boat they
planned to resurrect from the salvaged vessel. Then they
walked over to the Gulf Stream Dock.

Miami's Gulf Stream Dock is a gaudy spectacle. Gaudy
even against the neon-spangled harbor and the perfervid sky
line behind it. It extends three hundred feet into Biscayne Bay
and has mooring slips for fifty boats. Behind each cruiser is a
placard bearing its name. Lights glitter on wet planks, on the
functional bodies of the day's catch, and floodlights beglam-
our the colored dresses and the pastel beach costumes of the
crowds that stroll there. Small lights wink from slowly swinging portholes, and brighter bulbs illuminate cockpits and the
fishing tackle—delicate gear affected by masters of the craft,
and the appalling equipment with which sea giants are

fought; reels as big as ice-cream freezers and rods as thick as baseball bats.

Here the public comes to rent deep-sea fishing boats. Here, every morning, wild-eyed expectation puts out toward the South Atlantic and returns at night as triumph, or alibi. The place reeks of romance and fresh fish.

Voices from the busy brilliance greeted the boat builders— friendly voices and grudging ones: "Hi, Crunch! Hello, Desperate!"

"Hello, fellows!" Crunch's eyes found Mr. Williams. He was standing beside the scales with a group just back from the Stream.

"Thirty-two pounds, Mrs. Merson!" He chuckled. "Nice dolphin!"

The woman's eyes sparkled. "I thought I'd go overboard!"

Mr. Williams nodded as if Mrs. Merson's dolphin were something unprecedented and altogether amazing. He turned. "Hi yuh, boys!"

"Fine."

Crunch gazed thoughtfully at the water, the theatrical clouds, the rigid volplane of a homebound pelican. "Be a light northeaster tomorrow. About like today."

Mr. Williams said, "Yup. Plenty of sailfish off the whistling buoy."

There was a pause. Crunch had spent two years in the prize ring. Light-heavy. He hadn't liked it, but he'd needed money. Rather, his mother had. At the moment, he would have preferred taking a ten-round shellacking.

He said, "We bought that hull."

Mr. Williams' two hundred and thirty-eight pounds seemed to condense. His usually jovial voice was strangled. "I know it! I saw you two fools tow her up to the river this morning!"

"She was a good boat," Desperate said unevenly.

"Sure, she was! So was the *Merrimac* before the *Monitor* went to work on her!"

"We wondered, if maybe, when we got her fixed up—"

Mr. Williams interrupted. In his tone was pain that ached

through the soft and fervent evening: "This is like a judgment for trying to help my fellow man! I take you two birds off freighters! I teach you how to fish! How to do everything from cut baits to nurse seasick schoolteachers! I knit your reputations by hand! I offer you my own boat to run—the *Porpoise* herself—which is the *Normandie* of the charter business. But no. Oh, no! You have to prog up a derelict—burned in the bargain!"

"She's only been under a few days," Desperate murmured.

"It's not you I blame!" Mr. Williams compromised even that small solace. "It's Crunch! Thirty years old! A big guy! A tough guy! But no wise guy! What are you going to build her with?"

Crunch blushed and slowly flexed his right arm. The makers of his shirt had designed it amply, but, even so, the material was strained perilously around his biceps.

It did not impress Mr. Williams. "I suppose you've considered that it generally takes about four thousand bucks—in money—to build anything a normal human being would risk his neck in!"

"We got some tackle lined up," Desperate began. "Rudders, a swell mast, outriggers. Sam's letting us use his place when we're ready to haul out."

"You intend to pedal her?" Mr. Williams chuckled.

"I'm—we're—Sari and I are going to have a baby."

"Fine time to start thinking of that!"

Crunch leaned against a piling. It was as bad as he had expected it would be. But he was beginning to feel sore. It wasn't exactly soreness, either, but a deep, burning sensation—the kind that had won him his nickname. Won it in small boxing clubs, where nicknames are more like to be "Drop" or "Fade-out." Light fell on his eyes; Crunch had eyes like the blue flames of a welder's torch.

"We're building this boat, see?" he said. "I'd have worked for you this season—only I want my own boat more. Especially with a kid coming. I thought when we got her ready—"

"Which'll be about 1960!"

"—if you were going to have a place on the Gulf Stream

Dock, you might let Desperate and me—"

"—tie up here? Why, man, they won't know it's a fishin' boat! They'll think it's a case of mossbunkers!"

Crunch shrugged. "O.K. If that's the way you figure." He turned to walk away. He'd set his heart on the Gulf Stream Dock, but there were other anchorages.

Then he felt Mr. Williams' hand on his shoulder. Mr. Williams' other hand was held out straight. "I'll talk to the corporation next week! I hope you build a solid-gold boat and catch every four-eyed fish in the sea! I wish I had some dough—"

"Thanks," Crunch said.

That was all. Mr. Williams tried to decide whether his reticence was normal, or due to the fact that Crunch couldn't say any more; it meant a great deal to be on the Gulf Stream Dock. He wondered, too, how he could persuade the corporation's committee to save room for a nonexistent cruiser to be raised, like the *Phoenix*, from burned boards. And by grit alone.

Crunch and Desperate made a tour of the dock and gleaned from their friends a summary of the status quo in fishing. From those who were not their friends they gathered black looks and a few mediocre wisecracks. That group included several captains and mates; the charter business is competitive, uncertain, and highly individualistic. But all their conversation was stuff to make a fisherman's heart beat harder.

Marcy was hosing down the *Willalou*. He waved and shot water at them before he shut it off. "Nice outside today! The sails are swarming. Mac hit into an Allison's tuna. He was fishing a party from Pahk Avenoo. Some fat dame hung it, and you could hear her squeal clear to Fowey Light. We trolled by, hoping to hook its pal, and she was doing all right. On it for over an hour, screaming and yelling, and then I guess the tuna did the usual."

Crunch and Desperate nodded. The usual. Dove deep, wrapped his tail in the leader wire, kinked it, pulled hard, and went on alone to wherever Allison's tunas go.

Randy said, "Hear you've bid in on a fire sale! I saw the *Evangeline* hit and explode. A big woof—and that rich play-boy who owned her was in the water with his friends. Coast Guard picked 'em up. What's left of her?"

"You'll see soon enough," Desperate replied.

Randy sliced the port side fillet from a mackerel. "Yeah? Say, listen, you guys! You fished Mr. Perkins on the *Porpoise*, but I've got him now. If you bring that cremated derelict over here, don't try to take him away from me!"

Neither of them responded.

A cluster of people stood around the stern of the *Valkyrie*. They pushed their way through—poor people from the fringes of Miami, eager to buy fresh fish; rich men and their ladies, come down from the Beach to arrange for a day of trolling in the Stream; tourists, natives, kids; and a man who kept repeating, "A self-respecting trout fisherman wouldn't touch this marine stuff!" There was also a pretty blonde girl who didn't say anything, but kept staring incredulously at the sawed-off bill of a sailfish which she held in her hand.

"What's the attraction?" Desperate called.

Squeak Parsons pointed disgustedly with his mop. On the dock behind the *Valkyrie* lay the formidable carcass of a nine-foot shark.

"Caught him on a big rig," Squeak said—and his voice was like his gesture.

Fishing for sharks, excepting one or two breeds, is con-sidered no sport at the Gulf Stream Dock. It's like—they say —hunting cows in a New England pasture. Horrid, sharks may be, but game they certainly are not.

"My party wanted to see what it was like," Squeak ex-plained.

Blubber Ellis was splicing a line. He merely nodded.

Crunch grinned a little There had been some disaster for the placid Mr. Ellis that day. Usually he was on the dock in the midst of the crowd, dilating the dramas of his past.

"What'd you get?" Crunch asked.

Blubber made a noise—a noise like that of a saw on a knot.

"Skunked?" Desperate sounded sympathetic.

The note appealed to the huge and unhappy captain. "Is it mah fault if these rich damn Yankees ain't got the brains of a crawfisherman? This morning some guy from Boston comes up and charters me foah the day. Said he'd fished in every sea except the Caspian. So Ah don't advise him none. An' what happens? A white marlin comes along an' hits his bait. It'd of been the first caught this year! 'Drop back to him!' Ah yells. Does he drop? No, sir! You can see the marlin turn to gobble that little bittie ballyhoo. Sun's overhead an' the water's clear as gin. But this half-wit yanks the bait right away from him. You'd think the marlin would have gone off scared then. But he comes back. An' the fellow yanks the bait away. The third time the marlin tries to gulp it—Ah can see th' expression in his eye, which is plumb furious—but Mister Yankee feels the spike tap, an' still don't let out line! He strikes so hard instead that the dinged ballyhoo—hook, leader an' all—snaps back an' whips around the outrigger, clean out the water!"

"Tough," Desperate said. He sounded like a man who was on the verge of a great emotion.

"Tough!" Blubber gazed ruefully at them. "Tough! Before that marlin leaves, he cuts twice at the ballyhoo swingin' in the air! An' Ah can't get the line free in time to hook him!"

Crunch and Desperate walked away. "It's a lie," the latter said, after a while.

"Maybe," Crunch answered. "And maybe not. I saw a white marlin take a swipe at a flying gull, once."

THEY CAUGHT a trolley car out to the Northwest section, where faded apartment houses and small frame cottages vied for unattractive prominence with garages and ironwork shops and half-forgotten, vine-choked lime groves. Sari was standing in the door of their small apartment. She'd tied up her hair in a ribbon from an old middy blouse and her dark curls stood like a coronet. She wore a hibiscus at her waist, held by her apron strings.

"Did you get the boat?"

Crunch nodded.

"Swell! How was the fishing?"

"How do we know? We won't be doing any for a long time." He hugged her shoulders hard with one arm and said the habitual things. "Imagine a fishin' skipper with a wife named Sari! Or even one that looks like you!" The teasing of his voice camouflaged his everlasting awe.

"Did you bring any fish?" Sari asked.

They looked at each other guiltily.

"Well, we've got plenty without it. But the boys'll give you all we can eat, and we're going to be able to eat quite a lot, from now on."

They sat down to dinner at the kitchen table—which was also the living-room table. Crunch refused a second helping of beets. Sari ate them—"just to get rid of 'em." And afterward he said, "What's at the movies?"

She chuckled. "We could go over and look at the posters. But we can't give the man three quarters and go in."

"That's right. Not till 1960, Mr. Williams says."

MR. WILLIAMS looked down at the *Ev ng I ne IV*. The boys hadn't heard him come along the riverbank through the palms and Australian pines. They were too busy; Crunch assiduously following a pencil line along a piece of mahogany with a keyhole saw, and Desperate tacking canvas around the forward hatch. Already, moss and barnacles and sea mats had attached themselves to the hull. Every sign of its accident was gone, but the once-doughty cruiser was a shambles. Mr. Williams swallowed hard. He didn't like unpleasant things in life. They were pretty nice fellows too. Lunatics, maybe, but the kind you had to admire. Crunch's blond hair flew with his sawing. *Wife cuts it,* Mr. Williams thought. Desperate materialized copper tacks between his teeth with the regularity of a metronome.

"Hi yuh, sailors!"

Saw and hammer stopped. "Come aboard!" Crunch yelled happily.

The older man laughed. There wasn't any deck in the cockpit. Just crossbeams and braces. Doubled, he noticed, for extra strength. But no place for a fat man to stand.

"Look at her!" Crunch said. "A fellow gave us that mast! Aluminum! We're going to get some fancy linoleum for the deck. Lady on a yacht refused it. Wrong shade of gray. Desperate swapped three sweaters for a mess of cleats and brass strips. They're used, but we're having them chromed. I picked up a wheel from a racing car in a junk yard, and enough glass to make side panels. Real plate glass! Last week we took a skiff out where the *Ellen B.* sank, and dove up—" he pointed —"a bell, and a lot of wire, and fifty fathoms of new inch rope, still wrapped."

"Barracudas didn't bother you?"

Crunch snorted. "They don't come near you, if you don't splash too much! I got an octopus on my leg, but he was a little guy. Portuguese man-o'-war's worse!"

"Where'd you get that steering rig? Looks new."

"It is new, though I talked the chandler into a discount. You gotta have A-1 steering equipment."

"He gave you credit?"

Crunch shook his head. "If we could get credit at a marine hardware store, we'd be on velvet. We paid hard cash. Didn't you hear? We ran into a fellow needed his house painted. Offered us a hundred bucks. We got a couple of flood lamps on long cords off a photographer I know, and finished the whole shebang in two days and three nights. How do you like the trunk cabin?"

Mr. Williams knew boats. He also had a vision. "Going to be all right. In fact—if you don't mind my saying so—I'm surprised. If you can get her finished this way, and find a power plant—" He broke off. "I talked to the corporation."

"Yes?"

"I hate to disappoint you, Crunch. They just don't believe you two birds can build anything that'll be good enough for the Gulf Stream Dock."

"When they see her—"

"That's the trouble. When they see her, I'll be booked solid for another year. Everybody wants to get on that dock! I had to tell 'em you didn't know where your next nail was coming from. They just gave me a ha-ha for suggesting it."

"But, Mr. Williams, I've run your boat at the Gulf Stream Dock for a long time. The only customers I know fish out from there."

"That's another thing. The fellows on the dock—most of 'em—would hate to see you roll up with a boat. They're dividing your business now, and times are none too good. Besides, look at the record you made the last couple of years in the fishing tournament. If you start repeating that—"

"It was just luck."

"Yeah? Then they'll be scared your luck'll hold. Scared you'll take some of their trade. They raised the deuce when I said I was going to hold a place for you."

Crunch shrugged. "Nice guys! Though I can't say I blame 'em. And quite a few have been over here, giving us stuff, lending us tools."

"I'm sorry. Say, how's Sari? Haven't seen her around for quite a while."

"Not coming around these days." Crunch looked at Desperate, who had been sitting on the cabin during the parley.

"Well, son, that just makes it so much tougher!" Mr. Williams went away, then, precipitately.

"He's a good-hearted guy," Crunch said.

"We won't be on the Gulf Dock," Desperate answered slowly. "How we going to get back our old customers?"

Crunch was a little grim. "Write 'em letters."

"Yeah. We can try." Desperate pounded a tack.

SAM'S BOAT YARD was some distance upriver from the cove where they berthed the *Ev ng l ne*. That was where Sari phoned, and Sam himself came running through the weeds. It was on one of the black days, too. The day when they'd come down by trolley at 5:30 in the morning—tired, as usual; thin, from working too hard and eating too little—and found the boat on the bottom. Holes drilled through the planking in every compartment. Somebody—one of the fearful and jealous captains, doubtless—had spent a couple of hours there at night. They'd been diving down all morning, putting corks in the auger holes, and then pumping. Their backs ached and their hands were not just blistered but bleeding. Desperate had been close to crying, and Crunch had been talking about killing somebody if he ever found somebody.

Sam ran through the weeds. He hadn't bothered to drop his blowtorch. "Hurry!" he yelled. "Oh, Lord, hurry!"

"Sari?" Crunch said.

Sam gulped and nodded. "Gone to the hospital already!"

Crunch picked up some waste and tried to clean his hands. Desperate blew his nose. It is not funny when a squarehead cries. Crunch put on his jacket and considered changing his pants, but didn't. He went away, and Desperate kept pumping. All afternoon. All night, finally. He forgot he was pumping. He thought he was just waiting for something, and toward dawn he had trouble remembering what it was.

Eventually the pump sucked air. He got a sponge and began sloshing water overboard. The *Ev ng l ne* was floating again. He sat down and smoked a cigarette. Vaguely, he heard the first trolley stop. And Crunch came running through the weeds in the track Sam had made, nodding his head, for some ridiculous reason. His bellow scared up a pair of mockingbirds. "A boy! And Sari's fine! Eleven pounds, even!"

Desperate fumbled in his watch pocket. "Great," he said. "Look, Crunch. I been hoarding a little on the side." The bills were sweat-wadded. "Twenty-two bucks. Not for hospital bills or the dock. We can handle that later. For Sari and the kid. Maybe even some flowers."

Crunch saw, as he took the bills, that the *Ev ng l ne* was dry. A palsy seized him. His teeth chattered. His arm muscles quivered.

"Get some water," he said, "and pour it over me."

Desperate poured.

"Another bucket."

Crunch sat down, dripping. "A big little guy, like his old man. Look, Desperate! Do you mind if we name him—"

"After me?" The squarehead cursed softly. "I do. Though, if you can't think of anything, being in a sort of tizzie, you can use my middle name."

"What's that?"

"William."

"Bill," said Crunch. "That's a good name for a tough guy, isn't it?"

"Oh, probably he ain't so tough."

"No?" The blue eyes blazed with outrage for a moment. Then he laughed. "Bill Adams. It's O.K. I'll tell Sari tonight. Let's work!"

Desperate knew, then, how tired he was. But he whistled while he worked, and stopped only when he heard Crunch chuckle. He couldn't whistle then, because the sound made him grin.

BILL WAS six weeks old when his father decided to give up his dream. Everything that could be borrowed and begged, everything that could be created by human energy, had been tenderly bestowed upon the derelict. She was a trim cruiser again, forty feet long, not counting the harpoon pulpit, with aluminum-painted outriggers, mahogany cabin walls, a registry number, a sky-blue trunk cabin, cream interior, bunks, galley, stove, two day beds bought on time, top controls, and even a new name, which Sari had remembered from high-school ancient history—*Poseidon*. "He's the Greek god of the sea," she had said. "And that includes fish." Even the most bitter of their rivals had admitted it was a spectacular job. Only, there were no engines in the *Poseidon*.

Sari had named her and, in another sentence, reluctantly relegated her to limbo: "The milkman wouldn't leave anything for Bill this morning."

Desperate had walked out of the house, then, and spent his last quarter at the grocery store.

And Crunch had walked out later too.

When Desperate came back, Sari was playing with Bill, and she kept her head down. "Where do you think he went? Maybe he'll kill the milkman! Maybe he'll get drunk—and I wouldn't blame him! Or you, Desperate! Starving, working like that!"

"A guy," Desperate replied with difficulty, "offered us

two thousand for the *Poseidon*, as is."

Sari didn't answer.

Crunch took a trolley downtown. The guy might be at the Gulf Stream Dock. If he weren't, it was only a short walk to his hotel. Crunch dropped slowly from the trolley—one hand on the rail sufficing for the maneuver—and strolled out on the pier. The boats were all in, lights on. The sun had gone, but the sky was still carmine. With two thousand bucks he could pay up everything and start young Bill out decently in life. He and Desperate could get jobs; if not in the fishing fleet, then ... well— There'd be an advertisement for trolley motormen. He'd run one in Schenectady.

He strolled out, thinking of a bell clanging, streams of automobiles separating, the hiss of air brakes. "Plenty of room in the rear!"

People were crowded around Randy's *Vanity*. Must be something special. Mechanically, he pushed in to observe.

A big man with a café-society accent began yelling at Randy. "In my opinion, you cut off that fish deliberately! Criminal negligence! It was a record fish! A monster!"

Randy blinked and looked palely at the crowd. "I'm sorry, Mr. Closser. I didn't do it intentionally."

"I was Randy's passenger," another man said. "It wasn't his fault. He was getting a hook out of my sleeve, and his mate was helping."

The big man was breathing hard and growing redder. "I don't want to hear the fool's excuse! My fish had taken out a lot of line! He ran his boat over the line and broke it."

Suddenly he swung and knocked Randy back into the water. There was a silent, suspended instant. Randy came up, swimming in the tide. Someone threw a rope. Closser looked at his fist, smiled, and walked down the dock.

Crunch followed him. So did Randy's passenger, although Crunch did not notice that. He didn't notice anything. He had never liked or trusted Randy. But Randy was a little guy. And it was more than that. For three months Crunch had been fighting against odds that had proved insuperable. The gall of disappointment and frustration seethed inside him. He

walked, and kept whispering, "The lug. The mean lug." He
followed the lug into the parking yard, watched him unlock a
long yellow roadster, walked closer, and spoke. "That's the
right color car for you, Mr.—Closser."

The man whirled around. "Look here!"

"Randy's a fisherman, mister. He wouldn't of lied. If he
cut off your fish, he's sorrier than you are. His customer said
the same thing."

"Do you want what he got?"

Crunch came to his senses a little then. He had been a
fighter. Fighters don't fight with the laity.

The big man mistook his silence for circumspection. "I
thought not! It isn't healthy! When I was in Harvard I was the
intercollegiate heavyweight champion."

Then Crunch felt the burn again, deep, terrible and glorious. "A man who had the opportunity to go to Harvard," he
replied, "should know better than to be a louse." At least
afterward he maintained he had said, "louse."

They all came up—captains, mates, customers, rich men,
poor women, sportsmen, the newspaper boy—everybody.
They said it was a better fight than the promoters had ever
staged in Miami. They said Crunch hit him so hard he took off
the crushed coral in the parking yard like a hooked mako.
They said he went so high you could see the sky line under
his feet. It wasn't so, but he did fall flat, and got up a while
later and drove off without troubling anyone.

Mr. Williams took Crunch into his office and called a
doctor. Two bones were sticking through the back of Crunch's
right hand.

"You shouldn't have done that," Mr. Williams said. "Captains fighting passengers! Give us a bad name!"

"I'm not a captain any more! I guess I had a bellyful of life!
Had to hit somebody!" They poured iodine on his hand, and
his eyes turned gray. "Sorry."

Then Randy's passenger came in. He looked at the torn
blue shirt, the iodine and the gray eyes—which were coming
back again to blue. "You a captain down here?"

"Was," said Mr. Williams fearfully.

"Got a boat?"

"Have one. No engine."

The man nodded. He was a tallish man, thin, no sunburn, and he wore gold-rimmed glasses. He looked like a banker, or, maybe, a broker. One of those New York men, alert, quick; good fishermen, sometimes. This one was about fifty.

"No engine?" he said after a while.

Mr. Williams tried to make an excuse: "He and his mate were tops at the charter business till they got swelled heads and tried to build their own boat. They got licked on dough. He's through! It's too bad, but I guess he couldn't take it. And he just plain had to sock somebody."

"My name," said the man, "is Taylor. This was the first day that I ever tried deep-sea fishing. And I like that right of yours. I like it. I've been run out of my office by my doctor for a couple of months. If I chartered you in advance—say four weeks—would that? ..."

Crunch looked at his hand. "Yeah," he said, "it would."

"How soon could you be ready?"

"A week?"

"I'd like to get in on the first day of the Miami tournament. Is it possible?"

"We'll try. But with this mitt ..."

WHEN HE returned to his home and opened the door with his left hand, Sari raised her eyes and stared for a minute. Then she whispered to Bill, "There's your father. He's been fighting. And he's drunk. Maybe he isn't quite as good a guy as I've been telling you he was."

So Crunch grinned. "Not drunk. Not a drop. I got this goofy expression from being happy." He took out a ten-dollar bill. "Where's the squarehead?"

THEY LOST track of time. Slip Wilson and Bugs Holover and Cap Johnson came to help them. Slip even gave up a charter on one of the days. Bugs worked all night. The engines were lowered on the blocks. The reduction gears were attached to the shafts. Desperate put in the panels and hooked them up.

Mr. Williams drove over to the river on the eve of opening day. "I have your number in the parade. Think she'll be ready?"

"Try to be," Crunch said.

"Wish I had a berth for you at the dock. Looks like you've had a break. I suppose you know this Taylor owns a newsreel company?"

Crunch shrugged and lent his good hand to holding a storage battery. "I don't care what he owns, so long as it pays dividends and he likes fishin'!"

"Did he tell you he was taking two cameramen out with him to shoot the boat parade and any fish he catches?"

Crunch looked down at Desperate, whose arms knotted as he turned a bolt. "Hear that?" He wasn't pleased. "First trip, and we get a job put up on us! What if we don't have a strike all day? It's happened before! Every sport page will run the news that the *Poseidon* entered the tournament with two cameramen, and came back with all her bait! That's a sweet handicap for her maiden voyage!"

Desperate grunted. "Can't we make the guy wait till after our first trip?"

"It is kind of putting the lug on you boys," Mr. Williams agreed. "I'd hate to drag baits for two cameramen all day. But, then, it's really not the boat's maiden voyage. She was the *Evangeline*, remember! Kind of a 'widow' voyage!" He laughed.

"Maybe we won't have her ready anyhow," Crunch said dispiritedly. And he went back to work.

At 8:30 the next morning, Mr. Taylor was waiting on the sea wall near the Gulf Stream Dock. Waiting anxiously. The fifty fishing cruisers were wound with crepe paper, spangled with gold and silver paper stars, and bristling with fishing tackle. A vast throng on the pier yelled, sang, waved, took pictures, and prepared to embark for the flotilla parade. A band struck up "Dixie" aboard the glass-bottom boat, and the fleet pushed off. Once every year, to open its fishing tournament, Miami decks itself in bunting, and sails out on its in-

digo ocean in everything floatable, from rowboats with
kickers to yachts with crews of fifty.

As the crowd thinned and vanished, Mr. Taylor fidgeted.
His cameramen drove up and unloaded their equipment.

"The boys'll be along," he said convincingly. "Soon. Very
soon, now."

It was 9:15 when the *Poseidon* appeared, cutting across the
bay, both motors roaring, a wave at her bow. Mr. Taylor felt
weak with relief.

And Crunch made a bleak apology as he held his boat off
the sea wall: "Sand in our gas, friends! We can still make the
parade, I hope." They did, by a narrow margin. They were last
in line, but, Mr. Taylor thought, far from least.

It was a peaceful day outside, with wheeling gulls and
golden sargasso weed floating on the fantastically blue water.
Slow fishing—which is not unprecedented in January—and
Mr. Taylor relaxed. It was midafternoon before he bothered to
think that his two cameramen had photographed no piscato-
rial drama worthy of national release. Nothing but the boating
of a kingfish, and a long shot of a dolphin shaking out the
hook.

He understood the effect of such failure only when
Crunch traded places with Desperate at the top controls, and
said, "Well, at least she behaves all right."

"Sure," Mr. Taylor said. "Best boat in the fleet! You two
birds have genius! So why worry about a sailfish? We've got
plenty of days to get 'em in."

Crunch gazed into the two blue distances of sea and sky.
"Yeah. But it's a pity, since we have these photographers—"

"We can take 'em again." Mr. Taylor tried to smile away
Crunch's disappointment.

"I guess so. But it's the first day of the contest. And our
first trip. Besides, nobody has a sail yet."

"How can you tell that?"

"When we catch one we run up a flag." He scanned the
fleet. "Haven't seen any."

Then Mr. Taylor knew chagrin. He shouldn't have brought
the photographers. They interfered with the mysterious thing

called "luck." They were an embarrassment to Crunch. He began praying for a sailfish.

And he was deep in some mystic ritual when Desperate's voice rang thrillingly from above: "Watch it!"

"Watch it!" eventually became unforgettable to Mr. Taylor. He looked at his bait, trolling under the clear water, occasionally breaking the surface. He looked, and grew tense from head to foot. There was something behind and underneath it. A mere shadow.

Crunch was whispering, "Get ready to drop back when he taps it."

Then the tap, as the sailfish slapped the bait with his bill. Mr. Taylor tremblingly threw down the lever that let the reel spool turn free, and his bait, as if killed by the sail's slap, drifted astern. There was a silence. The reel unwound. He tried to count to ten. Then suddenly the unwinding reel sped faster. "He's got it," Crunch whispered at his shoulder. "Slam on the drag and sock it to him."

After that, Mr. Taylor became confused. The reel stopped unwinding. The line went taut. He remembered vaguely that he stood up and whipped back the rod, that there came an alarming answering pull, that Crunch half carried him to the big center chair and sat him down. He remembered that the reel was making a sound like a wounded banshee. He remembered how the rod bent and how he struggled to hang on. He remembered being afraid that all the line would be run off the reel, and that presently, with sickening suddenness, the line went slack. He thought it had broken.

But Crunch yelled, "Wind, man! Wind! He's coming up to jump!"

So he wound, and looked out on the water, and saw what some men have spent months to witness—the awesome leap of a sailfish, sword flailing, jaws wide, indigo dorsal spread full, the wide-forked tail churning itself free of the water. The fish hung in the air for a second; huge, scintillant, miraculous. Then it was gone. It came again, walking across the sea on its tail.

He remembered other things. A surging dive that melted line from his spool. Exhausting efforts to regain it inchmeal by heaving back slowly on the rod and lowering it quickly to crank back precious inches of slack thus created. Cramps in his reel hand. Sweat running down his face, and Crunch wiping it away without taking his eyes from the place where the line sizzled through the sea. He remembered the first time he managed to heave the leader wire out of the water and thought he had the fish, only to see it rush away again, a hundred yards in a few seconds.

And at last—it seemed hours later—the intensity of the struggle decreased. The fish was drawn near the boat. Its sail broke water. It lay over on its side. Crunch begged him to "keep it coming," and, paradoxically, to "take it easy." Then Crunch reached, grabbed the wire in a gloved hand, bent low and lifted. The sailfish, beating the bulwarks with its tail, was heaved bodily across the gunwale and dispatched by a single blow, which Crunch administered with a milk bottle.

"Didn't have time to turn up a billy on Sam's lathe," he explained.

It seemed a fantastically trivial statement to Mr. Taylor, until he realized it was Crunch's effort to hide his own excitement. They stretched out the fish, ecstatically praised its colors, and bent it into the seven-foot fish box. Only then did Mr. Taylor realize that his cameras had been grinding all the time. The *Poseidon*'s widow voyage would make the newsreels.

THREE DAYS later the *Poseidon* was standing on the ways at Sam's Boat Yard. Desperate and Crunch were toiling underneath her stern, putting on bigger rudders and otherwise preparing for a trip with their customer to the Keys. Sari had brought Bill down; he lay on the grass, watching the white clouds navigate the southeast trades. His mother unpacked a far from frugal lunch and listened while her husband filed noisily on a dull piece of bronze, and talked above the sound: "You're going to be a widow, honey, like the boat! This

spring. Guy saw us in the newsreels yesterday and wants us
for several weeks in Bimini!"

A car stopped. Mr. Williams stepped out. His expression
was secretive. "Got a note for you, Crunch." He studied the
Poseidon's naked planking. "You guys ought to quit fishing
and build boats! Nobody ever got rich in the charter business!"

"We like it!" Crunch opened the note, read it and handed
it to Desperate. "Dear Adams," it said. "Ever since you
cleaned up on the Closser rat, I've felt like a heel. Business has
been slow for me. I figured if you got a boat you'd take
Perkins back. I bored those holes. Now I got a chance at a
good berth in Key West for the spring and I'm pulling out.
Maybe Mr. Williams will give you my spot at the Gulf Stream.
Randy Forbes. P.S. You can't prove I sunk your boat."

Desperate giggled. "The dumb Benny! Doesn't this note
kind of prove it?"

Crunch took the note from his mate. He tore it slowly into
many pieces. He tossed them into the air, and the wind carried them out onto the oily river. He looked up, then, at Mr.
Williams.

"Randy's left my pier," he said, "for the reason of 'business elsewhere.' And other reasons not known, but suspected,
by me. Want the place, Crunch? Thirty bucks a month, including light and water." His eyes were twinkling. "Nice
dock; be a credit to the *Poseidon*."

Another car stopped on the road beside the ways. Mr.
Taylor walked over. He gazed at Sari, at Bill and at the lunch.
Then he called to his chauffeur, "I'm eating here! Come back
at six!"

The mate looked surprised. Mr. Taylor untied a bundle.
There were work clothes in it. "Thought I'd help you guys do
a little painting, Desperate. Nobody in my business knows it,
but I painted signs for a living once." He grinned at the
squarehead. "Which reminds me of a query that crossed my
brain last night. I don't know what your real name is."

"Smith."

"I mean, first name."

Desperate glanced about to be sure Sari and Crunch and Mr. Williams were beyond earshot. He stared doubtfully at Bill for a moment. Then he gathered himself. His eyes met Taylor's. "Nobody in my business knows my name." He paused again. "Desmond," he said truculently.

Selected Bibliography

This bibliography lists the major works by each writer represented in this collection and secondary sources that provide information on the life of the authors and their works, particularly the short stories included here.

STEPHEN CRANE

Works

Maggie: A Girl of the Streets. New York: n.p., 1893.
The Red Badge of Courage. New York: Appleton, 1895.
The Open Boat and Other Tales of Adventure. New York: Doubleday, 1898.
Whilomville Stories. New York: Harper, 1900.

Secondary Sources

Edwin H. Cady. *Stephen Crane.* New York: Twayne, 1962.
Donald B. Gibson. *The Fiction of Stephen Crane.* Carbondale: Southern Illinois University Press, 1968.
Joseph Katz, ed. *Stephen Crane in Transition.* DeKalb: Northern Illinois University Press, 1972.
R. W. Stallman. *Stephen Crane: A Biography.* New York: George Braziller, 1968.
Robert Wooster Stallman, ed. *Stephen Crane: An Omnibus.* New York: Knopf, 1958. (This work has newspaper accounts of the shipwreck that gave Crane the idea for "The Open Boat.")

HARRY CREWS

Works

The Gospel Singer. New York: Morrow, 1968.
Naked in Garden Hills. New York: Morrow, 1969.
This Thing Don't Lead to Heaven. New York: Morrow, 1970.
Karate Is a Thing of the Spirit. New York: Morrow, 1971.
Car. New York: Morrow, 1972.
The Hawk Is Dying. New York: Knopf, 1973.
The Gypsy's Curse. New York: Knopf, 1974.
A Feast of Snakes. New York: Atheneum, 1976.
A Childhood: The Biography of a Place. New York: Harper & Row, 1978.
Blood and Grits. New York: Harper & Row, 1979.
Florida Frenzy. Gainesville: University Presses of Florida, 1982
All We Need of Hell. New York: Harper & Row, 1987.
The Knockout Artist. New York: Harper & Row, 1988.

Secondary Sources

Steve Oney. "The Making of the Writer," *New York Times Book Review,* 24 December 1978, pp. 3, 17.
Frank W. Shelton. "A Way of Life and Place," *Southern Literary Journal* 11 (Spring 1979): 97–102.
Allen Shepherd. "Matters of Life and Death: The Novels of Harry Crews," *Critique: Studies in Modern Fiction* 20 (September 1978): 53–62.
V. Sterling Watson. "Argument Over an Open Wound: An Interview with Harry Crews," *Prairie Schooner* 48 (Spring 1974): 60–74.

EDWIN GRANBERRY

Works

The Ancient Hunger. New York: Macaulay, 1927.
Strangers and Lovers. New York: Macaulay, 1928.
The Erl King. New York: Macaulay, 1930.
A Trip to Czardis. New York: Trident Press, 1966.

Secondary Sources

Kenneth P. Kempton. *The Short Story*. Cambridge: Harvard University Press, 1948, pp. 197–200.

_____, ed. *Short Stories for Study*. Cambridge: Harvard University Press, 1953, pp. 226–31.

Mary B. Orvis. *The Art of Writing Fiction*. New York: Prentice Hall, 1948, pp. 89–90.

ERNEST HEMINGWAY

Works

In Our Time. New York: Boni & Liveright, 1925.

The Sun Also Rises. New York: Scribners, 1926.

Men Without Women. New York: Scribners, 1927.

A Farewell to Arms. New York: Scribners, 1929.

Death in the Afternoon. New York: Scribners, 1932.

Winner Take Nothing. New York: Scribners, 1933.

Green Hills of Africa. New York: Scribners, 1935.

To Have and Have Not. New York: Scribners, 1937.

For Whom the Bell Tolls. New York: Scribners, 1940.

Across the River and Into the Trees. New York: Scribners, 1950.

The Old Man and the Sea. New York: Scribners, 1952.

Islands in the Stream. New York: Scribners, 1970.

Secondary Sources

Anselm Atkins. "Ironic Action in 'After the Storm,'" *Studies in Short Fiction* 5 (1968): 189–92.

Carlos H. Baker. *Ernest Hemingway*. New York: Scribner, 1969.

James McLendon. *Papa: Hemingway in Key West, 1928–1940*. New York: Popular Library, 1972.

Jeffrey Meyers. *Hemingway, A Biography*. New York: Harper & Row, 1985.

Arnold Samuelson. *With Hemingway: A Year in Key West and Cuba*. New York: Random House, 1984.

Robert G. Walker. "Irony and Allusion in Hemingway's 'After the Storm,'" *Studies in Short Fiction* 13 (1976): 374–76.

JAMES LEO HERLIHY

Works

The Sleep of Baby Filbertson and Other Stories. New York: Dutton, 1959.

All Fall Down. New York: Dutton, 1960.

Midnight Cowboy. New York: Simon and Schuster, 1965.

A Story That Ends with a Scream and Eight Others. New York: Simon and Schuster, 1967.

The Season of the Witch. New York: Simon and Schuster, 1971.

Secondary Sources

Benjamin W. Griffith. "Midnight Cowboys and Edwardian Narrators: James Leo Herlihy's Contrasting Voices," *Notes on Contemporary Literature* 2, i (1972): 6–8.

Charles D. Peavy. "Songs of Innocence and Experience: Herlihy's *Midnight Cowboy,*" *Forum* (Houston), 13, iii (1976): 62–67.

ZORA NEALE HURSTON

Works

Jonah's Gourd Vine. Philadelphia: Lippincott, 1934.

Mules and Men. Philadelphia: Lippincott, 1935.

Their Eyes Were Watching God. Philadelphia: Lippincott, 1937.

Tell My Horse. Philadelphia: Lippincott, 1938.

Moses, Man of the Mountain. Philadelphia: Lippincott, 1939.

Dust Tracks on a Road. Philadelphia: Lippincott, 1942.

Seraph on the Suwanee. New York: Scribners, 1948.

Secondary Sources

Harold Bloom, ed. *Zora Neale Hurston.* New York: Chelsea House, 1986.

Robert E. Hemenway. *Zora Neale Hurston: A Literary Biography.* Urbana: University of Illinois Press, 1977.

Lillie P. Howard. *Zora Neale Hurston.* Boston: Twayne, 1980.

SARAH ORNE JEWETT

Works

A Marsh Island. Boston: Houghton, Mifflin, 1885.

The King of Folly Island, and Other People. Boston: Houghton, Mifflin, 1888.

Tales of New England. Boston: Houghton, Mifflin, 1890.

A Native of Winby, and Other Tales. Boston: Houghton, Mifflin, 1893.

The Life of Nancy. Boston: Houghton, Mifflin, 1895.

The Country of the Pointed Firs. Boston: Houghton, Mifflin, 1896.

Secondary Sources

L. Auchincloss. *Pioneers and Caretakers: A Study of Nine American Women Novelists.* Minneapolis: University of Minnesota Press, 1965.

R. Cary. *Sarah Orne Jewett.* New York: Twayne, 1962.

Josephine Donovan. *Sarah Orne Jewett.* New York: Ungar, 1980.

F. O. Matthiessen. *Sarah Orne Jewett.* Boston: Houghton, Mifflin, 1929.

Gwen L. Nagel and James Nagel. *Sarah Orne Jewett.* Boston: G. K. Hall, 1978.

Margaret F. Thorp. *Sarah Orne Jewett.* Minneapolis: University of Minnesota Press, 1966.

DONALD JUSTICE

Works

The Summer Anniversaries. Middletown, Conn.: Wesleyan University Press, 1960.

The Collected Poems of Weldon Kees. Iowa City: Stone Wall Press, 1960.

A Local Storm. Iowa City: Stone Wall Press, 1963.

Contemporary French Poetry, coedited with Alexander Aspel. Ann Arbor: University of Michigan Press, 1965.

Night Light. Middletown, Conn.: Wesleyan University Press, 1967.

Sixteen Poems. Iowa City: Stone Wall Press, 1970.
From a Notebook. Iowa City: Sea Mark Press, 1972.
Departures. New York: Atheneum, 1973.
Selected Poems. New York: Atheneum, 1979.
Platonic Scripts. Ann Arbor: University of Michigan Press, 1984.
The Sunset Maker. New York: Atheneum, 1987.

Secondary Sources
"The Effacement of Self: An Interview with Donald Justice," *The Ohio Review* 16, 3 (Spring 1975): 40–65.
"An Interview with Donald Justice," *The Iowa Review* 11, 2–3 (Spring-Summer 1980): 1–21.
Michael Ryan. "Flaubert in Florida," *New England Review and Bread Loaf Quarterly* 7, 2 (Winter 1984): 218–32.
Thomas Swiss. "The Principle of Apprenticeship: Donald Justice's Poetry," *Modern Poetry Studies* 10, 1 (1980): 44–58.

MACKINLAY KANTOR

Works
Long Remember. New York: Coward-McCann, 1934.
Andersonville. Cleveland: World, 1955.
Spirit Lake. Cleveland: World, 1961.
Story Teller. Garden City: Doubleday, 1967.
Beauty Beast. New York: Putnam's, 1968.
The Day I Met a Lion. Garden City: Doubleday, 1968.
Missouri Bittersweet. Garden City: Doubleday, 1969.
I Love You, Irene. Garden City: Doubleday, 1972.
The Children Sing. New York: Hawthorn Books, 1973.
Valley Forge. New York: M. Evans, 1975.

Secondary Sources
William B. Hesseltine. *"Andersonville Revisited,"* *Georgia Review* 10 (Spring 1956): 92–100.
"Mackinlay Kantor." *Wilson Bulletin for Librarians* 7 (September 1932): 82, 86.
W. J. Stuckey. *The Pulitzer Prize Novels.* Norman: University of Oklahoma Press, 1966, pp. 175–80.

William Van O'Connor. "Go West, Young Man . . . to the Massacre," *Saturday Review*, 21 October 1961, pp. 23, 38.

RING LARDNER

Works

You Know Me Al. New York: Doran, 1916.
Gullible's Travels, Etc. Indianapolis: Bobbs-Merrill, 1917.
The Young Immigrunts. Indianapolis: Bobbs-Merrill, 1920.
Symptoms of Being 35. Indianapolis: Bobbs-Merrill, 1921.
The Big Town. Indianapolis: Bobbs-Merrill, 1921.
How to Write Short Stories. New York: Scribners, 1924.
The Love Nest and Other Stories. New York: Scribners, 1926.
Round Up: The Stories of Ring Lardner. New York: Scribners, 1929.
June Moon, coauthored with George S. Kaufman. New York: Scribners, 1930.
Lose with a Smile. New York: Scribners, 1933.
First and Last, edited by Gilbert Seldes. New York: Scribners, 1934.

Secondary Sources

Matthew J. Bruccoli and Richard Layman. *Ring Lardner: A Descriptive Bibliography*. Pittsburgh: University of Pittsburgh Press, 1976.
Donald Elder. *Ring Lardner: A Biography*. Garden City: Doubleday, 1956.
Elizabeth Evans. *Ring Lardner*. New York: Ungar, 1979.
Otto Friedrich. *Ring Lardner*. Minneapolis: University of Minnesota Press, 1965.
Ring Lardner, Jr. *The Lardners: My Family Remembered*. New York: Harper & Row, 1976.
Walton R. Patrick. *Ring Lardner*. New York: Twayne, 1963.
Jonathan Yardley. *Ring: A Biography of Ring Lardner*. New York: Random House, 1977.

ANDREW LYTLE

Works

Bedford Forrest and His Critter Company. New York: Minton, Balch, 1931.

The Long Night. Indianapolis: Bobbs-Merrill, 1936.

At the Moon's Inn. Indianapolis: Bobbs-Merrill, 1941.

A Name for Evil. Indianapolis: Bobbs-Merrill, 1947.

The Velvet Horn. New York: McDowell, Obolensky, 1957.

A Novel, a Novella and Four Stories. New York: McDowell, Obolensky, 1958.

The Hero with the Private Parts. Baton Rouge: Louisiana State University Press, 1966.

A Wake for the Living: A Family Chronicle. New York: Crown, 1975.

Secondary Sources

Ashley Brown, "Andrew Nelson Lytle," in *A Bibliographical Guide to the Study of Southern Literature,* edited by Louis D. Rubin, Jr. Baton Rouge: Louisiana State University Press, 1979, p. 243.

Noel Polk, "Andrew Nelson Lytle: A Bibliography of His Writings," *Mississippi Quarterly* 23 (Fall 1970): 435–91.

JOHN D. MACDONALD

Works

The Brass Cupcake. Greenwich: Fawcett, 1950.

All These Condemned. Greenwich: Fawcett, 1954.

The Deep Blue Goodbye. Greenwich: Fawcett, 1964.

Condominium. Philadelphia: Lippincott, 1977.

The Green Ripper. Philadelphia: Lippincott, 1979.

Free Fall in Crimson. New York: Harper & Row, 1981.

(For a complete listing of MacDonald's seventy books and dozens of stories and articles, see Shine below.)

Secondary Sources

Frank D. Campbell. *John D. MacDonald and the Colorful World of Travis McGee.* San Bernadino, CA: Borgo Press, 1977.

David Geherin. *John D. MacDonald*. New York: Ungar, 1982.

Edgar W. Hirshberg, *John D. MacDonald*. Boston: Twayne, 1985.

The JDM Bibliophile, an irregular journal about MacDonald, is published by the University of South Florida, Tampa, FL 33620.

Walter Shine and Jean Shine, *A Bibliography of the Published Works of John D. MacDonald*. Gainesville, FL: Patrons of the Libraries, 1980.

THEODORE PRATT

Works

Big Blow. Little, 1936.
Mercy Island. Knopf, 1941.
The Barefoot Mailman. Duell, 1943.
The Flame Tree. Duell, 1950.
The Big Bubble. Duell, 1951.
The Story of Boca Raton. Roy Patten, 1953.
Seminole. Gold Medal, 1954.
Florida Roundabout. Duell, 1959.

Secondary Source

Margaret N. Montague, "Theodore Pratt: The Florida Trilogy (*The Barefoot Mailman, The Flame Tree,* and *The Big Bubble*)." M.A. thesis, Florida Atlantic University, Boca Raton, 1978.

MARJORIE KINNAN RAWLINGS

Works

South Moon Under. New York: Scribners, 1933.
Golden Apples. New York: Scribners, 1935.
The Yearling. New York: Scribners, 1938.
When the Whippoorwill. New York: Scribners, 1940.
Cross Creek. New York: Scribners, 1942.
Cross Creek Cookery. New York: Scribners, 1942.
Jacob's Ladder. Coral Gables: University of Miami Press, 1950.

The Sojourner. New York: Scribners, 1953.

The Secret River. New York: Scribners, 1955.

The Marjorie Rawlings Reader, edited by Julia Scribner Bigham. New York: Scribners, 1956.

Secondary Sources

Samuel I. Bellman, *Marjorie Kinnan Rawlings*. New York: Twayne, 1974.

Gordon E. Bigelow, *Frontier Eden: The Literary Career of Marjorie Kinnan Rawlings*. Gainesville: University of Florida Press, 1966.

Gordon E. Bigelow and Laura V. Monti, eds. *Selected Letters of Marjorie Kinnan Rawlings*. Gainesville: University Presses of Florida, 1983.

ISAAC BASHEVIS SINGER

Works

Satan in Goray, translated by Jacob Sloan. New York: Noonday, 1955.

Gimpel the Fool and Other Stories, translated by Saul Bellow and others. New York: Noonday, 1957.

The Magician of Lublin, translated by Elaine Gottlieb and Joseph Singer. New York: Noonday, 1960.

The Spinoza of Market Street, translated by Martha Glicklich, Cecil Hemley, and others. New York: Farrar, Straus & Cudahy, 1961.

Enemies, a Love Story, translated by Aliza Shevrin and Elizabeth Shub. New York: Farrar, Straus & Giroux, 1972.

Conversations with Isaac Bashevis Singer by Isaac Bashevis Singer and Richard Burgin. Garden City, NY: Doubleday, 1985.

Secondary Sources

Edward Alexander. *Isaac Bashevis Singer*. Boston: Twayne, 1980.

Marcia Allentuck, ed. *The Achievement of Isaac Bashevis Singer*. Carbondale: Southern Illinois University Press, 1969.

Irving H. Buchen. *Isaac Bashevis Singer and the Eternal Past*.

New York: New York University Press, 1968.

Paul Kresh. *Isaac Bashevis Singer*. New York: The Dial Press, 1979.

Irving Malin, ed. *Critical Views of Isaac Bashevis Singer*. New York: New York University Press, 1969.

Irving Malin. *Isaac Bashevis Singer*. New York: Ungar, 1972.

Ben Siegel. *Isaac Bashevis Singer*. Minneapolis: University of Minnesota Press, 1969.

GORE VIDAL

Works

Williwaw. New York: Dutton, 1946.

In a Yellow Wood. New York: Dutton, 1947.

The City and the Pillar. New York: Dutton, 1948.

Myra Breckinridge. Boston: Little, Brown, 1968.

Burr. New York: Random House, 1973.

1876. New York: Random House, 1976.

Kalki. New York: Random House, 1978.

Secondary Sources

John W. Aldridge. *After the Lost Generation: A Critical Study of the Writers of Two Wars*. New York: McGraw-Hill, 1951.

Bernard F. Dick. *The Apostate Angel: A Critical Study of Gore Vidal*. New York: Random House, 1974.

Robert F. Kiernan. *Gore Vidal*. New York: Frederick Ungar, 1982.

Ray Lewis White. *Gore Vidal*. New York: Twayne, 1968.

PHILIP WYLIE

Works

When Worlds Collide, by Wylie and Edwin Balmer. New York: Stokes, 1932.

Finnley Wren. New York: Farrar & Rinehart, 1934.

Generation of Vipers. New York: Farrar & Rinehart, 1942.

Opus 21. New York: Rinehart, 1949.

Triumph. Garden City: Doubleday, 1963.

The End of the Dream. Garden City: Doubleday, 1972.

Secondary Sources

Robert Howard Barshay, *Philip Wylie.* Washington, DC: University Press of America, 1979.

Clifford P. Bendau, *Still Worlds Collide: Philip Wylie and the End of the American Dream.* San Bernardino, CA: The Borgo Press, 1980.

Truman Frederick Keefer, *Philip Wylie.* Boston: Twayne, 1977.

Library of Congress Cataloging in Publication Data

Florida stories.

  Bibliography : p.
  1. Florida—Fiction. 2. Short stories, American—Florida.
I. McCarthy, Kevin.
PS558.F6F65   1989   813'.01'0832759   89-4710
ISBN 0-8130-0910-3

University Presses of Florida is the central agency for scholarly publishing services of the State of Florida's university system, producing books selected for publication by the faculty editorial committees of Florida's nine public universities: Florida A&M University Press (Tallahassee), Florida Atlantic University Press (Boca Raton), Florida International University Press (Miami), Florida State University Press (Tallahassee), University of Central Florida Press (Orlando), University of Florida Press (Gainesville), University of North Florida Press (Jacksonville), University of South Florida Press (Tampa), University of West Florida Press (Pensacola).

  Orders for books published by all member presses should be addressed to University Presses of Florida, 15 NW 15th Street, Gainesville, FL 32603.